1

Through the classroom's grimy windows, Eleonor watches the bushes and trees bend in the stiff breeze as dust is blown along the road. It almost looks like a river is flowing outside the school, murky and silent.

The bell rings, and the students gather up their books and notes. Eleonor gets to her feet and follows the others out of the classroom.

She watches Jenny Lind button her jacket in front of her locker. Her face and blonde hair are reflected in the dented metal.

Jenny is pretty, different. She has intense eyes that make Eleonor feel nervous, make her cheeks flush.

Jenny is artistic. She likes taking photos, and she also happens to be the only person in school who actually enjoys reading. When she turned sixteen last week, Eleonor said happy birthday to her.

But no one cares about Eleonor. She isn't attractive enough, and she knows it, even if, Jenny once said she wanted to take a series of portraits of her.

It was after PE, as they stood in the showers.

Eleonor grabs her things and follows Jenny towards the main doors.

The wind whips up the sand and dry leaves along the white walls of the building, scattering them across the playground. The rope snaps against the flagpole.

When Jenny reaches the bike racks, she pauses and shouts something. She gestures angrily and then sets off on foot without her bike.

Eleonor had punctured her tyres that morning, hoping it would mean she could walk home with Jenny. They would start talking

about photography again, about how black and white photographs are like sculptures made of light.

She has to rein in her imagination before she pictures them kissing.

Eleonor follows Jenny past the Backavallen sports centre.

The seating area outside the restaurant is empty, the white umbrellas flapping.

She wants to catch up with Jenny, but doesn't dare.

Eleonor is about two hundred metres behind her on the footpath running parallel to Eriksbergs Road.

The clouds race by above the spruce trees.

Jenny's light hair whips around and blows back into her face as one of the green line buses drives by. The ground shakes as it passes.

They leave the built up area behind, passing the ranger station. Jenny cuts across the road and continues on the other side.

The sun breaks through, and the remaining clouds cast shadows that seem to dart across the fields.

Jenny lives in a nice house down by the lake in Forssjö.

Eleonor knows this because she once came by after she found Jenny's missing book – a book she herself had hidden. In the end, she didn't dare ring the doorbell, and after waiting outside for an hour she just left it in the postbox.

Jenny pauses beneath the power lines to light a cigarette, then sets off again. The buttons on the cuff of her sleeve glint in the light.

Eleonor can hear the rumble of a big lorry behind her.

The ground trembles as a huge lorry with Polish number plates thunders past at high speed.

Its brakes screech, and the trailer careers to one side. The lorry turns sharply off the road and swings straight up onto the grassy verge, rolling onto the footpath behind Jenny before the driver manages to bring the heavy vehicle to a halt.

'What the hell!' Jenny shouts.

From the roof, water streams down the blue fabric on the side of the trailer, cutting a slick channel through the dirt. The engine is still running, and the smoke from the chrome exhaust pipes rises in thin columns.

The cab door opens and the driver climbs down. His black leather coat has a strange grey patch on the back and fits his broad frame snugly. His tight curls are almost to his shoulders.

He strides towards Jenny.

Eleonor stops dead and watches as the driver hits Jenny in the face.

A few of the straps on the side of the lorry have come loose, and a section of the fabric covering the trailer catches the breeze, obscuring Jenny from view.

'Hello?' Eleonor shouts, moving forward again. 'What are you doing?!'

As the thick fabric goes slack, she sees that Jenny has fallen to the ground and is lying flat on her back.

Jenny raises her head and gives a confused smile, her teeth streaked with blood.

The loose section of fabric starts flapping again.

Eleonor's legs are trembling as she steps into the wet ditch. She realises she should call the police and reaches for her phone, but her hands are shaking so much that it slips from her fingers. It falls through to the ground.

Eleonor bends down to retrieve it, and when she glances up again, she sees Jenny's legs kicking as the driver picks her up.

A car sounds its horn as Eleonor steps out into the road and starts running towards the lorry.

The driver's sunglasses flash in the sunlight as he wipes his bloody hands on his jeans and climbs back into the cab. He closes the door, puts the lorry into gear and pulls away, one wheel still on the footpath. The dry strip of grass smoulders as the lorry thunders into the road, quickly gaining speed.

Eleonor comes to a halt, gasping for air. Jenny Lind is gone.

A trampled cigarette and her bag of books are all that are left on the ground.

2

Jenny Lind is lying in the bottom of a small, tarred boat on a dark lake. The rolling waves make the wood beneath her creak.

She wakes with a sudden urge to throw up. The floor is rocking.

Her shoulders are aching, her wrists burning. She realises she must be inside the lorry.

Her mouth is taped shut. She's lying on her side with her hands bound above her head.

She can't see much – it's as if her eyes are still asleep. Lines of sunlight break through the tarpaulin.

She blinks, and her vision blurs.

She feels unbelievably sick. Her head is pounding.

The huge tyres roar against the tarmac beneath her.

Her hands have been bound to one of the poles holding up the trailer's covering.

Jenny tries to work out what happened. She remembers being knocked to the ground, someone holding a cold rag over her mouth and nose.

A wave of anxiety washes over her.

She looks down and sees that her dress is bunched up around her waist, but she is still wearing her tights.

The lorry is speeding along a straight stretch of road, the engine steady.

Jenny desperately searches for some kind of logical explanation, a source of misunderstanding, but deep down she knows exactly what is happening. She is in the very situation everyone fears

most. This is the kind of thing that only ever happens in horror films.

She left her bike at school and was walking home, pretending not to notice Eleonor following her, when the lorry pulled up across the footpath behind her.

When the driver hit her, it was so unexpected that she didn't have time to react, and before she could get back on her feet, he shoved a wet rag in her face.

She has no idea how long she was unconscious. Her hands feel numb from the lack of blood. Her head is spinning, and her vision disappears completely for a moment. She rests her cheek against the floor. She tries to keep her breathing calm. She knows she can't afford to throw up while her mouth is taped shut.

There is a dried fish head wedged next to the tailgate, and the air in the trailer smells sweet and heavy.

Jenny raises her head again. Blinking, she notices a padlocked metal cabinet and two large plastic troughs at the very front of the trailer. The troughs have been secured with thick straps, and the floor around them is wet.

She tries to remember what women who have survived serial killers say about fighting back or trying to forge a bond by talking about orchids or something.

There is no point trying to shout through the tape. No one would hear her.

If anything, she needs to keep quiet. It's better if he doesn't know she is awake. She shuffles upright, tenses her body and raises her head to her hands.

The trailer lurches, making her stomach turn. Vomit fills her mouth.

Her muscles start to shake.

The cable tie around her wrists is cutting into her skin.

She manages to grip the end of the tape with her numb fingers and pull it from her mouth. She spits and slumps back onto her side, trying to cough as quietly as she can.

Whatever was on the rag has affected her vision.

She peers up at the metal frame holding up the tarpaulin that runs down either side of the lorry. It feels like she is looking through a sack.

5

Each of the poles runs up to the ceiling, where it makes a sharp ninety-degree turn, and then continues beneath the roof and down the other side.

Like roof trusses, linked together with horizontal bars along the sides.

She blinks, trying to make her eyes focus, and sees that the bars are missing on the other side of the trailer, where the curtain is reinforced with five rows of sewn-in poles instead.

Jenny realises that it must be so that the side can be rolled up for loading.

If she can follow the metal pole across the roof with her bound hands, she might be able to get to the other side and open the cover, and shout for help.

She tries to lift the cable tie up the post, but immediately gets stuck. The sharp plastic digs into her skin.

The driver changes lane, and Jenny loses her balance, hitting her temple on one of the struts.

She slumps to the floor again, swallowing several times, and thinks back to that morning. To the breakfast table, with toast and marmalade on plates. Her mother was talking about her aunt, saying that she'd had four stents placed in her heart the day before.

Jenny's phone was on the table beside her mug. It was switched to silent, but the notifications on the screen still caught her eye, and that annoyed her father. He thought she was being disrespectful, and she had been frustrated by the unfairness of it all.

'What did I do? Why are you always on my case? Just because your life is so miserable!' she'd shouted, storming out of the kitchen.

The floor tilts and the lorry slows, changing gear as they drive uphill. Occasional flashes of sunlight burst through the tarpaulin, making the filthy floor shine.

Lying among the lumps of dry mud and dark leaves, Jenny notices a front tooth. Adrenaline surges through her.

Her eyes scan the trailer.

No more than a metre away from her, she spots two broken nails, painted with red polish intact. There is a trickle of dried blood on one of the poles, broken strands of hair still clinging to a dent in the tailgate.

'Oh God, oh God, oh God,' Jenny mumbles.

She gets to her knees and sits still, taking the weight off the cable tie around her wrists and feeling the blood come flooding back to her fingers with thousands of tiny pinpricks.

Her body is shaking all over, and she tries to get up, but the plastic tie has caught on something.

'I can do this,' she whispers.

She needs to remain calm. She can't allow herself to panic.

Wiggling her hands, she moves to one side and realises that she can shuffle along the bottom bar.

She is breathing too quickly as she works her way forward, past bumps in the pole, reaching the front section of the trailer. She grips the bar with both hands and tries to pull it free, but it has been welded to the front post and is impossible to bend.

Jenny peers over to the metal cabinet. The padlock is open, swinging on its shackle.

Another wave of nausea rises up inside her, but she doesn't have time to wait. The journey could be over at any moment.

She leans as far as she can towards the cabinet, stretching her arms to their full length and managing to reach the padlock with her mouth. She carefully lifts it clear and carries it back, crouching down to drop it into her lap. She slowly parts her thighs and it falls to the floor without a sound.

The lorry turns, and the cabinet door swings open.

The shelves inside are full of brushes, pots, pliers, hacksaws, knives, scissors, cleaning products and rags.

Her heart rate increases, and her pulse thunders in her ears.

The sound of the engine changes, and the lorry seems to slow down.

Jenny gets up again, leaning to one side, and holding the cabinet door open with her head. She spots a knife with a dirty plastic handle on a shelf between two tins of paint.

'Dear God, please save me, dear God,' she whispers.

The lorry swerves, and the metal door slams shut on her head with such force that she loses consciousness for a few seconds, dropping to her knees. She throws up.

She gets back onto her feet and notices that blood has started dripping from her wrists to the filthy floor.

Jenny leans forward, reaches the handle of the knife with her mouth, and bites down on the plastic as the lorry comes to a halt with a hiss.

There is a soft scraping sound as she lifts the knife from the shelf.

She carefully lowers her head to her hands and presses the rusty blade to the plastic tie with as much force as she can.

3

With the rusty knife between her teeth, Jenny tries to saw through the cable tie around her wrists. When she realises that the blade has made only a faint nick in the white plastic, she bites down harder on the handle, increasing the pressure.

She is thinking about her father. About his sad face as she shouted at him that morning, the scratched glass on his wristwatch, his resigned gestures as she stormed out.

Her mouth is hurting even more, but she keeps sawing. Saliva trickles down the handle of the knife.

A sudden wave of dizziness hits her, and she is just about to give up when the plastic snaps. The knife has cut through the tie.

Trembling, she slumps onto her side and hears the knife clatter across the floor. She quickly gets up and finds it, then moves over to the right-hand side of the trailer and listens.

She can't hear a thing.

Jenny knows she needs to act quickly, but her hands are shaking so much that at first she struggles to even push the knife through the fabric.

She hears a buzzing sound that lasts only for a few short seconds.

Jenny adjusts her grip on the knife and makes a vertical cut in the fabric, right next to the last post. She parts the material slightly and peers out.

They have stopped at an unmanned lorry park. The ground is strewn with pizza boxes, oily rags and condoms.

Her heart is pounding so hard that she can barely breathe. There is no sign of anyone else nearby, no other cars.

The wind carries a plastic cup over the pavement.

Jenny's stomach cramps, but she manages to repress the urge to throw up, swallowing hard.

Beads of sweat trickle down her back.

With trembling hands, she makes a horizontal cut in the fabric, just above the bar.

Her plan is to climb out, run into the woods, and hide.

She hears heavy footsteps, a metallic scraping sound. Her vision blurs again.

She climbs out, teetering on the edge of the trailer with the wind in her face. As she clings on to the tarpaulin, she sways and drops the knife. The dizziness seems to ripple through her head, and as she peers down at the ground it feels like the entire lorry might topple over.

She feels a searing pain in her ankle when she lands, but takes a step forward anyway, managing to maintain her balance.

She is so dizzy she can't walk straight.

Her head pounds more fiercely with every step she takes. The diesel pump pulses loudly.

Jenny blinks and starts walking just as a huge figure appears around the edge of the trailer and spots her. She stops dead and takes an unsteady step back. She feels like she is going to throw up again.

She ducks down beneath the muddy connection between the trailer and the lorry and crawls underneath, watching the figure hurry in the other direction.

Her mind is racing – she needs to find somewhere to hide.

Jenny gets up on shaking legs and realises she won't be able to run away from the driver into the woods.

She no longer knows where he is. Her pulse is throbbing in her ears.

She needs to make her way back to the main road and flag down a car.

The ground sways and lurches, the trees swirling around her, and the yellow meadow grass at the roadside pitches in the strong wind.

The driver has disappeared. She thinks he might have gone around the lorry, or maybe he is hiding behind the line of huge tyres.

Her stomach cramps again.

She glances in every direction, clinging on to the tailgate, blinking hard and trying to work out where the entrance to the main road is.

She hears a shuffling sound. She needs to run, to hide.

As she moves back along the trailer, she feels like her legs are about to give out. She spots a couple of rubbish bins, an information board and a footpath leading into the woods.

There is a rumbling engine somewhere nearby.

She looks down at the pavement, tries to compose herself, and considers calling for help as she sees a shadowy movement to one side of her leg.

A large hand grips her ankle, pulling her down. She lands on her hip, and something in her neck cracks as her shoulder hits the ground. The driver is beneath the trailer, dragging her towards him. She tries to cling on to a tyre, rolling onto her back and kicking out with her free leg. She hits the suspension and grazes her ankle, but manages to get away and crawl back out.

Jenny struggles to her feet, but the entire landscape swings to one side. She swallows the bile in her throat, hears the thud of footsteps, and assumes the driver must be running around the trailer.

She staggers forward, ducking beneath the hose from the diesel pump, moving as fast as she can towards the edge of the woods. As she glances back over her shoulder, she runs straight into another person.

'Hello, what's going on here?'

The voice belongs to a policeman, urinating into the long grass. She grabs his jacket, about to fall and drag him down with her.

'Help me . . .'

She lets go of him and staggers to one side. 'Take a step back,' he says.

She swallows, trying to grab hold of his jacket again. He shoves her away and she falls into the grass, dropping to her knees and breaking her fall with both hands.

'Please,' she breathes before throwing up.

The ground sways, and she slumps to her side, looking up at the officer's motorcycle through the grass. She can see movement reflected in the shiny exhaust pipe.

It's the lorry driver, striding towards them. She turns her head and sees his filthy jeans and leather jacket, her vision still blurred as though she's looking through scratched glass.

'Help me,' she repeats, struggling to hold back the cramps.

She tries to get up and vomits again, hears them talking as she spits into the grass. A voice says, 'She's my daughter,' explaining that it isn't the first time she has run away and gone on a drinking spree.

Her stomach turns. She coughs and tries to speak, but vomits again.

'What can you do, you know? Threaten to confiscate her phone?'

'Sounds familiar,' the police officer laughs.

'There, there, honey,' says the driver, patting her on the back. 'Get it all out, you'll feel better soon.'

'How old is she?' the officer asks.

'Seventeen – in a year, she'll be able to make her own decisions . . . but if she listened to me, she'd stick with school so she doesn't end up driving a lorry.'

'Please,' Jenny whispers, wiping the slimy mucus from her mouth.

'You can't put her in a drunk cell for the night, can you?' the driver asks.

'Not if she's seventeen,' the police officer replies before answering an emergency call on his radio.

'Don't go,' Jenny coughs.

The police officer walks calmly back to his bike as he finishes the call. A crow caws somewhere nearby.

The long grass bends and quivers in the wind, and Jenny watches as the police officer pulls on his helmet and gloves. She knows she needs to get up and presses her hands to the ground. The dizziness comes close to knocking her sideways again, but she fights it and manages to get onto her knees.

The police officer climbs onto his motorcycle and starts the engine. She tries calling to him, but he doesn't hear her.

The crow flaps up into the air as he puts the bike into gear and drives away.

Jenny slumps back into the grass. She hears the sound of gravel crunching beneath his tyres as he rides off into the distance.

4

Pamela enjoys the loose ice crystals that form when the snow starts to melt on the slopes. They make the skis' grip almost frighteningly sharp.

She and her daughter Alice have been using sunscreen, but they still both have a bit of colour on their cheeks. Martin, on the other hand, burned his nose and the skin beneath his eyes.

They ate lunch outside earlier, and it was so warm in the sun that both Pamela and Alice took off their coats and sat in their T-shirts.

All three have aching legs, so they have decided to take a break from the slopes tomorrow. Alice and Martin are planning to go fishing for trout, while Pamela pays a visit to the hotel spa.

When Pamela was nineteen, she and her friend Dennis travelled to Australia together. She met a man named Greg in a bar one night, and slept with him in his bungalow. When she got back to Sweden, she realised she was pregnant.

Pamela sent a letter to the bar in Port Douglas, addressed to Greg with eyes as blue as the ocean, and a month later he replied, explaining that he was already in a relationship. He was, however, willing to pay for an abortion.

It was a difficult birth, ending in an emergency Caesarean. She and the girl both survived, and when the doctors advised Pamela not to have any more children, she decided to get an IUD. Dennis was there for her during her pregnancy and delivery, supporting her and encouraging her to fulfil her dream of studying architecture.

After five years of training, Pamela found a job with a small firm in Stockholm almost right away. She met Martin while she was working on the plans for a villa in Lidingö.

Martin was the developer's building contractor. He looked like a rock star, with intense eyes and long hair.

They kissed for the first time at a party at Dennis's place. When Alice was six, they moved in together and got married two years later. Alice is now sixteen and in her first year of high school.

It's eight in the evening, and the sky is dark. They have ordered room service, and Pamela is hurrying to straighten up all of their discarded clothes and dirty socks before it arrives.

She can hear Martin singing 'Riders on the Storm' in the shower.

The plan is to lock their door once Alice falls asleep, open a bottle of champagne and have sex.

Pamela gathers up her daughter's clothes and takes them to her room.

She finds Alice sitting on her bed in her underwear, phone in one hand. The girl looks just like Pamela did at that age, with the same eyes, the same chestnut-red hair and the same tight curls.

'The lorry's number plates were stolen,' Alice says, glancing up from the screen.

Two weeks ago, the media reported that a girl around Alice's age had been assaulted and abducted in Katrineholm.

Her name is Jenny Lind, like the legendary opera singer.

It feels like all of Sweden has joined the search for her and the lorry with Polish number plates.

The police have appealed for help, and tips have been flooding in from the general public, but they still haven't found a single trace of the girl.

Pamela returns to the living room, straightening the cushions and picking up the remote control from the floor.

The darkness outside seems to be pressing up against the windows, and she jumps when she hears a knock at the door.

She is just about to answer when Martin emerges from the bathroom, singing and smiling. He is completely naked, with a hand towel wrapped around his damp hair.

She shoos him back into the bathroom and can still hear him singing as she opens the door to the woman with the serving trolley.

Pamela checks her phone as the woman sets the table in the living room, thinking that she must be wondering about the singing in the bathroom.

'He's fine, I promise,' she jokes.

But the woman doesn't smile, she simply hands Pamela the bill on a silver plate and asks her to write the total sum and sign before she leaves.

Pamela tells Martin it's safe to come out now, then goes to fetch Alice. They sit down on the enormous bed with their plates and glasses, and watch a recent horror film as they eat.

An hour later, both Pamela and Martin are asleep.

When the film ends, Alice switches off the TV, lifts Pamela's glasses from her nose and cleans up the plates and glasses. She then turns out the lights, brushes her teeth and heads to her own room.

* * *

Before long, the little town in the valley falls silent. At around three in the morning, the Northern Lights appear in the sky, shining like silvery tree branches.

Pamela is torn from her sleep by the sound of a young boy crying in the darkness, but his soft sobs fade before she has time to work out where she is.

She lies perfectly still, thinking about Martin's nightmares.

The sound came from the window by the bed.

When they first started dating, he often had nightmares about dead boys. Pamela found it touching that a grown man was willing to admit he was afraid of ghosts.

She remembers one night in particular. He woke up screaming. They sat in the kitchen, drinking chamomile tea, and her hair stood on end as he described one of the ghosts in detail.

The boy's face was grey, and he had slicked his hair back with rancid blood. His nose was broken, and one of his eyes was hanging from its socket.

She hears another sob.

15

Now wide awake, Pamela slowly turns her head.

The radiator beneath the window hisses softly, the warm air making the curtain bulge out as though a child were hiding behind it, pressing their face to the fabric.

She wants to wake Martin, but doesn't dare speak.

The crying starts again on the floor right next to the bed.

Her heart starts beating harder, and she reaches out for Martin in the darkness, but no one is there; the sheets on his side of the bed are cool.

Pamela pulls her knees up to her chest, curling up, suddenly convinced that the sobbing is moving around to her side of the bed before it stops abruptly.

She cautiously reaches for the lamp on the bedside table. The room is so dark that she can't even see her own hand.

The lamp feels like it's further away than it was when she went to bed.

Pamela listens tensely for the slightest sound, groping for the switch. She finds the base of the lamp and follows the cable upwards.

As her fingers reach the switch and turn on the light, she hears the sobbing again, over by the window.

Pamela squints in the sudden glare and puts on her glasses. She climbs out of bed and finds Martin on the floor in his pyjama bottoms.

He seems to be dreaming about something upsetting. His cheeks are streaked with tears. She sinks to her knees beside him and places a hand on his shoulder.

'Honey,' she says quietly. 'Honey, you've . . .'

Martin cries out, staring at her with wide eyes.

He blinks in confusion, scanning the hotel room and then turning back to her. His lips move, but he doesn't utter a word.

'You fell out of bed,' she says.

Martin shuffles up against the wall, wipes his mouth and stares blankly ahead.

'What were you dreaming about?' she asks.

'Don't know,' he whispers.

'A nightmare?'

16

'I don't know, my heart is beating so damn fast,' he says, climbing back up into bed.

Pamela lies down on her side and takes his hand.

'You shouldn't watch horror films,' she says.

'No.' He smiles, meeting her eye.

'But you know it's all fake, don't you?'

'Are you sure?'

'It's not real blood; it's just ketchup,' she jokes, pinching his cheek.

She turns out the light and pulls him close. They make love as quietly as they can, falling asleep with their limbs still entwined.

5

After breakfast the next morning, Pamela lies in bed reading the news on her iPad while Martin and Alice get ready.

The sun has risen, and the icicles outside are glowing, water already dripping from their tips.

Martin loves ice fishing and could talk for hours about lying on his stomach, blocking out the light as he peers down into the hole, watching the enormous trout approach from below.

The hotel concierge recommended driving out to Kallsjön, part of the Indalsälven River basin. There is plenty to catch, and it's easily accessible by car, but quiet enough that you can still fish in peace.

Alice puts down her heavy backpack by the door, hangs a pair of ice prods around her neck and laces up her boots.

'I'm starting to regret this,' she says as she straightens up. 'A massage and a facial sound pretty good right now.'

'I'm going to enjoy every second of it,' Pamela says from bed, smiling. 'I'm going to—'

'Stop!' Alice interrupts her.

But Pamela continues. 'Swim, use the sauna, get a manicure . . .'

'Please, I don't want to know.'

Pamela pulls on her bathrobe and moves over to her daughter, giving her a hug. She kisses Martin and wishes them shitty fishing – something she has learned to say instead of good luck – an old fisherman's tradition.

'Don't stay out there too long, and be careful,' she says.

'Enjoy your alone time,' Martin replies smiling.

Alice's skin looks almost luminous, her reddish curls peeping out from beneath her hat.

'Do your jacket all the way up,' Pamela tells her.

She pats her daughter on the cheek, her hand lingering though she can sense the girl's impatience.

The two moles beneath Alice's left eye have always made Pamela think of tears.

'What?' Alice grins.

'Have fun with Dad.'

They head off, and Pamela stands in the doorway, watching them disappear down the corridor.

She closes the door and returns to the bedroom, freezing when she hears a sudden scraping sound.

A heap of wet snow slides from the roof and rushes past the window in the blink of an eye, crashing down to the ground.

Pamela puts on her bikini, a bathrobe and a pair of slippers, and then grabs her tote bag with her room key, phone and a book, and leaves the suite.

* * *

Everyone else seems to be out on the slopes, so Pamela has the spa all to herself. The water in the large pool is as flat as a mirror, reflecting the snow and the trees outside.

She dumps her tote bag on a table between two lounge chairs, hangs up her bathrobe, and goes over to the bench of clean towels.

She lowers herself into the warm water and starts swimming slowly. After ten lengths, she pauses by the panoramic windows at the far end.

She wishes that Martin and Alice were here with her.

This is magical, she thinks, looking out at the mountains and the forest in the sunlight.

She swims another ten lengths, then climbs out of the pool to sit down and read.

A young man comes over and asks if she would like anything to drink, and though it is still morning, she orders a glass of champagne.

Heavy snow tumbles to the ground from a large tree outside. The branches quiver while small white flakes dance in the sunlight.

19

She reads another few chapters of her book and finishes her champagne. Then she takes off her glasses and heads into the sauna, where she thinks about Martin's recurring nightmares.

His parents and two brothers died in a car accident when he was just a boy. Martin was thrown through the windscreen and onto the tarmac, and though his back was badly grazed, he survived.

When she and Martin first met, her best friend Dennis was working as a psychologist in a youth clinic while he pursued a specialisation in grief counselling. He helped Martin open up about his loss and process the feelings of guilt he'd been dragging around like a ball and chain ever since the accident.

Pamela stays in the sauna until she is drenched in sweat, then takes a shower, puts on a dry bikini, and heads to the massage room. She's welcomed by a woman with scarred cheeks and sad eyes.

She takes off her top and lies face down on the table. The woman spreads a towel over her hips.

Her hands are rough, and the warm oils smell like green leaves and wood. Pamela closes her eyes as her thoughts start to drift away.

She pictures Martin and Alice disappearing down the quiet corridor without glancing back.

The woman's fingertips follow her spine down to the edge of the towel. She massages her upper glutes, and spreads her thighs apart.

When she's finished her massage, Pamela plans on getting a facial and then going back to the pool and ordering a glass of wine and a prawn sandwich.

The woman pours more warm oil onto her body, her hands moving up from her waist, across her ribs to her armpits.

A shiver passes through Pamela, despite how warm the room is. Maybe it's just her muscles loosening up.

Her mind turns to Martin and Alice again, but this time she is looking at them from above.

She sees Kallsjön tucked between the mountains, the ice as grey as steel. Martin and Alice are just two tiny black dots.

When the massage is over, the woman covers her in hot towels and leaves the room. Pamela remains on the bed for a moment, then slowly gets up and puts on her bikini top.

Her slippers are cold and damp as she pushes her feet into them. She can hear the sound of a helicopter in the distance.

Pamela walks over to the next room and says hello to the beautician, a blonde woman no older than twenty.

She dozes off during the deep cleanse and peel. The woman is busy preparing a clay mask when there is a knock at the door.

She excuses herself and leaves the room.

Pamela hears a man speaking quickly out in the corridor, but can't make out what he's saying. After a moment or two, the woman returns with a strange look on her face.

'I'm sorry, but there seems to have been an accident,' she says. 'They said it's nothing serious, but you should probably go to the hospital anyway.'

6

Pamela doesn't notice that her bathrobe is flapping open as she hurries through the hotel. She calls Martin, listening to his phone ring and ring with a rising sense of panic.

When no one answers, she starts running. She loses one of her slippers, but doesn't bother stopping to grab it.

The soft carpet dulls her footsteps, muting them almost like she is under water.

Pamela tries Alice's phone, but it goes straight to voicemail.

She presses the button for the lift and kicks off her remaining slipper. Her hands are shaking as she calls Martin again.

'Pick up,' she whispers.

She waits a moment or two then takes the stairs instead, clinging on to the handrail, hurling herself up two steps at a time.

On the second floor landing, she almost trips over a forgotten bucket.

She swings around and keeps going, trying to process exactly what the beautician said to her.

She told her it was nothing serious, but if that were the case, then why is no one answering?

Pamela stumbles out into the corridor on the third floor, steadying herself against the wall before breaking into a run again.

When she reaches the door to their suite, she comes to a stop, gasping for air. She inserts the key and steps inside, heading straight for the desk and accidentally knocking over the brochure stand as

she picks up the phone. She calls down to reception and asks them to book a taxi for her.

She pulls her clothes on over her bikini, grabs her bag and her phone and leaves the room.

In the taxi, she continues to call and text Martin and Alice.

She eventually gets through to the hospital, and speaks to a woman who refuses to give out any information.

Pamela's heart is racing, and she has to stop herself from screaming at her.

The road is wet and slushy. Tree trunks and melting piles of snow fly past the car window. Dark pines packed together glow in the sunlight. Hare tracks disappear into clearings.

She clasps her hands and prays to God that Alice and Martin are OK.

Her thoughts are racing. She pictures their rental car skidding in the snow before rolling down an embankment. She sees a mother bear charging out from the trees, a fishing hook flicking up and catching an eye, a leg snapping at the top of a boot.

She has made at least thirty calls to Alice and Martin, sent text messages and emails as well, but as the taxi pulls into Östersund, she still hasn't managed to get any answers.

The hospital glitters in the bright sunlight. It's a huge complex with brown walls and glazed walkways.

Melted snow runs across the pavement.

The driver pulls up by the ambulance bay, and she pays and climbs out, anxiety drumming in her head.

Pamela hurries along a brown wall decorated with strange blood-red wooden planks that lead her to the emergency room. She staggers over to reception and hears her own voice from afar as she gives her name.

Her hands are trembling as she pulls out her ID to give to the bearded man behind the desk.

He tells her to take a seat in the waiting room, but she stays on her feet, staring down at her shoes on the black carpet.

She realises she could search for information about car crashes on her phone, but she can't bring herself to do it.

23

She has never been so afraid in her life.

She takes a few steps, turns around and looks back at the bearded man.

She knows she won't be able to wait for long. She wants to go and search for her family in the intensive care rooms.

'Pamela Nordström?' a nursing assistant asks, approaching her.

'What's going on? No one is telling me anything,' says Pamela, swallowing hard as they walk.

'You'll have to talk to the doctor. I don't have any information.'

They walk down corridors full of stretchers and through automatic doors with dirty glass panels.

In one of the waiting rooms, she sees an old woman crying. The fish in the aquarium beside her dance in shimmering shoals.

They keep walking until they get to the intensive care unit.

Staff members hurry past the closed doors along the corridor.

The vinyl flooring is cream-coloured, and there is a strong smell of disinfectant in the air.

Another nurse appears from one of the rooms and greets Pamela with a reassuring smile.

'I know you must be beside yourself,' she says, shaking Pamela's hand, 'but there's nothing to worry about, I promise. Everything will be fine. The doctor will be here to speak to you soon.'

Pamela follows the nurse into one of the intensive care rooms. She can hear the rhythmic hiss of a respirator.

'What happened?' she asks, her voice barely above a whisper.

'We're keeping him sedated, but he's out of danger now.'

Pamela sees Martin lying in the bed, a plastic tube in his mouth. His eyes are closed, and he is hooked up to various machines measuring his cardiac activity, his pulse and his oxygenation.

'But . . .' Her voice deserts her, and she reaches out to brace herself against the wall.

'He'd fallen through the ice and was hypothermic when he was found.'

'But Alice,' she mumbles.

'What was that?' the nurse asks, smiling.

'My daughter, where is my daughter Alice?'

The nurse can hear how agitated she sounds. She turns pale as she listens to the uninhibited desperation in Pamela's voice.

'We don't know anything about . . .'

'They were on the ice together!' Pamela shouts. 'She was right there with him, you can't have left her out there, she's just a child! You can't . . . you can't!'

Five Years Later

7

They say that when one door closes, another door opens – or a window, at least. But when certain doors close, the saying seems more mocking than comforting.

Pamela pops a mint into her mouth and crushes it between her teeth as the lift shuttles her up towards the psychiatric ward at Sankt Göran's Hospital.

The mirrors on either side of her create an endless chain of faces.

She shaved her head before the funeral, but her chestnut-red locks are now down to her shoulders again.

On Alice's first birthday after her death, Pamela had two small dots tattooed beneath her left eye, exactly where her daughter's birthmarks had been.

Dennis convinced her to go to the Crisis and Trauma Centre, and since then, she has slowly learned to live with her loss. She no longer needs to take antidepressants.

The lift comes to a halt and the doors glide open. Pamela walks through the empty entrance hall, signs in at the reception desk and hands over her phone.

'So, today's the day,' the woman behind the desk says smiling.

'Finally,' Pamela replies.

The woman puts her phone into a pigeonhole, gives her a numbered tag, then gets up and opens the door by swiping her card in the reader.

Pamela thanks her and starts making her way down the long corridor. On the floor beside a cleaning trolley, she spots a bloody latex glove.

She turns off into the day room and says hello to a carer before sitting down to wait on the sofa, just like always. It sometimes takes Martin a while to get ready.

There is a young man sitting at a chessboard, anxiously muttering to himself as he adjusts one of the pieces.

An old lady is standing in front of the TV, her mouth hanging open, while a woman who looks like her daughter tries to talk to her.

The morning light gleams on the vinyl floor.

The carer pulls out his phone, answering in a subdued voice and leaving the room. Pamela can hear angry cries through the walls.

An older man in bleached jeans and a black T-shirt comes into the room, glances around and then sits down in the armchair opposite Pamela.

He must be somewhere around sixty. His thin face has deep furrows. He has bright green eyes, and his grey hair is gathered in a ponytail.

'Nice blouse,' he says, leaning towards her.

'Thanks,' she replies curtly, pulling her jacket around herself.

'I could see your nipples through the fabric,' he goes on in a low voice. 'They'll be stiffening now that I've mentioned it, I know that . . . My brain is full of toxic sexuality . . .'

Pamela's heart starts to race. She's uncomfortable, and she debates getting up and heading back to reception. She knows she can't show any fear.

The old woman by the TV laughs, and the young man at the chessboard knocks his black king over. Through the wall, she hears clattering from the pantry kitchen.

Strings of dust flutter from the vent by the ceiling.

The man in front of Pamela adjusts the crotch of his jeans and then holds out his hands in an inviting gesture. She notices that he has a number of deep scars running the length of his forearms, right down to his palms.

'I can do you from behind,' he says softly. 'I've got two dicks . . . I swear, I'm a sex machine, you'll be screaming and crying . . .'

He trails off and points to the doorway out onto the corridor.

'On your knees,' he says with a grin. 'Here comes superman, the patriarch . . .'

He claps his hands and laughs excitedly as a caregiver wheels a heavyset man into the day room.

'The prophet, the messenger, the master . . .'

The man in the wheelchair seems indifferent to his heckling, and simply says a quiet thank you as he is positioned on the other side of the chessboard. He straightens the silver cross hanging around his neck.

The carer leaves the wheelchair and comes over to the other man, who is now on his knees with a strained smile on his face.

'Primus, what are you doing here?' he asks.

'I've got a visitor,' he replies, nodding to Pamela.

'You know you have restrictions.'

'I got lost.'

'Get up, and don't look at her,' says the carer.

Pamela doesn't raise her eyes, but she can feel that he is still staring at her as he gets up from the floor.

'Take the slave out,' the man in the wheelchair says quietly.

Primus turns around and follows the carer out of the room. The lock buzzes and the door into the patients' area swings shut behind them, their footsteps fading across the vinyl floor.

8

Pamela turns her head as the door to the patients' corridor opens again. A carer carrying Martin's backpack follows him into the day room.

In the past, Martin's blond hair was always long, and he seemed so relaxed in his leather trousers, black shirts and pink mirrored sunglasses. But these days, his short hair is matted and his face is pale and anxious. He's heavily medicated and has put on weight. He's wearing a blue T-shirt, Adidas tracksuit bottoms and a pair of white sneakers with the laces removed.

'Honey.' She smiles, getting up from the sofa.

Martin shakes his head and stares in terror at the man in the wheelchair. Pamela moves over to him and takes his backpack from the carer.

'Everyone here is so proud of you,' the carer tells him.

Martin smiles nervously and shows Pamela the flower he has drawn on the palm of his hand.

'Is that for me?' she asks.

He gives her a quick nod and then clenches his fist.

'Thank you,' she says.

'I couldn't get any real ones,' he says without looking at her.

'I know.'

Martin tugs at the carer's arm, his lips moving silently.

'You've already gone through your bag,' the carer tells him. He turns to Pamela. 'He wants to check his bag to make sure he has everything.'

'OK,' she says, passing the bag to Martin.

He sits down on the floor, takes out his things and lines them up in a neat row.

Nothing is physically wrong with Martin's brain. It wasn't damaged during his time under the ice, but after the accident, he practically stopped talking. It seems as though every word he utters is followed by a wave of anxiety.

Everyone seems convinced he is suffering from post-traumatic stress disorder with elements of paranoid delusion.

Pamela knows that he isn't mourning the loss of Alice more than she is. That would be impossible. But she is fundamentally strong, and has learned that since everyone is different, they react differently. Martin's entire family died when he was just a child, and after Alice drowned, his trauma became increasingly complex.

She looks out through the window and sees that an ambulance has pulled up outside the emergency entrance to the psychiatric ward. But she can't really register the fact. She's drifting back in time to five years ago in the intensive care unit at Östersund Hospital.

* * *

'They were on the ice together!' she shouted. 'She was right there with him, you can't have left her out there, she's just a child! You can't . . . you can't!'

The nurse stared at her and opened her mouth to speak, but could not produce a single word.

The police and the emergency search and rescue team were informed right away, and they flew back out to Kallsjön with divers to search the lake.

Pamela couldn't keep her thoughts in order and paced restlessly around the room, repeating that it was all just a misunderstanding, that Alice was fine. She told herself that soon the three of them would be sitting at the dinner table in Stockholm, talking about this day. She imagined this despite knowing it would never come to pass. Despite knowing deep down exactly what had happened.

She was standing by Martin's bed when he woke up from his sedation. He opened his eyes briefly then closed them again for a moment or two before peering up at her. He studied her with a heavy gaze as he tried to return to reality.

'What's going on?' he whispered, licking his lips. 'Pamela? What is it?'

'You went through the ice,' she said, swallowing hard.

'No, it should've held,' he said, trying to raise his head from the pillow. 'I drilled a test hole and it was ten centimetres thick . . . You could've driven a motorcycle on it, that's what I told . . .'

He trailed off, suddenly staring up at her intensely.

'Where's Alice?' he asked, his voice trembling. 'Pamela, what's going on?'

As he tried to get out of bed, he fell to the floor and hit his head, splitting his brow.

'Alice!' he shouted.

'Did you both go through the ice?' Pamela asked, raising her voice. 'I need to know. They're up there with divers right now.'

'I don't understand, she . . . she . . .'

Beads of sweat were trickling down his pale cheeks.

Pamela took hold of his chin. 'What happened? Talk to me, Martin!' she said firmly. 'I need to know what happened.'

'Please, I'm trying to remember . . . We were fishing, that's what we were doing . . . it was perfect, everything was perfect . . .'

He rubbed his face with both hands and made his brow bleed again.

'Just tell me what happened.'

'Hold on . . .'

He gripped the edge of the bed so tightly that his knuckles turned white.

'We were talking about cutting across the lake to another bay, so we packed up our things and . . .'

His pupils widened, and his breathing became rapid. His face was suddenly so tense that she almost didn't recognise him.

'Martin?'

'I went through,' he said, meeting her eye. 'There was no sign that the ice was thinner, I can't understand it . . .'

'What did Alice do?'

'I'm trying to remember,' he said in a broken voice. 'I was walking ahead of her when it gave way . . . It all happened so damn fast, and suddenly I was under the water. There was so much broken ice, so

many bubbles, and . . . I'd started swimming back up when I heard the noise . . . Alice crashed into the water, she had fallen through the ice . . . I surfaced and filled my lungs, then dived back down and saw that she'd lost her sense of direction, she was moving away from the hole . . . I think she must've hit her head, because it was like there was a red cloud around her.'

'Oh God,' Pamela whispered. Tears started rolling down her cheeks.

'I dived deeper and thought I'd be able to catch up with her when she suddenly just stopped struggling and sank.'

'What do you mean she sank?' Pamela cried. 'How could she sink?'

'I swam after her, I was so close, and I reached out to try and get a hold of her hair, but I missed . . . and she disappeared into the darkness, I couldn't see anything, it was too deep, everything was black . . .'

Martin stared up at Pamela like he was seeing her for the first time. The blood from his eyebrow trickled down his face.

'But you dived again, didn't you . . . ? You went after her, right?'

'I don't know what happened, I don't understand . . .' he whispered, pausing for a moment. 'I didn't want to be saved.'

Pamela later found out that a group of cross-country skiers had spotted his bright yellow ice drill and backpack by the open hole. About fifteen metres away, they saw a man beneath the ice, and quickly broke the surface to rescue him.

A helicopter transferred Martin to the hospital in Östersund. His body temperature was just eighty degrees, and he was immediately sedated.

They had to amputate three toes on his right foot, but he survived.

The ice shouldn't have broken, but currents had weakened it in the area where they fell through.

That day, just after he first came to, was the only time Martin ever talked about the accident in its entirety.

Afterwards, he virtually stopped speaking, and became increasingly paranoid.

On the anniversary of the accident, he was found barefoot in the middle of the snowy main road near Haga Park.

The police took him to the emergency psychiatric ward at Sankt Göran's, and he has had around-the-clock care practically ever since.

Five years have now passed, and Martin still hasn't been able to accept what happened.

Over the past few years, he has been carefully shepherded back into outpatient care. He has learned how to cope with his fears, and has even spent a couple of weeks at home without asking to return to the unit.

Now, in consultation with the chief psychologist, Pamela and Martin have decided that he should come home for good.

All three believe it is time to take the next step in his recovery. But that isn't the only reason he's coming back.

For over two years now, Pamela has been volunteering with a children's rights organisation, taking calls from children and young people who are going through hard times. That was how she came into contact with social services in Gävle and first heard about a seventeen-year-old girl no one else wanted, Mia Andersson.

Pamela began discussing the possibility of opening up her home to Mia, but Dennis warned her that she will be rejected if Martin is still not well enough to live at home.

When she told Martin about Mia, he was so happy that he started crying. That was when he first promised to make a real effort to permanently move back.

Mia Andersson's parents were both heavy drug users, and died when she was seven.

For most of her life, she has been surrounded by drugs and criminal behaviour, and none of the homes where she has been placed over the years have worked out. At seventeen, she is now too old for anyone to want to take her in.

Certain families are struck by tragedy, and Pamela has come to realise that those left behind should seek out others with similar experiences. All three of them – Pamela, Mia, and Martin – have lost their closest relatives; they can understand one another, and could start a healing journey together.

'It's time to zip your bag back up now,' says the carer.

Martin does as he is told, folding the flap over the zip and standing up with his bag in one hand.

Pamela smiles at him.

'Are you ready to come home?'

9

The room is dark, but the peephole is glowing on the patterned wallpaper like a small grey pearl.

Just an hour or so ago, it had been invisible, as it had been for quite some time.

Jenny lies in bed, perfectly still, listening to Frida's breathing. She can tell that she is still awake.

Out in the yard, the dog barks.

Jenny hopes Frida won't assume it is safe to talk yet.

It hasn't been long since they stopped hearing steps on the floor above. It might have been nothing but the wood contracting, but they can't afford to take any chances.

Jenny stares at the glowing pearl, trying to see whether there are any shadows moving in the room next door.

There are small holes everywhere here.

You learn to pretend not to notice them darken while you're in the shower or eating soup in the dining room.

Being watched has become a natural part of life here.

In fact, Jenny remembers feeling like she was being watched for several weeks before she was abducted.

Once, when she was home alone, she thought she could sense someone else in the house with her, and when she woke up in the darkness, she had the chilling feeling that she had been photographed in her sleep.

A few days later, her bloodstained pale blue silk underwear vanished from the laundry basket. It was no longer there when she finally got around to buying some stain remover.

On the day she was taken, someone had let the air out of her bike tyres.

She screamed until her voice was hoarse when she first noticed someone watching her in the basement through the hole at the top of the concrete wall.

The police will be here soon, she had shouted.

But after six months, she finally accepted that the police officer on the motorcycle was never going to put two and two together and realise that the girl throwing up in the long grass was the same one who had been reported missing. He had never taken a good look at her, after all. He just dismissed her as another drunk teenage girl.

Jenny hears Frida roll over onto her side.

They have been planning their escape for two months now. Every night, they wait until they can no longer hear any footsteps upstairs and the shouts from the basement cease. Once they are sure everyone else is sleeping, Frida tiptoes over to Jenny's bed so that they can continue their discussion.

Jenny has always struggled to hold back all thoughts of escape, though she has known from the very beginning that she needs to run away from this place.

Frida has only been here eleven months, but she is already impatient.

For five years, Jenny has been gathering information and waiting for the right moment.

At some point, all the doors will be open, and she will walk out without looking back. But Frida seems desperate to break out.

Only a month ago, she snuck into the utility room and took the spare key to their door.

One of the walls is covered with dark keys hanging on hooks, and there are so many that no one seems to have realised one is missing. It was a big risk, but it was necessary, because their door is always locked at night and the shutters are nailed shut from the outside.

But they haven't packed anything, because that's the kind of thing someone might notice.

38

When their moment comes, they will simply vanish. The house has been quiet for at least an hour now.

Jenny knows that Frida wants them to escape tonight. The only problem is that the nights are still very light at this time of year. They would still be fully visible in the yard before they can disappear among the trees.

Their plan is a simple one: they will get dressed, unlock the door, walk down the hallway to the kitchen, climb out of the window and then make their way into the forest.

Jenny has made sure to approach the guard dog whenever she can, giving some of her food to him in the hopes that he will get used to her and keep quiet when she finally escapes.

From the house, you can see the silvery electrical towers over the treetops.

Jenny's idea is to follow the towers to avoid getting lost. The ground beneath them also tends to be kept clear to prevent any trees from damaging the lines during storms, and that means the terrain will be much easier to traverse than the dense forest floor. They will be able to maintain a faster pace and put more distance between themselves and Granny.

Frida has someone she trusts in Stockholm, someone she swears will help them with money, a place to hide and train tickets home.

They can't go to the police until they are safely back with their families.

There's a gold-framed photograph on the bedside table, and Jenny knows that it's a warning. Caesar had to have gone to her parents' house to take that photograph of them sitting on the back patio one summer morning.

Frida's picture is of her little sister wearing a bike helmet. It is taken straight on so that her pupils glow red.

Caesar has so many contacts within the police and the Amber alert system that he'll know if they try to call emergency services. He'll kill their families if they do.

The thought of escaping tonight is so tempting that adrenaline starts pulsing through Jenny's veins, but her gut tells her they should wait until mid-August.

The house is sleeping, and it has been several hours since Granny last checked in on them. The copper rooster weathervane on the roof creaks as it turns in the wind.

Frida's gold bracelet clinks as she reaches out in the darkness.

Jenny waits a few seconds, then takes Frida's hand in hers, squeezing it gently. 'You know what I think,' she says softly and without taking her eyes off the glowing pearl on the wall.

'Yeah, but it's never going to feel one hundred per cent right,' Frida replies impatiently.

'Keep your voice down . . . Let's wait a month, we can handle that. A month from now, it'll be pitch-black at this time of night.'

'But then there'll be something else that doesn't feel right,' says Frida, letting go of her hand.

'You know where I stand. I promise I'll come with you once it's darker.'

'But I'm not sure you actually want to leave. I mean . . . Are you going to stay here? What for? All the gold, all the pearls and emeralds?'

'I hate that stuff.'

Without a sound, Frida climbs out of bed and takes off her nightgown to create a fake body out of her duvet and pillows.

'I need your help getting through the forest. You know that part much better than I do . . . but without me, you won't be able to get home,' she says as she puts on her bra and a blouse. 'For God's sake, Jenny, let's do this together. If you help me, I can help you get money, train tickets . . . but I'm leaving right now. This is your only chance.'

'I'm sorry,' Jenny whispers. 'I can't. It's too dangerous.'

She watches Frida tuck her blouse into her skirt and zip it up. As she puts on her tights and boots, her feet softly drop against the floor.

'You have to check the ground in front of you with a stick,' Jenny whispers. 'All the way to the towers. I'm serious. Go slowly. Be careful.'

'OK,' Frida replies, tiptoeing over to the door.

Jenny props herself up in bed. 'Can I have Ramon's number?' she asks.

Frida doesn't reply. She just unlocks the door and steps out into the hallway.

There is a click as the catch springs back into place, then silence.

Jenny lies down, her heart racing.

She imagines desperately getting dressed and hurrying after Frida. Running through the woods, catching a train, coming home.

She holds her breath and listens.

By now Frida must have passed Caesar's door on her way to the kitchen, but she can't hear a thing.

But Granny isn't usually a deep sleeper.

Whenever one of them makes a sound, it never takes long before they hear her footsteps on the stairs.

But the house is still silent.

Jenny's heart skips a beat when the dog starts barking. She realises that Frida must have opened the window at the back of the house, that she is climbing out now.

The chain goes taut, straining against the dog's neck, and his barks abate before stopping altogether.

It doesn't sound any different when he catches the scent of a deer or a fox.

Jenny stares at the peephole, the spot still bright on the wall.

Frida must be in the forest now.

She made it past the network of bells.

But she still needs to be careful.

Jenny should have gone with her, she thinks. Now she has no key, no contact, no plan.

She closes her eyes and pictures a dark forest.

Everything is quiet.

Suddenly the toilet upstairs flushes, and she shudders and opens her eyes. Granny is awake.

There are heavy footsteps on the stairs.

The handrail creaks.

A bell rings softly in the utility room. It often happens when it's windy, or when an animal sets it off.

The peephole is still glowing.

Jenny hears Granny pulling on her jacket on the porch, leaving the house and locking the door behind her.

The dog is whimpering and yelping.

Another bell rings.

41

Jenny's heart is now racing.

Something must have gone wrong.

She closes her eyes tight and hears creaking from one of the rooms next door.

The weathervane on the roof turns with a screech.

Jenny opens her eyes when the dog starts barking in the distance. He sounds frenzied.

She hopes Granny assumed that Frida didn't dare go through the forest, that she took the road towards the mine.

The barking is drawing closer now.

Jenny knows deep down, long before she hears the voices in the yard, before the front door flies open, that Frida has been caught.

'I changed my mind,' Frida shouts. 'I was on my way back, I want to stay here, I'm happy . . .'

An aggressive slap stops her mid-sentence. It sounds like she was slammed into the wall and has slumped onto the floor.

'I just wanted to see my mum and dad.'

'Shut up,' Granny grunts.

Jenny knows she has to pretend to be sleeping deeply, that she has no idea Frida has attempted to escape.

She hears footsteps down the marble hallway drawing closer. The door to the boudoir opens.

Frida is sobbing, promising it was all a mistake, that she was on her way back when she got caught in the trap.

Jenny lies still, listening to the sound of metallic clicks and heavy sighs, but she can't work out what is going on.

'You don't have to do that,' Frida begs. 'Please, wait, I swear I won't ever . . .'

Suddenly, she screams. It is like nothing Jenny has ever heard before, a shriek of unfathomable pain, ending as abruptly as it began.

There is a thud against the wall, the sound of furniture being moved.

Jenny hears a pained wail between rapid breaths, then silence.

She lies perfectly still, her pulse pounding in her ears.

She has no idea how long she has been staring into darkness when the white pearl on the wall disappears.

Jenny closes her eyes, opens her mouth slightly, and pretends to be asleep.

She probably can't trick Granny, but she doesn't dare open her eyes again until she hears footsteps in the hallway.

It sounds like someone walking slowly, kicking a wooden block in front of them.

The door opens, and Granny comes in with heavy footsteps. The chamber pot clinks against the leg of the bed.

'Get dressed and come to the boudoir,' she says, prodding Jenny with her stick.

'What time is it?' Jenny mumbles drowsily.

Granny sighs and leaves the room.

Jenny quickly gets dressed, pulling on her jacket as she leaves the room. She pauses in the hallway, tugging her tights up higher before making her way into the boudoir.

The bright summer sky is hidden behind the dark curtains, and the only source of light in the room is coming from the reading lamp.

Just inside the door, there is a bloody plastic bucket.

Jenny feels her legs turn weak as she steps into the room.

The air is heavy with the scent of blood, vomit and faeces.

As she passes the bucket, she sees that Frida's feet are inside.

Her heart is racing.

It is only as she rounds the Japanese screen with the cherry blossoms that she sees the room in full.

Granny is sitting down in an armchair, and the mosaic floor around her is slick with blood. Her lips are pressed tightly together in a bitter expression. Her thick arms are streaked with blood right up to her shoulders, and it is dripping from the hand holding the saw.

Frida is lying flat out on the sofa.

She is being held in place by two ratchet straps looped under the seat at her torso and thighs.

Her entire body is shaking.

Her feet have been sawn off above the ankles, the wounds tied off, but the blood is still flowing from her stumps. The velvet

43

cushions and the pillows are soaked through, and a steady stream of blood is trickling down the legs of the sofa onto the floor.

'Now she never needs to worry about getting lost again,' Granny says, getting up with the saw in her hand.

Frida is wide-eyed with shock, and keeps lifting her mutilated legs in the air.

10

Light filters into the boudoir through the lace curtains and orange veils. It's early morning, but it feels like the sun is already setting.

Specks of dust shimmer in the light from the window.

Jenny has been trying to tend to Frida while Granny is in the kitchen.

Frida's pearl necklace, flecked with spattered blood, rises and falls with each shallow breath she takes. Her eyes are closed and the areas around them are pink, her lips chewed to shreds.

Sweat has turned her blouse translucent between her breasts and under her arms, and her black bra is plainly visible. Her checked skirt is bunched up around her waist.

Her pain is overwhelming; she doesn't seem to understand what has happened to her.

One of her calves is mangled and bluish-purple above the sutures. Jenny guesses she must have stepped in a bear trap in the woods. Maybe that was why Granny decided to amputate her feet.

Jenny has loosened the straps around her body and bound her bloody stumps. Twice she has stepped into the kitchen to explain to Granny that Frida needs to go to the hospital, but to no avail.

Frida opens her eyes and peers down at her maimed ankles. She lifts one stump and starts to panic.

'Oh God,' she cries.

She screams until her voice breaks and hurls herself to one side, collapsing onto the damp rug as she's silenced by the excruciating pain.

Jenny tries to hold Frida still, but she can feel the panic pulsing through her. She thrashes her head in desperation as her entire body trembles.

'I don't want . . .'

The stitches on her left leg burst, and she starts bleeding heavily again.

'My feet . . . she sawed off my feet . . .'

Frida's blonde hair is lank with tears and sweat. Her pupils are huge and her lips have lost all colour. Jenny strokes her cheek and repeats that everything is going to be OK.

'We'll get through this,' she says. 'We just need to stop the bleeding.'

Jenny moves the sofa, gently lifting Frida's mangled legs up onto the seat cushion to help stem the flow.

Frida closes her eyes, her breathing hurried.

Jenny turns to look at the peephole by the mirror, but the boudoir is too bright for her to be able to see if she is being watched.

She waits, listening.

Frida's boots and her white socks have been tossed under the table.

When she hears the clatter of china in the kitchen, Jenny bends down over Frida and carefully searches the pockets of her skirt.

She thinks she hears something and spins around.

Granny's red footprints lead away from the substantial pool of blood on the mosaic floor, past the plastic bucket and out into the hallway.

Jenny tries to make out the doorway through the gap between the two sections of the Japanese screen.

She hesitates for a moment, then hooks a finger inside Frida's skirt, feeling along the waistband. Hearing footsteps in the hallway, she quickly pulls her hand away.

Granny passes the boudoir and continues on to the porch.

Jenny gets onto her knees and undoes two of the buttons on Frida's blouse. Out in the yard, the dog starts barking.

Frida opens her eyes and watches as Jenny reaches into her sweaty bra. 'Don't leave me,' she mumbles.

Jenny feels beneath her right breast and finds a small scrap of paper. She pulls it out and gets to her feet.

The light coming in through the curtains seems to shift, becoming brighter for a moment.

Blood is still dripping from the sofa.

Jenny glances down at the scrap of paper and sees the phone number for Frida's contact, then turns away and pushes it into the waistband of her underwear.

'Please, you have to help me,' Frida whispers, gritting her teeth in pain.

'I'm trying to stop the bleeding.'

'Jenny, I don't want to die, I need to go to hospital. This isn't going to work.'

'Just lie still.'

'I can crawl, I swear I can,' says Frida, now gasping for air.

The front door opens, and Granny's footsteps draw closer. Jenny can hear her heavy shoes and the click of her cane on the marble floor.

The keys jingle on her belt.

Jenny moves over to the display case and starts making a new compress. The footsteps slow, the handle turns, and the door to the boudoir swings open.

Granny is leaning heavily on her stick as she comes into the room. She pauses by the screen, her stern face in shadow.

'It's time to go home,' says Granny.

Jenny swallows hard. 'She's bleeding less now,' she tells her.

'There's room for two in there,' Granny replies curtly, turning to leave the room.

Jenny knows what she has to do if she wants to survive, but she pushes back any thought of specifics. She moves over to Frida and avoids meeting her eye as she bends down and grips the edge of the embroidered gold rug.

'Wait, please . . .'

Jenny drags the rug carrying Frida across the mosaic floor, slipping in the blood as she shuffles backwards out into the hallway. Frida is sobbing and whimpers in pain at every bump, but says over and over again how much stronger she feels now.

47

Jenny pulls her past Caesar's room and towards the porch, forcing herself to ignore her cries and pleading.

Frida tries to cling to a gilded stool, and it follows them for a few metres before slipping out of her fingers.

'Don't do it,' she begs Jenny.

Granny is waiting in the doorway to the yard. The morning light behind her is hazy. Jenny can smell the soft scent of smoke on the porch, and she realises Granny must be burning something in the incinerator behind the seventh longhouse.

Frida screams in pain as Jenny drags her down the two steps and out into the yard.

Blood has started pulsing from one of her stumps, collecting in a small pool in the bunched-up rug. It leaves a dark trail across the gravel.

The dog whines anxiously as Granny ties its long leash to the rusty rubbish bin.

She unlocks the door to the sixth longhouse and props it open with a rock. The smoke curls over the tin roof and between the crowns of the trees.

Frida whimpers as Jenny loses her grip on the rug. Her pearls strain against her throat, her eyes desperate.

'Help me,' she pleads.

Jenny bends down and notices as she grips the edge of the rug again that her nails are broken. Without emotion, she continues dragging Frida inside, over the concrete floor.

Daylight filters in through the row of filthy windows beneath the beams and the tin roof.

There is an old train station clock leaning against one wall, and Jenny sees her slender shadow reflected in the domed glass.

The floor is dotted with dry leaves and pine needles.

A coiled fly trap swings gently above the workbench, next to which rusty bear traps sit in a plastic tub.

Jenny drags her friend past the drums and containers of fish by-products and into the large execution cage.

Frida can no longer hold back her fear of dying, and starts sobbing uncontrollably. 'Mum, I want my mum . . .'

Jenny pauses in the middle of the cage and drops the rug. She turns to leave and does not look back. With downcast eyes, she moves past Granny and out into the cool air of the yard.

The dog barks a few times as it snaps at his leash, circling and stirring up dust before settling down on the ground, panting.

Jenny grabs a broom from a wheelbarrow and hurries past the row of longhouses.

She knows that Granny will assume she has gone back to her room to bury her face in her pillow and cry.

Granny thinks she has scared her so badly that she will never try to escape.

Jenny is shaking with fear, but she turns off between the old lorry and the semi-trailer, kicking the broom head from the shaft and walking away.

While Frida is being gassed to death, Jenny makes her way into the forest without looking back.

She knows she has to fend off her sense of panic. She can't allow herself to start running.

She slowly makes her way through the bilberry bushes between the tree trunks. The wind rustles the leaves overhead.

Spiderwebs tickle her face.

Jenny is breathing too fast in the cool morning air. She knows Granny might already have started looking for her.

She makes her way forward, prodding the ground with the shaft of the broom and pushing branches out of the way with her free hand.

The forest becomes thicker, more tangled.

Up ahead, a tree has fallen between two others, blocking her path. She ducks beneath its trunk, and is just about to stand up on the other side when she spots something glittering in the light. A series of nylon threads have been strung up between the trunks.

Jenny knows they are in some way linked to the bells in the utility room.

She moves back, stands up again, and makes her way around the fallen tree. A branch cracks as it snaps underfoot.

She forces herself to move slowly and spots a pit as she passes by. The interwoven branches and moss have collapsed on the pointed stakes inside.

Jenny knows she only has one shot.

But if she can just make it out of the forest, she should be able to hitch a ride to Stockholm, where Frida's contact can help her get home.

She won't take any risks. She and her parents will need police protection until Caesar and Granny have been arrested.

A hundred or so metres up ahead, the forest opens out onto the line of electrical towers. The strip of land has been cut clear, and the power lines run from tower to tower overhead.

She moves around an uprooted tree and has just stepped into a small glade when she hears something thudding against the ground behind her.

A crow flaps up from a tree, cawing ominously. Huge ferns cover the ground.

Jenny wades through them, using her broom handle to repeatedly jab in front of her. The ferns come up to her thighs and are so thick that she can't see her own feet.

She can now hear agitated barking and is just about to start running when the broom handle is torn from her hand, hitting the ground with a loud crack.

Without moving her feet, she bends down and pushes back the ferns with one hand.

The broom handle is caught in a bear trap.

Its rough teeth have slammed together with such force that they have almost sliced the handle in two, and Jenny only needs to wiggle it back and forth twice before it snaps.

She slowly crosses the glade, poking at the ground with the broom handle, and makes her way between the final few trees and out into the cleared area.

She walks through yellow grass and between young birch trees with thin pink branches, pausing and listening behind her before setting off again.

11

It rained heavily overnight, but the sun is now shining and the leaves on the trees have finally stopped dripping.

Inside the three greenhouses, the greenery presses up against the glass streaked with condensation.

Valeria de Castro puts down her wheelbarrow outside the shed so she can grab fertiliser for the plants.

Her emergency alarm swings on its cord around her neck.

Joona Linna drives the spade into the ground with his foot, then straightens up and wipes the sweat from his brow with the back of his hand.

The neck of his knitted grey sweater is visible beneath his unbuttoned raincoat. His hair is ruffled, and his eyes are like tarnished silver until they catch the sunlight filtering down between the branches.

Every day still feels like the dawn after a stormy night, like stepping out in the first light to take stock of the destruction while hope permeates the air for those who survived.

He visits the graves regularly, taking flowers from his greenhouse. Time has the ability to soften grief and make it seem translucent. You slowly learn to cope with what's changed, with the fact that life goes on even if it looks nothing like what you had hoped.

Joona Linna is back working as a detective with the National Crime Unit, and has reclaimed his old office on the eighth floor.

All attempts to find the man who called himself the Beaver have led nowhere, and after eight months, the NCU still has nothing to go on but the blurry CCTV footage from Belarus.

They don't even know his name.

Every place they have linked him to has turned out to be a dead end.

No one in any of Interpol's 190 member countries can find a trace of him. It's as though he only existed for a few short weeks last year.

Joona pauses and looks over to Valeria, not realising that he is smiling. She is pushing the wheelbarrow towards him along the gravel path, her curly ponytail bouncing against the black nylon of her muddy padded jacket.

'Radio goo goo,' she says as their eyes meet.

'Radio ga ga,' Joona replies, starting to dig again.

Valeria is flying to Brazil the day after tomorrow for the birth of her eldest son's first child. Her youngest has agreed to take care of the plants in the nursery while she is away.

Lumi, his daughter, has come to visit from Paris, and will spend five days with Joona in Stockholm after Valeria leaves.

Two days ago, they watched the Swedish women's football team beat England and take bronze in the World Cup, and last night, they grilled racks of lamb.

Lumi seemed lost in thought during dinner, and when Joona tried to talk to her, she was distant, answering as though he were a complete stranger.

She went to bed early while Joona and Valeria watched a film about Queen on the sofa. The music has been playing in their heads non-stop ever since. Neither has been able to shake the melody.

'All we hear is radio ga ga,' Valeria sings over by the raised beds.

'Radio goo goo,' Joona replies.

'Radio ga ga,' she says with a smile, heading back towards the greenhouse.

Humming, Joona digs another few spadefuls of earth. The thought that everything is finally starting to get better has just crossed his mind when Lumi emerges from the house, stopping on the porch steps.

She is wearing a black windbreaker and a pair of green rubber boots.

Joona drives the spade into the ground with his foot and makes his way over to her. He is just about to ask whether there are any

tunes she can't get out of her head when he notices that her eyes are red and puffy.

'I've rebooked my tickets, Dad . . . I'm going home this afternoon.'

'Can't you give it another chance?' he asks her.

She lowers her head, and a lock of brown hair falls over her eyes.

'I came because I hoped things would feel different once I was actually here, but they don't.'

'I hear what you're saying, but you only just got here, so maybe—'

'Dad, I know,' Lumi interrupts him. 'I already feel bad. I know it's not fair after everything you've done for me, but I've seen a side of you that scares me, one I never wanted to see, and I've been trying to forget it ever since.'

'I know how it must've looked from where you were standing, but I had no choice,' he says, feeling dirty inside.

'Maybe that's true, but, either way, I feel unsafe in your world,' she explains. 'All I see is violence and death, and I don't want to be a part of that. I want a different kind of life.'

'I don't see my world that way, and maybe that means you're right, that I'm damaged . . .'

'I'm not trying to say that we need to decide one way or the other,' she says.

They both fall silent.

'Why don't we go in and have some coffee?' Joona asks hesitantly.

'I'm leaving now. I'm going to get some work done at the airport,' she replies.

'I can drive you,' Joona offers, making a move towards the car.

'I've already called a taxi,' she says and heads back inside to grab her bag.

'Are you fighting?' Valeria asks, stepping up beside Joona.

'Lumi's going home,' he says.

'What happened?'

Joona turns to her. 'It's me. She says she can't stand my world, and . . . I respect that,' he says.

Valeria frowns, and a deep furrow appears between her brows. 'But she's only been here two days.'

'She's seen who I am.'

53

'You're the best,' says Valeria.

When Lumi reappears, she's changed into her black lace-up boots and is carrying her bag in one hand.

'What a shame that you're leaving,' Valeria tells her.

'I know, I thought I was ready, but . . . it's just too soon.'

'You're always welcome back here.' Valeria holds out her arms. Lumi gives her a long hug.

'Thanks for having me.'

Joona takes Lumi's bag and follows her up to the turning circle. They stand side by side next to his car, looking out at the road.

'Lumi, I understand what you're saying, and I think you're right . . . but I can change,' he says after a moment. 'I can quit the force. It's just a job, it's not what I live for.'

But she doesn't reply. She quietly stands beside him watching the taxi approach along the narrow road.

'Do you remember when you were little and we used to pretend I was your pet monkey?' he asks, turning to her.

'No.'

'Sometimes I wondered whether you actually knew I was a person . . .'

The taxi pulls up and the driver gets out and says hello. He loads Lumi's luggage into the boot and opens the back door for her.

'Aren't you going to say goodbye to your monkey?' Joona asks.

'Bye.'

She climbs into the car, and Joona waves as the taxi wheels around, tyres crunching.

Once it has disappeared around the corner, he turns to his own car and sees the sky reflected in the windscreen. He leans against the bonnet and lowers his head.

He doesn't hear Valeria approaching until he feels her hand on his back.

'No one likes cops,' she tries to joke.

'I'm starting to realise that,' Joona says, looking up at her.

She sighs deeply. 'I don't want you to be sad,' she whispers, resting her forehead on his shoulder.

'I'm not, don't worry.'

'Do you want me to call Lumi and talk to her?' she asks. 'She went through some truly awful things, but if it wasn't for you neither of us would be alive today.'

'If it wasn't for me, you wouldn't have been in danger in the first place. That's worth thinking about.'

She pulls him to her and wraps her arms around him, cheek against his chest, listening to his heartbeat.

'Shall we have lunch?'

They walk back over to the raised beds. On a stack of empty pallets, there is a Thermos, two bowls of instant noodles and two bottles of beer.

'Fancy,' says Joona.

Valeria pours hot water from the Thermos into the plastic bowls, puts the lids back on, and uses the edge of the top pallet to open the two bottles.

They split their chopsticks and wait a few minutes before sitting down on the heap of gravel to eat in the sun.

'Now I don't feel anywhere near as happy to be leaving tomorrow,' says Valeria.

'It'll be great.'

'But I'm worried about you.'

'Because I can't get a certain song out of my head?'

Valeria smiles and opens the zip on her burgundy fleece. Her enamelled daisy necklace rests between her collarbones.

'Radio goo goo,' she sings.

'Radio ga ga.'

Joona takes a swig of beer and turns to look at Valeria as she drinks the stock from her noodles. There is dirt beneath her short nails, a deep frown on her face.

'Lumi just needs time. She'll be back,' she says, wiping her mouth with the back of her hand. 'You put up with years of loneliness because at least you knew she was alive . . . You didn't lose her then, and you won't lose her now.'

12

Tracy hears the rain approaching as it reaches Stockholm's metal rooftops. The first few drops hit the windowsill, and soon the neighbourhood is enveloped in the clatter of the downpour.

She is lying naked in bed beside a man called Adam. It's the middle of the night. His apartment is dark and he is asleep.

They met at a bar while she was out with her colleagues.

He flirted with her and bought her a few drinks. Eventually they started joking with each other, and when the others went home, she stayed behind.

Adam has thick, straggly bleached hair with dark roots and kohl beneath his eyes.

He told her that he worked as a high school teacher and claimed to come from an aristocratic family.

They staggered back to his apartment beneath an ominous night sky. Tracy lives in Kista, but his place is in the centre of town.

The apartment is small, with well-worn floorboards and dented doors, peeling paint on the ceiling and a shower above the bath.

He has crates of vinyl records on the floor and black silk sheets on his bed.

Tracy thinks back to when they first got back to his place, and he sat down on the edge of the mattress holding a red toy bus.

It was around twenty centimetres long with black wheels and had two rows of tiny windows.

She picked up her tights, her blouse and her silvery skirt, draping them over the back of a chair before moving towards him in her underwear.

When she approached, he nonchalantly reached out and rolled the front of the bus up her thigh.

'What's going on here?' she asked, trying to smile.

She couldn't hear his reply. He avoided eye contact and pressed the windscreen between her legs, slowly moving the bus back and forth.

'Seriously,' she said, taking a step back.

He mumbled an apology and put the bus on the bedside table, though his eyes lingered on it as though he could see the driver and passengers inside.

'What are you thinking about?'

'Nothing,' he replied, turning to her with half-closed eyes.

'Are you OK?'

'It was just a bit of fun,' he said, smiling up at her.

'Why don't we start over?'

He nodded, and she stepped forward again and caressed his shoulders, kissing him on the forehead and lips. She kneeled in front of him and started unbuttoning his black jeans.

It took him a while to get hard enough to put on a condom.

When he was ready, Tracy felt aroused as he pushed into her. She was lying on her back, holding his hips, trying to enjoy herself and groaning a little too much.

He thrust into her over and over again.

Her breathing quickened, and she tensed her thighs and toes. Adam suddenly stopped moving, still squeezing her breast with one hand.

'Keep going,' she whispered, trying to catch his eye.

He reached for the toy bus from the bedside table and tried to push it into her mouth. It hit her teeth and she turned away, but he tried again, pressing it against her lips.

'Stop, I don't want to,' she said.

'OK, sorry.'

They continued having sex, but she had lost interest and just wanted it to end, faking an orgasm after a while to hurry things along.

Adam grew sweaty as he climaxed and rolled to the side when he had finished, quietly saying something about breakfast before falling asleep with the bus in his hand.

Tracy is now lying awake, staring up at the ceiling. She realises she really doesn't want to wake up here with Adam.

She gets out of bed, grabs her clothes and goes to the bathroom to pee, clean herself up and get dressed.

When she comes back out, he is still sleeping, mouth open. His breathing is heavy and drunken.

The rain is now lashing down against the window.

Tracy goes out into the hallway and notices that her feet are still tender as she pushes them into her red pumps.

In a blue ceramic dish on top of a chest of drawers, she spots Adam's keys, wallet and the signet ring he was wearing earlier.

She grabs the ring and studies the coat of arms, which features a wolf and two crossed swords, and pushes it onto her ring finger. She heads for the front door, glancing back to his dark bedroom.

The entire building hums with the crashing downpour.

Tracy unlocks the door and steps out into the stairwell, closing it behind her and hurrying down the stairs.

She doesn't know why she stole his ring. She's not the kind of person who lifts things casually, and in fact, she hasn't stolen anything since preschool, when she took a small plastic cake home with her.

Outside, the rain is pelting the pavement and making it glisten.

The water is spurting out of drainpipes and flooding the road.

The drains are overflowing.

Tracy has only made it a few steps when she notices someone walking at the same speed as her on the other side of the road.

She catches glimpses of them between the parked cars. The cold water splashes onto her calves as she tries to pick up the pace.

Her footsteps echo between the buildings.

She turns off onto Kungstensgatan and starts running along the edge of Observatory Grove Park.

She hears the bushes rustling.

The lights are out in the windows on the other side of the street.

There is no sign of anyone.

Tracy calms herself down, but she is still out of breath as she hurries down the stone steps towards Saltmätargatan.

It's dark, and she clings on to the handrail as Adam's ring scrapes against the wet metal.

Tracy reaches the bottom, and glances back up the steps.

The glow of the street light at the top of the steps seems grey in the rain, and she blinks, but can't tell whether anyone is following her.

Without thinking, Tracy takes the short cut to the bus stop through the playground behind the Stockholm School of Economics.

The far street lamp is the only one working, but it isn't so dark that she can't see.

The water is now trickling past her collar and down her back.

In the playground, the muddy puddles ripple with the pounding rain. Behind the huge university building, soaked cardboard boxes lie strewn across the grass.

She regrets taking this route.

The rain is drumming down on the jungle gym. It almost sounds like there is a dog trapped inside the playhouse, panting and throwing itself against the walls. Its windows glitter in the dark.

The ground is saturated, and Tracy tries to avoid the worst of the mud in an attempt to save her shoes.

The rain hisses through the trees' bare branches, making a hollow clang whenever a large droplet hits the low metal fence surrounding the playground.

Something crosses Tracy's field of vision. At first, she doesn't realise what is happening.

An instinctive fear courses through her, making it difficult to breathe.

She slows down, her legs now heavy, trying to take in what she is seeing.

Her heart is pounding in her chest.

The seconds seem to stop ticking by.

Beneath the monkey bars, a girl hovers like a ghost in the darkness.

There is a steel cable around her throat, blood staining the front of her dress.

Her blonde hair is wet and clings to her cheeks as she holds her eyes wide open, her bluish-grey lips parted.

The girl's feet are perhaps a metre and a half above the ground. Her black sneakers lie beneath her.

Hands shaking, Tracy drops her bag to search for her phone and call the police when she sees the girl move.

Her feet have started twitching.

Tracy gasps and runs over to her, slipping in the mud. She reaches the girl and sees that the steel cable around her throat runs up to the very top of the jungle gym and down the other side.

'I'm going to help you,' Tracy shouts, moving around the back.

The cable is wound up by a winch that has been screwed into one of the wooden posts supporting the jungle gym. Tracy grips the crank, but it seems to have been locked somehow.

She pulls at it, fingers desperately searching for a catch.

'Help!' she shouts at the top of her voice.

She tries to open the panel covering the mechanism, but her hand slips and she cuts her knuckle. She pulls at the winch, trying to prise the entire thing out from the post, but it won't budge.

There is a homeless woman in a wet fur coat standing nearby, watching Tracy with a blank look. She has a couple of plastic bags draped over her shoulders, and a white rat's skull strung around her neck.

Tracy runs back around to the girl, gripping her legs and lifting her up, feeling the cramp-like twitches in her calves.

'Help! I need help!' Tracy shouts to the homeless woman.

She steps on the black sneakers, trying to get the girl to stand on her shoulders so that she can loosen the wire around her throat, but her body feels stiff and slips off her, swinging to the side.

The bar above them creaks.

Tracy lifts her again, holding her up. She stands like that in the darkness, in the rain, until the girl stops moving and the heat from her body fades. In the end, Tracy can't keep holding her any more, and slumps to the ground in tears. She doesn't know that the girl has been dead for some time.

13

Large parts of Observatory Grove Park have been cordoned off with officers stationed on the perimeter to keep journalists and curious members of the public away from the crime scene. Joona has just got back from the airport where he dropped Valeria off, and parks his car by Adolf Fredriks kyrka. As he walks the short distance to Saltmätar street, a journalist with a white moustache and furrowed face pushes over to him.

'I recognise you – aren't you from the National Crime Unit?' he asks with a smile. 'What's going on?'

'You'll have to speak to the press officer,' Joona tells him as he walks past.

'So can I write that there's a danger to the public, or . . . ?'

Joona shows his ID to the officer by the tape who lets him inside. The ground is still wet from last night's rain.

'Can I just ask one question?' the journalist shouts from behind him.

Joona heads straight for the inner cordon to the rear of the university building, and sees that they have already put up a protective tent around the jungle gym.

He can make out the movements of the forensic science technicians through the white vinyl.

A man in his mid-twenties with thick eyebrows and a neat beard waves to Joona and makes his way over.

'Aron Beck, Norrmalm Police,' he says, introducing himself. 'I'm leading the preliminary investigation.'

They shake hands before lifting the cordon and walking along the path to the playground.

'I'm pretty anxious to get started,' says Aron, 'but Olga said no one should touch anything before you'd seen the victim.'

They walk over to a young woman with a freckled face, red hair and light-coloured eyebrows. She is wearing a pinstripe coat and black boots.

'This is Olga Berg.'

'Joona Linna,' he says, shaking her hand.

'We've spent all morning trying to obtain footprints and other evidence, but the weather hasn't exactly been on our side. Most of it's gone, but I guess that's just part of the job,' she says.

'A friend of mine, Samuel Mendel, always used to say that if you can think about something that doesn't exist, you've just changed the rules of the game.'

She studies him with a smirk.

'They were right about your eyes,' she says, leading them over to the tent.

A path of step plates has been laid out on the ground around the main crime scene.

They pause outside as Olga explains that forensics have emptied every rubbish bin in the area, including down in the metro station and as far away as Odenplan. They have taken photographs, found multiple sets of fingerprints on the playground, and secured shoe prints from a muddy trail and along the edge of the footpath.

'Did she have any ID on her?' Joona asks.

'Nothing. No driver's licence, no phone,' Aron replies. 'Ten girls were reported missing overnight, but you know how it goes – most of them will turn up as soon as they've charged their phones.'

'You're probably right,' says Joona.

'We just spoke to the woman who found the victim,' Aron continues. 'She got here too late to be able to save her, and she's pretty fucking shaken up. She kept talking about a homeless woman, but so far we don't have any witnesses to the crime itself.'

'I'd like to take a look at the victim now,' says Joona.

Olga steps into the large tent and tells her colleagues to take a break. A moment later, the forensic science technicians start streaming out in their white single-use overalls.

'It's all yours,' says Olga.

'Thanks.'

'I won't tell you what I think yet,' says Aron. 'I wouldn't want to hear that I've gotten everything wrong.'

Joona pushes back the plastic, steps into the tent and pauses. The bright spotlights make the details and colours of the jungle gym pop, as though they were in a saltwater aquarium.

A young woman is hanging by her neck from the jungle gym. Her head is tipped forward, her damp hair covering her face.

Joona takes a deep breath and forces himself to look at her again.

She is a little younger than his daughter and is wearing a black leather jacket, a plum-coloured dress and thick black tights.

Her filthy sneakers are on the ground beneath her, and the fabric of her dress is dark with blood from the wound on her neck.

Sticking to the step plates, Joona moves around the jungle gym to examine the winch fixed to one of the posts.

The killer likely used a combi drill, because the screw heads look pristine, free of the damage typically caused by a screwdriver slipping out as it turns.

He studies the winch and sees that the catch has been deliberately bent to prevent it from being loosened.

An unusual murder. An execution.

A demonstration of power.

Whoever did this screwed the winch to the jungle gym, threw the wire over the top, and created a noose using the hook.

Joona moves to the front of the jungle gym again, pausing in front of the young woman.

Her blonde hair is wet but untangled, her nails are broken, and she isn't wearing any makeup.

He looks up and sees that the steel cable has slipped sideways, damaging the crossbar.

She was alive when the noose was put around her neck, he thinks. Then the killer went back to the winch and turned the crank.

63

Together the gears made her almost weightless as the killer turned the crank.

The spool rotated, hauling the young woman up by her neck. She struggled to break free, kicking with such force that the steel wire shifted along the crossbar.

A gust of wind causes the rustling flaps of the tent to bulge.

Joona's eyes remain unwaveringly on the victim as Aron and Olga come into the tent and stand beside him.

'What are you thinking, Joona?' Olga asks after a moment.

'She was killed here.'

'We knew that already,' Aron replies. 'The woman who found her said she was still alive. She saw her legs moving.'

'I can understand the mistake.' Joona nods.

'So I'm wrong after all?' he says.

Since the killer had already left the scene by the time the witness arrived, Joona knows that any signs of life she thought she saw were most likely nothing but idiomuscular contractions. The steel wire must have completely cut off all blood flow to the young woman's brain. She probably had about ten seconds to try to loosen the noose and kick her legs in panic before losing consciousness. She would have died shortly after that, but her nerve pathways may have continued to send signals to her muscles for several hours.

'My feeling is that the killer wanted to show just how helpless the victim was – whoever she may be – while also demonstrating their own power,' says Olga.

The girl's right ear, waxy and white, is visible between the strands of her blonde hair. The lining of her leather jacket is stained inside the collar.

Joona studies her small hands and short nails, the pale tan lines on her skin left by jewellery.

He slowly raises his hand and pushes the damp hair back from her face. Meeting her wide eyes, a profound sense of sadness washes over him.

'Jenny Lind,' he says quietly.

14

Joona is deep in thought as he passes through the glass entrance to the National Police Board.

Jenny Lind was executed in a playground. Hanged in the rain.

He continues through a set of revolving doors before turning right into a waiting lift.

Jenny vanished on her way home from school in Katrineholm five years ago. The search for her was intense and lasted for weeks.

The girl's picture was everywhere, and in the first year of her disappearance, they received a huge number of tips from the public. Her parents pleaded with the abductor not to hurt their daughter, and a substantial award was offered.

The perpetrator drove a lorry with stolen number plates, and despite having clear tyre tracks and a composite drawing of the driver from Jenny's classmate, they were never able to trace the vehicle.

There was a high level of engagement from the police, the public and the media, but the case eventually went quiet.

No one believed Jenny could still be alive.

But she had been, until only a few hours ago.

She is now hanging in the middle of a brightly lit tent, like something in a display case at a museum.

The lift comes to a stop with a ping, and the doors open.

The former head of the National Crime Unit, Carlos Eliasson, was forced to retire after taking full responsibility for Joona's actions in the Netherlands last year. He saved Joona from prosecution by claiming that he had personally authorised every step of the operation.

His replacement is Margot Silverman, a former chief inspector whose father was once the county police commissioner.

As Joona walks down the empty corridor, he takes off his jacket and drapes it over his arm.

His boss's door is open, but Joona still knocks before he enters, pausing just inside.

Margot shows no sign of having noticed him.

Her fingers dart across the keyboard, the nail polish on her right hand messier than the left.

Her skin is pale, with a smattering of freckles over her nose. Her eyes look dark and puffy, and her light-coloured hair is braided.

Among the legal books, police regulations and bills on the bookshelf, there is a small wooden elephant, a twenty-year-old trophy from a riding competition, and several framed photographs of her children. Her freshly laundered jacket is hanging on a hook by the door, her bag is on the floor.

'How are Johanna and the kids?' Joona asks.

'I'm not going to talk about my wife and children,' she replies as she types.

'But you wanted to talk about something?'

'Jenny Lind has been murdered,' she says.

'And Norrmalm Police have asked for our help,' he says.

'They can manage on their own.'

'Maybe,' he replies.

'You may as well sit down, because I think I'm about to repeat myself . . .' she says. 'When you're the boss no one dares tell you you're doing it. That's one of the privileges of the role.'

'Is that so?'

She looks up from her screen.

'Yes, you're entitled to steal other people's ideas and jokes, and everything you say is incredibly interesting by right of office, even though you're repeating yourself.'

'So you've said,' Joona says, not moving.

Margot's mouth has turned up into a smirk, but her eyes are as serious as ever.

'I know you always got your way under Carlos, and I have no intention of arguing about that, even though I do think it's an old-fashioned way of doing things,' she explains. 'You produce extraordinary results – but in both a positive and negative sense . . . You're too expensive, you leave behind a trail of destruction, and you take up more resources than anyone else.'

'I've arranged to meet Johan Jönson to go through the footage from the CCTV cameras around the playground.'

'No, you're going to drop this now,' says Margot.

Joona leaves the room. He knows that this case goes much deeper than any of them yet understand.

15

Joona steps out of the lift on the top floor of the Nyponet apartments on Körsbärsvägen and finds Johan Jönson waiting for him.

His colleague is in his underwear and a faded T-shirt with the word 'Fonus' printed on the front. He is almost entirely bald, but he has a beard that's flecked with grey, and his eyebrows are thick.

Despite having the entire floor of the building to himself, Johan has set up his computer on a small table with two collapsible chairs in the stairwell.

'You can't even get in there anymore,' he says, gesturing to the apartment door behind him. 'When it comes to IT equipment, I'm a hoarder.'

'Wouldn't it be nice to have a bed and a bathroom?' Joona grins.

'It's not easy when it's hard,' he sighs.

Joona already knows that the playground itself isn't covered by any CCTV cameras. It's in a blind zone behind the university building. But since this is central Stockholm, most of the streets nearby are covered.

Based on Jenny Lind's body temperature, the forensic science technicians from Norrmalm Police have estimated that the time of death was three ten in the morning. Nils Åhlén will make the final judgement once all the contributing factors have been determined from the evidence.

'We haven't exactly hit the jackpot,' Johan begins. 'None of the cameras are pointing at the playground, and we don't see anyone walking towards the crime scene or leaving afterwards . . . But we do

see the victim for a few seconds, and we've got a clear witness, if we can find him.'

'Good work,' says Joona, taking the seat next to him.

'So, we've followed the people who were in the area before and after the murder. Some of them appear on several cameras before disappearing.'

Johan picks up a pack of Pop Rocks, tears off one corner and tips the contents into his mouth. They crackle between his teeth, popping and hissing as he keys up the footage.

'What time frame are we looking at?' asks Joona.

'I've been checking from nine o'clock the evening before and onwards. There are a lot of people milling around then – several hundred pass the playground during the first hour . . . And I stopped at four thirty the next morning, when the place is crawling with cops.'

'Perfect.'

'I've cut together the relevant clips, person by person, to make it a bit more manageable.'

'Thanks.'

'Let's start with the victim,' says Johan, hitting play.

The dark CCTV footage fills the screen, a time stamp in the top corner. From the far side of Svea Road, the camera captures the entrance to Rådmans Street metro station. At the edge of the screen, a section of the park and the rounded facade of the university building are visible.

The resolution is fairly sharp, despite the darkness.

'She's coming soon,' Johan whispers.

The time stamp shows three in the morning, and in the glow of the street lamp, the heavy rain looks like a series of sloping scratches.

Outside a shuttered convenience store and the steel door of the public toilets, the pavement is glistening.

A man in a thick coat and a pair of yellow rubber gloves searches the rubbish bin and then shuffles off along the wall of torn posters and jet-washed graffiti.

Otherwise, the city is almost deserted. A white van drives by.

Three men drunkenly stagger towards McDonald's.

The city seems to darken as the rain becomes heavier.

A paper cup trembles on the low wall surrounding a pond. The water surges through a grate.

A person enters the shot from the left, rounding the entrance to the metro station and pausing beneath the overhanging roof, her back to the glass doors.

A taxi passes by on Svea Road.

Its headlights sweep over her face and her blonde hair. Jenny Lind.

In just ten minutes' time, she will be dead. Her face is in shadow again.

Joona thinks about her brief struggle, legs kicking so hard that her shoes come off.

When the blood supply to the brain is cut off, the feeling of suffocation is nowhere near as gradual as it is when you hold your breath. Before the darkness finally overtakes you, the feeling is explosive and panicked.

Jenny hesitates and then steps out into the rain, turning her back to the camera and walking past the convenience shop, down the path at the end of the pond. Then she disappears from view.

One of the security cameras from the City Library has captured her from a distance.

The resolution is poor, but her hair and face catch the light from a street lamp before she enters the blind spot around the playground.

'That's all we have of her,' says Johan Jönson.

'Understood.'

As Joona plays the footage back in his head, he realises that Jenny knew exactly where she was going, only she hesitated – perhaps because of the rain or because she was early.

What was she doing in the playground in the middle of the night?

Had she agreed to meet someone?

He can't escape the feeling that it's a trap.

'What are you thinking?' Johan asks, breaking the silence.

'I'm not sure yet. I'm just trying to hold on to my first impressions for a moment,' Joona replies, getting up from his chair. 'This footage

might not mean anything right now, but it could prove crucial later on . . . some part of what we saw and felt the first time.'

'Just let me know when you want to continue.'

Johan opens another pack of Pop Rocks and knocks them back.

Joona stares at the wall, thinking about Jenny's slender hands and the pale bracelets of skin glowing against her tan.

'Play the next one,' he says, sitting down again.

'This one follows the woman who found the victim. She gets to the playground just a few minutes after the murder.'

A CCTV camera has caught the woman running along the pavement in the rain, between the line of parked cars and the wall around the edge of the park.

She slows down and glances back over her shoulder as though she is being followed. The rain is hammering the roofs of the cars.

She is now walking quickly, breaking into another run before disappearing down the steps and into the blind zone near the playground.

'Here we cut to fifty minutes later,' says Johan, 'once she finally realises she can't save the girl.'

The camera on screen switches back to the entrance to the metro station. The puddles have grown around the drains by the crossing.

The woman reappears on the saturated grass behind the convenience store. She steps onto the pavement holding a phone to her ear and steadies herself with one hand on an electrical box near the public toilets. She slumps to the ground, her back against the dirty yellow wall.

She speaks into the phone, then lowers it and sits perfectly still, staring out into the rain until the first police car arrives.

'She was the one who made the emergency call – have you heard the recording?' Johan asks.

'Not yet.'

Johan clicks on a sound file, and they hear the operator's calm voice asking what has happened against the pouring rain.

'I couldn't hold her any longer, I tried,' the woman says, her voice breaking.

71

The recording covers what was said as she left the playground, crossed the grass, and sat down against the wall.

'Could you tell me where you are?' the operator asks.

'I found a girl, I think she's dead now . . . God, she was hanging, but I tried to hold her up . . . no one helped me, and I . . .'

Her voice breaks again, and she starts crying.

'Could you repeat what you just said?'

'I couldn't hold her any longer, I couldn't hold her,' she sobs.

'In order for us to help, you need to tell us where you are.'

'I don't know, Sveavägen . . . by, by the pond . . . What's it called? Observatory Groves.'

'Can you see anything recognisable?'

'A convenience store – it's a Pressbyrån.'

The operator continues trying to talk to the woman until the police arrive, but she stops responding and eventually lowers the phone to her knee.

Johan Jönson tips more Pop Rocks into his mouth and clicks on the final video.

'Want to take a look at our potential witnesses?' he asks. 'There were only three people near the playground at the time of the murder.'

A new camera shows a tall woman in a long white raincoat walking down Kungstensgatan on the other side of the university building. She drops a cigarette on the ground, and the tip glows for a moment before fading away. With no sense of urgency, she then continues along the street and disappears out of the camera's view at 3.02.

'She doesn't come back out,' says Jönson.

The image on screen changes again, growing darker. From the distant camera, a homeless woman wearing multiple layers of thick clothing is visible behind the City Library.

'I don't think she would have been able to see the playground from where she's standing, but I included her anyway,' says Jönson.

'Good.'

The camera angle changes again, covering the entrance to the metro station this time. The homeless woman is just discernible in the darkness beyond the Pressbyrån.

'And here's number three,' says Johan.

A man with an umbrella walking a black Labrador steps into the shot between the lifts to the train platform and the station entrance. The dog starts sniffing the mailboxes outside the Pressbyrån, and the man waits for a moment before they move past the toilets and onto the footpath.

After about twenty metres, he stops, his face turned towards the playground.

The time-stamp shows 3.08.

Jenny Lind has two minutes left to live. The noose is likely being put around her neck at that very moment.

The dog tugs at its leash, but the man stays still.

The homeless woman is moving around on the footpath, rummaging through a black rubbish bag and vigorously stamping on something.

The man with the umbrella and the dog glances over at her before turning back to the playground.

He should be able to see everything that is happening, but he shows no sign of witnessing a murder.

A taxi appears on Svea Road, sending up a wave of filthy water as it passes.

At 3.18, the man drops the dog's leash and walks slowly forward until he disappears behind the Pressbyrån.

'The girl is dead and the killer has likely already left the playground,' says Johan.

The dog starts sniffing around the lawn, its leash trailing behind it. The heavy rain makes the puddles look like they are bubbling. The homeless woman has walked out of frame in the direction of the library.

It is 3.25 when the man reappears, his face lowered. The water from his umbrella is pouring down behind him as he ambles back the same way he came.

'In theory, he could have gone right up to the body in that time,' says Joona.

The dog follows him back down onto Svea Road, and when they reach the metro station, the man bends down and picks up the leash. His calm face is visible for a moment in the grey light.

'You need to find him,' says Johan, pausing the image.

'His lack of reaction to the murder made me think he was blind, but he's not; he noticed the homeless woman when she started moving,' says Joona.

'He saw everything,' Johan whispers, meeting Joona's icy grey eyes.

16

Without any sense of urgency, Pamela clears the table, tidies up the kitchen and starts the dishwasher.

She drinks the last of her vodka, lowers the glass to the counter and moves over to the tall panelled window that looks out onto Ellen Keys Park. A group of people with picnic baskets and blankets is still lingering on the grass below.

The heatwave that has been sitting over central Europe since early June drove away the early summer rain overnight. The Swedes know that they have a limited number of sunny days to enjoy, so the parks and outdoor seating at every restaurant and bar quickly filled up.

'I think I'm going to go to bed soon,' she says. 'What are you doing tonight?'

Martin doesn't reply. He is still sitting at the table, playing a game on his phone, stacking geometric shapes until they collapse.

Pamela studies his pale face. He has been unusually anxious all day, and when she woke up at eight that morning, she found him curled up on the floor.

She puts the cold leftovers into the fridge, and wets the dishcloth to wipe up the table before she drapes it back over the tap.

'Really tasty,' Martin says, squinting up at her with a smile.

'You enjoyed your dinner, I noticed,' she replies. 'Which part was the tastiest?'

Martin looks down in terror, focusing on his phone.

Pamela turns back to the counter, wiping down the stovetop with cold water to make it shine. She tosses the paper towel into the rubbish bin, ties the handles of the bag and carries it out into the hallway.

Martin is still staring down at his phone when she returns. The only sound comes from the swishing of the dishwasher.

Pamela pours herself another vodka and sits down opposite him, opening a small jewellery box.

'I got these from Dennis. They're nice, aren't they?'

She holds up one of the earrings, a teardrop-shaped aquamarine, and shows it to Martin. He studies it, his mouth moving like he is searching for the right words.

'I know you know it's my birthday . . . and sometimes, in the past, you've had a present for me,' she says. 'You know that you absolutely don't need to, but if you do have one, now's the time to get it, because I'm going to go read in bed before I get too tired.'

Martin stares at the table, whispering to himself. He sighs and runs a hand over the tabletop.

'I wanted to give . . .' He trails off and turns to look at the window. He slumps to the floor, making his chair slide back behind him with a screech.

'It's OK,' she says, reassuring him.

Martin crawls over to her beneath the table, wrapping his arms around her legs like a child trying to get their parent to stay.

Pamela runs her fingers through his hair, takes a sip of her vodka and puts down the glass. She gently removes Martin's hands, gets up, and moves over to the window, looking out onto Karla Road. Her eyes refocus, and she sees herself reflected in the uneven glass.

Her thoughts have drifted to another email exchange she had with the supervisor from social services. They seem to have cleared the first hurdle. According to the supervisor, Pamela can provide a financially and socially stable environment; the office in their apartment can be turned into a bedroom, and Pamela's boss has said that she can take time off in order to attend any meetings with social services, schools or the care system.

She and Mia have a Skype meeting scheduled for the day after tomorrow. A chance to 'sound each other out', as the supervisor put it.

* * *

Martin crawls back up onto his chair and looks over towards Pamela, who is still standing by the window. He has been wanting to buy her a pearl necklace for almost a year, but hasn't dared. Instead, he bought her fifteen red roses today, but had to leave the shop empty handed when he realised that the boys would want the flowers on their graves instead.

'Hey,' he says.

He sees her wipe the tears from her cheeks before turning to look at him.

He can't tell her that he is afraid of birthdays because the boys will want to celebrate their birthdays too.

They get jealous whenever he buys presents for her. They want the breast whenever anyone talks about food.

He knows these are obsessive thoughts, but every time he tries to say something, he has to stop himself and think through how the boys will react.

He understands that it all stems from the car crash that killed his parents and two brothers.

Martin has never really believed in ghosts, but somehow he managed to open the door to them when he lost Alice. Now they are out there in the real world, and they can touch him with their cold fingers. They can shove him and bite him.

He has learned to be cautious, to avoid tempting or taunting them.

If he says a name, they want it, no matter whose it is. If he mentions a place, they want to be buried there.

But as long as he sticks to the rules, they keep quiet. Unhappy, but not angry.

'You should probably take the Lout out now,' she says to no one, as though she assumes he isn't listening. 'I don't like you being out in the middle of the night.'

He needs to find a way to tell her about the roses without drawing any attention to himself. Maybe she could pick them up from the shop tomorrow on the way to the office.

'Did you hear me, Martin?'

He should say something, or nod, but all he can do is look into her eyes, worried that she used his name.

'OK,' she sighs.

Martin gets up and steps into the hallway, turning on the lights and taking the leash from the hook.

His body has been trembling strangely all day. Almost like there is someone squirming inside him.

Maybe he is coming down with something, or maybe he's just tired.

The dog needed to go out in the middle of the night yesterday, and when they got back Martin was shaking so much that he had to take thirty milligrams of Valium. He can't remember what happened, but the boys were incredibly threatening and forced him to spend the rest of the night on the floor.

That had never happened before.

Martin shakes the leash and goes to the living room. The dog, fast asleep in his armchair as always, doesn't hear him. Martin crouches down beside him and gently wakes him.

'Shall we go for a walk?' he whispers.

The dog gets up, licks his chops, shakes and follows him into the hallway. His real name is Loke, but when he got old and weary, they started calling him the Lout instead.

He is a black Labrador, with such bad hips that he can no longer manage stairs. He spends almost all his time asleep, often smells less than great, can't hear very well and has pretty bad eyesight, but he still enjoys going for long walks.

*　*　*

In the bathroom, Pamela tries on the earrings. She takes them off again and goes back to the bedroom to put them on the bedside table. She gets into bed, picks up her glass of vodka and opens her book, only to close it again a moment later to call Dennis.

78

'Happy birthday,' he says, answering.

'Were you sleeping?' she asks, sipping from her glass.

'No, I'm actually still working – I'm going to Jönköping tomorrow.'

'Thank you for the present,' she says. 'They're beautiful, but you really shouldn't have. You know that, don't you?'

'Yes, but when I saw them, I thought maybe you could do with them, because they look like tears.'

'I've already tried them on – they're fantastic,' she says, before taking another sip and putting down her glass.

'How are things with Martin?'

'Pretty good, he's out with the dog right now. It's working.'

'And you? How are you?'

'I'm strong,' she replies.

'That's what you always say.'

'Because it's true, I've always been strong. I can cope.'

'But you don't have to—'

'Stop,' she interrupts him.

She hears Dennis take a weary breath before he shuts his laptop and moves it out of the way.

'You never change,' he says.

'Sorry . . .'

Dennis has always made this observation, usually with a sense of joyful amazement – though occasionally with a critical note in his voice.

Pamela's thoughts turn to Alice's sixteenth birthday. Martin had made a pasta dish that evening, with prawns and parmesan, and Dennis and his girlfriend stayed for dinner.

Dennis gave Alice a necklace he'd bought at the great bazaar in Damascus, and told her that she looked just like her mum when they first met in high school.

'She was the coolest, prettiest girl I'd ever seen.'

'But now, tons of pasta and one Caesarean section later . . .' Pamela said, patting her belly.

'You never change,' he said.

'Sure,' she laughed.

Pamela remembers they talked about children, that she had said she wasn't afraid of anything other than a new pregnancy. She and Alice had both come close to dying during the birth.

In the few seconds of silence that followed, their eyes turned to Martin. Pamela will never forget the genuine honesty in his voice as he said that Alice was the only child he had ever wanted.

'You're a bit quiet,' Dennis says on the other end of the line.

17

It is late on a Wednesday night, and despite the lingering warmth from the day, the streets of Östermalm are deserted. Martin and Loke are walking along the footpath between the avenue of trees in the middle of Karlavägen.

The only sound is the crunching of gravel beneath his shoes. The darkness pools between the old-fashioned lamp posts.

Since Martin always lets the dog stop and sniff anything he wants to, taking his time and peeing to mark the important places, they have already been out for an hour and a half.

The boys don't usually bother following him when he goes out with the dog. Instead, they wait for him at home, because they know he will be back.

More often than not, they hide in the walk-in wardrobe where they can see out between the slats in the doors. There is an old air vent behind the clothes, with a small metal cover that can be adjusted using a string.

He assumes that must be how they get in.

The last time he went on a business trip, before he took a leave of absence, they tried to cut his face to shreds. They held him down with twisted bath towels, stamped on a razor and pulled out one of the sharp blades. When they eventually got bored, he drove to the A & E in Mora and was given eleven stitches. He told Pamela he had fallen over.

'Ready to head back?' Martin asks Loke.

They turn off by Östra High School and start walking home. The street lights hanging overhead swing in the breeze, their white glow filtering through the branches of the trees and moving like cracks over the pavement.

Martin is suddenly struck by the mental image of a silvery grey lake. The sun is high above the spruce trees, and the ice around them is making soft creaking, thudding sounds. Alice's cheeks are rosy. She says that this is the most beautiful place she has ever been.

He hears the screech of brakes in the distance, tyres skidding on the tarmac.

Martin glances to the right and sees a taxi no more than a metre away from him.

The driver swears through the windscreen and presses his hand against the centre of the wheel, angrily sounding the horn.

Martin realises he is standing in the middle of Sibylle Street.

He crosses to the other side and hears the taxi speed away behind him.

Fragmented memories of Alice's accident occasionally force their way to the surface.

It always hurts so much.

He doesn't want to remember, though he knows that it would help Pamela. He doesn't want to talk about what happened.

It is one o'clock by the time he gets home. He locks the door and slides the chain behind him. He walks to the kitchen and dries off the dog's paws and feeds him.

Martin crouches down and puts his arm around the old dog, checking that he is eating and drinking properly before following him back to his armchair in the living room.

Once Loke has dozed off, Martin brushes his teeth and washes his face.

He will lie down beside Pamela and whisper that he longs for her, that he's sorry he let her down on her birthday.

He tiptoes into the dark bedroom.

Pamela has turned out the reading light, and her glasses and book are both on the bedside table.

Her face is pale, and she hisses softly with each breath.

Martin peers over to the wardrobe door, at the darkness behind the horizontal slats. The curtains sway in the breeze as he moves around the bed.

Pamela sighs and rolls over onto her side.

He keeps his eyes locked on the wardrobe doors as he quietly folds back the duvet.

There is a low creaking sound coming from inside the wardrobe, and he knows it is the cover on the old vent opening.

One of the boys must be coming in that way. Martin won't be able to sleep here.

He picks up the box of Valium from the bedside table and slowly walks towards the hallway, his eyes still on the wardrobe and one hand on the wall, supporting himself as he backs away. He doesn't turn around until his fingers reach the door frame. A shiver passes down his spine as he enters the hallway, steps over the dog's leash on the floor, and makes his way into the living room.

He switches on the floor lamp and sees its glow spread across the room. The dog is fast asleep in his armchair.

Martin crosses the creaking parquet floor and sees his own reflection in the dark glass of the balcony doors.

He senses movement behind him.

Without turning around, he moves slightly to one side so that he can see further down the hallway in the reflection.

The thick varnish on the bathroom door gleams in the light behind him.

The sheen seems to move sideways, and Martin realises that the door is opening. A child's hand lets go of the handle and quickly vanishes into the darkness.

Martin wheels around, his heart racing. The hallway is dark, but he can see that the door to the bathroom is now wide open.

He retreats to the corner of the living room and slouches down onto the floor with his back to the wall.

From where he is sitting, he can see the windows, the closed door to the kitchen and the dark opening into the hallway.

All day he has been fighting back a sense of desperation.

Martin doesn't want to risk derailing the process with Mia. He can't tell Pamela that his anti-psychotic medication doesn't work because the boys are real.

On the coffee table in front of him, next to a stack of paper, there is a glass full of pens, pencils and black pieces of charcoal. He occasionally uses his art materials to write messages to Pamela, though he suspects the eldest boy can read.

Still, it's better than talking.

He stares at the dark hallway and forces down four Valium. His hands are shaking so much that he drops the pack of pills.

Hunched up in the bright living room, his eyes are tired and aching.

He drifts off, dreaming about golden shafts of sunlight filtering through the ice. The bubbles around him seem to clink together, as though they were made of glass.

A sudden creaking sound wakes him.

The noise lasts less than a second, but his pulse immediately starts drumming in his ears. He knows it was the door to the wardrobe opening.

Someone has turned out the floor lamp, and the living room is dark.

The faint bluish glow of the TV spreads across the furniture like a thin layer of ice.

The entire wall by the door into the hallway is black.

The broken fairy lights from Christmas flutter in the wind on the railing around the balcony.

Martin reaches beneath the sofa for the pack of Valium. His hand gropes the floor, but it isn't there.

The boys clearly have no intention of leaving him in peace tonight.

As Martin shuffles closer to the coffee table, he feels the dizzying effects of the pills. He grabs a sheet of paper and a piece of charcoal and decides to draw a cross that he can hold up in front of him until sunrise.

His hand moves slowly and heavily as he draws. It's tricky to see in the darkness, and as he studies his drawing, he realises that the crossbar is too long on one side.

He hesitates, then adds another bar across, although he isn't quite sure if it helps.

With a drugged sense of having lost his free will, he lowers the charcoal to the paper again and draws another post alongside the first.

He shades in the surfaces of the wood, drawing until his eyelids grow heavy.

Martin takes another sheet of paper and manages to draw a lopsided cross. He starts again, but soon pauses when he hears frantic whispering in the hallway.

Without a sound, he shuffles backwards, pressing up against the wall and staring into the darkness.

The boys are coming.

One of them kicks away the dog's leash, making the steel links clatter against the parquet.

Martin tries to keep his breathing soft.

He spots movement in the doorway.

Two small figures step into the living room.

One of the boys is just three, the other around five.

In the TV's soft blue glow, he sees their sulphur-yellow skin straining over their skulls and creasing around their jaws.

Sharp bones protrude between membranes and tissue, visible just beneath their skin, almost on the verge of breaking through.

Martin looks at his drawings on the coffee table, but doesn't dare reach for any of them.

The younger boy is wearing nothing but a pair of polka dot pyjama bottoms. He glances at the older boy, then turns to Martin with a smile.

He slowly moves forward, bumping against the table and making the pencils rattle against the glass.

Martin tries to shrink back further.

The young boy comes to a halt right in front of him, blocking out the faint light. His head tilts forward slightly, but Martin doesn't realise that the boy has dropped his pyjamas until he feels the stream of urine hitting his crotch and legs.

* * *

Pamela wakes before the alarm, her entire body trembling and her head aching. She feels a strong urge to call in sick, fill a mug with vodka and stay in bed all day.

It's quarter to seven.

As she lowers her feet to the floor, she notices that Martin's side of the bed is empty.

He must be out with the dog.

She feels a wave of nausea as she pulls on her bathrobe, but tells herself she can handle this.

She sees the dog's leash on the floor in the hallway and continues to the living room.

The floor lamp is on, the coffee table askew, and there is an empty pack of Valium beneath the sofa.

'Martin?'

She finds him slumped against the wall in the corner, fast asleep, with his chin tucked into his chest. He stinks of urine, and his trousers are soaked.

'Jesus, what happened?'

Pamela hurries over to him and cradles his face in her hands.

'Martin?'

'I fell asleep . . .' he mumbles.

'Come on, let me help you . . .'

He gets to his feet wearily while Pamela supports him. He struggles to walk and stumbles into the sofa.

'How many pills have you taken?'

Martin doesn't want to go into the hallway, and tries to turn around, but Pamela refuses to give in, and he eventually follows her.

'Martin, you have to tell me,' she says.

He pauses outside the bathroom, wiping his mouth and looking down at the floor.

'I'm going to call an ambulance right now if you don't tell me how many pills you've taken,' she says sharply.

'Only four,' he whispers, glancing up at her with terrified eyes.

'I can't believe this is happening. You can't do this to me.'

She helps him undress and get into the shower. He sits down on the rough stone floor, leaning back against the tiles with his eyes closed as the water washes over him.

Pamela watches Martin as she calls Poison Control and explains that her husband has taken four Valium.

The dose isn't dangerous if he is otherwise healthy, she learns. She thanks the operator and apologises for calling.

Pamela knows that Martin takes a lot of sleeping pills and anti-anxiety medication, but this is the first time he has ever overdosed.

He seemed more anxious than usual yesterday, glancing back over his shoulder constantly like he thought someone was watching him.

She takes off her bathrobe and hangs it on the towel rack. She gets into the shower in her underwear and starts lathering him up, rinsing him off and drying him.

'Martin, you know that we won't be allowed to take care of Mia if you keep doing this kind of thing,' she says, leading him to the bedroom.

'Sorry,' he whispers.

She tucks him up in bed and kisses him on the forehead. The morning light is streaming through the curtains.

'Get some sleep now.'

She returns to the bathroom and loads his clothes into the washing machine. Next, she grabs some cleaning spray and paper towels and takes them to the living room.

The dog looks up at her from the armchair, licks his nose and immediately dozes off again.

'And how many pills have you taken, hmm?'

She wipes the floor where Martin was sitting and straightens the furniture. Replacing the pencils and charcoal back into the glass, Pamela sees Martin's drawings scattered across one side of the coffee table. She picks up a sheet of paper with a black cross drawn on it, and gasps when she notices the charcoal sketch beneath.

Martin has drawn a sturdy-looking frame consisting of two posts and double crossbeams. From the top beam, a person is hanging by

their neck. It's a quick sketch, but from her dress, and the long hair covering her face, it's clear that the figure is a girl.

Pamela picks up the drawing and takes it to the bedroom. She finds Martin wide awake and sitting up in bed.

'How are you feeling?' she asks.

'Tired,' he mumbles.

'I found this,' she says calmly, showing him the picture. 'I thought you might want to talk about it.'

He shakes his head and glances anxiously towards the wardrobe.

'Is it a girl?' she asks.

'I don't know,' he whispers.

18

The Department of Forensic Medicine at the Karolinska Institute is a red-brick building with blue awnings, and every fleck of dirt on the windows is visible in the bright sunlight. Outside the Department of Neuroscience on the other side of the road, the flag hangs limply from its pole.

Joona has just been to Norra begravningsplatsen to leave flowers on the graves.

Turning into the car park he sees that Åhlén's white Jaguar is parked neatly in its space for once, and pulls into the spot next to it.

The outdoor furniture has been brought out for the summer, and placed in the sheltered inner corner of the L-shaped building.

Joona walks up the concrete stairs to the entrance and through the blue door. He finds Åhlén waiting in the corridor outside his office.

Åhlén, known as the Needle, is Professor of Forensic Medicine at the Karolinska Institute, and one of Europe's leading experts in his field.

'Margot called to say you're not on this case,' he says in a subdued voice.

'A simple mistake,' Joona replies.

'Fine, I'll interpret that to mean that she was wrong, and not that you think it's a mistake you're not on the case.'

Åhlén opens the door to his office and welcomes Joona in. A young woman in a scuffed leather jacket is sitting inside at the computer. Frippe, the Needle's former assistant, moved to London

to start a band, but Åhlén maintains that his replacement, Chaya Aboulela, is just as good – even though she isn't a fan of hard rock.

'This is Chaya, my new colleague,' Åhlén says, introducing her with a theatrical gesture.

Joona steps forward and shakes her hand. Chaya has a slender, solemn face and sharp brows.

She gets up and swaps her leather jacket for her white lab coat as they head out into the corridor.

'So what's going on with the investigation?' she asks.

'I think we've got an eyewitness . . . but he hasn't been in touch yet, oddly enough,' Joona replies.

'So what's going on?' Chaya repeats.

'I'm waiting on the results of the autopsy as a matter of fact.'

'You are, are you?' she says with a wry smile.

'How long do you think you'll need?' Joona asks.

'Two days,' says Åhlén.

'If we're lazy,' she adds.

Åhlén opens the heavy doors to the chilly autopsy room, where there are four stainless steel tables. The polished surfaces of the sinks and various containers gleam beneath the fluorescent lights.

Jenny Lind is lying on the table at the far end of the room, fully dressed. She looks shrunken and chillingly still.

As Åhlén and Chaya put on their protective clothing, Joona walks over to the body. Her blonde hair has been combed back from her pale grey face.

He studies her nose and the pierced lobes of her small ears. She has an old scar above her lips.

Joona remembers it from the picture they released when she first went missing. The whites of her wide eyes have turned yellow, and the deep wound from the noose looks like a bluish black arrowhead on her slender neck.

Joona watches as Åhlén cuts open her jacket and dress, packing both into evidence bags.

Chaya's camera flash glares on the metal surfaces.

'Norrmalm's technicians at the scene estimated the time of death to be three ten in the morning,' Joona tells them.

'Could be,' Åhlén mumbles.

Chaya photographs Jenny in her bra and tights before Åhlén removes them as well, and she continues taking pictures of the body in her underwear before they too are bagged up.

Joona looks down at the naked young woman.

She is thin but not emaciated, and there are no visible signs of any abuse. Because rigor mortis is a factor of gravity, it always appears in the lowest parts of the body first, so when someone has been hanged, their legs, hands and genitals are the first to darken.

Brownish marbling has started to develop on her thighs and both sides of her torso.

Her hands and toes are bluish red.

'Chaya, what do you think?' asks Joona.

'What do I think?' she repeats, lowering the camera. 'What the hell *do* I think? I think she was alive when she was hanged, so it wasn't as if she were killed and then her dead body were placed in that position, as we sometimes see . . . and the choice of location is also definitely sending a message.'

'And what do you think that means?' Joona asks.

'I don't know, maybe that the murder was a display of some kind . . . although it's not as extravagant as those usually are.'

'Maybe that in itself is the extravagance,' Joona suggests.

'A murder that mimics an execution.' She nods.

'I saw that her fingertips are damaged from trying to loosen the wire during the few seconds she was still conscious . . . but other than that, there's no sign of violence or any other resistance,' says Joona.

Chaya says something under her breath, raises the camera and continues to document every part of the body. The bright flash causes their shadows to shoot up the walls of the room.

'Åhlén?' asks Joona.

'Mmm, what does Åhlén think?' he asks himself, pushing his glasses back onto the bridge of his nose. 'We know the cause of death is a bilateral compression of the carotid arteries, a consequence of her hanging, which lead to the cessation of blood flow to the brain.'

'I agree,' Chaya says quietly, putting the camera down on a bench.

'We'll do the internal examination so that we can see properly . . . but I'm expecting fractures of the hyoid bone and the upper thyroid cartilage, ruptures to the carotid arteries, and damage to the trachea but not the cervical spine.'

Åhlén examines the base of her neck, by her larynx, checking how deep the wire has cut into her flesh.

'Bare steel cable,' he says quietly to himself. 'Even a small child would've been able to winch her up,' Joona says. The gears in the winch would have made it extremely easy to raise her up. They can't rule out any type of perpetrator yet.

He looks closely at Jenny's face, trying to picture her fear as the noose was placed around her neck, how she would have sweated and kicked her legs. He imagines her desperately searching for a way out knowing there was no way to actually escape. Perhaps she begged for mercy, hoping she would be pardoned at the last minute if she showed submission.

'Do you want us to step out?' Åhlén asks quietly.

'Yes, please,' he replies without taking his eyes off the young woman.

'The usual five minutes?'

'That'll do.' He nods.

Joona remains by the table, looking down at her as their footsteps recede over the plastic flooring and the door finally closes.

Silence descends over the large room. He takes a step closer and feels the cold air coming off of her body.

'This is no good, Jenny,' he says softly.

Joona remembers the time she went missing all too well. He offered to go to Katrineholm to help with the investigation, but the head of the regional police force declined his request.

It isn't that Joona thinks he would have been able to save her. But he wishes he could tell himself that he did all he could five years ago.

'I'll find whoever did this to you,' he whispers.

Joona would normally never make a promise like that, but as he looks down at Jenny Lind, he cannot understand why anyone could have decided that she had to die in that playground.

That there were no other options.

Who was responsible for that lack of mercy? Where did the desire to choose murder over any alternative come from? Who could muster that kind of ruthlessness?

'I'll find him,' he promises her.

Joona moves around the body, studying every detail; her smooth knees, her ankles, her small toes. He moves slowly along the table, not taking his eyes off her, until he hears Åhlén and Chaya come back into the room.

They roll her onto her stomach and take their time photographing her.

Åhlén pulls back the blonde hair from her neck so that Chaya can document the top of the wound caused by the noose.

The steel table beneath her lights up in the camera flash. As if backlit by sunlight flooding in through a window, her body is a dark silhouette for a moment.

'Hold on,' says Joona. 'She's got a patch of white hair . . . I just saw it when you took a picture . . . right there.' He points to a small area on the back of her head.

'Yes, look.' Åhlén nods.

At the very base of her skull, there is a small patch of colourless hair. The rest is so light that the difference is almost imperceptible at first glance.

Using a pair of clippers, Åhlén cuts the white hair down to her scalp, and drops it into an evidence bag.

'Change in pigmentation,' Chaya says, sealing the bag.

'Destroying the hair follicles,' Åhlén agrees.

He removes the last few millimetres of hair using a razor blade and then fetches a loupe from his desk. Joona takes it from him and bends down to study Jenny's bare scalp up close: pale pink skin with a pattern of sweat glands and hair follicles and a few stray strands missed by the razor.

Joona realises he isn't looking at a natural pigmentation change, but a kind of white tattoo in the shape of an elaborate 'T' – badly healed at the upper edge, and slightly lopsided.

'She's been freeze-branded,' he says, handing the loupe to Chaya.

19

Joona has closed the door to the corridor, but he can still hear the whirr of the printer and the murmur of his colleagues' voices in the kitchen. His pale blue shirt is tight across over his shoulders and upper arms. His jacket is draped over the back of a chair, and his Colt Combat and shoulder holster are locked in the weapons cabinet.

As he sits at his desk, indirect sunlight from the window falls onto his cheek and his solemn mouth, leaving the deep furrow between his brows in shadow.

He turns away from the computer and looks at the only picture on his otherwise bare wall: a photograph with enlarged detail of the back of Jenny Lind's head.

A letter T, with a broad base and sprawling arms, white against her scalp.

Joona has seen purebred horses with freeze marks before. A stamp cooled in liquid nitrogen is pressed against the animal's skin, allowing its coat to continue growing, but without any pigmentation. The low temperature destroys the follicle's ability to colour the hair but doesn't affect the growth of the hair itself.

If this were Joona's case, the walls of his office would soon be covered in a web of photographs, evidence, lists of names, lab results and pin-studded maps.

The image of the white mark would be the nexus that emerges in every investigation.

He turns back to his computer and logs out of the Europol database. Joona has spent hours searching criminal records, surveillance and

suspect databases, and the National Board of Forensic Medicine's files for any link to freeze-branding.

He hasn't found a single hit.

But Joona's gut feeling is that the killer is not done yet.

He branded the back of his victim's head, and a brand is meant to be used more than once.

Thinking through the details of the case, Joona sees that the evidence is like the choppy surface of the ocean. The mystery has not yet taken shape.

The samples taken by the crime scene investigators are currently being analysed at the National Forensic Centre in Linköping.

The autopsy only began this afternoon.

A team from Norrmalm Police is trying to trace the winch and track down anyone with the right equipment for freeze-branding.

Aron interviewed Tracy Axelsson, the woman who found the victim. According to his report, she described seeing a homeless woman wearing a rat's skull around her neck. The witness was still in shock, and initially claimed that the woman had murdered Jenny, but she later retracted that claim and repeated some twenty times that the woman had stared straight at her instead of helping.

A local police team has managed to track down and interview the homeless woman, comparing her answers to the CCTV footage in which she appears. It seems clear that she was too far from the playground at the time of the murder to have seen anything of importance.

The woman was unable to say what she was doing in front of the jungle gym when Tracy found the victim, but Aron's guess is that she was trying to steal Jenny Lind's belongings.

The investigation is in its frustrating opening stages, and they currently have no leads. Aside from the fact that they have an eyewitness, Joona thinks.

A man stood facing the playground, watching the entire murder take place. He looked away only once when he glanced over to the homeless woman, who was stamping on a box.

At exactly 3.10 in the morning, his eyes were on the playground, though he had no discernible reaction to what he was seeing.

Perhaps he was paralysed by shock.

It isn't unusual for a person to lose all power of action when they witness something incomprehensible or terrifying.

The man simply stared straight ahead until the hanging was over and the killer had left the scene. Only then did his paralysis subside, and he slowly moved closer to the jungle gym, disappearing for a moment into the blind spot.

The man saw everything.

Joona walks down the corridor, thinking about Jenny Lind's parents, about how they must now know that their daughter's body has been found. He imagines the wind being knocked out of them as all the tension from five years of searching for her is finally swept away.

Their grief suddenly immediate and overwhelming.

They will forever be racked with guilt for having given up the search and lost all hope.

Joona knocks on his boss's open door and steps into the spacious office. Margot is sitting behind her desk with a copy of *Aftonbladet* open in front of her. Her blonde hair is tied back in a thick plait, and her pale eyebrows have been filled in with a dark brown pencil.

'I don't know what the hell to say,' she sighs, turning the tabloid towards him.

A drone shot of the crime scene fills the entire two-page spread, Jenny Lind still hanging from the jungle gym.

'Her parents really didn't need to see that,' Joona replies soberly.

'The editor claims it's in the public interest,' Margot tells him.

'What did they write?'

'It's all speculation,' she sighs, throwing the paper away.

Margot's phone is lying on her desk beside her coffee cup, and her fingers have left small grey ovals all over the dark screen.

'This isn't an isolated murder,' Joona tells her.

'No, actually that's precisely what it is . . . and you should know that, because I hear you haven't dropped the case, despite my direct orders,' she says. 'Carlos lost his job because of you. Do you really think I'm going to let the same thing happen to me?'

'The Norrmalm Police need help. I've read their report from the interview, and it's full of holes. Aron doesn't listen as closely as he should. He doesn't consider the fact that the words make up only part of what's being said.'

'So what else am I saying right now?' she asks.

'I don't know,' Joona sighs, turning to leave.

'Because you're no Sherlock Holmes, are you?' she calls after him.

He pauses in the doorway, his back to her.

'I hope your father-in-law is OK,' he says.

'Are you stalking me?' Margot says, her voice serious.

Joona turns around and meets her eye. 'It's just that Johanna and your youngest daughter have been with him for over a week now.'

Margot's cheeks flush. 'I wanted to keep this private,' she says.

'You usually drive to work and park your car in the garage, but your shoes are a bit muddy today because you walked through the park on your way from the metro station,' he continues. 'And when we met on Wednesday evening, there was no horse hair on your jacket. I'm guessing that for Johanna to take the car, it must be pretty serious, because you need it to drive the older girls out to the stables on Värmdö ... You were an avid rider yourself at their age and so it's important that you never miss a chance to go ... And if Johanna has taken the car, then it can't be her mother who is ill, because she lives in Spain.'

'Riding was yesterday. What makes you think they've been with Johanna's dad for a week?'

'Johanna usually helps you paint your nails, so they are freshly done every other Thursday ... but this time the brushwork looks a bit shaky on your right hand.'

'I'm not so good with my left hand,' she mutters.

'Your phone is usually covered in tiny fingerprints because you often let Alva borrow it, but right now they're all yours. That's why I assumed she must have gone with Johanna.'

Margot closes her mouth, leans back and studies him. 'You're cheating.'

'OK.'

'I'm not very susceptible to your charms.'

'What charms?' he asks.

'Joona, I don't like to threaten disciplinary action, but if . . .'

But before she can finish he closes the door and starts walking back to his office.

20

Joona pauses in front of his wall, studying the elegant T. T: the Latin letter derived from the Greek *tau* and Phoenician *taw*, which in turn was once a cross.

As often happens with certain cases, Jenny Lind's disappearance became a national concern, while others ended up in the shadows. Her picture was everywhere. Social media went wild, with seemingly everyone deeply invested in the case, and many people volunteering to join the search for the teenager.

Joona remembers her parents, Bengt and Linnea Lind, from their first few heartrending press conferences to their last bitter statements. They eventually disappeared from view altogether.

Five days after she was kidnapped, the *Aktuellt* news programme invited them on as guests. Jenny's mother did almost all of the talking, her voice breaking with emotion. Whenever it became too much, she pressed her hand to her mouth. Her father was more taciturn and formal, carefully clearing his throat every time he spoke. Linnea Lind said she was convinced her daughter was still alive, that she could feel it in her heart.

'Jenny is scared and confused, but she's still alive, I just know it,' she repeated over and over again.

The segment ended with the couple making a direct plea to their daughter's abductor.

Joona knows that the police gave them guidance on what to say, but he doubts they followed the script as they stood in front of the cameras.

A picture of Jenny was behind them. Her father struggled to keep his voice steady.

'This is our daughter, Jenny. She's a happy girl who likes books, and . . . we love her,' he said, wiping the tears from his cheeks.

'Please,' her mother begged. 'Don't hurt my little girl, don't . . . If it's money you want, we'll pay, I promise. We'll sell the house and the car, we'll sell everything we've got, every last thing, just let her come home to us. She's our sunshine, our . . .'

She started sobbing and buried her face in her hands. Her husband wrapped his arms around her, trying to calm her down before turning back to the camera.

'Whoever did this,' he said, his voice breaking. 'I want you to know that we'll forgive anything if you just let her come back to us. We'll forget everything that's happened and go our separate ways.'

The intense search lasted weeks, and the press reported on new leads, tips and police missteps daily.

The Swedish government announced a reward of 200,000 euros for any information that led to the rescue of Jenny Lind.

Thousands of lorries were searched and checked against the tyre tracks from the scene.

Yet despite all the resources and the huge number of tips from the general public, the investigation eventually ground to a halt, and interest faded. Jenny's parents pleaded with the police not to give up, but in the end there were simply no leads left to follow.

Jenny Lind had simply vanished.

Her parents hired a private detective, racking up so much debt that they ultimately had to sell their house, only to withdraw from the public eye and be forgotten by the press.

Joona tears his eyes from the photograph as his phone starts ringing. He walks over to his desk and sees that it's Åhlén.

'You called several times?' Åhlén says in his rasping voice.

'I wanted to see how it was going with Jenny Lind,' Joona says, sitting down at his desk.

'I'm not allowed to talk to you about this, but, as it happens, we're finished . . . I'll send the report as soon as we've got the last few test results.'

'Is there anything I should know now?' Joona asks, reaching for a pen and paper.

'Nothing noteworthy other than the mark on the back of her head.'

'Had she been raped?'

'There was no physical evidence of that.'

'Can you confirm the time of death?'

'Absolutely.'

'Our technicians said ten past three,' says Joona.

'I'd probably guess that she died at twenty past,' says Åhlén.

'Twenty minutes past three?' Joona repeats, putting down his pen.

'Yes.'

'And when you say you'd guess, do you really mean that you're sure?' Joona continues, getting up from his chair.

'Yes.'

'I need to talk to Aron,' Joona says, before hanging up.

Joona doesn't have to rewatch the CCTV footage to know that the man with the dog could be their killer.

They need to put out an alert, maybe even nationwide. They have to find him as soon as possible. From now on, they will have to consider the eyewitness their prime suspect.

At 3.18, he dropped the leash and headed towards the playground out of view of the camera. Since Jenny Lind would be dead just two minutes later, he wouldn't have had time to attach the winch to the jungle gym, but he could have walked over and wound the crank. There is no doubt about it: he could be the one who killed her.

21

Pamela glances at her watch. It's late afternoon, and she is alone in the office. The air outside is so hot that beads of condensation have started to trickle down the cool windowpane. Her Skype meeting with Mia is due to start any minute now, and she drinks the last of the vodka from her glass, pops another mint into her mouth and sits down at the computer.

The screen darkens for a moment, then an older woman wearing a large pair of glasses appears. She must be the caseworker.

The woman gives Pamela a joyless smile and explains in a tinny voice how these types of meetings usually work. At the very edge of the screen, she catches a glimpse of Mia, her blue and pink hair hanging down over both sides of her pale face.

'What the hell, do I have to?' Mia asks.

'Come and sit down,' the caseworker tells her, getting up.

Mia sighs and does as she is told, still only half visible on-screen.

'Hi, Mia,' Pamela says, smiling warmly.

'Hi,' Mia replies, looking away.

'I'll leave the two of you to chat,' says the caseworker, walking out of the room.

For a moment, no one speaks.

'I know this is a pretty weird situation,' says Pamela. 'But the idea is for us to talk and get to know each other better; it's all part of the process.'

'Whatever,' Mia sighs, blowing the hair out of her eyes.

'So . . . how are you doing?'

'Fine.'

'Is it as hot in Gävle as it is here in Stockholm? There's a real heatwave here; no one can be bothered to work. People have actually started climbing into the fountains to cool down.'

'Life's tough,' Mia mutters.

'I'm in my office right now. Have I told you I'm an architect? I'm forty-one, I've been married to Martin for fifteen years, and we live on Karlavägen in Stockholm.'

'OK,' Mia says, without looking up.

Pamela clears her throat and leans forward.

'You should probably know that Martin has a few mental health issues. He's very kind, but he has OCD and a lot of obsessive thoughts, and that means he doesn't talk much. He sometimes suffers from anxiety too, but he's getting much better . . .' She trails off and swallows.

'We're not perfect, but we love each other and hope you'd like to live with us,' she says. 'Or to see how it feels, anyway. What do you think?'

Mia shrugs.

'You'd have your own room . . . with a really nice view out over the rooftops,' Pamela goes on, realising that her smile is no longer genuine. 'We're pretty ordinary otherwise, we like going to the movies, eating out, travelling, shopping . . . What kind of things do you like?'

'I like going to bed without having to worry about someone trying to hurt or rape me . . . YouTube, the usual.'

'What kind of food do you like?'

'Listen, I've gotta go,' says Mia, moving to get up.

'Do you have any friends?'

'A guy called Pontus.'

'Is he your boyfriend? Sorry – that's none of my business.'

'No.'

'I have to confess I'm a little nervous,' Pamela says.

Mia sits down again, blowing the hair out of her face.

'What about the future?' Pamela says, hoping a different approach might open the conversation up. 'What would you like to do? What are your dreams?'

103

Mia shakes her head as if exhausted. 'Look, I'm sorry, but I can't do this . . .'

'You don't have any questions for me?'

'Nope.'

'Nothing you'd like to know? Or anything you want to tell me?'

The girl looks up.

'I'm hard work,' she explains. 'I'm worthless. No one likes me.'

Pamela forces herself not to argue.

'I'm almost eighteen, and that means society can stop pretending to give a shit about me soon.'

'That's probably true.'

Mia gives Pamela a sceptical glance.

'Why do you want me to live with you anyway?' she asks after a moment. 'I mean, you're an architect. You're rich, you live in the middle of Stockholm. If you can't have kids, why don't you just adopt a cute little girl from China or something?'

Pamela blinks and takes a deep breath.

'I didn't tell your caseworker any of this,' she says softly, 'but I lost my daughter when she was around your age. I didn't say anything because I don't want to scare you or make it seem like I think you can replace her. I just think that people who've lost a lot can help one another, because they understand certain things.'

Mia leans forward.

'What was her name?' she asks, her face now serious.

'Alice.'

'Not Mia, at least.'

'No.' Pamela smiles.

'What happened?'

'She drowned.'

'Shit.'

They sit quietly for a moment.

'I started drinking too much afterwards,' Pamela admits.

'Drinking,' Mia repeats dubiously.

'This was full of vodka.' She holds up her glass. 'I had to drink it to be able to call you.'

Pamela can tell that Mia is more relaxed now. She leans back in her chair and studies Pamela's face on the screen for some time.

'OK, I understand a little better now . . . maybe it could work between us,' she says. 'But you need to stop drinking, and you need to get Martin to pull himself together.'

* * *

Pamela feels restless as she leaves the office and steps out into the warm air. She decides to go for a walk before heading home to Martin.

As she walks, she replays the conversation with Mia in her head, wondering whether it was wrong of her to mention Alice.

She pulls out her phone to call Dennis, passing the second-hand bookshop as it rings.

'Dennis Kratz,' he answers.

'It's me.'

'Sorry, I saw that . . . it just came out automatically. Muscle memory.'

'I know,' she says, smiling.

'How are things with Martin?'

'Pretty good, I think,' she replies. 'He's been a bit anxious at night, but . . .'

'Don't count on any miracles.'

'No, it's . . .' She trails off, allowing a couple of bikes to pass before crossing the road.

'What is it now?' Dennis asks, as though he can read her expression.

'I know you think it's too soon, but I just had a first chat with Mia.'

'What does social services have to say?'

'We've cleared the first hurdle, but, I mean, their decision-making process isn't finished yet, so nothing is final.'

'But you're really hoping it works out?'

'Yeah, I am,' she says, noticing a couple of young women sunbathing in their underwear on a patch of grass.

'And you don't think it'll all be a little much?'

'You know me, nothing is ever too much,' she says, smiling again.

'Just let me know if there's anything I can do.'

'Thanks.'

Pamela hangs up. She's walking past a pharmacy and a news-stand when something catches her eye.

She stops dead, turning back to stare at the front page of the latest *Aftonbladet*.

THE EXECUTIONER, shouts the headline.

In the main photo, the Observatory Grove playground is visible from above and to the side. The police have cordoned off the area with tape and riot barriers.

Towards one edge, she can make out a number of emergency vehicles. A girl in a leather jacket and a dress is hanging from the jungle gym. Her lank hair is covering most of her face.

Pamela's heart starts thumping so hard that she feels her throat contract.

The image is the same as Martin's drawing.

The one he did last night.

Almost identical.

He must have been at the playground before the police.

22

Pamela's legs feel like jelly as she turns on to a back street, passes a yellow skip and pauses in a doorway.

Stumbling on a dead girl would have been a shock for anyone.

Now she understands why Martin couldn't sleep. He must have been walking around with those images in his head, too afraid to share them.

Ultimately, he overdosed on Valium and ended up sketching the scene.

Her hands are shaking as she takes out her phone and pulls up the *Aftonbladet* website.

A barrage of ads for Volvo and betting companies pop up before she can even open the article.

Her eyes hop anxiously from line to line as she reads.

The dead girl was found in the Observatory Grove playground early on Wednesday morning.

According to Aron Beck, the lead detective on the investigation, they have not yet made any arrests.

Pamela brings up the Stockholm Police homepage and tries to figure out how she can get in touch with him. Next to the emergency number, she spots the line for general, nationwide tips and inquiries.

Following the automated menu, she eventually gets through to a real person and explains that she wants to speak to Aron Beck about the murder in the playground.

She leaves her name and number, then drops her phone into her bag. A lump has settled in her throat, making it difficult to swallow.

She knows she should go home and try to get Martin to talk about what he saw.

A girl murdered in the playground.

Pamela tries to calm herself down, leaning back against a door and closing her eyes.

She jumps when her phone starts ringing and fishes it out of her bag. The call is from an unknown number.

'Pamela,' she answers hesitantly.

'Hello, this is Aron Beck, I'm a detective with the Stockholm Police. I understand you tried to get in touch with me?' says a weary male voice.

Pamela peers down the deserted street.

'Yes, I just read about the murdered girl in the playground in *Aftonbladet* . . . it said you were leading the investigation?'

'What is this regarding?' he asks.

'I think my husband might have seen something when he was out walking the dog on Tuesday night . . . He can't call you himself, because of a mental illness.'

'We need to speak with him immediately,' Aron tells her, his tone of voice changing.

'The problem is that it's incredibly difficult to have a conversation with him.'

'Where is he right now?'

'He's at home, at Karlavägen 11,' she replies. 'I can be there in twenty minutes if it's urgent.'

Pamela hangs up and starts walking, passing the skip and turning onto Drottning Street, where she's almost mowed down by a man on an electric scooter.

'Sorry,' she automatically calls out.

She turns off behind Kulturhuset to make her way towards Regering Street, but there's roadworks on Brunkebergs Square, which forces her to turn back on to Drottning Street.

It's fine, she thinks.

She still has plenty of time.

* * *

Fifteen minutes after her call with the detective, Pamela is running down Kungstens Street. Her breathing is heavy, and her damp shirt clings to her back. She turns on to Karla Road and sees five or six police cars up ahead, blue lights flashing.

The entire street is blocked off, including the pavement around her door. A crowd of curious onlookers has already started to gather.

Two officers in bulletproof vests are pressed up against the wall of the building with weapons drawn, while another two are keeping watch on either side of the pavement.

When the first officer spots Pamela, he holds up a hand.

He is tall and stocky, with a blond beard and a deep scar across the bridge of his nose.

Pamela keeps walking, but she nods and tries to indicate that she needs to talk to him.

'I'm sorry,' she says, 'but I live here and—'

'You'll have to wait,' he interrupts her.

'I just wanted to say that I think there's been some kind of misunderstanding. I'm the one who called the police, because—'

She stops abruptly on hearing agitated voices from the stairwell. The door opens, and a police officer emerges, followed by two others in helmets and vests. They drag Martin outside shirtless and in his pyjama bottoms.

'What are you doing?' Pamela shouts. 'Are you out of your minds?'

'I'd like you to calm down, please.'

'You can't treat people like this! He's not well, you're scaring him . . .'

The policeman with the blond beard holds her back.

Martin's hands are cuffed behind him. His nose is bleeding, and he looks frightened and confused.

'Who's in charge here?' Pamela asks, her voice shrill. 'Is it Aron Beck? Talk to him, call him and ask if . . .'

'No, you listen to me now,' he barks.

'I'm just trying . . .'

'I want you to calm down and take a step back.'

Blood is trickling over Martin's lips and chin.

A young woman who works in a nearby gallery is standing on the other side of the cordon, filming everything on her phone.

'You don't understand,' Pamela shouts, trying to regain a modicum of authority in her voice. 'My husband has a mental illness, he suffers from a serious form of PTSD.'

'I'm going to arrest you if you don't calm down,' the police officer tells her, looking her straight in the eye.

'You're going to arrest me for being upset?'

The police officers have a firm grip on Martin's upper arms. He stumbles, and they pull him back up. His bare feet hover over the pavement. Martin gasps in pain, but doesn't speak.

'Martin!' Pamela shouts.

His eyes scan the crowd and it's clear he heard her voice, but he isn't able to find her before they push his head down and into the car.

Pamela tries to make her way forward, but the officer with the blond beard grabs her by the arm and forces her up against the brick facade.

23

The windowless interrogation room in the Norrmalm Police Station smells like sweat and dirt. Aron Beck looks closely at the man identified as Martin Nordström. His face is streaked with dried blood, and he has a wad of tissue stuffed in one of his nostrils. His grey hair is standing on end. The links of his handcuffs are looped through a sturdy metal fixture on the table in front of him, and he is wearing a police-issue T-shirt and green pyjama bottoms.

Everything he says and does is being recorded.

At first, he refused to say whether he wanted a lawyer, but when Aron repeated the question, he simply shook his head.

Both men are now sitting quietly.

The only sound comes from the low hum of the flickering fluorescent lights.

Martin keeps trying to turn around, as though he wants to check whether anyone is behind him.

'Look at me,' says Aron.

Martin turns back and briefly makes eye contact before looking down again.

'Do you know why you're here?'

'No,' Martin whispers.

'You took your dog out late on Tuesday night. At three o'clock Wednesday morning, you were on the grass by the School of Economics.'

Aron pauses for a moment.

'Right next to the playground,' he adds.

Martin attempts to get up, but the handcuffs stop him. The links rattle against the table as he slumps down again.

Aron leans forward. 'Do you want to tell me what happened there?'

'I don't remember,' Martin says, his voice so quiet it is almost inaudible.

'But you remember being there, don't you?'

Martin shakes his head.

'You remember something,' Aron continues. 'Start there, and just tell me what you do remember. Take your time.'

Martin glances back over his shoulder again, then peers beneath the table before straightening up.

'We're not going anywhere until you start talking,' Aron tells him, sighing when Martin looks back over his shoulder for a third time. 'What are you looking for?'

'Nothing.'

'Why did you get up when I mentioned the playground behind the university?'

He doesn't answer, just sits quietly, his eyes fixed somewhere to one side of Aron.

'I know it can be hard,' Aron continues, 'but most people actually feel a sense of relief once they finally tell the truth.'

Martin meets Aron's eye for a second, then stares at the door.

'OK, Martin, let's try this instead. Look at me, I'm right here,' Aron says, opening a black folder.

Martin looks at him again.

'Do you remember this?' Aron asks, pushing a photograph across the table. Martin leans back so far that his arms are outstretched, the skin around his wrists wrinkles against the cuffs.

His breathing is fast, and he squeezes his eyes shut.

The photograph is a sharp image of the dead girl, the flash capturing every last detail.

The raindrops hang bright and calm in the air around Jenny Lind.

Her wet hair, covering most of her face, is the colour of lacquered oak. The tip of her chin and her open mouth are visible between

the strands. The steel wire has cut into her skin, and the blood that has run down her neck has stained her dress almost black.

Aron returns the photograph to the folder. Martin's breathing slowly becomes calmer.

When he finally leans forward again, his hands are almost white. His pale face is clammy, his eyes bloodshot.

He sits quietly, staring down at the table.

His chin is trembling like he is holding back tears.

'It was me, I killed her,' he whispers, his breathing becoming faster again.

'Tell me what happened, in your own words,' says Aron.

But Martin shakes his head, anxiously rocking back and forth.

'Calm down,' says Aron, forcing a warm smile. 'You'll feel better once you get it all off your chest, I promise.'

Martin stops rocking and continues to breathe rapidly through his nose.

'What happened, Martin?'

'I don't remember.' He swallows hard.

'Of course you do – you clearly had a strong reaction to the picture of the victim, and just now you told me you killed her,' says Aron, taking a deep breath. 'No one is angry with you, but you need to tell me what happened.'

'Yes, but I . . .' He trails off and glances back over his shoulder, and beneath the table again.

'You've confessed to killing the girl in the playground.'

Martin nods and starts poking at the links between the handcuffs.

'I don't remember anything,' he says quietly.

'But you remember that you just confessed to the murder?'

'Yes.'

'Do you know who she is?'

He shakes his head and glances up at the door.

'How exactly did you kill her?'

'What?' Martin stares blankly at Aron.

'What did you do? How did you kill her?'

'I don't know,' Martin whispers.

'Were you alone? Or did you have help?'

'I can't tell you.'

'But you can tell me why you did it, can't you? Do you want to tell me that?'

'I can't remember.'

With a deep sigh, Aron gets up and leaves the room without another word.

24

Joona pushes his sunglasses into his shirt's chest pocket as he walks down a long corridor in Norrmalm Police Station.

Plain clothes and uniformed officers hurry past him in different directions.

He finds Aron Beck standing by the coffee machine, feet wide apart and hands behind his back.

'What are you doing here?' Aron asks.

'I'd like to sit in on the interview.'

'Well, you're too late, he's already confessed,' Aron tells him, holding back a smile.

'Good work.'

Aron cocks his head and looks Joona over.

'I just spoke to Margot, and she thinks it's time to let the prosecutor take over.'

'That sounds a bit hasty,' says Joona, taking a cup from the cabinet. 'You know he has mental health problems.'

'But he's been linked to the scene at the time of the murder, and he also confessed.'

'What's his motive? What's his connection to the victim?' Joona asks, making himself an espresso.

'He says he can't remember.'

'What doesn't he remember?'

'He can't remember anything from that night.'

Joona takes the cup and holds it out to Aron.

'So how can he confess to the murder?'

'I don't know,' says Aron, looking down at the cup in his hand. 'But he admitted to it pretty much straightaway. You can watch the recording if you want.'

'I will. I want to know what you made of the interview first, though.'

'What? What do you mean?' asks Aron, taking a sip of his coffee.

'Is there a chance you misunderstood what he was confessing to?'

'Misunderstood? He said he killed the girl.'

'And what preceded the confession?'

'What do you mean?'

'What did you say to him immediately before?'

'Am I the one being interviewed now?' Aron asks, the corners of his mouth turning down.

'No.'

Aron puts the empty cup into the sink and wipes his hands on his jeans.

'I showed him a picture of the victim,' he grumbles.

'From the crime scene?'

'He was struggling to remember. I wanted to help him.'

'I understand that, but now he knows the case is about a hanged girl,' Joona tells him.

'We weren't getting anywhere. I had no choice.' Aron's tone is blunt.

'Could what you interpreted as a confession actually be about something else?'

'Are you trying to tell me I'm wrong now?' he asks.

'I'm just wondering if he could have meant that he *indirectly* killed her, because he couldn't save her?'

'Stop.'

'We know he didn't have time to attach the winch to the post . . . Obviously there's a chance he went there earlier and did it then, took the steps down to the playground to avoid the cameras, but if that's the case, it's hard to see why he took the route he did when he actually went to kill her.'

'Jesus Christ, talk to him yourself, you'll—'

'Perfect,' Joona interrupts him.

'You'll see how easy it is.'

'Has he been violent or aggressive?'

'He's just confessed to a brutal murder. It's horrifying, it's ice cold; I'd hang him from a fucking winch myself if I could.'

25

Joona knocks on the door before stepping into the interview room. The burly prison officer sitting opposite Martin is playing on his phone.

'Take a break,' Joona tells him, holding the door for the officer.

Martin's face is pale yellow and swollen, and his faint stubble makes him look vulnerable. His hair is standing on end, his eyes look weary. His hands are clasped on the scratched table.

'My name is Joona Linna and I'm a detective with the National Crime Unit,' Joona tells him, sitting down in the chair opposite.

Martin's nod is barely noticeable.

'What happened to your nose?' asks Joona.

Martin reaches up and gingerly touches his nose. The bloody wad of paper drops to the table.

'Has anyone asked whether you have any health issues? Whether you need any medication and so on?'

'Yes,' Martin whispers.

'Can I take off your cuffs?'

'I don't know,' says Martin, quickly glancing back over his shoulder.

'Are you going to be violent?'

Martin shakes his head.

'I'll take them off now, but I want you to stay in your seat,' says Joona, unlocking the cuffs and shoving them into his pocket.

Martin slowly massages his wrists as his eyes drift past Joona towards the door.

Joona takes out a sheet of paper and places it on the table in front of Martin's clasped hands. He studies Martin's face as he looks down at a rendering of the stamp found on the back of Jenny Lind's head.

'What's this?' Joona asks.

'I don't know.'

'Have a good look.'

'I have,' he says quietly.

'I understand you're suffering from complex post-traumatic stress disorder, and have trouble with your memory and speaking ability?'

'Yes.'

'While you were talking to my colleague, you confessed to the murder of a young woman,' Joona continues. 'Could you tell me her name?'

Martin shakes his head.

'Do you know her name?'

'No,' Martin whispers.

'What do you remember from that night?'

'Nothing.'

'So how can you be sure you murdered this woman?'

'If you say I did it, I want to confess and take my punishment,' says Martin.

'It's good that you want to confess, but in order for you to do that, we need to work out what really happened.'

'OK.'

'We know you were there when she was killed, but that doesn't necessarily mean you were the one who killed her.'

'I thought it did,' he says, his voice barely audible.

'Well, it doesn't.'

'But . . .'

Tears start rolling down Martin's cheeks, dripping onto the table between his hands.

Joona pulls out a tissue and hands it to Martin, who gently blows his nose.

'Why do you speak so quietly?'

'I have to,' he says, glancing at the door.

'Are you afraid of someone?'

119

He nods.

'Who?'

He doesn't reply, just peers back over his shoulder again.

'Martin, is there anyone who might be able to help you remember?'

He shakes his head.

'What about your psychiatrist at Sankt Göran's?'

'Maybe.'

'We could try him, does that sound good?'

Martin gives a minimal nod.

'Do you often have gaps in your memory?'

'I can't remember,' he jokes, looking down when Joona laughs.

'No, of course.'

'I have these gaps pretty often,' he whispers.

Someone walks down the corridor outside, singing and jingling a set of keys. As they pass the interview room, their baton hits the door.

Martin flinches, looking terrified.

'I think you saw something awful that night,' Joona says as he studies Martin's face. 'Something so terrible that you can't bring yourself to think about it … but you and I both know that what you saw is still there in your mind, and I'd like you to start by telling me whatever you can remember.'

Martin looks down at the table, and his lips begin to move like he's searching for words he lost a long time ago.

'It was raining,' says Joona.

'Yes.' Martin nods.

'Do you remember the sound on your umbrella?'

'She was standing like …'

He falls silent when the lock clicks and the door swings open. Aron strides into the room.

'The interview's over, the prosecutor is taking over the preliminary investigation,' he explains, clearing his throat.

'Martin,' says Joona, ignoring Aron completely. 'What were you going to say?'

'What?'

Martin looks Joona in the eye, a blank expression on his face. He licks his lips.

'OK, that's enough now,' says Aron, gesturing for the prison officer to come back into the room.

'You were just about to tell me what you saw,' Joona continues, trying to hold Martin's gaze.

'I don't remember.'

Aron takes the prison officer's ledger and signs off on the transfer.

'Just give me a minute, Aron.'

'I can't, it's out of my hands now,' he replies.

The prison officer makes Martin stand up, and explains that he will be taken back to his cell and given something to eat.

'Martin,' Joona tries again. 'The rain was hitting your umbrella, you were looking towards the playground, and you saw the young woman, who was standing like . . . Tell me what you were going to say.'

Martin shakes his head as though he doesn't understand the question. Aron tells the officer to take him away.

'You saw her in the rain,' Joona continues. 'How was she standing? Martin, I want to know what you were going to say.'

Martin opens his mouth, but nothing comes out. The prison officer grips his arm and leads him out of the room.

26

Pamela parks her car outside Karolinska Hospital, crosses the road and enters Norra begravningsplatsen through the gates.

She has been to the cemetery so many times over the years that she takes the quickest route through the huge network of footpaths between the graves and mausolea automatically.

The police officer who pushed her up against the wall on Friday refused to tell her where they were taking Martin. Her entire body was shaking as she climbed the stairs to their apartment, finding the door wide open, pieces of broken lock scattered across the floor.

Pamela picked up the pieces, pulled the door shut and locked the security door behind her. Then she popped one of Martin's painkillers from the blister pack, swallowed it, and sat down in front of the computer. Before long, she had tracked down a phone number for prison services and learned that Martin had been taken into custody at Kronoberg Prison.

She quickly packed him a bag of clothes, grabbed his wallet and jumped into a taxi, but when she arrived the guard refused to let her in. He took the bag but ignored her requests to speak to someone about Martin's mental health and his need for medication and treatment.

Pamela spent three hours waiting outside the prison that day. When the first guard's shift ended and another began, she tried again before giving up and heading home.

Late that same evening, she found out that Martin was being remanded on suspicion of the murder of Jenny Lind.

The same girl who had gone missing five years earlier.

The immediate frustration Pamela felt has now subsided, giving way to a weary astonishment at the absurdity of the situation.

Martin saw the dead girl in the playground that night and possibly even witnessed her death, but rather than listening to him and gathering evidence that might lead to the real killer, the police have charged him with murder.

Pamela steps into the shade of the elm tree, where she keeps a folding chair hooked to one of its branches and carries it over to Alice's grave.

The sun glitters on the dark inscribed granite behind the violets and the small bowl of candy canes.

She can hear the buzz of a lawnmower somewhere near the north chapel and the hum of the main road like distant thunder.

Pamela tells Alice about everything that has happened over the last few days. She tells her that Jenny Lind has been hanged in the centre of Stockholm, that Martin drew a picture of the crime scene, and that she called the police because she thought he might be able to help them.

She trails off as a woman using a walker passes on the footpath, waiting until she is out of earshot before building up the courage to say what she came to say.

'Alice, I love you,' she begins, taking a deep breath. 'But there's something I . . . I don't want you take this the wrong way, but I've been talking to a seventeen-year-old girl. She lives in a residential home in Gävle, and I . . . I want her to move in with us so she can have somewhere safe to live . . .'

Pamela drops to her knees and presses her palms to the sun-warmed grass on the grave.

'I don't want you to think she could ever replace you – no one could ever do that . . . and I don't want you to be sad, but I feel like this would be good for her and for me, and probably even for Martin too . . . I'm sorry.'

Pamela dries her eyes and tries to hold back the sobs until her throat aches. She gets up and hurries along the narrow footpath, hiding her face as she passes an old man with a red rose in his hand.

A swallow cuts through the air, scouting the freshly cut grass from above before turning sharply upwards.

Pamela walks quickly past the line of trees, suddenly realising that she forgot to hang the chair in the tree, but she can't bring herself to turn back.

Her movements feel stiff as she follows the pavement back to the car park.

Tears well up in her eyes, and she hurries over to her car, burying her face in her hands and sobbing as her diaphragm cramps.

After a while, she brings her breathing back under control, composing herself enough to start the engine and drive the short distance home.

She parks the car in the garage and walks through the building, keeping her tear-streaked face turned to the ground.

By the time she gets to the apartment, she is so cold she is shaking. She locks the security door, hangs the keys on the hook just inside, and heads straight into the bathroom. She takes off her clothes, gets into the shower and lets the hot water embrace her.

Pamela closes her eyes and relaxes as her body slowly warms up.

When she leaves the bathroom, the evening sun is painting a bright path over the parquet floor.

She hangs her towel on a hook in the bedroom and stands naked in front of the mirror. She sucks in her stomach, stands on her tiptoes and studies her body: her wrinkled knees, her thighs and her auburn pubic hair.

Her shoulders are pink from the hot water.

Pamela wraps her bathrobe around herself, walks to the kitchen and sits down at the table with her iPad.

Her heart starts racing as she reads the newspapers' speculation about the murder of Jenny Lind. The police haven't commented on the case, but the remand order is already circulating online with Martin's name and picture.

Pamela opens the mail app and sees that she has a new email from social services.

She clicks on it.

Decision pursuant ch. 11, § 4 Social Services Act

We have today made the decision to reject Pamela Nordström's application, on behalf of the Social Welfare Board, to provide temporary or ongoing foster care to a minor.

In light of information received regarding Martin Nordström, the board concludes that the proposed family home represents a direct threat to the child's safety (ch 4 § 2, National Board of Health and Welfare Code of Statutes 2012:11).

An icy chill runs through Pamela. She gets up and walks over to the cupboard. She grabs the bottle of Absolut Vodka and a large glass, fills it to the brim and drinks.

They have been turned down because Martin has been taken into custody. Of course social services rejected her application, she thinks, taking another drink. It makes perfect sense from their perspective, but the decision feels rash and unfair. Martin is innocent. He'll be released any day now.

27

With shaking hands, Pamela refills her glass and drinks two large gulps that make her mouth go numb.

She returns to the table, accidentally slamming down the glass and bottle.

The vodka burns in her stomach, and she can already feel her eyes losing their focus. She concentrates, reading through the board's decision one more time and looking up the relevant articles in the statutes. As she understands it, she can appeal the decision at the administrative court.

Pamela drains the last of the vodka from her glass, picks up her phone and calls Mia.

'Hi, Mia, this is Pamela, I—'

'Hold on,' Mia interrupts her, turning her attention to someone else. 'No, stop it, I need to take this . . . OK, I hate you too . . . Hello?'

'What's going on?' asks Pamela.

'It's just Pontus, he's singing outside my window,' she replies cheerfully.

'I saw his picture on Instagram – he's really cute,' says Pamela. She can hear herself slurring slightly.

'I know, I should probably fall in love with him or something,' Mia sighs.

Pamela turns to the window and looks down at the park. Sunbathers lie in the grass, and children are playing around the small pool.

'I wanted to tell you about something before you heard it from someone else,' she says, trying to gather her thoughts. 'Mia, social services turned me down.'

'OK.'

'But it's based on a misunderstanding, and I'm going to appeal. Nothing is final yet, and I don't want you to think that this is over.'

'Got it,' Mia mumbles.

The line goes quiet. Pamela unscrews the lid of the bottle with her free hand and starts to fill her glass again, stopping when the bottle lets out a glugging sound. She drinks the small amount of liquid in her glass and then swigs from the bottle instead.

'It'll work out, I promise,' she whispers.

'People always make promises,' Mia says flatly.

'But this is all just a stupid misunderstanding. They think Martin was involved in a murder.'

'Wait, he's the guy they're talking about everywhere?'

'But he didn't do it, it's all just a stupid misunderstanding,' Pamela repeats. 'I swear. I mean, you know yourself that the police make mistakes sometimes, right?'

'I have to go.'

'Mia, you can call me any time you . . .'

Pamela hears a click, and trails off. She gets up on unsteady legs, grabbing the bottle and taking it into the bedroom. She puts it down on the bedside table and slumps onto the bed.

She knows that Martin hasn't asserted his right to a lawyer. The police probably manipulated him into saying things he doesn't know anything about.

Pamela reaches for the bottle and takes another swig. She can feel her stomach trying to bring the liquid back up, but she resists it, focusing on keeping her breathing under control.

She doubts it is even legal to interrogate a mentally ill person without someone with psychiatric expertise being present.

Pamela sits up in bed, grabs her phone, scrolls through her contacts and hits call.

'Dennis Kratz.'

'Hi,' she says.

'What's going on with Martin?'

'You've seen what they're writing – it's completely insane . . .'

She makes a real effort not to slur her words as she tells him about Martin's drawing and everything that happened afterwards.

'I was thinking . . . could you talk to the police?' she asks.

'Of course.'

'Because I don't think they've got . . . you know, the right skills to . . . to interview someone with complex PTSD.'

'I'll speak to them tomorrow.'

'Thanks,' she whispers.

'And how are you?' he asks after a brief pause.

'Me? Things are pretty tough,' she says, wiping the sudden tears from her cheeks. 'I've actually had a drink to calm myself down.'

'You need someone to talk to.'

'I'll be OK, don't worry . . .'

'Do you want me to come over?'

'Come over,' she repeats. 'I really do need to talk to someone, if I'm honest . . . it's all been a bit much, even for me.'

'That's understandable.'

'Just don't worry about me, I'll straighten it all out and it'll be fine . . .'

Pamela ends the call, and her cheeks flush. She gets up and stumbles into the door frame. She massages her shoulder as she staggers into the bathroom and crouches over the toilet, pushing two fingers down her throat to make herself throw up. She brings up some of the vodka, then rinses her mouth and brushes her teeth.

The room is spinning, and she can feel herself becoming increasingly drunk. She washes down her armpits and pulls on a thin blue dress with a wide belt.

Dennis could be here any minute now.

Pamela checks her makeup and puts her new earrings in.

As she walks to the kitchen and sees the iPad lying on the table, she feels an anxious jolt in her chest.

What was the point of any of it? How could she have imagined that Mia would ever be allowed to live with them? They may have

been rejected for the wrong reasons, but Pamela knows that deep down, they do deserve to be refused. She has a real drinking problem, and Martin's obsessive thoughts and paranoid delusions aren't just going to go away.

How could she have ignored all of that?

Hoping for a new life is nothing but a pathetic fantasy.

By dragging Mia into this mess, she has done nothing but let her down. And she has also let down Alice by fooling herself.

Pamela goes back into the bedroom and slinks into bed. She wants to call Mia and tell her the truth, that she and Martin aren't suited to be parents.

It feels like the room around her is shifting, the walls and windows racing by her.

Pamela thinks to herself that she should go out onto the balcony, wrap the old string of fairy lights around her neck and jump.

She closes her eyes, and lets the darkness envelop her. When she wakes up, the doorbell is ringing.

28

Pamela feels like she has been sleeping for hours, but as she walks down the hallway, the drunkenness seems to flow through her body like a warm breeze.

She unlocks and opens the door for Dennis.

He's wearing a charcoal tweed jacket and a blue shirt. His grey-flecked hair looks like it has just been cut, and when his eyes meet hers, his expression is warm.

'Now I feel bad for making you come all the way over here,' she says, hugging him.

'But I like being your handsome sidekick,' he says, grinning.

He leans against the wall with one hand as he unties his shoes, then follows her to the kitchen.

'Would you like a glass of wine?'

'At the very least,' he replies.

She laughs, fully aware of how forced it sounds, and takes a bottle of American cabernet sauvignon down from the rack.

In the living room, Pamela turns on the floor lamp and its yellow glow fills the room, mirrored in the high windows looking out onto Karlavägen.

'It's been a long time since I was last here,' he says.

'I guess it has.'

'It feels like all I ever see is depressing hotel rooms these days.'

Pamela's hands are shaking as she takes two wine glasses out of the display cabinet.

She is still incredibly drunk.

'How are you?' Dennis asks cautiously.

'Pretty shaken up, to tell you the truth,' she says.

She can feel his eyes on her as she opens the bottle, pours some wine and hands him a glass.

He thanks her quietly and turns to look out of the window.

'What's that green building?' he asks.

'Where did that come from?' she says, laughing.

She moves over to him, and the sudden closeness of his body sends a tingling warmth through her.

'Has it always been there?' he asks, smiling.

'For the last eighty years, at least . . .'

Dennis lowers his glass to the coffee table, wipes his mouth and then turns to her.

'They suit you, the earrings,' he says, reaching out to touch one of them. 'You look so beautiful in them.'

They sit down on the sofa, and he puts an arm around her shoulders.

'What if Martin actually did the things they're accusing him of,' she says quietly.

'But he didn't.'

'I know you warned me, but we've been rejected by social services,' she tells him, straightening her dress.

'You can appeal,' Dennis calmly points out.

'I'm going to, of course I am, but . . . God, I don't know anything anymore,' she says, lowering her head to his shoulder. 'They turned me down because of Martin, even though we're not *really* together. It's a marriage in name only.'

'And do you still want that?'

'What?' She looks up at him.

'I'm asking as your friend, because I care about you,' he says.

'What are you asking me?'

'Would you still marry him today?'

'Well, you're taken,' she says with a grin.

'Only while I wait for you.'

She leans forward and kisses him on the lips, immediately whispering an apology.

They look into each other's eyes.

Pamela swallows hard and feels a rising sense of panic. She has had too much to drink and wants things she doesn't really want. She knows she should tell him to leave, but something inside her wants him to stay.

They kiss again, hesitantly, softly.

'You know that this might just be a reaction to everything that's happened, don't you?' he says hoarsely.

'What, are you a psychologist now?'

'I don't want you to do anything you might regret . . .'

'No, it . . .' She trails off, her heart racing as it dawns on her that she is about to cheat on Martin.

Dennis runs his finger along the deep gash in the coffee table from the night Martin tried to drag all the furniture into the stairwell.

'I'll be right back,' she says quietly, leaving him in the living room.

Pamela puts her wine glass on the table in the hallway, steps into the bathroom and locks the door. She sits down on the toilet with a mixture of anxiety and longing.

The skin on her thighs feels prickly.

She finishes peeing, picks up the mug that holds their toothbrushes and fills it with lukewarm water, rinsing between her legs. She dries herself off and pulls up her underwear.

She neatens her lipstick and applies a few drops of Coco to her wrists before heading back to the living room.

Dennis is on his feet, looking through the glass doors to the balcony. He turns around when he hears her approaching.

'I like these handles,' he says, reaching out to touch the brass on the doors.

'Espagnolettes,' she says, placing her hand on top of his.

They stand still for a moment, caressing each other's hands. Their eyes meet and they smile. But Dennis's face turns serious and he opens his mouth, as though he is about to say something.

'I'm a little nervous,' she says, before he can speak. She anxiously pushes her hair back from her face.

They kiss again. Pamela strokes his face and opens her mouth slightly, as he places his hands on her back, her waist, the base of her spine.

She feels him harden and presses herself against him, breathing heavily. A warm, pulsing sensation spreads between her legs.

Pamela has always been embarrassed by how easily aroused she is.

Dennis kisses her throat and chin and starts to undo the buttons on her dress. She watches him, his focused eyes and trembling fingers.

'Shall we take this to the bedroom?' she whispers.

He carefully wipes off her lipstick with his thumb and follows her past the hallway and into the bedroom. Pamela's legs feel like jelly as she walks over to the bed to move the cushions and fold back the bedspread.

Dennis takes off his shirt and tosses it on the floor. He has a deep scar running across the left side of his chest, almost like a line drawn in the sand.

Pamela peels off her dress and drapes it over the back of the armchair, then unclasps her bra and puts it on top.

'You're so beautiful,' he says, moving to kiss her.

He gently squeezes one of her breasts, kissing her neck and bending down to suck on her nipples, filling his mouth with her breast. He straightens up and starts to unbutton his trousers.

'Do you have a condom?' she whispers.

'I can go and get some.'

'We'll just be careful,' she says instead of explaining that she has an IUD.

She pulls down her underwear, using them to discreetly wipe herself, then drops them to the floor and pushes them under the bed with one foot. She climbs onto the bed.

The mattress rocks as he follows and crawls on top of her, kissing her on the lips, between her breasts and on her stomach.

She lets him part her thighs, her fingers wandering through his hair, as her breathing quickens when he starts to lick her.

She feels his soft tongue on her clitoris and realises she is already close to orgasm. She pushes him away and presses her thighs together as she rolls to one side in an attempt to avoid looking completely starved of attention.

'I want to feel you inside me,' she whispers, guiding him onto his back.

She puts her hand on him as she straddles his body.

He slips inside her and she gasps, knowing that she won't be able to last much longer.

Pamela rocks her hips and grits her teeth. She breathes heavily through her nose, trying to hide her orgasm as it washes over her.

Her thighs are trembling, and she leans forward to support herself on the bed. Dennis starts thrusting harder as her orgasm continues.

The headboard thuds against the wall, dust floating down from an angel hanging above on a hook. Her teardrop-shaped aquamarines swing back and forth in her ears.

She notices that he is getting closer, his forehead growing damp before he stops abruptly in order to pull out in time.

'You can come inside me,' she whispers.

He thrusts harder, gripping her ass and whimpering. She groans as though she were the one having the orgasm, feeling the force of his ejaculation.

29

The Police Authority's main conference room hums with voices and the sound of scraping chairs as it starts to fill up with journalists. Microphones from the TV channels and radio stations line the narrow table at the front of the room.

Margot is standing by the wall to one side of the podium, looking down at her phone as Joona approaches. Her black uniform is tight over her chest. The oak leaves and crowns on her epaulettes glitter in the lights overhead. Joona walks towards her.

'I hope you're not about to announce that we've arrested a suspect,' Joona says.

'He confessed,' she replies without even glancing up.

'I know, but his confession is complicated. He has serious problems with his memory, with speaking – he was just trying to do what he thought was right when Aron put pressure on him. It doesn't add up.'

When Margot finally looks up, she's frowning impatiently.

'I hear what you're saying, but . . .'

'Are you aware that he's currently a patient at a psychiatric ward, and that he's only at home on a trial basis?'

'Sounds like a relapse to me,' she says, dropping her phone into her bag.

'Except his psychiatric issues have no violent elements whatsoever.'

'Just drop it, Joona. You're off the case.'

'Talk to the prosecutor. Tell them I need to talk to him, just one more time.'

135

'Joona,' Margot sighs. 'You should know how this works by now.'

'I do, but it's too early for court proceedings.'

'Maybe so, but even if that's the case, it'll come to light – that's the reason we have lawyers.'

'OK,' says Joona.

Up on the podium, the press officer taps the microphone, and the room quietens down.

'This is what's going to happen,' Margot quickly explains to Joona. 'Viola will welcome everyone, then I'll take over and announce that the prosecutor has requested a man be held in custody on suspicion of the murder of Jenny Lind. After that, I'll hand things over to the county police chief, and he'll say something about how Norrmalm's painstaking investigation led to a rapid arrest, and . . .'

Joona turns away and starts walking towards the exit before she has time to finish. He passes the journalists and reaches the door just as the press officer welcomes everyone.

* * *

High above the roar of the traffic, Joona stands behind his armchair, hands on the backrest. His black shirt is unbuttoned, hanging loose over his white undershirt and black jeans.

Nathan Pollock left the apartment in the Corner House to Joona in his will. A two-bedroom apartment on the top floor of the tall building. He had never even mentioned owning the place. Joona had only known about his house.

Through the large window, Joona looks down onto Adolf Fredrik's church. The shimmering brown copper of the domed roof is surrounded by green treetops.

Joona thinks back to Martin's compulsive movements in the interrogation room.

It was like he was incapable of dealing with the terrible things he had seen. Over and over, he had to check beneath the table and behind his back.

As though he were literally being chased.

Joona moves over to the other window. A full moon hangs in the bright sky above the soft hills of Haga Park.

136

He closes his eyes and pictures Jenny Lind's body on the autopsy table. With her unnaturally pale skin and the dark gash from the steel wire, the image resembles a black and white photograph.

Though he can remember her yellow eyes and tobacco-coloured hair, his memory of her feels washed-out somehow.

Colourless and alone, staring out into nothingness.

He promised her he would find the killer, and he will.

Even though they've pushed him off the case, he would never be able to let go of Jenny Lind.

He knows that.

That fire inside him is the same one that prevents him from leaving the police force, despite knowing he probably should.

Joona moves over to the chest of drawers, picks up his phone and calls Lumi. He hears it ring, and suddenly her clear voice is so close that it feels like she is right there with him.

'*Oui, c'est* Lumi.'

'It's Dad.'

'Dad? Has something happened?' she asks anxiously.

'No, it . . . How's Paris?'

'Everything's fine here, but I don't have time to talk right now.'

'I just needed to tell you something . . .'

'Yes, but I thought you understood that I don't want you to keep calling me. I'm not trying to fight, but I still really need a break.'

Joona runs a hand over his mouth and swallows, hard. He braces himself against the cool sheet of glass on top of the chest of drawers and fills his lungs.

'I just wanted to say that you were right, that I can finally see that you're right . . . I'm working on a new investigation – I'll spare you the details – but it made me realise that I can't stop being a police officer.'

'I never thought you would.'

'I think it's a good thing that you're staying away from my world . . . it's changed me, I think it's damaged me, but I—'

'Dad, all I'm asking is that you give me some time,' she interrupts him, clearly on the verge of tears. 'I've had an idealised vision of you for years, and now I'm really struggling to make sense of everything.'

Lumi hangs up, and Joona is left in silence.

She has turned away from him because she saw what really drove him. She saw what he was capable of. She saw him kill a defenceless man – without a trial, and without mercy.

Lumi will never understand that that act of cruelty was the price Joona had to pay. The price Jurek demanded.

His very last words were a testament to that fact, the mysterious whisper before he fell.

That was the moment Joona changed, and with each day that passes he understands better that he has indeed transformed.

Feeling completely empty, Joona peers down at the phone in his hand and dials a number he thought he would never call again. Not long later, he leaves the apartment.

* * *

Joona emerges from Vällingby metro station into the hot afternoon sun. He puts on his sunglasses and cuts across the huge white cobbled rings of the square.

The shopping centre consists of low buildings, housing, restaurants, supermarkets, a jeweller, a tobacconist and a betting shop.

At the news-stands, pictures of Martin's face are splashed alongside headlines shouting that the Executioner has been caught.

There are times when the job of a police officer feels like a long, lonely walk across a bloody battlefield. Joona pauses in front of each body he comes across, forced to relive the victim's suffering and to try to understand the killer's cruelty.

He sees a couple of young men in swimming trunks smoking outside a modern-looking church.

Joona passes two high-rises before he comes to a halt outside an apartment building with walls the colour of dirty foam rubber.

The same colour as the walls around Kumla Prison.

He studies the small, barred windows on the ground level. The curtains are drawn, but the light inside is seeping through the fabric.

Joona presses a button on the entryphone.

'Laila, it's me Joona,' he says quietly into the microphone.

The lock buzzes, and Joona opens the door. Inside, a man with sunken, grizzled cheeks is sleeping on the stairs. The neck of his T-shirt is damp with sweat, and as the door swings shut, he opens his heavy eyelids and stares at Joona with enormous pupils.

Joona heads down to the basement, to a door that has been propped open with a broom. He moves the broom and lets the door lock behind him.

Heavy as a vault.

He continues down more stairs, eventually coming into a spacious room with pale yellow concrete walls and industrial vinyl on the floor.

The air smells like bleach and vomit.

He finds Laila sitting at her computer, grading chemistry tests. She works as an supply teacher at the local high school.

She is almost seventy, her lead-grey hair cut short, and she has furrowed cheeks and dark circles beneath her eyes. She is wearing a pair of tight black leather trousers and a pink blouse.

Pushed up against the inner wall of the room, there is an old pull-out bed with a green tarp draped over the double mattress.

The world outside the small curtain-covered windows by the ceiling feels a long way away.

On the floor, there is a plastic tray of leftover sushi with a pair of chopsticks inside. The desk chair creaks as Laila spins around and studies him with her calm, pale brown eyes.

'So you want to start again?' she asks.

'Yes, I think so,' he says, hanging up his jacket and shoulder holster.

'Why don't you lie down then.'

He moves over to the bed, straightening the brown corduroy cushions beneath the tarp. He picks up a sheet sitting nearby, spreads it out and tucks it in at the edges.

Laila turns on the fan in the pantry, grabs a bucket from the cupboard under the sink, and puts it on the floor by the bed.

Joona kicks off his shoes and hears the tarp rustle beneath him as he lies back. Laila lights an oil lamp with a tapered metal funnel and puts it on the table beside him.

'The clock shop was nicer,' Joona tells her, attempting a smile.

'This is nice,' she replies, returning to the pantry.

She opens the fridge and returns with a small cellophane package, taking a seat on the edge of the bed. Once the screen of her computer goes to sleep, the oil lamp is the only source of light left in the room. Its flickering glow dances into the corners, and a sliver of sunlight cuts across the ceiling.

'Are you in pain?' Laila asks him, looking him in the eye.

'No.'

It has been a long time since Joona last felt like he needed to see Laila. He can usually manage his pain and grief without having to numb himself, but right now, he doesn't know how to process the knowledge that he has changed. He has been reluctant to admit it, but he can't keep hiding. He knows it's true, and he knows that Lumi saw it happen.

The bowl of the pipe looks like a sooty black lump the size of a lime. Laila examines it for a moment and then attaches it to the birchwood stem.

'I just need to relax,' Joona whispers.

She shakes her head, unwraps the plastic around the bronze-coloured raw opium, and pinches off a small piece.

Joona adjusts one of the cushions beneath him, rolls onto his side, and attempts to smooth out the crumpled tarpaulin.

He has come to realise that his world has changed him so much that he is incapable of leaving it – even for his daughter's sake.

To her, I am a part of the force that wants to do good, but actually does evil, he thinks.

But maybe the desire is irrelevant. Perhaps I'm simply part of the force that does evil.

He tries to get comfortable.

I need to leave myself to find my way, he tells himself.

Laila rolls the sticky ball of opium between her index finger and thumb, then pushes it onto a black needle and heats it over the lamp. Once it softens, she presses it down over the small hole in the bowl of the pipe and smooths out the edges.

She carefully pulls out the needle and passes him the pipe.

140

The last time Joona came to see Laila, he grew weaker with each day he spent with the pipe. Though he could feel the life running out of him, he didn't want to stop.

Laila started talking about how he needed to meet the old woman of the dead, Jabmeakka, before he was done. How the old woman had materials she wanted to show him.

He remembers he started dreaming about Jabmeakka. Her crooked back and wrinkled face.

With calm movements, she spread out different weaves in front of him, and he couldn't tear his eyes away from them.

Joona doesn't know how he managed to turn back towards life.

He has always felt incredibly grateful that he did, yet here he is again, taking the pipe in his hands.

A pang of anxiety rushes through him as he holds the pipe over the narrow column of heat rising from the funnel of the oil lamp.

He is about to cross a threshold he thought he would never pass again. Valeria would be so sad if she could see him right now.

The black substance starts to bubble and crackle, and Joona raises the pipe to his mouth and inhales the opium fumes.

The effect is immediate.

He exhales as a tingling sense of euphoria courses through his body. He moves the pipe back to the heat, and fills his lungs again.

Everything already seems beautiful and he feels a comfort he has only ever found with the pipe. Every movement is enjoyable, his thoughts free-flowing and harmonious.

He smiles when he sees Laila roll a new ball of opium between her fingers.

Joona takes another hit, closes his eyes and feels her take the pipe from his hand. He thinks back to his childhood, cycling to Oxundasjön with his friends after school, bathing in the water.

He sees the shimmering dragonflies darting over the flat surface of the lake.

The memory has a quiet beauty to it.

Joona smokes, listening to the bubbling of the pipe. He thinks back to the first time he saw two dragonflies mating in a so-called

wheel. For a few seconds, the circle formed by the insects' slender bodies took on the shape of a heart.

Joona wakes and takes the pipe again, holding it over the heat and hearing it crackle, breathing in the sweet fumes.

He smiles and closes his eyes, dreaming of a tapestry patterned with dragonflies.

Pale as full moons.

As the light shifts, he sees that one of the dragonflies resembles a delicate cross. A moment later, it is caught by another, forming a ring.

* * *

After eight pipes, he lies quietly, drifting in and out of dreams for several hours. But that wonderful somnolent state eventually turns into an anxious nausea.

Joona is sweating, so cold that he is shaking.

He tries to sit up, but immediately vomits into the bucket, slumping back down and closing his eyes.

It feels like the entire room is spinning, lurching in different directions.

He lies still, composing himself, then gets up from the bed. The room turns upside down, and he is tossed to one side, knocking over the bedside table and landing shoulder first on the floor. He lifts himself up onto all fours, only to throw up, crawl forward and collapse, unmoving, gasping for air.

'I need another pipe,' he whispers.

He vomits again, although this time he doesn't have the energy to even lift his head.

Laila comes over and helps him back onto the bed. She unbuttons his vomit-flecked shirt and uses it to dab his face.

'Just a bit more,' he begs her, shivering.

But rather than replying, Laila unbuttons her blouse. She drapes it over the back of her desk chair, unclasps her bra, and lies down behind Joona, using her body heat to warm him.

His stomach turns, but he doesn't throw up again.

She holds him still, softly clutching him to stop him from trying to parry the room's twists and turns.

His body is shaking, damp with cold sweat, and her breasts feel slippery against his wet back.

Laila whispers to him in Finnish.

He lies quietly, noticing the light eclipsing from time to time whenever someone walks past one of the low windows.

Little by little, her heat makes its way into his body.

The shivering stops and the nausea fades away. Laila's arm is still around his torso, and she is humming a song.

'You're back in yourself now,' she whispers.

'Thank you.'

Laila gets up and puts her blouse back on, while Joona remains on the bed, looking down at the thick layer of plastic on the concrete floor. There is a red bucket and a mop in the corner of the room beneath the window. On the floor by the desk is the box of leftover sushi.

The plastic lid reflects the light, painting a small white streak on the ceiling.

He tries to remember something that came to him between dreams of pale dragonflies.

Something to do with the murder.

He closes his eyes and remembers that he started thinking about three photographs he saw by chance years ago, taken by a pathologist in Örebro.

A dead girl lying on an autopsy table.

A suicide.

Joona has a clear memory of pausing to study one of the images: she was face down, and he remembers thinking that the photographer had taken the photograph from a bad angle. The flash had caused a reflection of a metallic object to shine onto her dark hair on the back of her head.

But what if it wasn't a reflection after all – what if the hair was simply white?

Joona forces himself to get up, and tells Laila he has to go. He staggers over to the kitchenette, cleans his face and rinses his mouth.

The photographs were on the Needle's desk, alongside a letter and a torn envelope.

143

Joona never found out the exact cause of death.

He remembers Nils telling him it was a suicide just as his colleague, Samuel Mendel, came into the room.

'I have to go,' Joona repeats, drying his face with a paper towel.

Laila grabs a white T-shirt from a cardboard box and passes it to him. He thanks her and pulls it on, the white fabric turning grey as it absorbs the beads of water on his chest.

'You know I don't want you to come here,' she says. 'You don't belong here; you've got more important things to do.'

'It's not that simple anymore,' he says, steadying himself against the back of the sofa. 'I've changed. I can't explain it, but there's something inside me that I can't control.'

'I noticed that much . . . and I'm here if you feel like you need to do it again.'

'Thank you, but now I have to get back to work.'

'Good – I think you should.' Laila nods.

He takes his gun holster from the hook on the wall, straps it over his right shoulder, and pulls on his jacket.

30

Joona takes a taxi straight to the police station in Kungsholmen. He needs to talk to Margot and the prosecutor about the photographs of the dead girl he remembers from the pathologist in Örebro.

This isn't over just because Martin Nordström has confessed. There is no time left to lose.

The car's tyres rumble against the pavement as they overtake a bus and pull in behind an older Mercedes in the right-hand lane.

Joona slept for a long time, but his body feels exhausted from the high. His hands are still shaking from the comedown.

He knows he can't tell Margot that he will never drop the Jenny Lind case.

Nor will he tell her that the interview with Martin – and his subsequent confession – was wrong in every way. Martin clearly had no memories from that night, and just said what he thought Aron wanted him to say.

A stone hits the windscreen, leaving a small, pale blue nick on the glass.

Joona thinks back to the photograph again and how he had taken for granted that the white patch on the back of the victim's head was just reflected light. But now he thinks otherwise.

The girl's death was labelled a suicide. Yet she had been freeze-branded and, in all likelihood, murdered – just like Jenny Lind.

Joona reminds himself that being humble and showing his respect for the work Norrmalm Police have done might help him persuade

Margot to give him another look at the case. He'll admit that he has trouble letting things go and then ask whether he can check this one last thing, purely for his own peace of mind.

It would be as simple as asking for permission to request information from the old case, a single telephone call.

But what am I going to do if she says no, he asks himself.

The car swerves, and the tall buildings cast long shadows across the pavement. Joona leans back in his seat, feeling a lingering sense of dizziness like the slick spheres of a ball bearing rolling around his head.

He pulls out his phone and calls the Bergslagen Police Authority. A moment later, he has been put through to someone named Fredrika Sjöström.

'Joona Linna?' she repeats after he introduces himself. 'How can I help?'

'Fourteen years ago, a girl committed suicide in Örebro. I don't remember all of the details, but I think it was in a changing room – possibly at a swimming pool.'

'Doesn't ring any bells,' says Fredrika.

'Well, I was wondering if you could dig out the report and the images from the autopsy.'

'And you don't have a name for this girl?'

'I wasn't involved in the investigation.'

'That's all right, I'll find her. It's not like there's much else going on around here . . . Just let me log in,' Fredrika tells him. 'Fourteen years, you said? That'll be . . .'

Joona hears his colleague muttering to herself as her fingers strike the keyboard.

'This must be the one,' Fredrika says, clearing her throat. 'Fanny Hoeg . . . She hanged herself in the women's changing rooms at the sports centre in Örebro.'

'She was hanged?'

'Yes.'

'Can you access the pictures?'

'They haven't been digitised . . . but I've got a case number – just give me a minute and I'll call you back.'

146

Joona ends the call, closing his eyes and feeling the gentle rocking of the car. Though this could be an important lead – potentially crucial for the preliminary investigation – he hopes he is wrong.

Because if he is right, and there is a pattern, then they are looking for a killer who has done this before, someone who might already be, or may become, a serial killer.

The phone rings. Joona is still clutching it in his hand, and he opens his eyes and answers.

'Hi, it's Fredrika again,' she says, clearing her throat briefly. 'There wasn't an autopsy, just an external examination.'

'But you have the pictures?' Joona asks.

'Yeah.'

'How many are there?'

'Thirty-two in total. Including close-ups.'

'Are you looking at them now?'

'Yes.'

'This might sound strange, but can you see anything unusual about any of them? Are there any processing issues, or strange reflections?'

'What do you mean?'

'Pale marks, bright patches, reflected light.'

'No, they look totally normal . . . wait, hold on, there's a small white patch in one of them.'

'Where?'

'At the top edge of the shot.'

'No, I mean *where* on Fanny's body?'

'On the back of her head.'

'Are there any other images of the back of her head?'

'No.'

The string of prayer beads hanging from the rear-view mirror swings as the taxi drives over a speed bump.

'What does the report say?' Joona asks.

'Not much.'

'Read it to me.'

The taxi pulls up to the kerb and parks alongside the rough stone wall on Polhemsgatan. Joona climbs out and steps aside for a family with a stroller full of inflatable flamingos, water pistols and umbrellas.

He crosses the road and heads through the glass entrance of the Police Authority building as he listens to Fredrika read the meagre notes about the young woman's death.

Fanny Hoeg had been in contact with the Church of Scientology, and when she ran away from home, her parents were convinced she had simply joined the sect. The police failed to track her down and, six months later, on her eighteenth birthday, stopped looking.

When she eventually reappeared, her parents were on vacation. By then, she had been missing for over a year.

Perhaps she needed help breaking away from the church, and felt like she was all alone without her parents.

The investigating officers' theory was that she had gone to the sports centre as a last resort, hoping to track down her old soccer coach, and that she had hanged herself when she failed to find her.

Both the crime scene investigators and the pathologist ruled the case a suicide, and the police closed their investigation.

Joona asks for the name of the pathologist, then thanks Fredrika for her help.

He pauses when he reaches the lifts, steadying himself against the wall as a shiver passes through him.

The large glass doors by the entrance open and close repeatedly.

A group of people hurry towards the inner courtyard talking loudly.

Joona listens to them as though in a dream, composing himself and finally pressing the button to go up. He wipes his mouth and runs a hand through his hair.

Fredrika confirmed that there were no flashes in any of the other thirty-odd images. Only the one of the back of Fanny's head.

Joona had probably been right during his high. She had been freeze-branded.

Then executed, by hanging.

It could be the same killer with the same modus operandi.

Joona steps into the lift and calls the pathologist who examined Fanny Hoeg's body fourteen years ago. At the time, he was working at the pathology lab that is now a part of the Department of Laboratory Medicine at Örebro University Hospital.

As the doors open and Joona starts walking down the corridor, a man with a croaky voice answers the phone.

'Kurtz.'

Joona pauses, feeling the lingering tail of the opium high hit him as he explains the reason for his call.

'Of course, I remember her,' the pathologist tells him. 'She and my daughter were in the same class at high school.'

'She had a patch of white hair.'

'That's correct,' the man replies, surprised.

'But you didn't shave her head?' Joona continues.

'I had no reason to, there was no doubt about what happened, and I was thinking of her family, who . . .' He trails off, breathing heavily. 'I just assumed she'd bleached some of it,' he says.

'You were wrong about almost everything.'

As Joona passes his office, he thinks about the fact that the murderer held both women prisoner before killing them. That means it is entirely possible that he might be planning to abduct another, or that he may already be imprisoning a third woman. He reaches Margot Silverman's door, knocks, and steps inside.

'Margot,' he says as she meets his eye. 'You know I have a hard time letting things go, and I can be a bit obsessive about finishing things myself. But I might have found a connection that links an old case to Jenny Lind's murder, and I'd like to ask your permission to request information about it.'

'Joona,' she sighs, looking up at him with bloodshot eyes.

'I know the prosecutor has taken over the preliminary investigation.'

'Look at this email,' says Margot, turning her screen towards him.

He moves forward and reads a message from the address rymond933, forwarded to Margot by Aron.

I read that you'd caught the bastard the press was calling the Executioner. If you ask me, he should be deported and sentenced to life.

The thing is, I drive a taxi and I was at the McDonald's on Sveavägen that night, recording a couple of crows through the window

149

doing something funny. But when I watched the video I saw that the bastard is visible in the background, so I thought I would share this and let his fucking lawyers try to save him now.

Joona grabs the mouse and clicks on the attached video. Through the bright reflections from the fast food joint, he can make out the empty pond and the wall and the end of the university building.

There are a couple of crows on the pavement outside, gathered around a closed pizza box.

In the distance, beyond the black birds and the pond, Martin is visible. He is standing perfectly still, holding his umbrella in one hand and the dog's leash in the other.

The playground is hidden from this angle. Martin drops the leash and takes a step forward.

That means the time is 3.18.

In just two minutes, Jenny Lind will be hanging from the jungle gym. Martin steps into the blind spot from the CCTV footage and continues forward over the wet grass.

These are the few moments they were missing.

They will finally be able to see whether he continued around the playhouse to the obscured part of the playground where the jungle gym is.

He could still have time to reach the winch and start turning the handle.

Martin pauses by the playhouse, staring straight at the jungle gym. He takes another few steps forward and then stops, still holding the umbrella over his head.

A white flash lights up the trees.

The water from the umbrella is running down onto his back.

The camera shakes.

Working together, the crows manage to open the lid of the pizza box.

Martin stands perfectly still for quite some time before turning away and walking back towards the Pressbyrån.

All he did was watch.

He never even got close to Jenny.

When Martin leaves the area, it is 3.25, and Jenny Lind has already been dead for five minutes.

With its leash trailing on the ground, the dog follows Martin as he disappears from the shot, heading back towards the metro station.

The camera stays still for a moment, then pans after one of the crows as it flaps away with a piece of pizza, abruptly ending the video.

'Do you want to take over the case, Joona?' Margot asks, her voice hoarse.

'I was right.'

'About which part?'

'We aren't looking at an isolated murder.'

31

Pamela takes an unopened bottle of Absolut Vodka from the pantry and peels off the plastic wrapper from the lid. She grabs a glass and sits down at the kitchen table.

She knows she shouldn't be doing this. She should stop drinking during the week, but she fills the glass to the brim anyway.

She studies the clear liquid and the dappled shadow it casts on the table. This is the last glass, she tells herself as her phone starts ringing,

'Dennis Kratz' flashes on the screen.

A rush of anxiety shoots through her. She was incredibly drunk when she invited him over yesterday. Fragmented memories from last night and this morning trickle through her head.

She cheated on Martin with Dennis.

* * *

Pamela stared up at the sconce on the ceiling as the room spun like a raft in a whirlpool. She eventually dozed off but later awoke suddenly with a deep sense of danger.

The room was almost pitch-black.

She was naked beneath the sheets, trying to remember what she had done last night.

Without moving, she listened to the whining of the old air vent in the wardrobe.

The curtains were closed, but the grey light from outside was seeping in through the gaps. Pamela blinked, trying to make her eyes

focus, and thought she could make out a child's handprint on the window.

The floorboards creaked behind her.

She turned her head and saw a tall figure in the middle of the room, holding her bra in one hand.

It took her a few seconds to realise it was Dennis, and she immediately remembered what had happened.

'Dennis?' she whispered.

'I took a shower,' he said, draping her bra over the back of the chair.

She sat up and felt the stickiness between her legs. She saw him picking up her dress from the back of the armchair, turning it right way out.

'You should probably go,' she said.

'OK.'

'It's just that I need to sleep,' she explained.

As he dressed, Dennis tried to tell her how he didn't want her to be disappointed in him, to regret anything.

'I mean, for me, it was perfectly logical,' he said as he buttoned his shirt. 'Because I guess I've always been in love with you – even if I haven't always admitted that to myself.'

'I'm sorry, but I can't have this conversation right now,' she said, her mouth dry. 'I can't believe we did what we did. It doesn't fit my self-image.'

'You don't always have to be the stronger person, you know. You really need to accept that.'

'Who else is going to do it?'

Once he had gone, she struggled to her feet and locked the door, took out her contact lenses, and went back to bed.

She slept deeply, dreamlessly, until the alarm went off. She took a shower, tidied away the wine glasses and changed the sheets. She put yesterday's clothes into the laundry basket, took the dog out, and hurried to work.

She had a busy work day. After a meeting at a building site on Narvavägen, she went up onto the roof and made a few sketches, and then got into the temporary construction lift.

The cramped metal cage clanking and shaking as it carried her back down to street level.

As Pamela took off her hard hat, her thoughts immediately turned to her betrayal, to the fact she would have to tell Martin everything.

* * *

She is now sitting at the kitchen table with a glass of vodka in front of her, phone ringing in her hand.

'Pamela,' she answers.

'I just spoke to the police, and the prosecutor is dropping the charges on Martin and releasing him,' Dennis tells her.

'Now?'

'It doesn't usually take long once they've made the decision. He'll probably be out within twenty minutes or so.'

'Thanks.'

'How are you?'

'I'm OK . . . but I don't have time to talk right now. I should probably go get Martin right away.'

They hang up and Pamela picks up her glass, wondering if she should try to pour the vodka back into the bottle. She decides she is too stressed, and empties it into the sink instead. She then hurries out into the hallway, grabs her bag and keys, locks the door behind her, and jumps into the lift.

Through the bars of the gate, she sees the floor rise up and disappear as the lift begins its creaking journey downwards.

The lights in the stairwell are out, but she spots a stroller outside the doors to one of the floors.

She wants to get to the prison before Martin is released.

Pamela turns to check her makeup in the mirror on the wall of the lift, and takes out her powder compact as she passes the third floor.

Right then, a bright light fills the entire lift, and she hears the whir of a rapid camera shutter.

She wheels around, but all she has time to see is a pair of black boots as the lift continues its descent.

Her heart is racing, and she doesn't understand her reaction. The stress must be making everything seem threatening. It was probably just an estate agent taking pictures of the building.

When she reaches the ground floor, she pushes back the gate and leaves. She runs down to the garage and jumps into her car, then hurries to the exit ramp and presses the button to open the doors.

'Come on,' she whispers as the garage door slowly folds to one side.

She drives up the ramp, swinging over the pavement, and out onto Karlavägen before picking up speed.

Her mind is racing.

They are dropping the charges and letting Martin go. She'll be able to appeal the decision by social services and call Mia to let her know everything is going to be OK.

The traffic lights turn to amber, and Pamela accelerates rather than slowing down. A woman in a burqa throws her arms up at the crosswalk, and someone blasts their horn.

She takes Karlbergsvägen, and has just turned off on to Dalagatan when a police officer on a motorcycle appears alongside her and signals for her to pull over.

Pamela comes to a stop by the kerb and watches the officer climb off his bike, take off his helmet and walk towards her.

She winds down the window as he approaches. He looks kind, with sceptical eyes and a tanned face.

'You were going a bit fast there – did you know?' he asks.

'Sorry, I'm just really stressed.'

'Could I see your licence?'

She rummages through her bag before dumping her keys and glasses case onto the passenger seat. She finds her wallet and manages to open it, but her hands are unsteady and she can't get her licence out of its compartment. She has to pull out several cards before it finally comes out.

'Thanks,' says the officer, comparing the image on her licence with her face. 'You were doing seventy-four kilometres an hour outside a school.'

'God . . . I didn't see it, I must've missed the signs.'

'Well, I'll have to seize your licence either way.'

'OK, I understand,' she says, noticing that her back is sweating.

'But I'm in a real hurry. I couldn't keep it a while, could I? Just today?'

'I think you should count on losing it for at least four months.'

She stares at him, trying to process his words.

'But . . . am I just supposed to leave the car here?'

'Where do you live?'

'On Karlavägen.'

'And do you have a parking space there?'

'A garage.'

'Then I'll follow you back to the garage.'

32

Martin is hunched up on the floor beside his bunk, arms wrapped around his knees. He is wearing his green prison-issue uniform, though the slippers they gave him are under the sink. He hasn't slept all night, and his tired eyes are stinging. The plastic-wrapped bedsheets and towel are lying untouched next to a bag containing soap and a toothbrush.

Before the jail was built in the 1970s, the site was Crown Princess Lovisa's Home for Poor Children, which meant the two dead boys were joined by gangs of other children last night. They stalked the corridors, banging on all of the doors before gathering outside Martin's cell.

The boys rammed at his door and pulled at it, eventually lying down outside and staring at him through the gap at the bottom.

Since they couldn't get in, they stared at him, but he turned away and covered his ears until daybreak.

Martin hears heavy footsteps approaching down the corridor outside, followed by the slow clinking of keys. He squeezes his eyes shut as one of the wardens opens the door.

'Hi, Martin,' says a man with a Finnish accent.

Martin doesn't dare look up, but he sees the man's shadow cut across the floor as he steps into the room and moves in front of him.

'My name is Joona Linna. We met briefly, in the interview room,' the man continues. 'I'm here to tell you that the prosecutor won't be pursuing the case against you; she's dropped the charges, and you're going to be released immediately. I want to apologise for everything that's happened to you. But, before you go, I'd like to ask whether

you would be willing to help us find the person who killed Jenny Lind.'

'If I can,' Martin mumbles, peering at the man's shoes and the hems of his black trousers.

'I know you don't like to talk much,' says Joona, 'but when we last met, you were about to tell me something. My colleague interrupted us, but you were about to describe Jenny Lind as she was standing in the rain.'

'I can't remember,' Martin whispers.

'We can do it a little later.'

'OK.'

Martin's body feels stiff as he gets up from the floor.

'Would you like me to call anyone to let them know you're being released?'

'No, thanks.'

He doesn't dare say Pamela's name, because the door into the corridor is ajar. The dead children will want to take her name if he says it. They'll be angry if they can't have it on their gravestones.

The officer with the Finnish accent takes Martin to a guard, who leads him to the booking desk, where he is given a bag containing his clothes, shoes and wallet.

Five minutes later, he steps out onto Bergsgatan. The gate behind him closes with a whirr, and he starts making his way down the street, along the row of parked cars glittering in the sunlight.

He can hear a dog barking in the distance.

A boy with a grey face is standing by the big fan grille, staring down at him. Water drips from his hair onto his grey jacket, and the knees of his filthy jeans are ripped.

The fingers on one hand are outstretched, straining.

Martin turns and starts walking in the opposite direction. He hears quick footsteps behind him, the sound of someone approaching, then feels a hand grip his clothes. He tries to pull away, but the person behind him hits him hard on the cheek. Martin stumbles to one side and loses his balance, grazing his hand on the pavement as he breaks his fall.

He hears a roar in his ears, just like when he crashed into the water.

He remembers that the sudden chill beneath the ice was like being knocked down. As he tries to get up, a man with wide eyes and a tense mouth hits him in the face. His fist strikes him just above the nose.

Martin puts his hands up to try to protect himself as he struggles back onto his feet. He can't see anything out of one eye, and he can feel blood trickling down over his lips.

'What the hell did you do with her for five years?' the man shouts. 'Five years! I'll kill you, you hear me? I'll . . .'

The man is breathing heavily, pulling at Martin's jacket, and they both stagger out into the road.

'Answer me!'

It's Jenny Lind's father.

Martin recognises him from TV, back when he saw the man and his wife plead with the abductor to let their daughter go.

'There's been a misunderstanding, I haven't . . .'

But the man hits him again, just above the mouth this time, and he stumbles backwards into a bicycle locked to a post. He hears the bell ring.

Two police officers come running over the grass from the swimming pool nearby.

'He took my daughter, he killed my daughter!' the man shouts, picking up a loose tile from the pavement.

Martin wipes the blood from his face and sees the smaller boy standing on the strip of yellow grass, filming him on his phone.

The sunlight catches the side mirror of one of the parked cars, blinding Martin. He looks away, thinking about the broken light filtering through the ice.

The officers shout for the man to drop the paving stone and calm down. His breathing is laboured, and he glances down at the slab as though he has no idea where it came from before dropping it to the pavement.

One of the officers takes Martin aside, asks if he is OK and checks whether he needs medical attention. The other checks the man's driver's licence, and explains that he will be charged with assault.

'It's all just a misunderstanding,' Martin mutters, hurrying away.

33

They have been listening to the sound of digging all day, the splash of the gravel as it hits the wheelbarrow. Caesar just decided that they should be building a bunker to take refuge in when the end comes. He seems much more uptight than he is usually. Yesterday, he pushed Granny over for being too slow.

Despite the heat in the cage, Kim shivers as Blenda starts combing her hair with her fingers. She doesn't like having anyone behind her, so she tries to focus on the sliver of light beneath the door.

In the walkway between the cages, flies buzz around the bucket of bread and dried fish. Granny brought it in yesterday and just left it there. They haven't been fed yet.

'Let me see your face,' says Blenda.

They are both thirsty, but Blenda takes the plastic bottle and shakes the last few drops into her cupped hand to wash Kim's face anyway.

'What do you know, there's a girl hiding under there after all.' She smiles.

'Thanks,' Kim whispers, licking the water from her lips.

Kim is from Malmö, and plays handball. Her team was en route to a match in Solna when they stopped for lunch in Brahehus. There was a long line for the toilets, and Kim couldn't wait.

She'd grabbed a napkin and set off into the woods. There were wads of used tissue everywhere, so she moved further into the trees until she could no longer see any of the buildings or cars.

She still remembers the glade where she stopped, the warm sunlight on the blueberry bushes and moss, the glittering spiderwebs and dark pines.

She lowered her trousers and underwear and then squatted, feet wide apart.

With one hand, she held her clothes away from the tiny droplets splashing up from the ground.

Somewhere nearby, a twig snapped.

She realised there was someone else nearby, but had no choice but to finish up.

The footsteps behind her drew closer as pine cones and sticks crunched underfoot, branches brushing against trouser legs.

It all happened so quickly.

Suddenly, he was right there, holding a rag over her mouth, pulling her onto her back. She tried to escape his grip and felt the hot urine trickling down her thighs before she lost consciousness.

That was two years ago.

She spent the first six months alone in the basement, but was eventually allowed up into the main house. She remembers the moment Granny told her that the search had been called off. Kim used to share a room with Blenda, who has been here much longer. Blenda wears a gold bracelet and has been taught how to drive the lorry. Their room was on the second floor, and they took care of all the cleaning and washing, but didn't have any contact with the other women in the house.

Out in the yard, the wheelbarrow creaks, and they hear Granny shouting at Amanda, telling her she won't get any food if she doesn't do any work.

'Do you know them?' Kim asks in a low voice.

'No,' Blenda replies. 'But I heard that Amanda ran away from home because she was bored and wanted to see the world. She wanted to travel around Europe and sing in a band.'

'What about Jasmin?'

'She's from Senegal and . . . I don't know much about her. She swears in French.'

Since Jenny Lind tried to escape, everything has changed. Everyone has seen the Polaroids of Jenny's final struggle, her dead body. Now

all the girls have been stripped of their privileges and are no longer allowed to sleep in the house.

Now they live in cramped cages like animals.

* * *

Blenda has just started plaiting Kim's hair when the crossbar is lifted from the door and Caesar steps into the longhouse.

They blink in the bright daylight and see the machete swinging by his thigh. The dull blade looks heavy.

'Kim,' he says, pausing in front of the cage.

She lowers her eyes as Granny has taught them, noticing that her breathing is rapid.

'Everything OK?' he asks.

'Yes, thank you.'

'What would you say to eating dinner with me?'

'That would be very nice.'

'We can have an aperitif right now, if you'd like?' he says, unlocking the cage.

Kim crawls over and climbs down onto the floor, brushing the straw and dirt from her tracksuit bottoms before following him out into the sunny yard.

The sudden flow of blood to her legs makes her toes tingle.

The wheelbarrow has tipped over, spilling the gravel, and Jasmin is lying on the ground beside it. Granny is hitting her with her stick, not saying a word. Amanda hurries over and rights the wheelbarrow, then grabs one of the spades and starts shovelling the gravel back into the barrow.

'What's this?' Caesar asks, pointing with the machete.

'Just an accident,' Amanda replies, looking up at him.

'An accident? Why was there an accident?' he asks.

Granny stops hitting Jasmin and takes a few steps back, breathing through her open mouth. Jasmin is still lying on the ground, staring blankly ahead.

'It's been hot, and we need water,' Amanda replies.

'Did you tip the gravel out just to get water?' asks Caesar.

'No, it . . .'

162

Amanda does up the top few buttons of her sweat-drenched blouse with trembling fingers.

'The minute I turn my back, you act as if the rules no longer apply,' Caesar continues. 'What's wrong with you? What would you do without me? Are you going to take care of yourselves? Get your own food and buy your own clothes?'

'I'm sorry – we just need water.'

'So you don't think the Lord knows what you need?' he asks, raising his voice.

'Of course He—'

'First you decide you're unhappy,' he interrupts her. 'And once you're unhappy, you start thinking about running away.'

'She didn't mean anything by it,' Granny speaks up. 'She's—'

'You're the one who forced me to turn to harsher punishments,' he barks. 'I don't want it to be this way, I don't want to have to lock any of you up.'

'I would never run away,' Amanda swears.

'Are you a dog?' he asks, licking his lips.

'What?'

'Dogs don't run away, do they?' he says, studying her. 'If you're a dog, shouldn't you be standing like one?'

With a blank expression on her face, Amanda lowers the spade to the wheelbarrow and gets down onto all fours in front of him.

Her blouse has come untucked from her skirt, and the sweat on her lower back is glistening in the sun.

'Fanny tried to run away, Jenny tried to run away – does anyone else want to try to run away?' asks Caesar.

He grabs Amanda's hair, pulls back her head, and brings the machete down on her neck. The sound it makes is like an axe hitting a chopping block. Amanda falls flat on her face. Her body twitches for a moment or two, then stops moving.

'I'll take care of her,' Granny whispers, raising a hand to her necklace.

'Take care of her? She doesn't deserve a burial – she'll rot by the side of the road,' he tells her, turning and heading towards the house.

Kim is still standing in the yard, close to Amanda's dead body, trembling. She watches as Caesar stretches an extension cord across the yard and plugs in an angle grinder.

The next hour passes in what feels like a haze. Caesar cuts up Amanda's body as Kim and Jasmin pack the pieces and place them into plastic bags. They secure the tops and carry them over to the trailer of the lorry.

Caesar tosses a water bottle, a few pieces of jewellery and a purse into the last of the bags, along with her head and right arm, and tells Granny to dump her somewhere far away.

34

Mia Andersson is sitting opposite her caseworker in one of the rooms on the ground floor.

The mug of coffee in her hands has grown cold.

A sense of loneliness seems to follow her with every step she takes.

She never had anyone to look after her when she was younger; it was up to her to keep herself clean and fed. When she was seven, she found both of her parents dead in the bathroom, overdosed on fentanyl. She was taken in by social services and placed with a family in Sandviken two weeks later, though she soon got into a fight with another child.

Mia is blonde like her mother, but she has dyed her hair pink and blue. She fills in her eyebrows, and wears a lot of eyeliner and mascara. Her face is quite sweet, but her crooked teeth make her look tough when she smiles.

She dresses in black jeans, boots and baggy sweaters.

Mia has come to realise that people are not kind; they just use one another. There is no such thing as real love, as genuine compassion, everything is just a superficial sales pitch.

Her life since her parents died has been a solution-oriented, 'salutogenic' approach derived from evidence-based methods – as it says in the brochure.

She hates this system.

There are certain kids no one wants, and that's fine. The few people who do want them are, of course, entirely unsuitable.

Mia didn't answer when Pamela called her earlier today, and when she tried again five minutes later, she blocked her number.

'What's on your mind, Mia?'

'Nothing.'

The caseworker is a woman in her fifties, with short grey hair and a pair of glasses that hang on a gold chain between her enormous breasts.

'I know you're upset because the board denied Pamela and Martin's application.'

'It doesn't matter.'

The only time Mia has ever felt like she had a family was when she was with Micke. But afterwards, once he went to prison, she couldn't believe she had ever actually been in love with him. He was only nice to her because she brought in money from drugs and robberies.

'You've been placed with two families since you arrived here.'

'And they didn't work out,' Mia replies.

'Why not?'

'You'd have to ask them.'

'I'm asking you.'

'People expect you to be sweet and nice all the time, but I'm not. I get frustrated sometimes, like when people try to make decisions on my behalf without understanding a fucking thing about me.'

'We're going to conduct a supplementary psychiatric evaluation.'

'I'm not crazy, I'm really not. I just haven't been put with a family where I fit in – as I am.'

'Well, you have a place here,' the caseworker says without smiling.

Mia scratches her forehead. The staff at the home claim to care about her, but they aren't her family, and they don't want to be; they have their own kids to worry about, and this is nothing but a job to them, a way to earn a living. There's nothing wrong with any of them, but ultimately her problems are just their pay cheque.

'I want to be in a real home,' says Mia.

The caseworker looks down at her notes.

'You're already on the waiting list, and I think you should definitely stay on it, but to be perfectly honest with you, you're almost eighteen, so your chances aren't great.'

'OK, got it, it is what it is,' says Mia, swallowing firmly.

She gets up and thanks the caseworker, shaking her hand and leaving the room before walking down the corridor and sitting down on the stairs.

Mia doesn't have the energy to go up to her room. Lovisa is having one of her outbursts.

She is busy scrolling through memes on her phone when a news alert pops up: Aron Beck, the lead detective in the investigation into the murder of Jenny Lind, says that the prosecutor made a mistake when she requested that Martin Nordström be held in custody. He has now been cleared, and is considered the key witness in the ongoing investigation.

Mia heads downstairs to the front door. The air outside is warm, and steam is rising from the grass, the rhubarb and the drooping lilacs.

She walks past the two cars parked outside and hurries down the driveway, taking the short cut to the left through the long weeds, and coming out on to Varvs Street.

She glances back over her shoulder.

An older man with long grey hair is standing by the side of the road, taking pictures of the bees flying around the tall lupins.

Mia walks along the edge of the trees, glancing in between the trunks. She still feels like she is being watched.

The road takes her around a small wood and into an industrial area full of building wholesalers and mechanics' workshops.

She walks past the old gas towers.

The hot air is quivering over their domed tops. She hears a car approaching from behind.

The gravel beneath its tyres crunches in its movement towards her.

Mia turns around, using her hand to block the sunlight, and sees that it's a taxi. It stops about twenty metres away.

She starts hurrying along the fence and hears the car following her, speeding up until it pulls alongside her.

She could climb the fence and run down to the docks, she thinks. But then the back window rolls down and she sees Pamela's face.

'Hi, Mia,' she says. 'I need to talk to you.'

The taxi comes to a stop, and Mia climbs into the back seat beside her.

'I saw that they let Martin go,' she says.

'It's been reported already? What did they say?'

'That he didn't do anything . . . but that he's, like, an important witness.'

'I could've told them that from the very beginning,' Pamela sighs.

Her face is pretty, but she has such sad eyes. A network of fine lines stretches across her forehead.

'I tried to call you a few times.'

'Did you?' Mia says, feigning surprise.

The car starts moving again, and Mia looks out through the window, smiling to herself when she realises that Pamela took a taxi all the way from Stockholm just because she didn't answer her phone.

'I've spoken to a lawyer, and we're going to appeal social services' decision.'

'Will it work?' Mia asks, inspecting Pamela from one side.

'I don't know what they'll say about Martin . . . He's a highly sensitive person, and he's had mental health issues – I told you about that, didn't I?'

'Yeah.'

'I'm just afraid of how being locked up might have affected him,' Pamela explains.

'What does he say?'

As they slowly drive through Gävle, Pamela tells Mia that Martin was assaulted by Jenny Lind's father outside the prison. She searched for him until two in the morning, calling all of the hospitals to see if he had been admitted. Early the next day, he was found asleep in a small boat by Kungsholms strand. When the police picked him up, he was confused and couldn't tell them what he was doing there.

'I went to the emergency psychiatric ward, but . . . Martin didn't want to talk. He said almost nothing, and seemed too scared to come home with me.'

'God, poor guy,' says Mia.

'I think he needs a few days to get himself together and realise that this was all just a mistake.'

They drive by the main square, where three small girls are running across the stone tiles, chasing bubbles.

'Where are we going?' asks Mia, peering out through the window.

'I don't actually know. What do you want to do?' Pamela grins. 'Are you hungry?'

'No.'

'Do you want to go to Furuvik?'

'Furuvik? The amusement park? You know I'm almost eighteen, don't you?'

'I'm forty-one, and I love roller coasters.'

'Me too,' Mia admits with a smile.

35

It is nine in the evening by the time Pamela climbs out of the taxi on Karlavägen. She heads straight inside and takes the lift to the fifth floor.

Her cheeks have gained some colour from the sun, and her hair is a mess. She and Mia rode the roller coaster more than ten times, and ate popcorn, cotton candy and pizza.

Pamela opens the security door, picks up the mail from the floor, and locks up behind her before hanging the key on the hook.

As she is untying her shoes, she thinks about taking a shower and getting into bed to read.

She flicks through the mail and feels a sudden chill. Between the envelopes, she finds a polaroid picture of Mia.

Her pink and blue hair is tucked behind her ear, and she looks happy. In the background, Pamela can make out the entrance to the haunted house at the amusement park.

The picture must have been taken only a few hours ago.

Pamela turns the image over and notices some tiny writing on the back, so small that she can't quite read it.

She takes the polaroid through to the kitchen, puts it down on the table and turns on the brightest light. She grabs her glasses and leans in close.

she'll be punished if he talks

Heart racing, she tries to process what this all means. There is no doubt this is a threat, someone trying to scare her and Martin.

170

The news sites and billboards that evening are all full of headlines and hastily written articles about how Martin is now considered the police's key witness.

Someone wants to frighten her, to make her stop Martin from testifying. It must be the killer.

He's watching them. He knows where they live, and he also knows about Mia.

The thought makes Pamela feel sick with panic.

She picks up her phone to call the police and explain what happened, to ask them to protect Mia. But she immediately recognises that it won't happen. They'll take her statement and explain that what happened isn't enough to warrant police protection.

In a way, she understands; it's just a photograph and a general threat. There aren't any names or specifics, after all.

But it means that the person who killed Jenny Lind is afraid of Martin's testimony. And Mia will be punished if he reveals what he saw.

Pamela puts down her phone and studies the photo again.

Mia looks so happy, the row of rings in her ear glittering in the bright sunlight.

Pamela turns the photograph over and runs a finger across the letters, watching as they disappear from the glossy surface.

Her fingertip is blue, and the words are gone.

She gets up and feels her hands shaking as she opens the cupboard and takes out the bottle of vodka. She looks at it for a moment and then pours it down the sink, running the tap until the smell disappears. She returns to the table to call Mia and tell her to be careful.

36

It takes Joona a little more than an hour to drive out to Kapellskär harbour and take a water taxi to the restricted military area on the north-east shore of Idö.

The Sea of Åland is as flat as a mirror and dazzling. Gulls lift off from the concrete jetty as the boat docks.

Joona walks up to a modernist tarred wood building and presses the buzzer. He shows his ID to the receptionist and then takes a seat in the cool waiting room.

The compound is an exclusive retreat for high-ranking politicians, members of the military and agency heads in need of various forms of rehabilitation.

After five minutes, a woman in uniform comes to get him, taking him to one of the eight suites.

Joona finds Saga Bauer sitting in an armchair with a bottle of mineral water in one hand. As ever, she is staring out towards the horizon through the enormous window.

'Saga,' he says, sitting down beside her.

During her first few months at the clinic, she paced back and forth like a caged animal, repeating that she wanted to die.

These days, she doesn't speak at all; she just sits by the window, looking out at the sea.

Joona comes to see her regularly. At first, he would read to her, but later he started talking about himself. It was only when he happened to mention a case at one point that he really noticed she was listening.

Since then, he has told her all about the investigations he has been working on, continually sharing his theories with her.

She listens to him speak, and on his most recent visit, she even smiled slightly when he mentioned the discovery of the freeze-brands.

Joona tells her about Martin Nordström, who watched the murder take place. He explains that the man has complex PTSD and paranoid delusions, and that he was pressured to confess to a murder they now know he didn't commit.

'He was assaulted outside the prison and is now back in the emergency mental health ward,' he continues. 'I doubt I'll be able to interview him . . . everything just feels so slow at the moment, but I've found an older case that seems to be linked to this one . . .'

Saga doesn't speak, just looks out at the water.

Joona puts two photographs onto the table beside her.

Fanny Hoeg's gaze is dark and dreamy. Jenny Lind is staring straight at the camera, and looks like she might be holding back a laugh.

'Fanny was hanged, just like Jenny, only fourteen years earlier,' Joona explains. 'We don't have any detailed pictures of the stamp, but it's clear she was freeze-marked too. A lock of her dark hair at the back of her head had turned completely white.'

Joona tells Saga that the two women were roughly the same age. They were both popular girls but weren't in romantic relationships and they were both active on social media.

'Their builds were different, they had different eye colours, and one was blonde, the other brunette,' he says. 'When Jenny was abducted, the general consensus was that she'd been chosen at random, but when I compare her with the image of Fanny, there's something similar about them . . . something about their noses and cheeks, their hairlines . . .'

Saga reacts to something Joona has shown her for the first time and turns to look at the pictures.

'Obviously we're searching for any other murders, suicides and disappearances that could be linked to the same perpetrator,' Joona continues. 'But based on what we know now, these two murders, he doesn't seem to be particularly active – he might not even be a

serial killer yet. But he does follow a pattern, he's got a method . . . and I know he's not going to stop.'

* * *

On the way back, Joona makes a detour to Rimbo to talk to a horse breeder called Jelena Postnova. The narrow road is flanked by trees and leads to a parking area by a roundpole fence. Aron Beck is leaning against a silver-grey Mercedes Benz, and he looks up from his phone as Joona parks and climbs out of his car.

'Margot thought I should come out here and apologise,' he tells Joona. 'So, sorry. I'm sorry I acted like an idiot. I should've let you interview Martin before getting the prosecutor involved.'

Joona puts on his sunglasses and looks over to the red wooden stables. In the paddock, a young man is riding a black stallion. The dust from the dry ground has been kicked up, and it paints the horse's legs brown.

'Margot says it's up to you whether I stay on the case, and I'd totally get it if you wanted me off,' Aron continues. 'But I want you to know I don't give a damn about making a name for myself. My only focus is stopping this bastard. If you give me a second chance, I'll work my ass off until you tell me to stop.'

'Sounds good,' says Joona.

'Really? Shit, that's great.' Aron sounds relieved.

Joona sets off down the gravel path towards the stables. Aron follows him, keeping up as they talk through the investigation so far.

The team from the National Crime Unit have searched the records going back twenty years, but haven't found any other murders, suicides or deaths fitting the same pattern.

An average of forty young women take their own lives in Sweden every year, roughly twenty-five per cent by hanging.

Other than Jenny Lind and Fanny Hoeg, only three women have been murdered by hanging in that time frame, each one within the context of an abusive relationship.

Extensive autopsies were carried out, but none of the reports mention freeze-branding or pigmentation changes.

The gravel track curves between the large building and a field with eight horses in it. It's hot in the bright sunlight. Grasshoppers chirp in the ditches, and swallows flutter high overhead.

'In terms of women suspected of having been abducted, it's trickier,' Aron continues. 'Once we filter out the clear-cut cases in which girls are trafficked out of the country, that leaves us with several hundred people.'

'We'll have to look into all of them,' says Joona.

'But only six of them seem like genuine abductions.'

An older woman emerges from the stable with a saddle in one hand. She throws it into the back of a rusty pickup and then turns towards them, squinting in the light.

She has cropped white hair and is wearing a pair of dirty jodhpurs, leather boots and a T-shirt picturing Vladimir Vysostky.

'I've heard you know pretty much all there is to know about breeding horses,' Joona says, holding up his ID.

'Dressage is my specialty, really, but I do know a bit,' she replies.

'It would be great if you could help us.'

'Absolutely – if I can.' She shows them into the stable, where the air is slightly cooler.

The heady aroma of horses and hay hits them as they step inside. Joona takes off his sunglasses and looks along the row of twenty or so stalls. Beneath the ridge of the roof, a powerful fan whirs away. The horses snort and stamp on the floor.

They walk past the tack room and the damp wash stall before stopping in front of one of the horses.

Daylight filters in through a line of small, dirty windows.

'How do you mark your horses?' asks Joona.

'If we're talking about the harness racers, microchips have replaced freeze-branding,' she replies.

'When did you stop freeze-branding them?'

'I'm not sure, maybe eight years ago . . . but we do still triangle mark them.'

'What's that?' asks Aron.

175

'If a horse is injured or gets too old to be used as a real riding horse, you can have a vet freeze-brand it with a triangle instead of having it put down. Look at Emmy,' Jelena continues, leading them over to one of the stalls at the far end of the building.

The old mare snorts and raises her head as they peer in. At the top of her left flank, a white triangle shines brightly against her reddish-brown coat.

'It means she's retired. She still potters around, and I ride her in the woods from time to time.'

A fly lands at the corner of the horse's eye, and she shakes her heavy head and stamps her feet, flank hitting the wall. The harnesses, reins and stirrups hanging above her clink softly.

'How does the marking work?'

'It varies, but we do it with liquid nitrogen, at almost two hundred degrees below zero. We deliver a local anaesthetic and then press the stamp to the skin for about a minute.'

'Do you know anyone who uses this mark?' Joona asks, showing her the close-up of the back of Jenny Lind's head.

Jelena leans in to the picture, a sharp crease between her brows.

'No,' she says. 'And I'd probably go so far as to say that no one uses that kind of mark on their horses in Sweden – or anywhere.'

'So what do you make of it?'

'I have no idea,' she says. 'I don't know how the meat industry works in other countries, but there are no numbers to identify and trace the animal on this mark.'

'No.'

'I'd associate it more with the type of marking cattle breeders used to use in America,' she says. 'They sometimes looked a bit like that, though maybe a little less elaborate.'

*   *   *

As they return to their cars, Joona realises that Jelena is probably right: the victims' markings are about ownership, not identification. The perpetrator wants to show that the marked women belong to him, even after death.

'We're moving too slowly. More women are going to die if we don't find him soon,' Joona tells Aron, opening his car door.

'I know, it makes me feel sick.'

'He might already have his next victim.'

37

Pamela pays the driver and climbs out of the taxi in front of Sankt Göran's Hospital. She enters through door one, pausing for a moment to check whether anyone is following her before taking the lift to ward four. She signs in at reception and hands over her phone.

Martin is in the day room, playing cards with a stocky man in a wheelchair. She recognises him, the man called the Prophet by the others, a repeat patient in the ward. He has a small cross tattooed on every fingertip.

'Hi, Martin,' she says, sitting down at their table.

'Hello,' he mumbles.

She reaches out to touch his forearm, managing to catch his eye for a second or two before he turns away. He still has a Band-Aid on his forehead, but the bruise on his cheek has already started to turn yellow.

'How are you?' she asks.

'No feeling,' the Prophet replies, slapping his thigh.

'I was talking to Martin.'

. The Prophet pushes his thick glasses up the bridge of his nose, gathers up all the cards and starts to shuffle them.

'Are you in?' he asks her, cutting the deck.

'Do you want to play?' Pamela asks Martin.

He nods, and the Prophet deals out the cards. An orderly with muscular arms is standing by one of the other tables nearby, watching an older woman colour in a mandala.

A man with a grey beard is dozing in front of the TV. The applause from a syndicated quiz show rings out faintly from the speakers.

'Tens,' Martin whispers, eyes darting over to the glass doors.

'You want my tens?' Pamela says smiling.

'Are you sure? You could choose nines instead . . .' the Prophet says.

He hurriedly shakes his head, and she hands him three tens.

Pamela glances up at the clock and feels a knot of anxiety when she realises that it won't be long until Martin is shouting and convulsing.

'Go fish, go fish,' the Prophet says as a door opens.

Pamela looks up and sees Primus – the man who was harassing her during her last visit – step into the day room, followed by an orderly. His grey hair is hanging loose, and a sports bag is slung over one shoulder.

He bows deeply to the Prophet, adjusts the crotch of his tight jeans, and pauses behind Pamela's chair.

'Admitted today, discharged today,' he says with a grin.

'You do as you're told,' the Prophet says, lowering his eyes to his cards.

'Man, I'm going to do so much fucking,' Primus whispers, sucking on his index finger.

'Come over here with me,' says the orderly.

'OK, but what's the time?'

As the orderly checks his watch, Primus reaches out and strokes Pamela's neck with his wet finger.

'Time for you to walk on out of here, so say your goodbyes,' the orderly tells him.

'I don't need to walk, I can fly,' says Primus.

'But you're not free,' the Prophet points out, his voice grave. 'You're just Caesar's lackey, a fly buzzing around his king . . .'

'Shut up,' he whispers anxiously.

Pamela watches Primus as he follows the orderly, who swipes his card, enters a code and opens the door.

Martin is still clutching his hand of dog-eared cards.

'Your threes,' he mumbles.

'My threes,' says the Prophet, picking up his cards from the table. 'Yes.'

'Go fish,' he says, turning to look at Pamela. 'Could I have your sevens?'

'Go fish.'

'You know, they're doing a lot of research into gynoids – female androids, in other words,' the Prophet tells her, using the cards to scratch his chin. 'A researcher by the name of McMullen has built a sex robot that can actually listen and remember what you say. It can talk, frown and smile.'

He puts down his cards and holds up his palms. Pamela can't help but glance at the ten small crosses on his fingers.

'Give me all your kings,' says Martin.

'Before long, you won't be able to tell the difference between a gynoid and a real woman,' the Prophet continues. 'It'll be the end of rape, prostitution and paedophilia.'

'I'm not so sure about that,' Pamela mutters, getting up from the table.

'The new generation of robots will be able to scream, cry and beg,' says the Prophet. 'They'll fight back, they'll sweat in fear, they'll throw up and wet themselves, but . . .' He trails off as a nurse with a wide face and laughter lines around her mouth comes into the room and asks Martin and Pamela to follow her.

'You haven't eaten anything today?' she asks as Martin lies down on one of the beds in the waiting room.

'No,' he replies, glancing over to Pamela.

His face is a mess, and he closes his eyes as the nurse inserts a needle into the crook of his left arm before leaving the room.

Dennis has explained what electroconvulsive therapy involves. Using an electrical current, doctors induce a controlled seizure in an attempt to restore the balance in the brain.

Given that Martin had to return to the ward after just a few days at home, his psychiatrist believes that the treatment is their last resort.

'Primus said that . . . that I'm . . . going to prison.'

'No, that was the detective, Aron. He tricked you into confessing to things you didn't do,' she explains.

'Right,' he whispers.

She pats his hand and he opens his eyes.

'You don't have to talk to any more police officers, just so you know . . .'

'It's OK.'

'But you have every right to say no after what they put you through.'

'I want to, though,' he whispers.

'I know you want to help, but I don't think . . .' She trails off as the nurse's assistant comes in and announces that it is time for the procedure to begin. Pamela walks alongside Martin as they move him into the treatment room.

An arc of cables loop between a yellowed plug socket and a row of monitors.

At one side of the room, an anaesthetist with greying eyebrows is sitting on a stool, adjusting the angle of the screens.

Martin is moved into position, and a nurse anaesthetist links him up to the various machines.

Pamela can see that he is worried, and she takes his hand.

'The treatment takes around ten minutes,' the other nurse explains, administering the anaesthetic.

Martin closes his eyes, and his hand goes limp.

The nurse waits a few seconds, then injects a muscle relaxant.

Martin is now sleeping deeply, his mouth slightly sunken. Pamela lets go of his hand and moves back.

She watches as the nurse anaesthetist places an oxygen mask over his mouth and nose and starts the oxygen supply.

The psychiatrist comes into the room and immediately moves over to Pamela. He has deep-set eyes and prominent cheekbones, a shaving rash on his throat and five clear pens in the chest pocket of his white coat.

'You're welcome to stay,' he says. 'But some relatives find it unsettling to see the patient's muscles react to the electricity. I promise it doesn't hurt, but I just want you to be prepared.'

'I am,' she says, looking him in the eye.

'Good.'

The nurse hyperventilates Martin in order to increase the oxygen levels in his brain, then takes away the mask and places a mouth guard between his teeth.

The psychiatrist starts the ECT machine, adjusting the power, the pulse width and the frequency. He steps forwards and holds the two electrodes to Martin's head.

The ceiling light flickers, and Martin's arms bend towards his body in a sudden spasm.

His hands shake unnaturally and his back arches.

His jaw tenses as his chin presses against his chest, the corners of his mouth curving downwards and the tendons in his neck straining.

'Jesus,' Pamela whispers.

It almost looks like he's wearing a distorted mask. His eyes are so tightly shut that a new set of creases has appeared on his face.

His pulse is racing.

The nurse gives him more oxygen.

His legs start to jerk.

The bed beneath him creaks and the protective cover bunches up revealing the cracked artificial leather beneath.

Martin's convulsions end suddenly, like someone blowing out a flame. A coil of smoke curls slowly towards the ceiling.

38

Martin turns his head and sees the window and the lamp drift out of his field of vision like flowing water.

He hasn't eaten anything since the cheese sandwich and strawberry juice he was given when he woke up from the anaesthetic.

Pamela spent a while sitting by his side, but eventually had to hurry off to work.

He got up the minute his legs felt strong enough, and went to the therapy room to paint. He is no artist, but painting has become an important part of his routine.

Martin puts down his brush and paint next to the palette, takes a step back and studies the canvas.

He has painted a small red cabin, though he no longer remembers why. Behind the curtains in one of the windows, a face is visible.

Martin washes the acrylic paint from his hands and forearms and leaves the therapy room.

Strictly speaking, they aren't allowed to eat between meals, but he occasionally sneaks into the dining room to search the fridge.

He starts walking down the empty corridor.

The group room is quiet, but as he passes the doorway, he sees that the chairs have been rearranged as though an invisible audience is watching a performance.

The boys have been lying low ever since Martin arrived here. He hasn't even heard them at night. Maybe they think it's a good thing that he is back in the ward.

He pauses and peers through the glass panel on the door into the psychiatrists' office. Dr Miller is standing in the middle of the room, staring blankly ahead with his pale eyes.

Martin wonders whether he should knock and say that he wants to go home, but suddenly can't even remember his own name.

The doctor's name is Mike, he can remember that. They call him M & M.

What's happening? He knows he is a patient in ward four, that he is married to Pamela and lives on Karlavägen.

'Martin, my name is Martin,' he reminds himself, setting off down the corridor again.

A new wave of dizziness rushes through his head, and the large metal cabinets seem to swirl into the corner and disappear.

He passes one of the new orderlies – a short woman with pale upper arms and stern creases around her mouth – who doesn't even notice him.

When he reaches the door to the patients' dining room, he turns around and sees a restraint bed outside the group room.

It wasn't there a moment ago.

He shudders and slowly opens the door.

The thick curtains have been drawn to block out the sunlight, and the room is submerged in a murky gloom.

The plastic chairs are grouped around the three round tables, which have waxed tablecloths topped with napkin holders full of summer napkins.

He hears a click somewhere nearby, followed by a faint creaking. It sounds like a seesaw tipping from one side to the other.

He sees the fridge behind the low bench and its stainless steel canteens.

Martin crosses the glossy plastic floor, pausing when he spots a movement in the far corner.

Holding his breath, he slowly turns towards it.

He sees an unnaturally tall person standing perfectly still, arms raised. Their fingers are the only part of them that is moving.

Martin recognises the figure as the Prophet. He is standing on a stool, taking something down from one of the cupboards.

Martin slowly backs away and watches as the Prophet climbs down with a packet of sugar in one hand, then sits down in his wheelchair.

The seat groans beneath him.

Martin reaches the door, carefully pushes it open and hears the hinges creak softly, like a mosquito, right by his ear.

'Think of it as one of God's miracles,' the Prophet says behind him.

Martin stops, letting go of the door and turning around.

'I needed to grab a few things before I leave,' the Prophet tells him, moving over to the sink.

He pours the sugar into the sink, retrieving a plastic bag containing a mobile phone that was hidden in the bottom. He brushes it off and pushes it into a pocket before turning on the tap.

'I'm being discharged in an hour.'

'Congratulations,' Martin whispers.

'We all have different callings in life,' the Prophet says, moving over to him. 'Primus is a flesh fly who needs bodies to lay his eggs, I lay mine in people's souls . . . and you, you're trying to erase yourself with electricity.'

39

It is five o'clock, and Pamela is alone in the office. She has closed the curtains and is sitting at her computer, preparing drawings of a row of windows that face out on to a lush green roof terrace when her phone rings.

'Roos Architects,' she answers.

'This is Joona Linna from the National Crime Unit. I want to start by saying just how sorry I am for what my colleagues put you and your husband through.'

'OK,' she says, her voice strained.

'I'm sure that you've lost all faith in the police, and I know you've said you don't want to talk to us, but please think of the victim and her family – withholding evidence pertinent to the case really only affects them.'

'I know,' she sighs.

'Your husband is our sole eyewitness; he saw everything at close range,' says Joona. 'And I think most people find it hard to carry things that—'

'What, so now you care about him?' Pamela interrupts Joona.

'All I'm saying is that it was a gruesome murder and now Martin carries the burden of those images in his head.'

'I didn't mean . . .' She trails off and thinks about the threat to Mia, how it has made her start looking over her shoulder, just like Martin.

She has actually bought some pepper spray to give Mia, so that she can protect herself if anyone attacks her.

'We think the perpetrator held Jenny Lind captive for five years before killing her,' the detective continues. 'I don't know whether you remember when she went missing – there was a huge amount of press coverage at the time, and her parents turned to the media to beg for her release.'

'I remember,' Pamela says meekly.

'They've just had to see their daughter in the morgue.'

'I can't talk right now,' she says, a sense of panic welling up inside her. 'I have a meeting in five minutes . . .'

'Afterwards, then – just give me half an hour.'

Pamela reluctantly agrees to meet him in an Espresso House at six fifteen just to get off the phone. By the time she locks herself in the toilets, the tears have already begun spilling down her cheeks.

She doesn't dare tell the detective about the threat. Doing so could mean putting both Mia and Martin in danger. All she wanted was to give Mia the chance at life Alice never had, but instead she has put her squarely in the killer's sights.

* * *

Joona looks Pamela over as she sips her coffee, holding the cup with both hands as she lowers it to the saucer in order to avoid shaking too much. She seemed anxious when she first arrived, and insisted on switching to a table on the second floor, at the very back of the room.

Her auburn curls are hanging loose over her shoulders. He can see she has been crying, though she has tried to hide it with makeup.

'I know mistakes happen,' she says, 'but this . . . You forced him to confess to murder. I mean, this experience has set him back more than you can imagine.'

'I agree, that should never have happened. The prosecution authority will be launching an internal investigation.'

'Jenny Lind has . . . I don't know, a special place in my heart . . . and I really do feel for her family, but . . .' She pauses, swallowing hard.

'Pamela, I need to talk to Martin in a comfortable, non-threatening setting . . . ideally with you there.'

187

'He's back in twenty-four-hour care,' she says.

'I understand he suffers from complex PTSD?'

'He has paranoid psychoses, and you locked him up and terrified him. It was the worst thing you could have done for his condition.' She turns to the window and looks down at the people walking along Drottning Street.

Joona sees her smile softly as her eyes follow two young women. A tear-shaped aquamarine swings from her ear lobe.

She turns back to him, and he realises that what he initially thought were two birthmarks just beneath her left eye are in fact tattoos.

'You said that Jenny Lind has a special place in your heart,' says Joona.

'When she disappeared, she was the same age as my daughter Alice,' she says, swallowing hard again.

'I understand.'

'And then just a few weeks later, my own daughter died.'

Pamela looks into the detective's pale grey eyes. It feels like he knows her, like he understands what such losses can do to a person.

Before she has time to ask herself why, she moves her cup aside and tells him all about Alice. Her tears drip onto the table as she talks about the trip to Åre, right up to the day her daughter drowned.

'Most of us will experience huge loss at some point in our lives,' she says. 'But we get through it. It never feels that way at first, but it is possible to move on.'

'Yes.'

'But with Martin . . . it's like he's still stuck in that first phase of pure shock. And I don't want him to get any worse than he already is.'

'What if it helps him?' asks Joona. 'I can come to the ward and talk to him there. We'll be careful, do things on his terms.'

'But how are you going to interview someone who doesn't even speak?'

'We could try hypnosis?'

'I don't think so,' she says, smiling involuntarily. 'That's probably the last thing Martin needs.'

40

Mia gives her clothes a once-over, tucks her hair behind her ear, and can't help but smile to herself as she knocks on the half-open door to the office.

'Come in, sit down,' her caseworker tells her, without looking up.

'Thanks.'

Mia crosses the creaking floor, pulls out the chair across from the caseworker, and takes a seat.

After yet another day of temperatures hovering around ninety-five degrees, the room is hot and stuffy. The window out on to the trees is open, thudding softly against its rusty latch. The caseworker finishes typing something and then looks up.

'So, I checked with social services, and Pamela Nordström hasn't lodged any appeals.'

'But she said . . .' Mia forces herself to stop, lowering her eyes and picking at the chipped nail polish on her thumb.

'As I understand it,' the caseworker continues, 'the rejection was based on the fact that the home environment was considered unsafe, because of her husband.'

'But he's innocent, for God's sake, it's all over the news.'

'Mia, I don't pretend to know the details of the board's decision, but there haven't been any appeals . . . and that means that the rejection stands.'

'OK.'

'There's nothing we can do about it.'

'I said OK.'

'But how do you feel?'

'Like the same thing happens every time.'

'Well, I'm glad that this means you'll be here with us a while longer, at the very least,' the caseworker says encouragingly.

Mia nods and gets up, shaking the woman's hand like always. She closes the door behind her as she leaves and starts making her way upstairs.

Even from a distance, she can hear Lovisa shouting and swearing, throwing things onto the floor. She has ADHD, and she and Mia are always getting into arguments that can escalate dramatically.

Lately, Mia has started to wonder whether Lovisa might actually be capable of killing her.

Just last night, she woke up to the sound of Lovisa sneaking around her room in the dark. Mia heard her footsteps on the floor and sensed her pause by the bed and sit down on the chair by the chest of drawers.

She reaches the top of the stairs, heads into her room and sees that the bottom drawer is open. She looks down into it.

'What the fuck,' she mutters, leaving the room again.

The old wooden floor creaks beneath her boots. She flings open the door to Lovisa's room and stops dead.

Lovisa is on her knees, and has tipped the contents of her purse onto the floor in front of her. Her hair is knotted, and she has scratched herself on the backs of her hands.

'Do you want to tell me why you stole my underwear from my room?' Mia asks.

'What the fuck are you talking about? You're sick,' Lovisa snaps, getting to her feet.

'You're the one who actually has the diagnosis.'

'Just shut up,' she says, scratching her cheek.

'Can I have my underwear back now, please?'

'I think it's you who's the thief. You're the one who's been taking my Ritalin,' says Lovisa.

'OK, so you've lost your pills again – is that why you stole my underwear?'

Lovisa stomps around the room, tugging at the chewed sleeves of her blouse. 'I haven't touched your gross panties.'

190

'But you have, like, zero impulse control, and—'

'Shut up!' Lovisa shouts.

'You're so fucking wound up you don't even know what you're doing when—'

'Shut up!'

'You probably just hid your pills somewhere and forgot where, and now you're blaming me because you can't find—'

'Go to hell!' Lovisa roars, kicking her things across the floor.

Mia walks out and heads back downstairs. She hears Lovisa behind her, screaming that she's going to kill everyone.

It's warm outside, but Mia pulls on her khaki jacket and goes out.

She takes her usual shortcut past the trees, down to the industrial area, turning off by the old gas towers. These days, the two cylindrical brick buildings are used for film screenings, theatre performances and concerts.

Mia tries to keep her disappointment at bay as she walks towards the water behind the biggest of the gas holders.

She hears the bass and the drums well before she reaches the abandoned plot of land.

Her jacket catches on a bush, but she keeps walking, pulling it free.

She spots Maxwell and Rutger, both staring down at a smoking disposable barbecue.

The two are part of a small gang of guys who dream of becoming famous rappers one day.

Maxwell has connected a speaker to his phone, and is trying to rap to the beat, though he soon breaks off and starts laughing.

There are a couple of beer bottles pushed into the sand beside them.

Rutger is busy sharpening a branch with his axe.

Mia steps over the low wall, approaches the two men, and notices two figures in the bushes on the other side of the old tracks.

She keeps walking and realises that one of them is Shari. She is on her knees in front of Pedro, and before Mia has time to look away, she catches a glimpse of his penis in her mouth.

A spotlight from one of the cranes at the dock casts shadows of the branches of a tree.

191

When Maxwell spots Mia, he grins and starts rapping again.

She dances slowly as she approaches them.

Though she actually finds them pretty embarrassing, she always pretends to be impressed, applauding after every verse. In truth, the only reason she ever hangs out with them is because they are willing to pay surprisingly well for the small amounts of uppers she manages to steal from the home.

'My contact is getting a bit worried someone will realise there's medication missing, but he wants to prioritise you guys. That's what he told me, anyway,' she explains, taking out a bag containing the ten Ritalin she stole from Lovisa.

'Mia, this is . . . I don't know. It's getting really fucking expensive,' says Maxwell.

By pretending to have a bona fide connection at the home, she's been able to drive up the price to a ridiculously high level.

'Do you want me to pass that on to my contact?' she asks, shoving the bag back into her pocket.

'If we beat the shit out of you, maybe he'll get the picture,' he replies.

'What's the drama?' asks Pedro, casually walking over to the barbecue.

41

A new beat thunders from the speakers. Rutger scratches his beard with his axe and says something under his breath to Pedro.

Mia makes a silent promise to herself never to sell drugs to these people again. They might be the dumbest people in Gävle, but they're also starting to get suspicious.

Shari comes over and casually nods to Mia, locking eyes with her for a moment. Her lipstick is smeared on her chin.

As she bends down to pick up one of the beers from the ground, Maxwell holds out a hand to stop her, laughing.

'Not mine, not after that.'

'Funny.'

Shari spits onto the ground, grabs Pedro's bottle and takes a swig.

'Not mine,' Rutger repeats, laughing.

The reflection of one of the harbour cranes ripples in the water between the barges.

'So do you want the stuff or what?' Mia asks.

'I want a better price,' says Maxwell. He flops six sausages onto the grill.

'There is no other price,' Mia tells him, starting to button her jacket.

'What the fuck, I'll pay for it,' says Rutger, spinning the black axe in his hand and dropping it to the ground. The metal clinks softly as it hits the sand.

He takes out his wallet and counts the notes, but snaps them back when Mia reaches out to take them.

'I have to go,' she says.

Rutger waves the notes in the air and starts rapping about how their dealer has to leave because she's so popular and busy. Pedro claps along with the beat, and Shari starts swaying her hips. Maxwell takes over, trying to freestyle about a girl who is so thirsty that she wants to drink from all the bottles.

'Idiot,' Shari mutters, giving him a shove.

'Suck my bottle,' he laughs.

Rutger gives Mia the money. She counts it, shoves it into her inside pocket and holds out the bag of pills.

'There's a party later. I want you to come,' says Maxwell.

'What an honour.'

Mia has no intention of ever partying with them again. It's unclear why he is even asking her. Once, at a party with them, Maxwell tried to rape her while she was passed out drunk on the couch. She woke up when he began to penetrate her and she pushed him away and told him she would go to the police, but he argued that it wasn't attempted rape because she hadn't said no.

He turns the sausages on the barbecue with his fingers and burns them, hopping on his feet and swearing.

'So you coming to the party or what?' he asks, shaking out his hand.

'Look at this,' Mia tells him, pulling out her phone. 'The Criminal Code says in chapter six, paragraph one, and I quote, that if a person tries to have sex with someone who is either sleeping or drunk—'

'Seriously, bitch, just drop it,' he interrupts her. 'You didn't fucking say no, did you? You were just lying there, and—'

'It's enough that I didn't say yes,' she butts in, holding the phone out to him. 'Read it. You tried to rape me, which means your prison sentence could be up to—'

Maxwell suddenly hits her so hard that she loses her balance. She slams into the ground and hits her head on the sand. She can't see anything, and rolls onto her stomach, breathing heavily and getting onto all fours.

'Chill out, Maxie,' Pedro tells him.

Mia's vision returns. Her cheeks sting. She manages to find her phone and tries to compose herself.

194

'You're not worth raping,' Maxwell shouts.

Mia gets up and starts walking back towards the gas towers.

'You're just a fucking whore, you know that?' he yells after her.

When she reaches the road, she stops to brush the sand from her hair and her clothes. She can taste blood in her mouth.

Mia walks through the industrial area, towards the large car park on Södra Kungsvägen. The red umbrellas outside Burger King are flapping in the breeze. She crosses the empty car park, steps through the glass doors, and breathes in the aroma of melted cheese and hot oil.

Pontus is behind the till, wearing a short-sleeved shirt and a cap.

They used to live in the same home, but since he was placed with a family, he has gone back to school and found a part-time job.

'What happened?' he asks.

Mia realises her cheek must be red, but she just shrugs.

'Got into an argument with Lovisa.'

'You should just steer clear of her – everything stresses her out.'

'I know.'

'You eaten?'

She shakes her head.

'The boss said he'd be leaving at six thirty,' Pontus tells her, keeping his voice low. 'If you can afford to buy something, you can wait inside.'

'A coffee.'

He enters her order into the till, she pays with one of Maxwell's notes, and Pontus hands her a cup of coffee.

Mia comes here to eat almost every evening when Pontus is working, always waiting outside the petrol station nearby until the end of his shift. They usually walk down to the park by the sewage treatment plant and kick a ball against the wall. In the past, they always used to talk about escaping together, heading to Europe, but now that Pontus has a family, he's no longer interested.

'How's it going with Stockholm?' he asks.

'It's not.'

'I thought you said she was appealing?'

'She never did it,' Mia tells him, feeling her ears turn hot.

'But why—'

'I don't know,' she snaps.

'Well don't take it out on me.'

'Sorry, I just wish she'd been honest with me instead. I actually really liked her, and I thought she meant what she said,' Mia says, turning away to hide her trembling chin.

'No one's honest. Are you?'

'When it suits me.'

'So tell me the truth: are you in love with me?'

'Honestly, I don't think I'm even *capable* of being in love,' she replies, looking up at him. 'But if I could fall in love with anyone, it'd be you, because you're the only person I actually like being around.'

'But you're sleeping with those rappers.'

'No, I'm not.'

'I don't trust you.' He grins.

'If this is all just about sex, we can do it.'

'It's not, and you know it.'

Mia takes her coffee over to one of the tables and looks out at the cars on the road.

She drinks slowly, and before long she sees the boss leave for the day. Ten minutes later, Pontus puts a bag down on the table in front of her, and tells her he'll be finished in half an hour.

'Thanks,' she says, grabbing the bag and heading out into the evening air.

A dirty pickup swings into the car park, coming to a stop by the entrance to the restaurant. Mia walks through the red glow of its tail lights, crossing a narrow strip of grass.

She takes her usual seat on the concrete block by the skips to one side of the petrol station, and peers down into the bag.

She carefully takes out the cup of Coca-Cola and puts it down on the ground, balancing the bag of fries on her knee as she unfolds the paper around the burger.

Mia is hungry, and swallows such a big mouthful that her throat starts to cramp. She has to wait a few seconds before she can take another bite.

A lorry pulls in to the petrol station, slowly passing in front of the pumps. The cab is strangely dark behind the windscreen, making

196

it look like there's no driver behind the wheel. One of the side mirrors has been knocked off, and is hanging loose on a couple of wires.

The lorry's headlights blind Mia as it swings around and starts rolling straight towards her.

She slurps her Coca-Cola and lowers the cup to the ground.

The heavy lorry parks right in front of her, blocking out the light from the petrol station with its high trailer.

It creaks to a stop.

The engine falls silent.

A chain swings against the steel frame of the trailer, clinking softly.

The brakes hiss.

The driver doesn't get out; maybe he just parked up to get some sleep.

Fumes continue to rise from the vertical exhaust pipes.

Mia brushes a few limp pieces of lettuce from her parka.

The door opens on the other side of the lorry.

She hears the driver climb down, huffing and puffing, and start walking towards the petrol station.

The shards of a broken bottle glitter in the ditch as a car passes through the roundabout.

Mia stuffs fries into her mouth and listens to the driver's fading footsteps.

When she bends down to pick up her Coke, she notices something on the ground beneath the cab.

A wallet, fat with notes.

The driver must have dropped it when he got out.

Over the years, Mia has learned never to hesitate, and she drops the rest of her burger into the bag and crouches down by the lorry, right by the front wheels.

She can make out a grimy axle, and the air smells like dust and oil.

Mia glances over to the pumps in front of the brightly lit forecourt and the toilets to the rear.

She can't see a soul.

She crawls under the trailer, wriggling forward to reach for the wallet. Just as her fingers close around it, she hears the driver's footsteps.

The gravel beneath his feet crunches against the pavement.

She lies perfectly still, flat on her stomach while her feet poke out from beneath the lorry.

The minute he climbs back into the cab, she will drag herself out and run between the containers and down to the footpath.

Her breathing is hurried, her pulse racing in her ears.

She can tell from the sound of his footsteps that he is right by her side now.

Someone grabs her legs.

It was all a trap.

They pull her out so aggressively that her chin scrapes against the ground.

She tries to get up, but a sudden blow between the shoulder blades knocks the wind out of her.

She kicks desperately, knocking over the cup of Coca-Cola and sending ice cubes skidding under the lorry.

Mia feels a heavy knee on her back before he grabs her hair and pulls back her head.

Her scream fades into silence as an icy sensation spreads across her face.

Her mouth burns, and then she loses consciousness.

* * *

When she wakes up, everything is dark. She is queasy, and can feel a series of strange jolts through her body.

Somehow, she knows she must be on the floor inside the lorry.

The air smells like rotten meat.

Her mouth is so tightly bound that her cheeks are aching. She can't move, but she tries to kick out all the same. She is too weak, and quickly loses consciousness again.

42

Pamela leaves the office at six forty, locking the door behind her, and sets off down Olof Palmes Street in the warm evening air.

She has arranged to meet her boss and one of their big clients at the restaurant Ekstedt at eight.

She knows that her caution since receiving the threatening polaroid is starting to verge on paranoia, but she really does feel like she is being watched, and it sends shivers down her spine.

The rush of city life around her, all the clattering footsteps and humming car engines, feel deafening to her.

She passes a young woman in frayed denim shorts getting an earful over the phone. It sounds like her ragged breathing and remorseful answers are right in Pamela's ears.

'But you're the only one I love . . .'

As Pamela turns back to look at her, she notices a young man in blue sunglasses. He is watching her, and raises his hand as though to wave.

She turns away.

A siren blares in the distance.

The wind blows downy tufts of some kind along the road.

Pamela hurries on, keeping track of the young man in the reflections of the shop windows on the other side of the street.

He isn't far behind her.

Her thoughts are swirling. She thinks about the polaroid of Mia, the vodka draining into the sink. She dreamed last night that someone blinded her with a flashlight.

Pamela knows she might only be imagining that the man is following her, but she still debates hailing the next taxi that comes by.

Cigarette butts and pouches of dip litter the pavement outside the back door of a restaurant.

A dove flaps away.

She dashes over Sveavägen just as the traffic lights turn green, provoking a blast of car horns.

People stop and stare, watching her.

She walks quickly past the popular Urban Deli and continues into the narrow alley leading to the Brunkeberg Tunnel.

Her breathing is quicker now.

As she opens one of the swinging doors into the underground walkway, she sees the young man reflected in the glass.

She hears the door swinging back and forth as she hurries inside.

The long tunnel is round like a wormhole, with a silvery ceiling and curved yellow panels.

Her frantic footsteps on the tiled floor echo down the walls.

She should have chosen a different route.

Pamela hears someone else come into the tunnel and glances back over her shoulder, sees the door swinging on its hinges.

The person behind her is nothing but a dark silhouette against the scratched glass.

The tunnel bends to the right, making her invisible to him until he rounds the corner himself.

The far end is still two hundred metres away.

She can see the hazy light shining in through the glass doors.

Pamela crosses over into the bicycle lane and presses up against the wall.

She can hear that the person behind her has broken into a run.

Their footsteps echo dully down the tunnel.

Pamela rummages through her bag for Mia's pepper spray in its small cardboard box and realises her hands are shaking as she tears it open. She looks down at the spray can, trying to figure out how to use it.

The footsteps are quickly drawing closer.

A shadow appears.

The man rounds the corner with his sunglasses on top of his head.

Pamela steps out from the wall and holds the spray can up in front of her. She presses down on it just as he turns to look at her.

The bright red spray hits him square in the face, making him scream and clutch his eyes. He staggers backwards into the wall.

His bag clatters to the floor.

Pamela follows him, still holding the button.

'Stop!' he shouts, trying to push her away with one hand.

She drops the can and kicks him between the legs. He drops to his knees and then keels over to one side, whimpering, both hands on his crotch.

His face is drenched in the blood-red spray.

Pamela pulls out her phone, takes a picture of him.

An elderly woman further down the tunnel is approaching, and she gasps in fear when she sees the man's face.

'It's just paint,' Pamela reassures her.

She picks up the man's bag, finds his wallet and pulls out his ID. She takes a picture of it, too.

'Pontus Berg,' she says. 'Before I call the police, do you want to tell me why you've been following me?'

'You're Pamela Nordström, right?' he groans.

'Yes.'

'Someone's taken Mia,' he says, sitting up with a sigh.

'What do you mean, "taken her"? What are you talking about?' she asks, feeling another shiver down her spine.

'This is going to sound crazy, but you have to believe me when—'

'Just tell me what happened,' she interrupts him, voice raised.

'I called the police in Gävle five times, but no one will listen to me. I'm in their databases for all kinds of crap . . . I didn't know what to do, I mean, I know the application went to shit, but she said you cared about her, so I thought—'

'Tell me why you think someone has taken Mia,' she interrupts him again. 'You know this is really, really serious, don't you?'

The young man gets to his feet, brushing himself off and picking up his bag with awkward movements.

'It was last night, I'd just finished my shift and went to meet Mia . . . she usually waits for me behind the petrol station right next door.'

'Go on.'

'But as I was walking over there, I nearly got mowed down by a lorry driving out of the lorry park . . . and when it pulled out onto the Seventy-six, the tarpaulin on the side flapped up – one of the straps was loose . . . so I could see, like, straight into the trailer. It was just for a few seconds, but I'm ninety-nine per cent sure I saw Mia lying on the floor inside.'

'In the back of the lorry?'

'It was her clothes, anyway. You know, that army jacket she's always wearing . . . And I'm sure I saw a hand bound up with black tape around the wrist.'

'Oh God,' Pamela whispers.

'It was too late to run after it or shout or whatever . . . it was like, I couldn't really believe what I'd seen, but when I got to the concrete block where Mia normally sits to wait, her food was there, and her Coke had been knocked over . . . and now it's been twenty-two hours and she's not answering her phone and she didn't go back to the home last night.'

'And you told the police all this?'

'The thing is, I'd taken my medication just before, and it kicked in right then . . . I'm not an addict or anything, I've got a prescription, but I'm always a little weird for the first hour or so,' he says, wiping his mouth. 'I know I was slurring, and I lost my focus . . . And when I called back, it was pretty obvious they already knew that Mia has run away a bunch of times . . . They just said they were sure she'd turn up once she was out of money. I didn't know what to do – I know how it must look to them, so I thought that, like, the police would listen if you called them.'

Pamela pulls out her phone and calls Joona Linna at National Crime.

43

It's ten thirty by the time their car reaches Gävle. When Pamela called Joona earlier that evening, she explained all about the polaroid of Mia and the explicit threat that had been made against her.

She had been worried that he might reproach her for withholding information, but he just asked about the image, the handwriting and the exact wording of the message.

On the drive north, Pontus told Joona what he saw and patiently answered his questions about every last detail. He's stuck to the same story throughout, and it is clear that he's worried, that he really cares about Mia.

'Is Mia your girlfriend?' Joona asks him.

'I wish,' he replies with a crooked smile.

'Pontus likes to stand beneath her window and sing,' says Pamela.

'Ah, that might explain it,' Joona jokes.

Pamela makes an effort to be casual during the conversation, but her anxious heart is racing. She tries to tell herself that this is all just a mistake, that Mia is already back at the home.

'I need to wash this paint off before I go home,' says Pontus.

'You look like Spiderman,' Pamela tells him, managing a smile.

'Do I?'

'No,' says Joona, pulling to the petrol station next to Burger King.

The red trim along the flat roof glows in the hazy darkness. The car park is empty, dusty.

Joona knows that they will soon learn whether Mia Andersson has been abducted or not.

If she has, they are probably looking at the same perpetrator.

But that will also mean that his modus operandi has changed.

It started with the hanging of Fanny Hoeg, which he staged as a suicide. Fourteen years later, he took a far greater risk by killing Jenny Lind in a public place, and now he has abducted a third woman in an attempt to silence an eyewitness.

The threat against Pamela and Martin changes everything. It's a new piece of the puzzle. The killer suddenly seems affective – the murders are emotional outbursts rather than cold-blooded acts. Either way, something has changed; he has become both bolder and more active than before. Perhaps on some level he knows the end is near, but he's desperately fighting off anything or anyone who could stop him.

There was one good witness at Jenny Lind's abduction, a classmate who had been walking some forty metres behind the lorry, and she was able to tell investigators about the blue side curtains and the Polish number plates.

She saw a well-built man with tight black curls down to his shoulders, wearing sunglasses and a leather jacket with a grey patch resembling flames or the leaves of a willow tree on the back.

The night air is warm and smells of fuel as Joona, Pamela and Pontus climb out of the car. A bus makes its way around the roundabout, its headlights sweeping over the cracked tarmac.

'Mia usually sits on that concrete thing over there,' says Pontus.

'And you came from that direction?' Joona points.

'Yeah, I came over the grass, past all the trailers. I stopped right there, just as the lorry was pulling out.'

'And it turned that way, towards the E4?'

'The same direction we just came from,' Pontus confirms.

They head into the petrol station, its shelves full of sweets. The walls are lined with fridges and coffee machines, and sweet buns and rotating hot dogs sit behind the glass counter.

Joona undoes the top button of his jacket, takes out his wallet and shows his ID to the young woman at the cash register.

'My name is Joona Linna. I'm with the National Crime Unit,' he says. 'I'm going to need your help.'

'OK,' she replies with a curious smile.

'I want to be a police officer too,' Pontus says under his breath to Pamela.

'We need access to your security cameras,' Joona tells her.

'I don't know anything about them,' the woman says, cheeks turning pink.

'I'm guessing you have a contract with a security company?'

'Securitas, I think . . . but I can call my boss.'

'Please.'

She pulls out her phone, scrolls through her contacts and makes the call.

'He's not answering,' she says after a moment or two.

Pamela and Pontus follow Joona behind the counter. The young woman makes eye contact with Pontus but quickly lowers her gaze.

Joona studies the monitor by the cash register. Eight small squares, one for each camera. Two of the cameras are covering the inside of the shop, four are positioned around the pumps, one on the car wash, and one on the parking spaces for trailers.

'Is there a code?' asks Joona.

'Yeah, but I don't know if I've got the, you know, authority to give it out.'

'I'll call the security firm.'

Joona dials a number and explains the situation to the Securitas operator. Once they have verified his identity, they help him log in.

He clicks on one of the miniature images, and the camera feed fills the screen.

Between a pillar holding up the flat roof and a washer fluid pump, the blue bins are visible. One of the flagpoles is too.

None of the other cameras are pointing in that direction.

Joona scrolls back through the footage to the period when Mia was taken. Pontus leans forward.

A figure walks into shot from the left of the screen. A young woman, with pink and blue hair. She is wearing a loose khaki jacket and a pair of black boots.

'That's her, that's Mia,' says Pamela, swallowing hard.

205

The girl's face seems thoughtful, and she is walking slowly. As she passes the pumps, she vanishes from view, but reappears as she sits down on the concrete block.

She carefully lowers a cup to the ground, pushes her hair back from her face, lifts the burger out of the bag and folds back the wrapper.

'I don't know why she always wants to sit there to eat,' Pontus says quietly.

Mia peers out at the road as she shovels fries into her mouth. She takes another bite of her burger and then peers over to the turn off for the petrol station.

A set of headlights dazzle her for a moment, the light flashing on the blue container behind her.

She picks up her Coke, takes a sip and then lowers the cup to the ground as a lorry pulls up and obscures her completely.

Pamela clasps her hands and quietly prays to God that nothing bad is going to happen to Mia, that this is all just a misunderstanding.

The vehicle comes to a stop, the hot air quivering in front of the engine's air vent.

Mia is no longer visible on any of the cameras.

The driver's cab is hidden behind the various pumps and hoses, and they can see the door opening and someone climbing out but they can't make out his features.

They watch as the driver's baggy black tracksuit bottom move around the side of the vehicle.

Something catches the light on the ground beneath the lorry.

After a while, the man reappears, walking past the cab and back to the semi-trailer, hitting the coverings with one hand.

The nylon fabric shakes.

He moves to one side so that his back is now visible.

On the man's black leather jacket, there is a patch resembling grey flames.

'It's him,' says Joona.

The man climbs back into the cab, starts the engine, revs it for a moment in order to increase the pressure in the braking system, then pulls away.

The lorry swings around and moves out of the petrol station.

Mia is gone.

Her drink is now lying on its side, ice cubes glistening on the concrete.

'Is he the one who killed Jenny Lind?' Pamela asks, her voice trembling.

'Yes,' Joona replies.

She can't breathe, and hurries out from behind the counter, accidentally bumping into a shelf and scattering bags of candy across the floor. She keeps going, out into the night air, straight over to the concrete block where Mia was sitting.

Pamela can't make sense of this.

She can't understand why he took Mia.

Martin hasn't talked to the police.

After a while, Joona comes out and stands beside her. They look out at the traffic circle and the industrial area bathed in yellow light.

'We've put out a nationwide alert,' he says.

'Surely it must be possible to trace the lorry?'

'We'll try, but he has a bigger head start on us this time.'

'You don't seem convinced the nationwide alert will be enough.'

'It won't.'

'So everything hinges on Martin?' she says, more to herself than anything.

'We don't have any forensic evidence, we can't identify the driver from any of the CCTV footage, and there are no other eyewitnesses.'

She takes a deep breath, trying to keep her voice steady: 'And if Martin helps you, Mia will die.'

'I'm sure the threat against her was genuine, but that also tells us that the killer is convinced Martin will be able to identify him.'

'But I don't understand – what would you do if you didn't have Martin? I mean, you're the police. Surely there must be another way? There's DNA, the on-board computer in the lorry, the footage we just watched ... Not to sound horrible, but ... just do your fucking job.'

'That's what we're trying to do.'

Pamela sways, and Joona grabs her arm.

'Sorry, I'm just worried,' she says quietly.

'It's OK, I understand.'

'So you really need to talk to Martin?'

'He saw the murder.'

'Yeah,' she sighs.

'We can do it all in secret, all in the ward . . . no visible officers, no contact with the media whatsoever.'

44

The meeting room in ward four darkens as the sun passes behind a cloud. Martin is sitting on the sofa, eyes downcast and hands clamped between his thighs. Pamela is standing by his side, holding a teacup.

Joona walks slowly over to the window and peers out at the brick facade over the ambulance bay and the entrance to the emergency psychiatric ward.

Dr Erik Maria Bark shuffles forward in his chair, leaning over the low table and trying to catch Martin's eye.

'I don't remember anything,' Martin whispers, glancing over to the door.

'We call that . . .'

'Sorry.'

'It isn't your fault. We call it retrograde amnesia, and it's very common in complex PTSD,' Erik continues. 'But given the right help, you'll start to remember and be able to talk again – I've seen it many times.'

'Do you hear that?' Pamela asks softly.

Erik Maria Bark specialises in psychotraumatology and disaster psychiatry, and is part of a team that aims to help acutely traumatised and post-traumatic patients.

Strictly speaking, he is currently on leave in order to write a comprehensive standard work on clinical hypnosis, but he has made an exception for his friend Joona.

'Hypnosis may seem a little mystical, but it's really nothing but a natural state of relaxation and inner focus,' Erik goes on. 'In a moment,

'I'll explain how it works in practice, but, in essence, it involves relinquishing much of your attention on the world around you – a bit like when you go to the movies . . . only, with hypnosis, you turn your focus inwards, rather than following a film . . . That's really all there is to it.'

'OK,' Martin whispers.

'And once you're relaxed enough to reach that state, I'll help you sort through your memories.'

Erik studies Martin's tense, pale face. He knows that the hypnosis could be incredibly frightening for him.

'We'll do this together, you and I,' says Erik. 'I'll be with you the whole way, and Pamela will be right here too. You can turn to her and talk to her whenever you like . . . or break the hypnosis, if you want to.'

Martin whispers something in Pamela's ear, then looks up at Erik.

'He wants to try,' she says.

'Martin, lie back on the couch and I'll explain what happens next,' Erik tells him.

Pamela moves to one side as Martin kicks off his slippers and lies down, his head at an uncomfortable angle on the armrest.

'Joona, could you draw the curtains?' asks Erik.

The curtain rings scrape against the wooden pole, and the room is soon submerged in a soft darkness.

'Try to get comfortable, move the cushion under your neck,' Erik says with a smile. 'Your legs should be uncrossed, and your arms by your sides.'

The curtains sway for a moment before falling still. Martin is on his back staring up at the ceiling.

'Before we get into the hypnosis itself, I'd like to do a few relaxation exercises, so we can try to get your breathing nice and calm.'

Erik always starts by getting his patients to relax before gradually moving on to the induction and then the deep hypnosis, never telling them where the transitions are. He does this partly because there are no absolute limits, and partly because the process is much trickier if the patients are actively waiting for the change, trying to pay attention to the shift.

'Think about the back of your head. Feel its weight and the way the cushion is almost pushing it up,' Erik says in a calm voice. 'Let your face and cheeks relax, your jaw and your mouth . . . feel your eyelids growing heavier with every breath. Let your shoulders sink back and your arms rest against the cushions, let your hands become soft and heavy . . .'

Erik calmly moves through each body part, checking for any visible signs of tension and returning several times to Martin's hands, neck and mouth.

'Breathe slowly through your nose, close your eyes and enjoy the heaviness of your eyelids.'

He tries not to dwell on the fact that a girl's life is at stake, that they need Martin to produce a description of the perpetrator.

Erik has read up on the case and watched the footage of Martin by the playground. He knows that he saw the murder. Everything is saved in his episodic memory, and the difficulty will be in bringing up coherent observations, because the trauma itself will put up a fight.

Erik allows his voice to become increasingly monotone, repeating how relaxing and calm Martin is and how heavy his eyelids feel, before leaving the relaxation exercises behind and moving on to the induction.

He tries to get Martin to stop thinking about his surroundings, about the other people in the room and what is expected of him.

'Just listen to my voice telling you that you are deeply relaxed . . . nothing else matters now,' he says. 'If you hear any other sounds, you'll simply become more relaxed, more focused on my voice and what I'm saying.'

A thin slice of the summer sky is visible between the pale blue curtains.

'In a moment, I'm going to start counting backwards. I want you to listen to each number, and with each number you hear, you'll feel a little more relaxed,' says Erik. 'Ninety-nine . . . ninety-eight, ninety-seven.'

He studies Martin's stomach, following his slow breathing, and counts in time with each rise and fall, slowing down slightly.

'Everything is incredibly comfortable right now, and you are focused on my voice . . . Imagine you're walking down a set of stairs, and with every number you hear, you take another step and feel calmer and heavier. Fifty-one, fifty, forty-nine . . .'

Erik feels a pleasurable tingle in his gut as he lowers Martin into a deep state of hypnosis, approaching the limits of catalepsy.

'Thirty-eight, thirty-seven . . . you are still walking down the stairs.'

Martin seems to be sleeping, but Erik can see that he is listening to every word he says. Step by step, they descend ever deeper into an enclosed state of inner consciousness.

'When I reach zero, you will be walking your dog along Sveavägen. You turn off by the School of Economics, heading towards the playground,' Erik says, his voice still monotone. 'You feel calm and relaxed. You can look around and tell me everything you see at your own pace . . . nothing here is dangerous or threatening.'

Martin's feet twitch.

'Five, four . . . three, two, one, zero . . .You are now walking along the pavement, past the wall and out onto the grass.'

45

Martin's face is unmoving, like he can no longer hear Erik's voice. He is lying back on the sofa with his eyes closed, and everyone in the dark meeting room is watching him attentively. Joona is standing with his back to the window, and Pamela is sitting in the chair, arms wrapped around herself.

'I've now counted down to zero,' Erik reminds Martin, leaning forward. 'You are standing on the lawn next to the School of Economics.'

Martin opens his eyes a fraction, his gaze flickering beneath his heavy eyelids.

'You are deeply relaxed . . . and can tell me what you see right now.'

Martin's right hand shifts slightly, his eyes close, and his breathing slows.

Pamela gives Erik an unsure glance.

Joona is standing perfectly still.

Erik studies Martin's expressionless face and wonders what could be holding him back. It's almost as though he lacks the strength to take the first step. He wonders whether he should try giving Martin hidden commands instead, suggestions expressed as commands.

'You're standing next to the School of Economics,' he says again. 'You're perfectly safe here, and if you're ready, you can tell me what you see.'

'Everything is glistening in the darkness,' Martin says quietly. 'The rain is falling on my umbrella, and the grass is rustling with the downpour.'

The meeting room is utterly silent. Everyone seems to be holding their breath.

Martin hasn't spoken this coherently in five years. Pamela's eyes well up. She had thought he would never be able to express himself like this again.

'Martin,' says Erik. 'You've taken the dog to the playground in the middle of the night . . .'

'Because it's my responsibility,' he says, gaping strangely.

'Taking the dog out?'

Martin nods, steps forward onto the wet grass.

The rain is coming down hard.

Loke wants to keep going, pulling his leash taut. Martin sees his own hand lift slightly.

'Tell me what you see,' says Erik.

Martin peers around and spots a homeless woman in the shadows on the slope up towards the observatory.

'There's someone on the path . . . with loads of bags in a shopping trolley.'

'Turn back to the playground,' says Erik. 'You can watch exactly what happens there without feeling any fear.'

Martin's breathing becomes shallow, and beads of sweat cling to his forehead. Pamela gives him an anxious glance and covers her mouth with her hand.

'Your breathing is calm, and you are listening to my voice,' Erik tells him, maintaining a measured tempo. 'None of this is dangerous; you're perfectly safe here. Take things at your own pace and . . . tell me what you see.'

'There's a red playhouse, further back, with a small window. The rain from the roof is pouring onto the ground.'

'But to the side of the playhouse, you can see the slides,' Erik continues. 'The swings, the jungle gym, and . . .'

'The mothers are watching the children play,' Martin mumbles.

'Remember, it's the middle of the night – the light is from a street lamp,' Erik explains. 'You drop the leash and approach the playground . . .'

'I'm walking over the wet grass,' says Martin. 'And then I reach the red playhouse and stop . . .'

Through the rain, Martin can make out the playground in the dim glow of the street lamp. The heavy raindrops make the illuminated puddles by his feet bubble.

'What do you see? What's happening?' asks Erik.

Martin studies the playhouse and sees the floral curtains in the dark window. He is just about to turn towards the jungle gym when everything goes black.

'What colour is the climbing frame?'

He hears a rhythmic thudding against his umbrella, but can't see a thing.

'I don't know.'

'From where you are standing, you can see the jungle gym,' says Erik.

'No.'

'Martin, you're looking at something that is difficult to process,' Erik goes on. 'But there's no need to be afraid. Just tell me what you see, even if it's only small fragments.'

Martin shakes his head slowly. His lips have turned pale, and sweat is now trickling down his cheeks.

'There's someone in the playground,' says Erik.

'There is no playground.'

'In that case, what do you see?'

'It's just dark.'

Erik wonders whether something could be physically blocking Martin's view. Perhaps he is holding the umbrella at such an angle that he can't see up ahead.

'There's a street lamp in the distance.'

'No . . .'

Martin stares into the darkness, angling the umbrella back and feeling the cold rain drip down his spine.

'Look at the playhouse again,' Erik tells him.

Martin opens his weary eyes and stares up at the ceiling. The armchair creaks as Pamela shifts.

'He had ECT recently, and I think it must've had an effect on his memory,' she says softly.

'When was this?' asks Erik.

'The day before yesterday.'

'I see.'

Erik knows it is very common for a person's verbal episodic memory to deteriorate immediately after ECT. But if that were the case, Martin shouldn't simply be staring into darkness; he should be fumbling through hazy islands of memory.

'Martin, let your memories come through as they are, don't worry about the darkness between them. You know you are standing in front of the slide, the rope ladder and the jungle gym ... but if you can't see them right now, perhaps you can see something else?'

'No.'

'Let's go deeper into the relaxation ... When I count down to zero, you are going to open your mind to all the images you associate with this place. Three, two, one ... zero.'

Martin is just about to say that he can't see anything when he notices a tall man with something strange on his head.

He is standing in the darkness, a few steps away from the pale circle of light cast by the street lamp.

There are two boys sitting on the muddy ground by his feet.

Martin hears a metallic clicking sound, like someone winding a mechanical toy.

The man turns to Martin.

He is wearing a top hat and clothes from an old TV show for children.

A red velvet curtain hangs from the brim of his hat, obscuring his face. Grey tufts of hair poke out from beneath the frayed hem. He starts walking towards Martin with curious steps.

'What do you see?' asks Erik.

Martin's breathing quickens and he shakes his head.

'Tell me what you see.'

Martin raises his hands as though he is trying to shield himself from a punch, and he rolls off the sofa, falling heavily to the floor.

Pamela cries out.

Erik is already by his side, helping him back onto the couch.

Martin is still deep in hypnosis. His eyes are wide open, but he is looking inwards.

'No need to worry, it's all OK,' Erik says in a calming voice, picking up the cushion from the floor and placing it beneath Martin's head.

'What's happening?' Pamela whispers.

'Close your eyes and relax,' Erik continues. 'None of this is dangerous, you're completely safe here . . . I'm slowly going to bring you out of the hypnosis now, step by step, and once I've done that, you'll be fine, you will feel rested.'

'Hold on,' says Joona. 'Ask him why it was his responsibility to go to the playground.'

'It's because I wanted him to take the dog out,' says Pamela.

'But I want to know whether anyone else made him go to that particular place that night,' Joona persists.

Martin mumbles something and tries to sit up.

'Lie back down,' says Erik, his hand firm on Martin's shoulder. 'Let your face relax, listen to what I say and breathe slowly through your nose . . . Do you remember saying that you went to the playground with the dog . . . and that it was your responsibility?'

'Yes . . .' Martin's mouth curls into a taut smile, and his hands begin to shake.

'Who said it was your responsibility to take that route?'

'No one,' whispers Martin.

'Did anyone mention the playground before you went there?'

'Yes.'

'Who?'

'It was . . . Primus, he was in the phone booth . . . talking to Caesar.'

'Do you want to tell me what they said?'

'They said different things.'

'Did you hear both Primus and Caesar?'

'Only Primus.'

'And what exactly did he say?'

'*It's too much,*' Martin says, his voice dark.

217

His lips keep moving, but all that comes out is a faint whisper. His eyes snap open and he stares blindly ahead, repeating Primus's words:

"'I know I said I wanted to help, Caesar . . . but going to the playground and sawing off Jenny's legs while she's hanging there, kicking . . .'"

Martin interrupts himself with a pained noise. He lurches up off the sofa on unsteady legs, knocking over the lamp, staggers forward and throws up on the floor.

46

Joona walks quickly down the corridor with one of the orderlies, waiting as she enters her code on the lock and then following her to the administrative offices.

The ventilation duct on the low ceiling hums.

It was obvious that Martin had seen and heard far more than he was able to share, but the little that did come out may well be all they need.

Something is stirring inside Joona, as though someone has stoked the dying embers and the fire has flared up again.

The investigation has just entered a new phase. They now have two names linked to the murder.

None of the staff Joona has spoken to so far remembers a patient by the name of Caesar, but Primus Bengtsson has been admitted on seven occasions over the past five years.

As Joona follows the woman down an identical corridor, he thinks about the complexity of Martin's situation.

The patients aren't permitted to have mobile phones in the ward, but there is a phone booth for them to use. Martin happened to overhear Primus while he was on the phone with Caesar, discussing their plans for Jenny Lind. Hearing that, it became his responsibility to try to save her.

His obsessive compulsive disorder prevented him from telling anyone what he heard, and he had no choice but to go to the playground that night, in an attempt to stop the murder.

But when he arrived, he became completely paralysed. He froze right where he was as Jenny was executed before his eyes.

The orderly takes Joona through the staff dining room. Sunlight floods in across the tables, revealing streaks from where they were recently wiped down. The pale blue curtains are grubby at the hems, blowing in the breeze from the air-conditioning unit.

They continue into the next corridor, where there is a whiteboard on one wall and a trolley stacked with boxes of printer paper.

'It's just through there,' says the orderly, gesturing to a closed door.

'Thanks,' Joona says, knocking and stepping inside.

The chief psychiatrist, Mike Miller, is sitting at his computer. He flashes Joona a relaxed smile as he introduces himself.

'They used to tap those into the frontal lobe with a hammer, through the eye socket,' he says, pointing to a framed tool on the wall. It looks like a thin ice pick with a graduated shaft.

'Right up until the mid-sixties.' Joona nods.

'They did away with the antiquated methods and lived in the most modern of times . . . just like us,' the doctor says, leaning forward.

'You gave Martin electroconvulsive therapy.'

'Which is a bit unfortunate if you think he really did witness a murder.'

'Yes, but he managed to point out another of your patients who was directly involved.'

'Under hypnosis?' Mike asks, raising an eyebrow in amusement.

'Primus Bengtsson.'

'Primus,' the psychiatrist repeats, his voice affectless.

'Is he here now?'

'No.'

'Since we suspect he may have been involved in a murder, confidentiality no longer applies.'

Mike's face is solemn. He takes a pen from his chest pocket and then looks up at Joona. 'Tell me how I can help.'

'Has Primus been discharged? Does that mean he's healthy?'

'This isn't a forensic-psychiatric ward,' Mike replies. 'Almost all of our patients are here voluntarily, meaning the principle is to discharge anyone who wants to be discharged, even if we know they'll be back. They're people, after all; they have rights.'

'I need to know whether Primus was in the ward at three specific times,' Joona tells him, reeling off the dates when Jenny Lind disappeared, when she was killed, and when Mia was taken.

Mike jots down the dates on a yellow Post-it. Neither of them speak as he logs in and searches the records on his computer. After a while, he clears his throat and tells Joona that Primus was not in the ward on any of the three dates.

'So, no alibi from us,' he says.

'But he's here pretty often?'

The doctor turns away from the computer and leans back in his chair. The oblique sunlight paints the many wrinkles on his thin face in sharp relief.

'He has repeated psychoses, so it's a fairly cyclical process. He usually wants to stay for one or two weeks before being discharged again. Then after a few months of freedom, he forgets to take his medication and comes back to us.'

'I'm going to need his home address in order to contact him.'

'Of course, though I don't believe he has a fixed address . . .'

'What about a phone number, alternative addresses, a contact person?'

The doctor moves a small bowl with a rose floating in it, turns the screen towards Joona and shows him the empty contact form.

'All I know is that he often visits his sister Ulrike, who . . . he has something of an obsession with.'

'In what sense?'

'He can spend hours talking about how beautiful she is, the way she moves, and so on.'

'Have you ever had a patient or employee called Caesar here?' Joona asks.

The doctor scribbles down the name, puffs out his cheeks and runs two searches on the computer before shaking his head.

'Tell me about Primus.'

'We don't know much about his private life, but aside from his psychoses, he has been diagnosed with Tourette's syndrome and coprolalia.'

'Is he violent?'

221

'The only thing he does when he's here is talk about his grandiose and bizarre sexual fantasies.'

'Forward his notes to me,' says Joona, handing the doctor his card.

Joona turns to leave, but pauses and looks back at the doctor. There is something reticent about the man's deep-set eyes.

'What is it you're not telling me?' Joona asks.

'What aren't I telling you?' Mike repeats with a sigh. 'There's no mention of this in his notes, but lately I've been wondering whether Primus might actually believe his own words. I wonder whether the things we see as compulsive provocations are actually a case of a warped self-image, which in that case would point to an extreme variant of a narcissistic personality disorder.'

'Do you consider him dangerous?'

'Most people find him incredibly unpleasant . . . but if my suspicions are correct, then he could definitely be dangerous, too.'

Joona leaves the room with a strong sense that the hunt has finally begun. He hurries back down the corridor to reception, collects his phone and reads the messages from his team.

Primus Bengtsson doesn't appear in any of the police databases.

Since he doesn't have a phone registered in his name, they cannot trace his calls. He has no fixed address, but they do know that his sister lives in Bergvik in Södertälje.

After poring over the CCTV footage from the petrol station in Gävle, the only thing the team has been able to determine is the model of the lorry. They cannot rule out that Primus was the driver, but nor can they prove it.

Despite the nationwide alert, there still hasn't been a single sighting of Mia. But if they can find Primus, then there's a chance they can still find the girl.

Joona leaves the ward and steps out into the warm air. As he walks back to his car, he calls Tommy Kofoed, who worked on the National Murder Squad until his retirement two years ago.

Kofoed listens, humming sullenly as Joona tells him about the case.

'It doesn't seem like Primus is our killer, but he's involved in what happened at the playground somehow,' Joona says in conclusion.

'Sounds like a breakthrough,' Kofoed mutters.

'I'm on my way back to the station to talk to Margot about resources, but I want the surveillance to start right now.'

'Makes sense.'

'The sister is the only fixed point in Primus's life . . . Listen, I'm sorry to ask, but do you think you could head over there and keep me up to date?'

'I'll do anything to get away from the grandkids,' Kofoed replies.

47

It is evening by the time Joona parks outside the main entrance to the National Police Board building, hurries through the glass doors and runs over to the lifts.

He has just updated Aron on the latest developments, and they have decided to give Margot a joint briefing.

He walks quickly down the eighth-floor corridor, the sheets of paper on the bulletin board fluttering in his wake.

Aron is waiting for him outside Margot's door.

'Primus isn't in any of our databases,' he tells Joona. 'But I just found his sister in the surveillance database.'

'Why is she in there?'

'She's married to Stefan Nicolic, who's a member of a criminal biker gang's inner circle.'

'Good work.'

Joona knocks and opens the door, and they step into the room together. Margot takes off her glasses and looks up at them.

'The preliminary investigation has entered a new phase, and we've got a pretty alarming pattern,' Aron tells her. 'The killer isn't done yet. He abducts girls and holds them prisoner before executing them.'

'I heard about the girl in Gävle,' says Margot.

'Mia Andersson.' Aron holds up a picture of her. 'This is her, and she's probably our next victim.'

'I know.'

'But we've had another development related to Jenny Lind,' Joona says, taking a seat in one of the armchairs. 'We now know that the

reason Martin Nordström went to the playground that night was that he heard another patient in the psychiatric ward talking about the murder on the phone – before it actually happened.'

'What, so he went there to watch?' asks Margot.

'He's mentally ill, and when he heard that conversation, he felt like he had no choice but to go there and try to stop the execution. But he froze up when he saw it.'

Margot leans back in her chair. 'Have we identified the patient he overheard on the phone?'

'Yes, his name's Primus Bengtsson, and he was talking to someone called Caesar,' Aron tells her, sitting down in the other armchair.

'And have we brought this Primus Bengtsson in?'

'He'd already been discharged and doesn't have a permanent address,' says Joona.

'For God's sake,' Margot sighs deeply.

'Right now, Caesar is just a name, but we think he tried to get Primus to help with the murder,' says Aron.

'There are two killers?' asks Margot.

'We don't know. As a rule, serial killers work alone, but they do sometimes have followers – both passive and active,' Joona explains.

'So we're looking at a serial killer?'

'Yes.'

There's a cautious knock at the door.

'Oh, right, I invited Lars Tamm,' says Aron.

'Why?' asks Margot.

'Primus spends a lot of time with his sister Ulrike, who, according to our database, has links to a criminal biker gang.'

There is another almost inaudible knock at the door.

'Come in,' Margot shouts.

Lars Tamm peers in as though he was expecting a nice surprise. His face is dotted with pigmentation marks, and his eyebrows are white. He has been the lead prosecutor at the National Unit Against Organised Crime since its founding.

Moving cautiously, he steps into the room and shakes hands with each of them before taking a seat in the remaining chair.

'What do you know about the biker gang?' Joona asks him.

'It's known simply as the Club, and has a serious criminal presence in Sweden, Denmark and Germany,' he replies. 'Ulrike's husband Stefan Nicolic is one of the leaders of the Swedish branch, and . . . let's see, what else? The Club has links to Tyson, who dominates the drug trade around Järvafältet here in Stockholm, and the Polish Road Runners.'

'What do they do?' asks Margot.

'Underground gambling, money laundering, loan sharking, debt collection, weapons smuggling and a lot of drugs.'

'But no human trafficking?'

'Not as far as we know . . . though of course there's prostitution, and . . .'

Joona leaves the room, walking down the hallway to call Kofoed, but it goes straight to voicemail.

He sends a message about the connection to the Club and asks Kofoed to call him as soon as he can, turning and heading back to Margot's office.

'How on top of them are you?' Aron asks, getting up again. 'I mean, could Primus be a member of the Club without you knowing about it?'

'The Club belongs to the category of organised crime we call self-defining . . . they choose their level of involvement themselves, and it often takes several years to become a full member . . . though of course they do have a large base of lower-level members.'

'So he could be involved that way?'

'If he has anything to offer them,' Lars replies.

Joona tries calling Kofoed again. This time, it rings, and he is just about to hang up when he hears a click, followed by a rushing sound.

'I'm starting to understand what it's like to have a cop for an old man,' he answers, his voice low.

'Do I need to come and rescue you?' Joona asks, leaving the room again.

Kofoed lets out a subdued laugh.

'I haven't seen Primus yet,' he says. 'But Ulrike is on the ground floor. At first I thought she was alone in the house, but then I caught

a glimpse of someone else . . . I've been waiting and waiting, and just managed to get a picture of her . . . it's a terrible shot, but I think she looks like Mia Andersson.'

'Send me the picture and keep your distance. Be careful,' Joona tells him.

'OK.'

'Tommy? Take what I'm saying seriously now.'

'I haven't had this much fun in years.'

Joona's phone beeps, and he opens the image. He takes in the house's red facade and siding, the white window frames, cracked wood and peeling paint. In one of the windows, a young girl is partially visible.

Joona enlarges the image. The resolution is terrible, but he studies the shape of her face, the faint light above the tip of her nose. It could be Mia, just as Kofoed said. They certainly can't rule out having found her.

He returns to Margot's office with the phone in his hand, interrupting Lars Tamm mid-sentence.

'OK, listen,' he says. 'I put Tommy Kofoed on to watching Ulrike's house . . .'

'I shouldn't be surprised,' Margot sighs.

'And he just sent me this picture,' he says, passing her the phone.

'Who is that supposed to be?' Margot asks, putting on her glasses.

Aron moves over behind her and bends down over the phone. 'That could be Mia Andersson, right? It does look like her.'

'We'll have to give the picture to the technicians,' says Joona. 'But if it is Mia, she won't be there for long – that house is definitely just a stopover.'

'We should storm it now,' says Aron.

'I need to discuss this with CID and the Security Services,' Margot points out.

'*Discuss*,' Aron repeats, his voice raised. 'Then you can come and cut the wire when we find Mia's mutilated body hanging from—'

'Enough,' Margot snaps, getting up from her chair. 'I understand the gravity of this, the whole thing makes me furious – I will not

stand for any more deaths, but if we decide to set up a raid, we have to do it right.'

'But if we sit and wait . . .'

'We're not sitting and waiting, that's not what I'm saying, is it? We're not going to wait.' Margot's voice is sharp, and she wipes her mouth with the back of her hand. 'Joona, what do you think? What should we do?'

'We need to get people over there right now while we prepare for a raid.'

'OK, then let's do this,' says Margot. 'You two get in the car and drive over there, and I'll talk to the National Task Force.'

48

Joona buttons his grey windbreaker over his bulletproof vest and pushes his Colt Combat into a padded UPS envelope.

Aron is sitting on a stack of pallets nearby, one leg bouncing anxiously.

It is eight minutes past eleven, and the sky has grown dark.

There are three cars parked in the twilight on the sloping ground outside Södertälje Electric AB.

Margot Silverman has raised the status of the raid to a so-called special operation, despite the fact that their technicians have been unable to confirm whether or not the young woman in Kofoed's photograph really is Mia Andersson.

Two of the nine operatives from the National Task Force have already arrived, and are waiting behind a rusty pickup with the words 'Franzén Plumbing' on the tailgate.

The men introduced themselves as Bruno and Morris. They are almost as tall as Joona, and both are wearing blue work trousers and fleeces.

Bruno has a shaved head and a blond beard.

Morris has short dark hair and rosy cheeks, and is wearing a small crucifix on a chain around his neck.

Joona has taken minute-by-minute control of the operation, and is in constant contact with Margot and the rest of the command team.

Everyone is struggling to assess the situation.

No one but Ulrike and the young woman has been seen in the house, but it is a large building, and they have only been watching it from one vantage point.

'Our primary aim is to rescue the woman who may or may not be Mia Andersson,' says Joona. 'And our secondary aim is to arrest Primus if he is inside, and bring him in for questioning.'

It's dark between the cars on the slanting pavement, but on the mint-green wall of the building a lamp with a zinc shade casts a narrow circle of light.

The four men gather underneath it to study the map. Joona explains how the raid will work, taking them through their routes, their meeting point and where the ambulances will be waiting. He places a copy of the house's floor plans on top of the map, pointing to the front door, the hallway and the other rooms on the ground floor.

'The stairs are a problem,' says Morris.

'But you'll have to go up in pairs, even if it's cramped,' Joona tells them.

'Guess so,' Bruno replies, scratching his blond beard.

They are waiting for another seven operatives from the National Task Force. Three of them will take up strategic positions outside with sniper rifles while the others get into combat pairs and search the house.

Aron drops his phone, and it clatters to the ground beside the stack of pallets. He quickly picks it up, checking to see whether the screen has survived unscathed.

Morris examines the magazine of his automatic rifle, making sure all of the bullets are fully jacketed, and takes the sight out of his sports bag.

'Ugh, what the fuck,' he mumbles, turning the lens towards the light. 'There's some kind of crap on the lens.'

'Let's see,' says Bruno.

'Something sticky.'

'Maybe you can smoke it,' Bruno suggests.

The agents start joking about what Morris was like before he pulled himself together and joined the force. Whenever he couldn't get hold of weed, he would smoke anything, from banana skins to toadstools. Once, he even mixed ground nutmeg with white spirit, and left the paste to dry out in the oven.

Joona opens an envelope and passes photos of Mia Andersson, Primus, Ulrike Bengtsson and her husband, Stefan Nicolic, to the others.

'Nicolic is armed and extremely dangerous. Last year, one of our colleagues was shot in bed and he cropped up in the investigation that followed.'

'He's mine,' says Morris.

'They've got access to a lot of heavy weapons,' Joona says as his phone starts buzzing. 'I need to take this – it's Kofoed.'

He hears a scraping sound as he answers, followed by Kofoed catching his breath, right up close to the microphone.

'Can you hear me?' Kofoed asks, his voice low. 'A vehicle just pulled up outside the house – a van with tinted windows, it's just sitting on the driveway . . . My position's not great, so I can't see whether anyone got out or what's going on.'

'Stay where you are,' Joona tells him, ending the call.

'What did he say?' asks Aron.

'A van just arrived at the house. They might be about to move Mia,' Joona explains as he calls the command team again.

Talking them through the latest development, he notices the two agents whispering to one another, looking stressed.

Morris's eyes seem glassy, and his cheeks and ears have turned red. He blows the dirt from the Picatinny rail on his gun and attaches the sight.

The light from the zinc lamp illuminates Bruno's broad shoulders and back. Aron pushes a pouch of snus tobacco beneath his upper lip.

'OK, listen up,' Joona tells the three men. 'Margot wants us to go in ASAP.'

'The rest of the team are almost here,' says Morris.

'I know, but command has weighed that against the risk that Mia Andersson will be taken away in the van . . . the road blocks are late, and they want to avoid a car chase.'

'For fuck's sake,' Morris sighs.

'Our orders are to start the raid immediately,' Joona repeats.

'OK, what the hell,' says Bruno, giving Morris a reassuring glance.

'Aron and I will go in through the front door, and I want the two of you to block the exit using your pickup. Give us a hundred and twenty seconds before coming in after us. No stun grenades, no raised voices, but expect return fire.'

'The team will be here in twenty minutes,' Morris says, standing his ground.

'Come on, we don't have twenty minutes,' Aron tells him, raising his voice. 'Do you want to let them disappear with the girl? And then wait until we find her hanged somewhere a few years from now?'

'We have final orders to go in now,' says Joona, passing Aron one of the wireless earpieces. 'Make sure you can hear me and that you've got comms on direct mode.'

Joona starts walking, envelope in hand. Aron follows him, heading up towards Bergsgatan.

'You've got a Sig Sauer, right?'

'Last time I checked,' says Aron.

'Keep it hidden until we're inside.'

The two agents stay behind, watching them disappear into the darkness. They see Joona and Aron reappear in the glow of a street lamp in the distance.

Morris paces anxiously, then puts both hands on the mint-green wall and leans against it, taking deep breaths.

'I smoke two joints before I smoke two joints,' says Bruno.

'And then I smoke two more,' Morris replies, though he doesn't smile.

'We can do this,' Bruno tells him, his voice subdued.

'I know,' says Morris, picking up and kissing his crucifix.

'Did you get the crap off your sight?'

'Makes no difference – I'm not going to need it.'

They pick up the sports bags with their guns and place them in the bed of the pickup, then climb in and put the truck in reverse.

49

Silently, Joona and Aron turn left and start walking up to the crown of the hill, the street lamps illuminating patches of pavement. The slope is lined with villas from the early twentieth century, and the lights are on in some of the windows.

'When did you last do training on this kind of operation?' Joona asks, stepping over a fallen electric scooter.

'It's not something you forget,' Aron replies.

They cut across the road, into a narrow cul-de-sac where the pavement is cracked.

As they pass a small rock face, they see Ulrike Bengtsson's house at the top of the steep hill, its pointed roof rising up into the black sky.

Joona thinks about the photograph of Ulrike. She is tall and in her sixties, with blonde hair, pierced brows and tattooed arms. With their slender faces and crowded teeth, she and her brother look very much alike.

They pass the last street lamp, where a home-made basketball hoop is attached to the post, and their shadows grow longer, eventually merging with the darkness.

All they can hear is the crunching of their own footsteps.

There are two green bins beneath a small wooden shelter and, by the gate, a rusty sign reading ZOO & TATTOO.

The black van is parked on the steep driveway, and a faint light is visible in the bedroom window on the ground floor.

Joona steps forward and knocks on the tinted window of the van. Aron positions himself by the back door, pulling his gun from its

holster, turning off the safety catch and keeping it hidden by his side. Joona knocks again, then walks around the van and peers in through the windscreen.

'It's empty,' he says.

Aron secures his weapon and follows Joona up the stone steps to the house. He can already feel the sweat trickling down his temples.

The branches of a tree in front of one of the neighbouring houses sway in the breeze, making the light in one of the windows blink anxiously.

Aron's heart is pounding in his chest, his teeth gritted. He can feel his pulse thudding in his temples. He remembers the drills from his training sessions, but this is the first time he has ever actually taken part in a serious raid like this.

Joona turns towards the bedroom window on the ground floor. A movement inside catches his eye, something like a piece of black fabric falling from the ceiling to the floor.

They continue up the long set of steps to the porch beneath the balcony. Joona turns the door handle and tries the door.

'Locked,' Aron whispers.

Joona struggles to shrug his black backpack off and takes out a lock-pick gun. He pushes the rod into the keyhole, pulls the trigger until the pins are knocked out, then uses the tension wrench to turn the lock.

He opens the door slightly, peering into the dark hallway as he puts the lock-pick gun back into his bag. He pulls out a towel and a pair of bolt cutters, then spreads the towel in the crack between the door and the frame and cuts the chain lock.

The broken links fall into the towel without a sound.

'We're going in now,' Joona says into his radio.

He pulls his gun from the padded envelope, flicks off the safety catch, then, leaving his backpack on the steps, heads inside.

They step over a pair of red motorcycle boots and enter a long, narrow hallway.

There is a set of stairs leading up to the second floor, and an opening into the living room.

They hear a cooing sound, followed by muted birdsong.

Gun raised, Joona secures the room and gestures for Aron to follow him on the left. Their eyes slowly adjust to the darkness.

Aron peers up to the second floor between the bannisters.

Joona keeps moving forward, aiming at the dark clothing hanging on hooks on one wall.

There is a layer of down and dust covering the floorboards.

Aron crouches down, aiming his gun at the dark space beneath the stairs. He can hear a soft scratching sound from inside.

The gun starts to shake in his hands. Something faintly catches the light. Aron thinks he spots something moving, and shifts his finger from the trigger guard to the trigger.

He gasps in surprise as a large black bird flaps up out of the shadows. It collides with the dark ceiling light and crashes into the wall, feathers rustling, before flying into the next room.

Aron straightens up, gun pointing at the floor, trying to compose himself and bring his breathing under control.

He came a hair's breadth from firing his weapon.

Joona glances over to him without taking his gun off the doorway up ahead.

A few small birds flutter down the hallway and up to the second floor.

'What the fuck is this place?' Aron whispers, wiping the sweat from his eyes.

'Focus.'

Aron nods, raises his weapon and aims through the doorway. The floorboards groan beneath him as he starts moving.

On top of a chest of drawers, he notices a couple of rusty socket wrenches.

Joona gestures for Aron to stick to the left wall.

They can hear the cooing of birds from the dark living room straight ahead.

* * *

As Joona reports that he and Aron are entering the house, Bruno and Morris turn off onto Byggmästaregatan. Their rusty pickup rolls

forward, creaking, and comes to a halt across the road by the rubbish bins, preventing anyone from passing.

'I don't like this,' says Morris. 'I don't like this at all.'

'We're just doing our job,' says Bruno, swallowing hard.

'How, though? We can't secure the second floor and the kitchen unless we split up, or . . .'

'Take it easy,' says Bruno. 'Joona wants us to have his back when he goes in, so we'll just have to ignore the second floor to start with. There's no other way. We secure room after room and keep an eye out behind us.'

'I know, I know, I'd just rather wait for the others.'

'It's been a hundred and twenty seconds.'

Morris attempts a smile, pretending to take a drag on a joint before climbing out of the truck.

They walk slowly past the rubbish bins, up the slope to the house. Once they are no longer visible from any of the windows, they dump their bags by the garden path, put on their helmets and take out their automatic Heckler & Koch rifles. Without a sound, they run over to the house and up the steps to the front door.

Bruno adjusts his earpiece, opens the door and aims at the stairs in the darkness. Morris enters behind him, scanning the wall where the coats are hanging, followed by the doorway into the living room.

Everything is calm and quiet.

Bruno waits until Morris has secured the area beneath the stairs before he closes the front door.

On the spindles down the side of the stairs, the bird droppings have mixed with down and pooled along the edge of the bannister.

Bruno uses the barrel of his gun to poke at a hardened lump of the mixture. Dry flakes crumble to the floor.

'Maybe you could mix that with white spirit and smoke it?' Morris says quietly.

He drops to his knees and aims his gun into the darkness beneath the stairs, regretting that he didn't mount a light onto his rifle.

50

Blackout curtains cover the windows, leaving the large living room in a greyish umbra.

There are birds half-dozing on the pool table and chirping up by the ceiling.

Joona and Aron move slowly, four metres apart. The floor creaks softly underfoot.

Joona cautiously makes his way forward, glancing over to Aron and then ducking down to check beneath the pool table.

The last time he was at the shooting range, he noticed that the feed mechanism in his gun wasn't working properly. In order to avoid the firearm jamming, he replaced the magazine spring once he got home, but he hasn't had time to test the gun since.

Joona secures the room to the left as Aron steps inside. Tiny feathers and flecks of dust swirl through the air.

Joona notices that Aron's eyes are locked on a yellow parrot climbing on the dark chandelier.

Fixating on any detail for too long can be dangerous.

With his left hand, Aron reaches out and picks a downy white feather from the edge of the billiards table.

There is a light on somewhere up ahead.

They keep moving forward, past a gleaming tiled stove.

The floor is thick with seed casings, heaped up against the walls with the feathers and droppings.

'Looks like someone lost it,' Aron mumbles.

A green parrot hops between the bottles, carafes and glasses on a brass serving trolley.

As Aron secures the blind spots to the sides, he feels a sense of mortal dread growing inside him, swelling like nausea.

He watches Joona's calm movements, the way he sticks to the wall and keeps his gun pointed straight ahead, perfectly aligned with the hallway.

The lacquered floorboards give way to quiet green carpet as they step into the hallway.

Joona sees the curtain covering one of the windows flutter, and realises that Bruno and Morris must have closed the front door.

'Secure the service stretch between the kitchen and the living room,' he tells them over the radio.

He gestures to the hallway leading to the bedroom where Kofoed saw the younger of the two women.

They move slowly to avoid startling the birds.

Joona motions for Aron to stay just behind him.

Aron wipes the sweat from his upper lip. He knows he is supposed to be keeping an eye on the laundry room while Joona searches the bedroom.

A small bird flaps down the hallway.

Joona reaches out and pushes the door open. He steps inside and wheels around, gun raised, to the right and the left.

A large mirror has been mounted on the ceiling above the pine double bed, and a row of pale blue parakeets are perched on the curtain pole.

There is a used condom on the bedside table.

The woman is nowhere to be seen – assuming she isn't hiding in one of the wardrobes lining the wall to the right.

Joona glances back and sees Aron's pale face out in the hallway, and waits for him to take up position.

His colleague doesn't need to get any closer to the laundry room, just step to the other side of the hallway.

Back in the billiards room, a parrot starts screeching anxiously.

Aron meets Joona's eye. He nods, then moves over to the doorway to the laundry room and pauses.

Somewhere to the right, a light is glowing.

On the grey vinyl floor, there is some kind of fibreglass hatch, beneath which the pipes for the washing machine and drier have been laid.

Against the other wall, there is a shower stall with frosted glass walls.

Aron takes a step to the side, and his eyes lock onto a mirror with an ornate golden frame.

A white cockatoo shifts slowly over by the shower.

Right then, Aron's heart starts pounding so hard that it makes his ears ache. In the mirror, he can see a woman lying on a bed just to the left of the door. She hasn't spotted him yet. Her nightgown is pulled up to her breasts, leaving her lower body bare, and her legs are crossed at the ankles.

Her stomach slowly rises and falls with each breath.

Aron gestures to Joona, unable to tear his eyes away from the woman. Her shaved pubic area is red from an unfinished tattoo of a humming bird.

The plastic walls of the shower cubicle creak softly.

Joona's gun is still trained on the wardrobes when he turns back and sees Aron take a step into the laundry room without securing the area to the right of the doorway.

An unexpected movement sends dust and feathers swirling across the floor.

'Aron,' Joona whispers, 'you can't . . .'

He watches as a knife is driven straight through Aron's throat, the tip breaking through the skin just beneath his ear on the other side. A cascade of blood follows the blade as it is torn back out.

Aron staggers backwards, coughing blood.

Someone lets out a mirthless laugh, a piece of furniture topples over, and he hears the sound of quick footsteps disappearing.

Joona runs into the laundry room, scanning the space with his gun.

He sees a tall woman in her mid-sixties backing away from him, knife raised.

She bumps into the shower stall and keeps moving backwards until she hits the wall.

Someone must have left the laundry room through the other door, and they are now running towards the hallway.

Without lowering his gun, Joona notices the empty bed and the small table of tattoo ink.

He requests a medevac, emphasising the urgency of his colleague's injury.

Aron slumps down onto a stool, dropping his gun to the floor and coughing blood onto his chest. He gropes for something to lean against, knocking over a box of laundry detergent and making the white crystals spill across the floor.

The woman is gripping the knife with both hands, her eyes darting between Joona and Aron. She must have been hiding in the shower stall when Aron stepped into the room.

'Police,' Joona says quietly. 'Drop the knife.'

She shakes her head, and Joona holds up a reassuring hand. Her breathing is rapid, and she tries to close her lips over her crooked teeth.

'Ulrike, listen to me,' he says, slowly moving closer. 'I need to know how many people are in the house, so no one else gets hurt.'

'What?'

'Put the knife down.'

'Sorry,' she mumbles, lowering the knife in confusion.

'How many people are . . .'

She thrusts upwards with the knife, towards Joona's torso. The force of her attack takes him by surprise, but he manages to twist his body and sees the glittering tip of the blade slice through his windbreaker.

He catches her forearm in his left hand, ramming the butt of his gun into her collarbone and kicking her feet out from beneath her, causing her to fall backwards.

51

Morris moves through the billiards room towards the doorway into the kitchen, Bruno right behind him.

His realises that his mouth has gone dry.

Their job is to secure the kitchen without taking their eyes off the hallway.

Morris has his assault rifle raised, finger on the trigger. The red dot in his sight always corresponds to the point of impact.

A couple of birds lift up from the floor and flap into the hallway. Both men heard the brief commands being sent over the radio. Joona has requested a medevac. Aron is seriously injured.

They quickly secure the blind spots to the right and left, then Morris steps into the spacious kitchen with a dark-grey tiled floor.

The dishwasher door is open, and there is a pot of black plastic spatulas beside the stovetop.

Two small white birds are pecking at breadcrumbs on the counter.

Bruno watches Morris through the doorway. He gestures for him to wait and slowly moves closer.

A grey parrot with red tail feathers is hanging upside down from the lamp above the table.

They hear a series of thuds from the other side of the house. A woman cries out, and then Joona Linna's voice appears through their earpieces.

'There are two heavily armed men in the house,' says Joona. 'I repeat, there are . . .'

Right then, there is a deafening bang in the living room, and a moment later, their pickup explodes outside the house.

The shock wave blasts against their chests, making the windows rattle.

The birds in the kitchen start flying around the room.

The entire garden seems to be ablaze.

The bed of the pickup falls through the branches of the trees, landing on the neighbour's lawn. Tangled steel and engine parts rain down on the road. A tyre thuds down on the hill and bounces away. The engine itself lands on the roof of the van.

A cloud of smoke and dust hangs in the air.

All that is left on the driveway is a crater and a car door.

Morris keeps his breathing even and continues through the kitchen. The adrenaline is making his fingertips feel cold.

He saw only a glimpse of the explosion through one of the windows, but realises that a recoilless rifle must have been fired from somewhere inside the house.

The door to the living room has swung open by a few centimetres.

The larger parrots have started to return to their perches, but the canaries are still racing around in the air.

'I need to get Aron out – can you secure the hallway?' Joona asks over the earpiece.

Morris gestures to Bruno that he thinks the shooter is in the living room, and wants to force open the door.

Bruno shakes his head and motions for Morris to take cover, guard the door and wait.

But Morris licks his lips and takes a cautious step forward.

The darkness in the living room almost seems to be pulsing.

The birds on top of the fridge shift anxiously as he approaches.

Morris repeats to himself that he needs to stop the man with the recoilless rifle, that he can't allow him to shoot down the helicopter. He continues towards the door as though in a trance. The red spot in his sight quivers at chest height over the dark crack.

Behind him, Bruno says something in a raised voice.

Morris notices a movement from the corner of his eye.

A round-shouldered man with a plaited beard and a black shotgun steps out from his hiding place beside the fridge.

Morris turns his weapon on him. There is a deep crack, the muzzle flash reflected in the glass of the kitchen window. Morris is hit in the side of the head. His mangled helmet slams into the wall behind him before slamming to the floor. Blood sprays across the drawers beneath the counter. His body falls heavily into a half-sitting position against the open dishwasher. The vast majority of Morris's head has been blown away, but a small piece of the back of his skull remains, his lower jaw hanging slack over his chest.

'Jesus Christ,' the man with the semi-automatic shotgun gasps.

Joona drags Aron to the billiards room as Bruno returns to the kitchen with heavy footsteps. He feels his legs shaking beneath him. Over the ringing in his ears left behind by the blast, he can hear whistling birdsong.

The man who was hiding behind the fridge is now staring down at Morris's body and the blood on the walls and cupboards. His shotgun is pointing at the floor. He turns slowly towards the billiards room as Bruno pulls the trigger and feels the gun shudder in his hands. The jacketed bullets pass straight through the man's chest, shattering the window behind him. Shards of glass fly through the air, and the frame splinters. It takes no more than two seconds for him to empty his thirty-round magazine. Empty casings clatter onto the tiles.

The man with the plaited beard staggers backwards and crashes to the floor. A cloud of tiny blood drops seems to hang in the air.

Bruno backs up into the billiards room as he takes out the empty magazine. He thought he had his gun set to three-shot burst mode.

His pulse is thundering in his ears. His eyes focus on the shredded helmet and what is left of his colleague's head.

'For fuck's sake, Morris,' he pants, pulling out a new magazine.

A man with long blond hair and black-rimmed glasses kicks open the door to the living room up ahead. He is wearing leather trousers and a dark-green bulletproof vest. In his right hand, Bruno can see a Glock 17.

Bruno moves backwards, tripping over the edge of the green rug and hitting his head on the side of the billiards table. The magazine thuds to the floor, skidding away beneath the heavy table.

Joona lets go of Aron and runs forward, sticking to the wall, pausing to the right of the kitchen door.

Bruno moves out of the man's line of fire, shuffling backwards and searching his trouser pockets for another magazine.

Joona is standing perfectly still with his gun aimed at the doorway.

A barely perceptible shadow passes over the glossy paint on the door frame.

As he'd handcuffed Ulrike to one of the thick pipes in the laundry room, she told him there were two bodyguards in the house.

Joona had cut off a length of the shower hose and pushed it into Aron's throat, between his vocal cords, in an attempt to create a reasonably secure airway. Using the rug, he then dragged him through the laundry room and reached the billiards room just as the shooting began.

He can hear the hum of the helicopter overhead.

The scent of gunpowder is thick in the air.

The blond man with the Glock steps into the billiards room and fixes his eyes on Aron, who is lying on the floor with both hands on his throat.

Blood is seeping out between his fingers.

The man aims his gun to the left, but Bruno has managed to take cover behind the billiards table.

Joona moves quickly, grabbing the man's wrist from behind and tearing his arm back, pressing his Colt Combat to his shoulder and pulling the trigger. The man's body shakes and blood sprays across the wall; his arm goes limp, and his gun drops to the floor. He cries out in pain. Joona drags him to one side by his injured arm, spinning him around and ramming his left elbow into his cheek and chin in the process. He hits him hard, and the man's head snaps back, knocking off his glasses and sending a spray of sweat across the room. They stagger over together. The man crashes into the cue rack and then drops to the floor. He lands on his hip, breaking his fall with one hand before slumping down. The empty bullet case rolls in a wide half-circle, coming to a stop when it hits his nose.

Bruno has managed to find a new magazine, and slots it into his assault rifle before getting to his feet behind the billiards table.

Aron is pale and sweaty, desperately trying to draw in air through the pipe. He is about to go into circulatory shock.

52

Joona quickly frisks the man on the floor, then drags him over to the window and handcuffs him to the radiator. He then turns back to Aron, catching his panicked eye and repeating that everything will be OK. He grabs the rug and pulls him towards the hallway. Bruno follows him out, quickly securing the stairs and then keeping his gun trained on the billiards room.

They hear a series of heavy thuds from upstairs.

The blood from Aron's throat has seeped through the rug, leaving a glistening red trail behind them.

A white dove hops away, flapping up into the air when it realises it is trapped by the advancing rug.

The roar of the helicopter grows louder, making the windows rattle.

Joona drags Aron past the staircase.

Over the din, they hear a woman laughing upstairs. Bruno drops to one knee and aims his weapon at the dark opening on the landing.

'Take Aron out,' Joona tells him, holding the door open for them.

The helicopter is hovering over the garden, the choppy roar of its rotor blades bouncing between the houses. Dust and leaves are scattered in a circle, bushes bending in the powerful downdraught. A stretcher is slowly being winched down between the garden and the house.

Bruno hauls Aron up onto his shoulder and runs out, ducking down.

Joona closes the door behind them, dampening the noise of the helicopter slightly.

From the laundry room, Ulrike shouts something.

Joona starts making his way upstairs, his gun trained on the landing. The dry bird droppings crunch beneath his feet.

According to the plans, the second floor consists of a suite of rooms, including a large living room, a bathroom and a bedroom.

He hears the woman's languid laugh again, almost as though she is asleep, dreaming of something funny.

Joona continues until his eyes are level with the floor and he can see the entire living room.

The polished boards are covered in a layer of dust and down. The door to the bedroom is closed, but the bathroom door is ajar.

He wheels around, weapon still raised.

The spindles beneath the bannister flicker by in front of the seating area, the TV and the desk.

He continues up the stairs.

There is a faint scent of perfume and smoke hanging in the air.

The sound of the rotor blades grows louder, and he realises that the helicopter must be taking off.

The top step groans under Joona's weight.

He moves quickly across the room, pausing by the closed bedroom door and listening intently.

The hinges squeak softly as he slowly pushes it open.

He steps to one side, peering into the dark room and using the muzzle of his gun to nudge the door open further. He blinks, waiting for his eyes to adjust.

In the soft light, Joona can make out white walls and a white floor, the shape of a bed against the right-hand wall. A thin curtain is blowing in the breeze by the open window. The white fabric billows slowly.

The window frame creaks, the latch scraping against the metal, and a grey light spills into the room.

Joona notices a young boy standing perfectly still in the middle of the room, his hands clasped behind his back. He is wearing nothing but a pair of white silk pyjama bottoms.

His thin shoulders and combed hair catch a little of the light.

He looks straight at Joona, breathing quickly.

Up by the ceiling, ten or so pale yellow canaries are fluttering around. The sound of their wings is like dry leaves caught in a gust of wind.

The curtain ripples, letting more light into the room. Joona checks that there is no one else there, and is just about to take a step inside when he notices a bare foot on the window frame.

There is someone outside.

The curtain rises in the wind, opening slightly.

A young woman has climbed up onto the windowsill, and is standing right on the edge, clinging on with one hand, a dreamy smile on her face.

It isn't Mia, but she is likely the woman Kofoed photographed.

She is wearing a white nightdress, and the fabric is slick with blood over her groin. Her pupils are so small they are almost invisible.

Joona slowly crosses the white floorboards, keeping his gun trained on the doorway behind the boy.

The boy's chin has started to tremble.

'You can't kill my mum,' he says between shallow breaths.

'I'm not going to kill anyone,' Joona tells him. 'But I want her to come down from the window before she gets hurt.'

'Mummy, he's nice.'

She slips on the sill, and something hard strikes the glass as she regains her balance, letting out another dull laugh. The woman leans back, away from the house, one hand still gripping the frame.

The cracked wood creaks.

Joona notices that she is holding a small revolver in her free hand. He slowly moves closer.

The woman turns back to the bedroom and scratches her head with the barrel of the gun. 'Who are you talking to?' she asks, her voice drowsy.

'My name is Joona Linna. I'm with the police, I'm here to help you. I want you to drop the revolver and climb back inside.'

'You'll die so fucking much if you touch me,' she says.

'No one wants to hurt you. I'm going to come closer now, and help you down.'

'Pull the pin,' she mumbles.

There is a clinking sound as a small pin with a ring on one end falls to the floor. The curtain bulges again, illuminating the boy slightly.

He is holding a military issue Shgr 2000 grenade out to Joona, his pale hand gripping the spring-loaded lever. If he drops it, the grenade will explode after three and a half seconds.

'Don't let go of the lever,' says Joona.

'You can't kill her,' the boy sobs.

'We'll all die if you let go.'

'You're just trying to trick me,' says the boy, his breathing uneven.

'I'm a policeman,' Joona tells him, slowly moving forward. 'I want you to—'

'Stop!' the boy shouts.

His rapid breathing makes his flat chest rise, trembling. He is standing too far away for Joona to be able to lunge forward and snatch the grenade from him.

Joona looks over to the woman in the window. Her eyelids are heavy, the revolver hanging limply by her hip.

'Be careful now,' Joona tells the boy, pushing his gun back into the holster. 'We'll fix this, there's nothing to worry about, just keep hold of it exactly like you are now.'

'Throw it at him,' the mother mumbles.

'Don't do anything,' Joona blurts out. 'You can't let go, and you definitely can't throw it – no one in this room will survive if you do.'

'He's just scared.' The woman smiles.

'Don't listen to her . . . your mum doesn't understand how a hand grenade works, but I'm a policeman, and I'm telling you it'll kill everyone in this room.'

The boy starts crying, the hand clutching the grenade shaking.

'Throw it now,' she whispers.

'Mummy, I'm too scared . . .'

'Do you want him to rape me and saw off your legs?' she slurs.

'I promise I'm not going to hurt either of you,' says Joona.

'He's lying so fucking much.' She smiles, raising the revolver to her own temple.

'Sorry,' says the boy, throwing the grenade.

248

Joona takes a step forward, catching it mid-air in his left hand. He turns on his heel and throws it into the living room. The grenade hits the door frame and bounces off to one side in the adjoining room.

Joona hurls himself towards the boy to protect him as the detonator ignites the explosive hexotol.

The sharp bang is deafening.

The door is torn from its hinges and crashes into the bedroom.

The shock wave knocks the air out of them.

Splintered wood lashes at their skin.

Joona rolls to one side, pulls out his gun and aims it at the window.

The bedroom is full of dust and smoke.

The white curtain billows slowly out towards the darkness.

The woman is gone.

Joona gets onto his feet and runs over to the window. She is lying on her back in the grass down below, drowsily raising a hand to the sky. Two men from the National Task Force charge towards her.

The blast must have thrown her back, making her fall through the branches of the birch tree into the long grass.

He sees the revolver among the damp leaves in a gutter below.

The boy is on his feet, gawking at the bloody birds lying among the shards of the door and the door frame.

53

The recent heatwave has made the leaves on the trees in Vanadislunden darken and curl. Pamela and Dennis walk slowly around the large red-brick reservoir, dust from the dry trail swirling around their legs.

They decided last night to meet for lunch today, and Dennis has brought a bag of sandwiches and freshly squeezed orange juice.

A slim man with an old-fashioned hatbox beneath one arm was walking close behind them for a while, but Pamela can no longer see him.

They sit down on a shady park bench, and Dennis takes out a sandwich and hands it to Pamela.

She thanks him and studies the disused water park. A pile of rubbish and blackened leaves has built up at the bottom of the cracked slide.

It feels like just yesterday that she and Mia were riding the roller coaster together.

Pamela has finally submitted her appeal to the administrative court. It took her a while to gather all the necessary certificates and references, but the process is now underway, and social services' decision will likely be overturned.

The minute Martin was named as an eyewitness in the press, the threat arrived – and before Pamela even had time to process that fact, Mia was gone.

Over and over again, an icy rush of anxiety shoots through her as her mind drifts to the terrible things Mia might be going through right now.

She has no idea whether it was right to try to help the police. What if Mia suffers as a result?

But, at the same time, she knows that she has to do everything she can to find her.

Joona Linna claims Martin is the key.

His transformation during the hypnosis session was certainly eye-opening. Just like that, he could talk in coherent sentences, something he hasn't done in years, remembering fragments from the playground that night.

'You look sad,' Dennis tells her, pushing a lock of hair back from her cheek.

'I'm OK ... Actually, no I'm not,' she tells him. 'I'm not OK. I can't bear the thought that he's taken Mia, and it's all my fault.'

'No, it—'

'But it is,' she interrupts him.

'Why would it be your fault?'

'Because we've been helping the police.'

'*Have* you, really?'

'Martin told them he heard a patient in his ward talking about hurting Jenny Lind ... that's why he went to the playground in the middle of the night.'

'Were you there? Did you hear Martin say that?' he asks, dabbing at the corner of his mouth.

'It was under hypnosis,' she replies.

'Seriously – this is too much,' Dennis says, exasperated. 'First they force him to confess to murder, and now they're trying to—'

'It wasn't like that,' she interrupts again. 'It was ... I can't explain it, but they need to find Mia, and Martin could suddenly speak while he was hypnotised ... it was incredible, really, he was talking in long sentences ...'

'Was the person who hypnotised him at least a doctor?' Dennis asks sceptically.

'Yes, they were.'

'And did Martin agree to it?'

'Of course.'

'But did he really understand what it involved? Did Martin know he wouldn't be in control of his words, that he'd be manipulated into saying what the police wanted him to say?'

'But that's not how it was at all,' Pamela argues.

'Well, that's good . . . I just have serious doubts about hypnosis; I've seen patients become psychotic because they felt like the words coming out of their mouths weren't their own . . . and that feeling can sometimes break through several weeks later.'

'No one told us that.'

'I'm not saying it'll definitely happen, I'm just saying that there are risks, and that you might want to take a closer look at them before you agree to any more hypnosis.'

'There hasn't been any mention of doing it more than once. We gave it a chance, but . . . Martin has actually found it easier to talk since the session.'

'Though I'd guess that's probably because of the ECT.'

'Maybe.'

Pamela looks out at the rooftops, the hot air wavering above the glittering ventilation pipes. Mia is her responsibility, no matter what anyone says. None of this would have happened if she hadn't come into Mia's life.

'You're quiet again. It's like you're always shutting yourself off,' says Dennis.

'Sorry, I . . .'

'There's no need to apologise.'

She puts the bottle on the ground by the bench and takes a deep breath.

'It's just that everything happened at once, and I wasn't prepared. You know what I'm like, and this isn't me. I drank too much and then ended up in bed with you. I mean, what's going on with me?'

'Pamela,' he tries to interject.

'I know that you warned me. You tried to put the brakes on.'

'Because I didn't want you to have any regrets,' he replies, placing his hand on hers. 'I like Martin, but you're the one I care about, who I've always cared about.'

'I'm sorry for ruining everything,' she says, pulling her hand away.

'From the outside, what we did probably doesn't look like the kindest thing,' he says. 'But it was human, and it was understandable.'

'Not to me. I'm so ashamed, and I wish—'

'Well I'm really not,' he interrupts her. 'I'm not ashamed, because if I'm perfectly honest, I've always been in love with you.'

'Dennis . . . I know I must have been giving you mixed signals, I hate that about myself, and I . . .'

'Please, stop.'

'And I'm ashamed because I have no intention of leaving Martin . . . things would be different if I did, but that's not how it is.'

He brushes a few breadcrumbs from his lap.

'I respect what you're saying,' he says, swallowing hard. 'But maybe you shouldn't pin too much hope on Martin becoming the man he once was again . . . With ECT and the right medication, he might be able to manage without full-time care, but . . .'

'Dennis, I love you as a friend, and I don't want to lose you.'

'Don't worry,' he says, getting to his feet.

* * *

Pamela is sitting at her computer in the office, reading through old articles on the search for Jenny Lind.

She takes off her glasses and turns to the window, looking out at the red and black tin roofs and thinking about that terrible coincidence again: that Mia might die simply because Martin happened to witness Jenny Lind's murder.

Jenny is already dead, but Mia is still alive.

She has to believe that Mia will be OK.

She will be – so long as the killer doesn't find out they are trying to help the police.

If they give in to his threat, there will be no one fighting for Mia. She really will be all alone then. She doesn't have any worried parents to show up on TV and plead for her release, reaching the entire country and convincing the government to offer a reward.

Pamela tries searching for private detectives.

She had never really considered their existence before now. They run secret background checks, and investigate fraud, spying and

infidelity. All of them trace missing children, family members and friends, too.

She walks to the kitchen, opens the cupboard and stares at the bottles of alcohol lined up inside.

If there is even a chance she can help save Mia, she can't allow anything to get in her way.

She won't be drinking champagne in a spa this time; she would rather die than face her own self-hatred again.

Pamela wonders whether she should pour all of the vodka down the sink, but tells herself it would be better to leave the bottles where they are, tempting her. That way, the choice remains an active one.

She sits down at the kitchen table and calls Joona Linna. When he picks up, she can hear just how unbalanced she sounds as she asks him about the case, whether the information that came out during the hypnosis has led anywhere, and what the next steps are.

Joona patiently answers each of her questions and doesn't tell her to calm down even once – despite the fact she repeats herself and her voice breaks.

'I'm sorry for sticking my nose in, but I started thinking about Jenny Lind's parents and how active they were when she first went missing. It seems like they were everywhere, and then suddenly they just disappeared,' she says. 'I always assumed it was because the media lost interest once the trail went cold and there were no new developments to follow. I mean, that probably was the case, but nothing stops existing just because the media turns its attention to something else.'

'That's true.'

'And then I started thinking about the polaroid of Mia, how the killer was communicating with me before he even abducted her . . . Are you sure he never got in touch with Jenny Lind's parents? Have you talked to them recently, since Mia's disappearance?'

Pamela hears Joona shift in his chair.

'They refuse to have any contact with the police,' he says. 'And I can understand that – we failed to find Jenny, and now she's dead.'

'But what if they didn't tell you everything? It's the same killer, after all; imagine if he threatened them, told them not to cooperate with the police . . . maybe that's why they went quiet.'

'I did actually have the same thought myself, but—'

'Maybe they were sent – I'm sorry for interrupting, but maybe they were sent a picture of Jenny before she disappeared. They might never have noticed the text on the back – the writing was really small.'

'The problem is that they hang up the minute they hear it's us,' Joona explains. 'They don't want anything to do with the police.'

'But what if I got in touch with them?' she blurts out.

'I imagine it'll be the same.'

'But I was thinking that . . . that if I could just get them to listen to me for a moment, they would realise that we're talking about another girl's life here.'

The minute Pamela hangs up, she pulls up the website for *Katrineholms Kuriren* website, the Lind family's local newspaper, and clicks on the 'In Memoriam' tab. She searches their notices and eventually finds Jenny Lind's obituary, along with the date and time of her memorial service.

54

When Mia woke on the concrete floor of the cage, the shaky journey in the back of the lorry had felt like a dream. Her mouth had been taped, her hands and feet bound with black cable ties. She had been out cold for much of the journey, and lost all sense of how long they had been driving before they finally came to a halt.

Her last clear memory is of sitting on the concrete block outside the petrol station.

She was waiting for Pontus when the lorry pulled up in front of her.

It was a trap.

The driver dropped his wallet to the ground and walked around the trailer.

Maybe it made no difference that she had crawled under the vehicle, maybe he would have grabbed her anyway. But as she lay on her stomach beneath the lorry, she was a sitting duck, with no chance of escaping or defending herself.

He hit her and held a rag to her face – maybe even injected her with something later.

She has no idea how she ended up in the cage.

Fragments of a yard and a row of long, narrow buildings without windows flutter through her mind as she tries to recall.

She was only half-conscious when she felt the strange chill of something being pressed against the back of her head.

A few hours later, her scalp began to tingle and itch, and for the next two days, it felt like she had burnt herself.

She has been branded, like all the others.

Mia is now lying on the dirty straw covering the concrete floor, using her rolled-up parka as a pillow. She raises her head slightly and sips water from a plastic bottle.

Her fingers still smell like burger.

The sun has risen, making the tin roof of the building creak as it heats. It got so hot in here yesterday that her temples started to throb. Her clothes were drenched in sweat, and only dried overnight.

'Isn't there an inspection today?' Mia asks.

'She's coming,' Kim replies.

'Both of you, shut up,' Blenda hisses from the other cage.

Through the bars, Mia peers out at the bright rectangle around the locked door at the far end of the building. Next to it is a bucket of bread and corn, and a medicine cabinet hangs on the wall.

She shares a cage with a 22-year-old named Kimball, or Kim for short. Her parents are from Mexico, but she was born and raised in Malmö. Kim plays handball, and was abducted as her team was making its way to a match.

She looks just like her mother, but her face is much thinner.

A polaroid of their family has been taped to the bars of each cage. The picture of Kim's mother was taken while she was in bed. She must have woken up just before the flash lit up the room, because her eyes are wide and her mouth is open as if she's confused and afraid.

The photo of Pamela was taken in the mirror through the gate of a lift.

Caesar clearly doesn't know that her application was rejected.

Mia has asked Kim, but she still doesn't know what this is all about, whether there is an underlying reason or purpose for holding them prisoner.

Granny seems to do everything for Caesar.

Sometimes she disappears in the lorry for an entire day.

Gauging from the brutality of the attack and the black leather jacket the assailant wore, Mia initially assumed it was a man who abducted her. She now knows it was Granny.

From time to time, she shows up with new girls.

None of them ever seems to be sold or passed on elsewhere. This is somewhere you stay until you die.

Kim has no idea how long Granny and Caesar have been doing this, but when she arrived two years ago, there was a woman called Ingeborg who had been here for seven years.

Life has been pretty much the same the whole time. Very little ever happens. A number of women are forced to live here against their will, and Caesar shows up in his grey Valiant a few times a month to rape a handful of them.

Until recently, some of the girls got to live in the big house, and were given expensive clothes and gold jewellery. But since Jenny Lind tried to escape, Caesar has become incredibly violent, locking them all up in cages.

Everyone knows that Caesar has contacts within the police, and Blenda says that Jenny probably called the police when she got to Stockholm because she thought she was safe in the city.

They have all seen the pictures from that rainy night when she was given her punishment. In the first photo, she seems to think she will be forgiven. After that, the images show her struggle, her wide eyes and taut mouth, the blood streaming down her throat, and, finally, the heavy limpness of her body.

Kim claims that Granny has changed. At first, she could be nice sometimes, calling the girls her titbits, but these days she is only ever strict and angry.

She carries a stick with a poisoned tip. One deep jab is enough to knock you out for several hours, but if you only get a scratch or if the ampoule isn't quite full, you just lose your vision for a while.

Mia asked whether they could try to influence Caesar, to rouse his sympathy and convince him to free them, but everyone says he is far worse than Granny. He's the one who makes the decisions, they say.

Just last week, he got angry and killed Amanda.

Kim started crying when she talked about it, repeating over and over again that it felt like a nightmare.

The dog starts barking outside, and a woman begins screaming uncontrollably in one of the other longhouses. Kim whimpers in fear, and Mia takes her hand.

258

'Everything will be OK if you put your faith in the Lord,' Blenda tells them.

Blenda is the oldest of the women, and is always trying to get them to adapt to their new lives in order to avoid suffering. She's a bit like a big sister, making sure they wash as well as they can, forcing them to eat and drink properly – no matter how bad it tastes.

Blenda shares a cage with a Romanian girl called Raluca. She can't speak Swedish, but she knows a few words in English and German. She calls Granny Baba Yaga, as though she knew her from before.

'Sit up, she's coming now,' Blenda tells them.

The squeaking of Granny's wheelbarrow draws closer and stops outside. The dog is panting, and Granny shovels some food into a trough.

'I always dreamed of having a granny,' Mia jokes.

'Shut up.'

'Baba Yaga,' Raluca whispers, shrinking back.

They can hear Granny lifting the bar from the brackets and leaning it against the wall before she opens the door and lets the blinding sunlight flood in.

Dust swirls through the air.

Granny carries the trough inside and puts it down on the counter. She grabs her stick and comes over to their cage, opening the door and letting the dog inside.

Kim is wearing a pair of dirty red tracksuit bottoms and a T-shirt with a picture of Lady Gaga. She parts her legs as the dog approaches.

Her eyes are downcast, her face blank.

The dog sniffs her and turns away, licking his nose before moving on to Mia.

She is sitting with her legs crossed, looking at Granny as the dog pushes his nose into her crotch and then leaves the cage.

Once the inspection is over, they say grace and are given some beans with dried elk meat and a piece of bread.

Mia and Kim are the first to be let out into the yard today.

Their wrists are bound together with thick plastic ties that cut into their skin. It feels strange to stand up and move around, but

they try to get as much exercise as possible before they have to return to the cage.

In the middle of the yard, there is a girl lying in the white bathtub. Granny claims that long baths are calming. The girl used to cry all night, but after two weeks in the bath she fell silent.

'If Jenny got all the way to Stockholm, it must be possible to escape,' says Mia.

'Don't even talk about it,' Kim whispers.

'But I'm not going to just hang around here, waiting to be raped.'

The ground is dry, and their shoes kick up a cloud of dust. They hold hands to prevent the plastic tie from breaking their skin.

'Has anyone here actually seen the infamous traps in the woods?' asks Mia.

'You don't understand anything yet.'

As they pass the girl in the tub, she stares up at them with a vacant look on her face. Beneath the surface of the water, her skin has turned spongey, peeling away from her feet and knees.

'We're different . . . You know your parents are never going to stop looking for you,' Mia tells Kim. 'But there's no one looking for me . . .'

55

Martin follows the orderly towards the day room and steps into the telephone booth. It is a small room, with a single window looking out onto the corridor. He closes the door, sits down and picks up the receiver.

'Hello,' he says.

'How are you doing?' asks Pamela.

'I'm OK,' he replies, lowering his voice slightly. 'And you?'

'A bit tired, I'm in bed with a cup of tea.'

He hears a soft rustling sound as she changes position.

'Technical drawings?' he says.

'You heard them crinkling? I miss you lying beside me, looking at them and asking me to explain my thinking.'

Martin opens the door to the telephone booth, peeking out to check that the corridor is empty before he continues.

'Have they found Primus?' he whispers.

'No, it doesn't sound like it.'

'I don't understand why I can't remember hearing him say those things.' Martin looks down at the scratched tabletop, the pencil stub and the crumpled sheet of paper.

'There's a funeral and memorial for Jenny Lind on Monday. I'm thinking about going,' Pamela tells him.

'Won't that be strange?'

'It might be, but there's something I'd like to ask her mother.'

'Is it about Mia?'

'I just want to ask a few direct questions. It's up to them whether they answer or not. I won't be able to live with myself if I don't do

everything I can,' she says. 'Would you like to come with me? I think it might do you good.'

'Why?'

'You don't have to if you don't think you're up to it. It might make them feel guilty to see you.'

Martin chuckles. 'I can put a Band-Aid on my nose to make them feel sorry for me.'

'It's nice to hear you laugh,' says Pamela.

Martin peeks out into the corridor again. The boys will punish him now, he thinks. They'll claim he was laughing at the fact that they don't have graves.

'I'll come if you want me to,' he says.

'Do you think your doctor will say it's OK?'

'As though I'd been committed . . .'

'I just think it might be a good idea to check with him, since it's a funeral – I don't want it to make you feel worse.'

'I can handle it. I need to get out of here.'

'Dennis will give us a lift.'

'He's the best.'

56

Joona follows a prison officer with a food trolley to cell 8404, then picks up the tray and steps inside.

The door swings shut behind him, the lock rattling.

He puts the tray of food on the table and starts the recording, stating the time, date and the names of those present.

Primus's sister, Ulrike Bengtsson, is sitting on the bed in front of him. She is wearing loose prison-issue clothes and has her arm in a sling. Her jewellery has been confiscated, and her greasy hair is slicked back, not a scrap of makeup on her slender face.

Ulrike has been married to Stefan Nicolic for thirty-five years, and doesn't have any children.

She looks up at Joona with sluggish eyes, as though she lacks the energy to close her lips around her crowded mouth of teeth.

Joona's grey shirt is tight over his chest and shoulders. His jacket is back in the car, and he's rolled up his sleeves to his elbows.

The cold air gives him goosebumps.

His forearms and hands are streaked with pale scars from parachute lines and knife attacks.

'I hope you've got someone to feed the birds for you,' he says.

'Stefan'll have to do it, they're his project. I've never understood how anyone can love birds, they're just ugly little dinosaurs to me . . . But he's a trained ornithologist – you should hear him once he gets going: "they're perfect", "imagine being able to fly", "they fill their skeletons with air when they breathe", blah blah blah.'

'And you run a tattoo parlour?' Joona asks.

'Yeah.'

'Business going well?'

She shrugs.

'Well, you had one customer, at least,' he says.

'What, Lena? She's not exactly a customer – she's Stefan's girlfriend. She wanted to surprise him with a tattoo.'

'Your husband's girlfriend?'

'She's welcome to him . . . I've sucked off Stefan so many times that it's had evolutionary consequences,' she says, baring her teeth.

Lena Stridssköld is the young woman who fell from the window, and the six-year-old boy is her son.

Neither was seriously harmed in the blast.

The boy was taken in by social services, and Lena was brought to Kronoberg Prison in Stockholm – just like Ulrike and the surviving bodyguard.

'You're going to be held in custody on suspicion of attempted murder,' Joona tells her.

'Seriously, come on,' she sighs. 'It was self-defence. You sneak into my home – what the hell am I supposed to think? It's not like you introduced yourselves or showed any ID . . . I thought I was about to be raped and have my feet sawn off.'

'But that's not what happened, is it?'

One of the officers from the National Task Force was shot in the head by a bodyguard with a semi-automatic shotgun and died immediately. Ten seconds later, the shooter was killed by the officer's partner. Aron is still in a serious but stable condition. Joona saved his life.

It transpired that Mia wasn't in the house after all, and Margot feels like she was deceived. The National Task Force have already filed a report against her, and there will be an internal investigation into the raid.

'You broke my collarbone,' Ulrike mutters, gesturing to her sling.

'It'll heal.'

'What, are you a doctor now?'

Joona lifts the two bowls of soup from the tray, sets out the spoons and the glasses, tears the plastic wrapper from the plates of cheese sandwiches, and spreads the napkins.

'Why don't we eat before it gets cold?' he asks.

Modern interview technique calls for a listening phase early on in the session. Joona gives it more weight than most.

He is attempting to get Ulrike to the stage where she has already said so much that there is no point in holding back the rest.

Joona eats a spoonful of soup, pauses and smiles at her. 'It's good,' he says.

She picks up her spoon, stirs and tastes. 'What can you offer me if I cooperate?' she asks, wiping the soup from her lips with the napkin.

'In what way are you prepared to cooperate?'

'I'll tell you everything if I can avoid prosecution and get a new identity.'

'What's everything?' Joona asks, picking up his sandwich.

'I've seen and heard a lot over the years,' she explains.

'We know that the Club is involved in drug trafficking, money laundering and extortion.'

'The usual,' she mutters, eating more soup.

'OK, but do you know whether they abduct young women?'

The spoon clinks against her crooked teeth. 'They're not into human trafficking, if that's what you're asking,' she replies.

'But Stefan could be hiding certain things from you.'

'He's just a nerd who made the wrong kind of friends as a kid; he thinks he looks cool when he puts his gun on the table before sitting down . . .'

Joona finishes off his sandwich and sips his apple juice. 'Do you know Jenny Lind?'

'Nope, who's that?'

'Your brother knows her.'

She looks up from her bowl. 'Primus?'

'Yes,' Joona replies, meeting her eye.

Her mouth has turned down in a frown as she lowers her head to eat.

'Have you ever heard of Mia Andersson?' Joona asks.

Ulrike doesn't reply, simply keeps eating. After a while, she tips the bowl to get at the last of the soup.

'I want everything in writing before I say any more,' she says, lowering her spoon.

'What?'

'That I'm not going to be charged, that I'll get a new identity, a new life.'

'We don't have that system in Sweden; there are no crown witnesses, you can't escape prosecution by testifying against someone else.'

'Am I supposed to feel tricked now?'

'Maybe by yourself.'

'Wouldn't be the first time,' she mumbles.

Joona starts to clear the table. He knows she's realised she has already told him a fair amount of the truth. She simply needs to accept that this isn't a negotiation. It's one-sided.

'Shall we take a break?'

Joona remembers something the philosopher Michel Foucault once wrote, that the truth is not part of the order of power; it is bound up with freedom.

Confession is liberation.

'I tried to kill the cop who came into my studio,' she says, her voice subdued. 'I stabbed him in the neck and then I tried to stab you in the stomach.'

'Who are you afraid of?' he asks, pushing their paper napkins into one of the plastic cups. 'Is it Stefan Nicolic?'

'Stefan? What are you talking about?'

'All the lights were off in the house . . . you had a knife in the shower with you, and two bodyguards.'

'Doesn't everyone?' She smiles.

'Are you scared of Primus?'

'Are you sure you're really a detective?'

He stacks her bowl on top of his, places both spoons inside, and leans back.

'First, you wanted a new identity, and now you want to stay in prison,' Joona tells her. 'I might be able to help if you tell me who you're afraid of.'

266

She brushes a few crumbs from the table with one hand and then sits quietly for a moment or two, eyes downcast, before looking up at him.

'There's a man called Caesar,' she says.

Ulrike shakes her right foot, making her prison-issue slipper fall to the floor, then bends down and pulls off her sock. Just above her ankle, a wound loops around her leg. It looks like it has only recently been tended to, but the blood between the swollen edges has turned black, and the line of stitches make the gash look like barbed wire.

'He hid under my bed and crawled out in the middle of the night to take pictures of me.'

'Caesar?'

'I was asleep, and only woke up when he tried to saw my foot off . . . At first I didn't know what was going on, it just hurt so fucking much . . . I started shouting and hitting him, trying to push him away, but I couldn't do it, and he just kept sawing . . . the whole bed was covered in blood . . . I don't know how, but I managed to reach my personal alarm. He only stopped when it started wailing. He just tossed the saw to the floor, left a polaroid on the bedside table and ran off . . . Christ . . . I mean, who does that? You know? He must be out of his fucking mind, hiding under people's beds and trying to saw their feet off.'

'Did you see him?'

'It was dark.'

'But you must have got some kind of impression of him?'

'No idea, it was the middle of the night. I thought I was going to die.'

She gingerly pulls her sock back on.

'What happened once he left?'

'I pulled a belt tight around my leg to stop the bleeding . . . The security company showed up way before the ambulance, but by then Caesar was gone . . . There was a plastic bag under the bed, full of the tools he'd brought.'

'What kind of tools?'

'I don't know, I saw one of the guards take out some screwdrivers and something with a handle and a bit of steel wire.'

'A winch?'

'I don't know.'

'Where is this plastic bag now?'

'Stefan took care of it.'

'How do you know about Caesar?'

'Primus told me about him, afterwards. Stefan's convinced he's part of a rival gang – that's why we've got the bodyguards and all those guns.'

'But Caesar isn't someone you've met or heard of before?'

'No.'

'So what did Primus say about him? How do they know each other?'

'They got in touch over social media somehow . . . they share the same view of society, you know?'

'Doesn't sound like a rival gang.'

'I know, but Stefan's convinced. He told me and Lena we'd be raped.'

'And what do you think about all of this?'

Ulrike's face is weary, solemn. 'At first, Primus said Caesar was a king, but after what happened, he seemed scared. He burnt his phone in my microwave.'

'And you're so afraid of Caesar that you want to stay in prison?'

'He told Primus he'd saw off my head next time.'

'Why is he threatening you?'

'To punish Primus. He's always talking about how beautiful I am – it's just one of those things that goes around in his head. I mean, I was cute as a little girl, but that definitely passed.'

'And why does Caesar want to punish your brother?'

'I guess Primus made some promises he couldn't keep. He's always talking too much, just like me right now.'

'It's good that you're telling the truth.'

'For who?'

'You'll be safe in custody, and if you help me find Primus, I might be able to stop Caesar.'

'Find Primus?'

'Where does he live when he's not in the ward?'

'I don't know.'

'Does he stay at your place?'

'Stefan said no. He sleeps wherever he can – with friends, in stairwells, on the metro . . . though the Eagle's Nest is open today, so he'll be there.'

'The Eagle's Nest?'

'What, did that one pass the pigs by? You guys really are the best and brightest.' She smiles. 'It's where a bunch of people get together to lose all their money on – well, it used to be cockfighting. Guess who came up with that idea? But, like I said, most people aren't as interested in birds as Stefan, so these days it's mostly MMA and dog fights . . .'

'Where can I find this place?'

'Down by the docks, the southern dock in Södertälje. There's a freight company with a warehouse and loading area down there . . . Stefan's got a deal with the security firm.'

'And you think Primus will be at the Eagle's Nest?'

Ulrike leans back in her chair, arms folded. The dark circles beneath her eyes seem to have deepened, and she looks exhausted.

'Unless he's dead or locked up on a psych ward, he'll definitely be there.'

57

Martin avoids Pamela's eyes in the mirror as the lift carries them downstairs. His face seems so lonely to her, almost defenceless. The lights flicker as the lift slows and stops on the ground floor.

The doors open.

Martin picks his backpack up from the floor and slings the straps over one shoulder.

They walk out through the lobby together.

Dennis is waiting behind his car in the roundabout, wearing a charcoal suit and a pair of sunglasses.

'It's been a while,' he says, shaking Martin's hand.

'I know.'

'Good to see you.'

'Same,' Martin mumbles, glancing back over his shoulder.

'It's so nice of you to drive us,' Pamela tells Dennis as they walk towards the car.

'Pamela got a bit *Fast and Furious* recently,' Dennis jokes.

'I heard,' Martin replies.

'So how do you feel about leaving the ward?' Dennis asks him, taking his backpack.

'Good.'

He puts the bag into the boot and closes the lid.

'Do you want to sit in the front, Martin?' Pamela asks.

'I don't mind either way.'

'Go ahead. The two of you can talk,' she says.

Dennis opens the passenger side door for Martin, and waits until he is sitting comfortably before closing it and opening the back door for Pamela.

'Feeling OK?' he asks, his voice low.

'I think so.'

Before she has time to climb into the car, Dennis wraps his arms around her from behind and kisses the nape of her neck.

She anxiously squirms away from him and sits down, her heart racing.

Dennis closes the door and walks around to the driver's side, starting the ignition and pulling away from the psychiatric ward.

Pamela will have to talk to Dennis about not doing that kind of thing.

She looks out at the buildings speeding by and wonders whether she gave him the wrong idea when she called to ask for a ride. Maybe he mistook her energy for flirtation.

The traffic slows to a crawl on the bridges over Lilla and Stora Essingen. Fumes from the exhaust pipes and heat rising from the tarmac make the air thick and lifeless.

They are stuck behind a tanker, and someone has drawn an enormous penis in the dirt on its cylindrical tank. Pamela has always wondered what kind of person feels the urge to do that.

The traffic thins out as they pass Södertälje, and they gradually pick up speed as the suburbs, noise barriers and sports fields flash by.

'How did you like the hypnosis session?' Dennis asks Martin.

'I don't know, I just wanted to help, but I've been feeling a bit anxious ever since . . .'

'I can understand that – I guarantee hypnosis is not good for you.'

'But maybe I'm mixing it up with the ECT,' Martin continues, rubbing his nose.

'Martin, I commend your willingness to help the police, of course you should. But don't commit to any more hypnosis, that's all I'm saying,' Dennis tells him. 'You either remember or you don't . . . and trying to dig up repressed memories can easily turn into memories of things that never actually happened.'

'I remembered what Primus said, though.'

'But if the memories that come to you during hypnosis are real, they're there without hypnosis too . . . and then at least you know they aren't the product of suggestion.'

A taxi with a broken tail light cuts in just ahead of them and Dennis has to brake hard, making the seat belt cut into Pamela's shoulder.

It's incredible that Martin has started speaking in full sentences. Pamela wonders what the real source of this change was: the electric shocks, the hypnosis or the fact that he is trying to help the police find Mia.

'All I remember is taking the dog out in the rain,' he says.

Pamela leans forward between the seats. 'But you also drew a picture of what you saw when you got home,' she says.

'I don't remember that either.'

'No, but it proves you saw Jenny, at the very least. You might not have seen the murder, but you did see her hanging there.'

'You say that, but . . .'

'I just want you to really try to remember,' she tells him, leaning back again.

'I am. I'm trying, but it's all just black.'

58

The cool air inside the church smells like stone. Pamela sits down beside Martin and Dennis on an empty pew just before the ceremony begins.

The funeral is small, only family and close friends in attendance. There are no more than twenty people sitting on the creaking wooden benches.

Pamela catches a glimpse of Jenny Lind's parents at the very front of the church. As the bells ring out, she sees Jenny's father's back shaking with tears.

The summer sun moves slowly over the walls as the ceremony continues, making the stained glass in the choir glow.

Despite his best efforts to provide comfort and hope, the priest's sermon feels too subdued. Jenny Lind's mother has buried her face in her hands, and Pamela shudders at the thought that the girl was taken just a few minutes from where her coffin now lies.

She feels sick with anxiety hearing the soft patter of the priest sprinkling a cross of earth onto the lid of the coffin.

This is the first memorial she has been to since Alice's.

Martin takes her hand and squeezes it.

Pamela lowers her head and keeps her eyes firmly shut during the final psalm, and when the music stops, she hears Jenny's family stand up from their pews. She composes herself, opens her eyes and sees them moving forward in a slow line to leave flowers on the coffin.

* * *

The air outside the church is hot and almost too humid to breathe.

Two women are talking to the priest, a man in a wheelchair is waiting to be picked up, and a young girl is kicking up dust in the gravel.

Jenny's father has already taken his seat in the car, but her mother is still standing by the doorway, accepting people's condolences.

Pamela waits until the last few mourners have left the church before dragging Martin over to Jenny's mother.

Linnea Lind's face is frozen in an expression of permanent grief, her eyes puffy from crying.

'I'm so sorry for your loss,' Pamela tells her.

'Thank you,' Linnea replies, fixing her eyes on Martin. 'Aren't you . . . I . . . I'm so sorry for what my husband did.'

'Don't worry,' Martin replies, looking down at the ground.

'It's so unlike Bengt, he's usually very quiet.'

A handful of people are still lingering between the church and the car park.

'I know this isn't the right moment,' says Pamela, 'but I'd really like to talk to you sometime. Maybe I could call you tomorrow?'

'Come to the wake.'

'Thank you, but . . .'

'I heard you lost a daughter the same year Jenny disappeared . . . so you know what it's like. It's not easy.'

'You never get over it.'

* * *

Everyone attending the wake drives the short distance back to Linnea and Bengt's building and parks in the guest spaces outside.

'What are you going to do?' Pamela asks Dennis as she and Martin climb out of the car.

'I'll wait here,' he says. 'Need to reply to a few emails anyway.'

The small group steps into the pale-yellow apartment complex and takes the lift to the fifth floor.

Pamela follows Linnea to the kitchen and attempts to say something about how beautiful the ceremony was.

'It was, wasn't it,' Linnea replies flatly.

She switches on the coffee machine, opening a few packs of biscuits with shaky movements.

On the coffee table in the living room, there is an old-fashioned tea service, with small cups on matching saucers, a bowl of sugar cubes, a jug of milk and a three-tiered cake stand.

The old sofa creaks as the guests sit down.

There are little trinkets and holiday souvenirs everywhere, along with potted plants and crocheted tablecloths.

Bengt brings in four chairs from the kitchen and invites everyone to take a seat.

They attempt to make small talk, but the conversation keeps faltering. A spoon clinks against a coffee cup. Someone mentions the heatwave, and someone else tries to joke about climate change.

Eventually, Linnea holds up a framed photograph of her daughter and tries to say a few words about all the things that made Jenny different and special.

'All feminism and vegan food . . . everything that was wrong with us and our generation. We used the wrong words and our car ran on fossil fuels, and . . . oh, I just miss it so much . . .' She trails off, tears streaming down her cheeks. Her husband rubs her back.

When an elderly woman gets up and announces that she has to get home to take the dog out, the others all take the opportunity to thank their hosts and leave as well.

Linnea tells them to leave everything on the table, but they carry their cups to the kitchen anyway.

'Is everyone leaving?' Pamela whispers to Martin.

They hear voices from the hallway as guests make their goodbyes, then the sound of the front door closing and a moment of silence before Linnea and Bengt reappear.

'Maybe we should get going too,' Pamela tells them.

'You aren't going already, are you?' Bengt asks in a gravelly voice.

He opens a cupboard and takes out two bottles and four glasses, pouring vodka for himself and Martin, and cherry liqueur for the women.

'Martin, I want you to know that I'm sorry I hit you,' he says, pushing the glass over to him. 'There's no excuse, but I thought . . . well, you

275

know. And when I finally saw you in person, something inside me just snapped . . .' He empties his glass, and his face screws up as he feels the burn of the alcohol and clears his throat. 'Anyway, I'm really sorry . . . and I hope you'll accept my apology.'

Martin nods and glances over to Pamela, as though he wants her to reply for him.

'It was all the police's fault,' she says. 'Martin isn't well, and they tricked him into confessing to things he didn't actually do.'

'I thought that . . . you know,' says Bengt. 'Not that I'm trying to excuse myself . . .'

'No,' she says.

'Would you shake my hand?' Bengt asks, looking up at Martin.

Martin nods and holds out his hand, but seems slightly startled when Bengt takes it in his.

'Can we put all this behind us?'

'That works for me,' Martin says quietly.

Pamela pretends to sip her cherry liqueur and lowers the glass to the table. 'Did you hear that he's taken another girl?' she asks.

'Mia Andersson,' Linnea says immediately.

'It makes you feel sick,' Bengt mutters.

'I know,' Pamela whispers.

'But you saw him, didn't you?' asks Bengt. 'You were there, weren't you, Martin?'

'It was too dark,' Pamela explains.

'What do the police have to say about the whole thing?' Linnea asks.

'To us? Not much,' Pamela tells her.

'No, of course,' Bengt sighs. He picks up a crumb from the table and drops it into his mouth.

'There is one thing I've been wondering,' Pamela goes on. 'When he took Jenny, did he ever get in touch with you?'

'No, what do you mean?' Linnea asks anxiously.

'No letters or phone calls?'

'No, it . . .'

'He's just a madman,' says Bengt, looking away.

'But did he try to contact you before she disappeared?'

'I don't understand.' Linnea frowns.

'I might have misunderstood, but I think he took a photo of Mia – the girl who's gone missing – as a kind of warning,' Pamela explains, feeling like she is getting tangled up in her own words.

'No, nothing like that,' Linnea replies, setting her glass down harder than she meant to. 'Everyone said it was just an unhappy coincidence that our Jenny was walking home from school as the lorry drove past.'

'Mmm.' Pamela nods.

'The police were sure he only decided to take her when he saw her that day,' she continues, her voice shaking. 'But that's not what happened, it wasn't random. I tried to tell them that – I know I'd said all kinds of things, that I was angry and upset, but they still could've listened.'

'Yeah,' Bengt adds, filling his glass again.

'What makes you say it wasn't random?' Pamela asks, leaning in.

'Several years later, I found Jenny's diary. She'd hidden it under her bed, and I only found it when we moved here . . . I called the police, but by then it was too late, no one cared.'

'What did she write?' Pamela asks, looking her in the eye.

'Jenny was scared. She tried to talk to us, but we didn't listen,' Linnea replies, tears welling up in her eyes. 'It wasn't random, it was planned; he'd chosen Jenny, he had followed her Instagram account. He'd been spying on her, so he knew which way she came home when school was over.'

'She wrote all that?'

'He'd been in our house too, watching her, taking underwear from her chest of drawers,' Linnea continues. 'One night when we got home from salsa class, Jenny had locked herself in the bathroom . . . She was a total mess, and instead of figuring out where all this was coming from I banned her from watching any more horror films.'

'I would have done the same,' Pamela says quietly.

'But in her diary, I read what she'd actually been through. This was before we moved to the apartment and we were still in our house, and she was doing her homework in the kitchen as it got dark outside. We had a little lamp in the window, but it wasn't turned on . . . You know what it's like – if the lights aren't on inside, you can see out

into the garden even after dark – and she thought she saw someone standing between the trees.'

Pamela nodded.

'She thought she was just imagining it, that she was just scaring herself, so she turned on the light in the window . . . but when she did that, she saw the man clearly. They stared at each other for a moment, and then he turned and was gone . . . It took her a few seconds to realise that if she could see him when the light was on, then the window was acting as a kind of mirror – he must have been standing right behind her in the kitchen.'

59

Joona is walking through the muggy air beneath Centralbron. Cars whizz past in both lanes, and exhaust fumes linger around him. Filthy clothes and sleeping bags line the concrete abutment, mixing with the empty cans, discarded crisp packets and old needles.

Joona's phone is already in his hand when it starts ringing. It's Pamela Nordström.

Her voice is shrill and agitated as she recounts her meeting with Jenny Lind's parents and the revelations from Jenny's diary.

'He was right there in the kitchen behind her,' she says. 'Their eyes only met for a few seconds, and she didn't describe his face, but he was wearing a dirty coat with a black fur collar and green rubber boots.'

'Did you read the diary yourself?'

'Yes, but that's all she wrote about him. Though in several places she did say that she felt like someone was watching her . . . and this is the interesting part: one night, a bright light woke her up, but when she opened her eyes, the room was dark . . . She was convinced someone had been taking photos of her while she slept, that it was the flash that woke her up.'

Lead-grey dust swirls up from the kerb as a bus passes on the road.

'I've always struggled to believe that his victims were chosen on impulse,' Joona says. 'He must have seen them somewhere . . . and clearly started stalking them.'

'Yeah.'

'We haven't found Primus yet, but we need to speak to Martin again, if he's willing.'

'He wants to help, he keeps saying that, but a friend of ours – a psychologist – doesn't think we should agree to any more hypnosis. He worries that it could be detrimental to Martin.'

'Then we'll try without hypnosis,' Joona tells her, hanging up.

The echo of his footsteps fades as he emerges into the evening sun on the quay. A musty smell rises up from the water flowing slowly by.

The flags hang limply on their poles, and even the leaves of the aspen trees are still.

Joona walks along the water past the parliament building, looking down at Strömparterren Park and remembering the cold water all those years ago.

When he reaches Operakällan, a waiter in the restaurant leads Joona through the grand dining room, past a gold screen and onto the glass veranda with views out onto the water and the palace.

He spots Margot sitting at a secluded table with the head of the security services, Verner Zandén, the chief prosecutor Lars Tamm, and county police chief, Gösta Carlén.

Their champagne glasses are raised mid-toast when Joona reaches them.

'There was no need for you to come down here, Joona – the answer is still no,' Margot says before he even has time to speak. 'No one has even heard of the Eagle's Nest. I just asked both Verner and Lars here, and I also talked to Team 2022 and CID.'

'And yet it seems like it does exist,' Joona says, standing his ground.

'Everyone here is familiar with the case, up to the catastrophic raid on the villa that certain people claimed was so fucking necessary.'

'Three women have been abducted – two of whom have already been found murdered . . .' Joona trails off and steps to one side as the waiters arrive with their first course and top off their glasses.

He knows he has to tread carefully with his request. By now it is common knowledge that Margot ordered them to enter the house before backup arrived, and that it was this decision that led to their losses that night.

'Grilled duck liver with a licorice and ginger sauce,' the waitress announces. '*Bon appétit.*'

'Thank you,' says Verner.

'Sorry to eat while we talk,' says Lars. 'But we're giving Gösta a send-off – he's going to Europol.'

'It's my fault. I wouldn't be interrupting if it wasn't so urgent,' says Joona.

He stands quietly as they begin their meal, waiting until Margot looks up before continuing.

'The background is that our eyewitness, Martin Nordström, overheard a phone call between Primus and a man by the name of Caesar,' he explains. 'They were discussing Jenny Lind and the playground just a few days before the murder.'

'That much we know,' says Verner, coating a piece of duck liver in sauce.

'And you still think that Primus, or this Caesar man, killed Jenny Lind – correct?' asks Margot.

'I think it was Caesar.'

'But you're looking for Primus?' she says, dabbing her mouth with a napkin.

'What makes you think it was Caesar?' asks Verner.

'He punished Ulrike Bengtsson when Primus failed to blindly follow his orders . . . he turned up at her home in the middle of the night and tried to saw off one of her legs.'

Lars Tamm spears a piece of baked onion on his fork, but can't quite bring himself to raise it to his mouth.

'Does he fit the profile of our killer?' asks Gösta.

'He had a winch with him.'

'Then it's him,' Verner says firmly.

They pause for a moment when a waiter arrives to clear the table, brushing crumbs onto a silver plate and topping up their water glasses.

'What do we know about Caesar?' Margot asks once he's left.

'Nothing,' Joona tells her. 'There's no one in any of the databases that fits his description. If Caesar is his real name, then he's never been admitted to the psychiatric care facility where Martin and Primus sometimes are, and he hasn't worked in the system either . . . and there's no one with that name in Stefan's biker gang or in any of its rival organisations.'

'A complete unknown,' Gösta mumbles.

'I need to find Primus because he's the only one who can tell us who Caesar is,' Joona explains.

'Sounds logical,' Verner agrees in his deep voice.

'Primus is homeless, but his sister says you can always find him at the Eagle's Nest.'

Soundlessly, the waiters reappear, serving cold Riesling and oven-baked zander with roasted broccoli cream and pickled kohlrabi.

'Shall we try the wine?' asks Margot.

They each pick up their glass, share a casual toast, and sip.

'Very nice,' says Verner.

'Either way, you don't have enough evidence to call out the National Task Force,' Margot tells Joona.

'Yes, we should probably exercise caution in our dealings with them for a while,' Gösta mumbles.

'I'll go in undercover, then,' says Joona.

'Undercover,' Margot repeats, sighing.

'I'll find Primus if you authorise this.'

'Excuse me, but I doubt that.' She smiles.

'Besides, it's too dangerous,' Verner points out, taking another sip of his wine.

'We don't have any other option,' Joona explains. 'The Eagle's Nest is only open tonight. After today, we'll have to scour the city's stairwells and stations until he shows up at the psych ward again . . . and that could take months if he follows his usual pattern.'

'I'm still trying to make sense of this,' says Lars, putting down his cutlery. 'Does the Club order kidnappings and murders from Primus and Caesar?'

'I don't think so,' Joona replies.

'But the Club does sell drugs and organise gambling . . . And they increase their profits massively through their illegal loan business.'

'The usual,' says Verner.

'But to keep the whole thing going, they have to make sure the debts are actually collected,' Lars continues. 'If there's the slightest chance that someone won't pay, the whole business collapses.'

'But kidnapping young women sounds a bit over the top,' Margot points out.

'Not for them,' Lars argues. 'They just see it as a last resort for getting the money they're owed.'

'Regardless of the underlying causes,' says Joona, 'right now, there's only one person who can help move the investigation forward.'

'Primus,' says Verner.

'And why should we think that Primus will be there?' asks Margot.

'His sister says he never misses the Eagle's Nest,' says Joona.

'And if you do find him, how do you plan on getting him out of there?'

'I'll come up with something.'

'You have a tendency to improvise when . . .'

They pause again as the waiter returns to clear the table.

'Very good,' Gösta tells him quietly.

'Thank you,' the waiter replies before disappearing.

All eyes are on Margot as she slowly turns her wine glass in her hand. The refracted light spills across the white tablecloth.

'Running an undercover operation tonight feels a bit hasty,' she says, looking up at Joona. 'And it probably won't even lead us to Primus.'

'I'll find him,' Joona insists.

'But I'm not convinced . . . I always say that we should trust routine police work, the big, slow machinery.'

'But tonight's the only night . . .'

'Just hang tight, Joona. There'll be more nights at the Eagle's Nest, and then—'

'By then Mia Andersson might be dead,' he says, cutting her off.

Margot gives him a stern look. 'If you interrupt me again, I'll take you off this case.'

'OK.'

'Do you understand what I'm saying?'

'Yes, I do.'

An uncomfortable silence follows. Gösta tries to steer the conversation elsewhere by saying a few awkward words about

renovating a waterfront cabin on Muskö, but gives up when no one replies.

It is still unpleasantly quiet when their next course arrives. The waiter quickly tells them that they have Gotland lamb fillets with a ragù of lentils, hazelnuts and red wine from the western coast of the Gironde bay in Bordeaux.

'We'd like to continue with our meal now,' Margot tells Joona, picking up her cutlery.

'Can we talk again later, to discuss the plan?' Joona asks her. 'I only need a small team. We'll go in, keep a low profile, isolate Primus from the others and arrest him.'

As Margot raises her fork to point at him, a drop of sauce lands on her shoe.

'You're a smart man, Joona, but I've found your weakness,' she says. 'Once you get hooked on a case, you make yourself vulnerable because you're incapable of letting go. You're willing to do anything – break the law, lose your job, even die.'

'Is that a weakness?' he asks.

'I'm saying no to an undercover operation tonight.'

'But I need to . . .'

'Did you just interrupt me?' she snaps.

'No.'

'Listen, Joona,' she says slowly. 'I'm not Carlos, I have no intention of losing my job because of you. I need you to understand that I'm your boss, and that if I give you an order, you have to obey it, even if you don't agree with it.'

'I do.'

'Good.'

'You've got some sauce on your shoe,' Joona tells her. 'Do you want me to wipe it off?'

When she fails to reply, he grabs a white napkin from a serving trolley and gets onto his knees in front of her.

'This isn't funny,' Verner speaks up.

'I have to object,' says Gösta, sounding stressed.

Joona carefully wipes away the sauce and then polishes the rest of her shoe.

Someone mumbles unhappily at a neighbouring table; and everyone on the veranda has stopped talking. Lars's eyes suddenly look glossy, and Verner is staring down at the table.

With no sense of urgency whatsoever, Joona moves on to the next shoe, polishing it before getting to his feet and folding the napkin.

'You can have two people,' Margot tells him coolly, cutting into her dish. 'Tonight only. I don't want anything to go wrong, and I want you to report back to me tomorrow morning.'

'Thanks,' Joona replies, turning to leave.

60

Riding side by side, three motorcyclists drive through the industrial area in Södertälje's southern harbour, passing the petrol stations, lorry depots and logistics companies that line the southern harbour.

The roar of their one-cylinder engines ricochets between the flat facades of the buildings.

The night air is warm and humid. Looming on the other side of the bay is the huge heat and power plant.

Joona is on the centre motorcycle, flanked by two colleagues.

Their job is to infiltrate the Eagle's Nest, find Primus and pull him out of view to arrest him without drawing any attention to themselves.

Four hours earlier, Joona took Edgar Jansson and Laura Stenhammar through the plan for the evening.

He has never worked with either of them before, but he remembers Laura being removed from active duty with the Norrmalm Police a decade ago for throwing a hand grenade into a van carrying an amphetamine lab. After that, she was recruited to Säpo's constitutional defence unit, where she worked on identifying and infiltrating extremist groups.

Edgar is only twenty-five, but he works undercover for the drugs squad across the Stockholm region.

Each of the three has managed to obtain identity documents, money and a Husqvarna Vitpilen – a 700cc-engine motorcycle.

They have all changed their clothes for the operation too.

Laura was wearing a crocheted tunic when they met earlier that day, but is now in a pair of tight leather trousers, biker boots and a white tank top.

Edgar has swapped his pale-brown trousers and checked sweater for black jeans, cowboy boots and a ripped denim jacket.

Joona is wearing a pair of black and white camouflage trousers, bulky boots and a black T-shirt.

Laura was able to secure from one of her informants a key card that should function as some kind of entry pass to the Eagle's Nest.

They have studied the pictures of Primus Bengtsson and Stefan Nicolic and can now recognise them by sight. They've also pored over satellite images of the harbour to familiarise themselves with the relative positions of the buildings and roads, the high fences and docks, plus the loading area for shipping containers.

Three officers from the Special Operations Unit are waiting in a rigid inflatable boat on the canal, and can be at the harbour by the Eagle's Nest in under five minutes if Joona and the others find Primus.

The three of them pass beneath the high railway bridge and follow a fence covered in signs warning about security companies and nearby CCTV.

The motorcycles slow down in front of the gate to a loading terminal for containers and bulk cargo.

Laura takes out her key card and swipes it through a reader attached to a fencepost, feeling a mix of nervousness and relief as the gates swing open.

They roll inside, coming to a stop in a parking area that is already full of enormous motorcycles. From a hangar-like building nearby, they can hear shouting and noise.

'Put a tracker on Primus if you get a chance, but don't take any risks; give it time,' Joona repeats as they walk towards the door.

The plan is to split up and discreetly search for Primus.

The night sky is bright, but the area is still fairly dark, untouched by the harsh shadows from artificial light.

The three officers walk along the rusty train tracks on the concrete dock.

A group of bearded, tattooed men in leather vests is moving towards the security check in front of them.

Edgar smiles stiffly, straightening his denim jacket.

They follow the line over to the entrance. Laura unties her hair, letting her henna red locks spill down over her bare shoulders. There are four bouncers with assault rifles guarding the entrance.

The stocky man in front of them hands over his gun and receives a receipt, which he stuffs into his wallet.

From the hangar, the sound of shouting and clapping is louder now, like waves crashing in against the shore.

On the other side of the checkpoint, a tall blonde woman is greeting people, handing out drinks tickets which appear to be individual frames of film.

'Good luck,' she says, holding Joona's eye.

'Thanks.'

* * *

Inside the building, it's much darker. There is a crowd of people around a raised boxing ring in the middle of the hangar. A bell rings out, and the two boxers return to their corners. Both are breathing heavily, and the white tape around their hands is bloody at the knuckles.

The three officers force their way over to the bar, which is surrounded by tattooed arms, shaved heads, black leather, beards and pierced ears.

'I love cosplay,' Laura mumbles drily.

The floor is wet, littered with plastic cups, discarded snuff and spent drinks tickets.

As Laura holds up one of the frames of film to the light above the bar, she realises it's porn: a woman being penetrated by a dildo on a long pole, attached to some kind of machine.

They each exchange a square of film for a beer, then push back through the crowd, splitting up.

The boxing ring is illuminated, people thronging towards it, the faces of those at the front catching the light above.

Joona moves closer to the match.

He hears a series of rapid thuds as one fighter attacks the other. A bookie with long hair and a round brimmed hat moves through the crowd, taking bets.

On the other side of the hangar, the doors onto the dock are wide open. Swallows swoop deep into the building, hunting for insects.

Joona watches the two boxers for a moment, and ascertains who will win.

He glances back over to security at the entrance and to the bar, but can no longer see either of his colleagues.

One floor up, along one side of the hangar, there is an office with huge windows looking out onto the space. Joona can make out a number of people in the warm light inside, silhouettes moving behind the glass.

The man in the blue corner of the ring shouts something, delivering a low kick followed by a quick roundhouse to the cheek.

The other man's head sways, and he staggers to the side, dazed. He reaches the ropes and ducks away just as the round comes to an end.

The bookie in the bowler hat moves from person to person, quickly gathering bets and handing over receipts.

'Red corner to win on knockout,' Joona tells him when their eyes meet.

'That's 6/4,' he replies.

'OK.'

The man hands Joona a receipt for his bet before moving on.

The boxer in the red corner spits blood into a bucket. The air smells like sweat and liniment. His opponent pushes his mouth guard back into his mouth.

The bell rings again.

Their bare feet thud against the floor.

Joona systematically works his way through the crowd, looking carefully at every face, making sure he doesn't miss Primus.

Everyone is focused on the boxers.

On the floor behind the blue corner, he notices a thin man in a black sweatshirt, his hood up. Joona can't see his face, but he doesn't seem to be reacting to the match at all.

Joona starts pressing his way over to him.

The crowd roars, raising their arms.

The boxer in the red corner issues a barrage of hard jabs to the other's ribs.

Joona is shoved aside, and loses sight of the man in the hoodie.

The boxer in the blue corner backs up, trying to protect his ribs with his elbow. His hands dip slightly as the other man rolls beneath his jabs.

There is a smacking sound, like someone clapping their wet palms.

A right hook hits the blue boxer square on the cheek, making him reel to the side. One of his knees gives way as another right hook hits his temple. He crashes to the floor.

Joona pushes ahead, watching through the crowd's raised arms as the boxer in red stamps on his opponent's face.

The crowd cheers, a few people start to clap.

A half-empty beer is thrown into the ring, frothing as it splashes across the canvas. Joona can no longer see the man in the hood.

The vast majority of the crowd have thrown their betting slips to the floor.

Joona studies every face as he goes to hand in his receipt and collect his winnings.

He glances up towards the office again and sees a man who could be Stefan Nicolic standing in the window, looking down at the ring. He isn't much more than a silhouette, but some of the warm light behind him reaches his face.

61

Edgar leaves Laura at the bar. He spots Joona in the crowd by the boxing ring, and makes his way deeper into the hangar.

He follows the stream of people through the open doors, out onto the dock.

Somewhere nearby, a dog is barking aggressively.

Edgar scans the crowd for Primus, passing a long line of porta-loos and walking through a loading area for shipping containers.

He sees a thin man in a leather vest throwing up onto the lid of a rubbish bin. His jeans are drenched in urine, and Edgar has time to notice the track marks on both arms before he looks away.

Barges and cargo ships are moored along the dock.

Everyone seems to be moving towards a large warehouse with a vaulted roof. The doors are wide open, and he can hear shouting and barking from inside.

Edgar passes a large loader and follows the stream of people into the enormous warehouse.

It turns out to be a road salt depot. Inside, the floor almost looks like it's buried beneath a layer of snow.

The rear half of the space is full of firmly packed salt, reaching up to the yellowed Plexiglas ceiling some fifteen metres above the floor. Towards the front of the depot, there is a rectangular pen made from linked riot fences. The floor is white, with deep tyre tracks and salt piled up in drifts by the walls.

Fifty or so men are jostling around the fenced-off area.

There are cages of fighting dogs with muscular necks and jaws, restless and aggressive.

Edgar starts scanning the agitated faces in the crowd for Primus.

Through the throng, he sees one of the dog trainers step out into the pen. He is holding the dog's leash and collar with both hands, shuffling forward as the dog strains against its back legs, rearing up into the air.

An intense round of betting is currently underway, and the men in the audience are all shouting and pointing. The dogs bark, pulling so hard on their leashes that they start wheezing.

A judge in a checked coat holds up his hand.

The trainer unclips the leash but keeps hold of the dog's collar, shouting something as it drags him another few steps forward.

Edgar can't see the other half of the pen, but he assumes the second trainer is doing something similar.

The judge counts down and lowers his hand.

Both trainers let go of their dogs, and the animals lunge forward, snapping and growling, trying to sink their teeth into each other.

The crowd, in an uproar, presses up against the fence.

Both dogs are up on their hind legs, kicking up dust as they lean on the other's shoulders, biting repeatedly.

The dark brown dog manages to bite down on the other's ear, pulling and shaking his head with no sign of letting go. They drop down on all fours again, circling one another, blood dripping onto the white floor.

The lighter of the two dogs is whimpering.

Their stomachs rise and fall in time with their rushed breathing.

The dark brown dog still has its jaws clamped on to the other's ear, and keeps thrashing its head side to side. It tears off a piece of flesh and runs away with it.

The man beside Edgar laughs.

Heart racing, Edgar pushes forward. Right then, he spots Primus towards the rear of the depot. There is no doubt about it – he recognises him immediately from the photographs: that narrow face, the crooked teeth, the long grey hair.

He is wearing a red leather jacket, and seems to be having a heated discussion with a shorter man.

The trainers shout and the dogs snarl, lunging at each other again.

The lighter of the two dogs falls, landing on its back with the other dog on top of it.

Edgar sees Primus hand a thick envelope to the other man, who gives him a few notes back as a tip.

The dark brown dog has its jaws locked around the other dog's throat.

The crowd has started shouting.

The pale dog is trembling, bracing its legs against the other in panic, but the darker dog refuses to let go.

The scene is so upsetting that Edgar's eyes well up as he tries to make his way over to Primus.

He can still see his red leather jacket through the throng.

He wipes away the tears with his hand, thinking that it won't be too hard to put a tracker on Primus.

'The fuck's wrong with you?' a bearded man yells, gripping his upper arm.

'Nothing,' Edgar tells him, meeting the man's drunken eyes.

'They're just dogs,' he says, grinning.

'Go fuck yourself,' Edgar snaps, pulling free.

'You know what they do to people down in—'

'Just leave it,' he interrupts, barging past.

'Soy boy!' the man shouts after him.

Primus is gone. Edgar frantically scans the crowd and spots him making his way out of the depot. He forces his way ahead, apologising, and then follows in the gap in the crowd that opens up as the dead dog is dragged out of the pen by its trainer.

62

The dogs are still barking from inside the salt depot as Edgar steps out into the night air. There are people moving all over the dock now, some towards the stacked shipping containers and others around the doors into the main hangar.

He spots Primus up ahead and hurries after him.

An older man with a swastika tattooed on his forehead is downing Fanta from a plastic bottle. He burps and wipes his hand on his belly.

Edgar follows Primus as he turns off into one of the dark alleys between the containers. The change in acoustics is so sudden that it almost feels like he has gone deaf.

It smells like shit and vomit.

The red, yellow and blue metal walls rise fifteen metres into the air.

Down one of the intersecting passageways, he sees a line of men forming outside an open container. A naked woman is sprawled on the plastic-covered bed inside, a stocky man on top of her. Edgar sees another woman in a short pleather skirt being picked up and carried away.

A tall woman in a blonde wig staggers across the floor with a slack condom hanging between her legs.

Primus's ponytail bounces against the back of his red leather jacket as he continues through the labyrinthine corridors of the shipping containers. After another hundred or so metres, he turns and disappears into an open container.

Edgar keeps walking down the narrow passageway, hesitating before he follows Primus into the darkness. He cautiously makes his way along one wall, then stops. He can hear people moving nearby, hushed voices from several directions. There is a chemical tang of smoke in the breathless air. A hurricane lantern hanging from the ceiling gives off a faint brown glow.

As his eyes slowly adjust to the darkness, he can make out ten or so people sitting against the walls and lying on the floor. In the far corner, Primus is standing in front of a man with a braided beard.

Edgar pulls some money from his pocket, slowly crosses the bare plywood floor and watches as Primus buys a small plastic tube of what is most likely freebase.

The man with the braided beard counts the money a second time as Primus stamps impatiently, pushing a lock of grey hair back behind his ear.

Edgar steps over a sleeping man and approaches Primus, holding out a bill and pretending to have found it on the floor.

'You dropped this,' he says.

'Huh? Oh, thanks. Shit, that's nice of you,' Primus says, pushing it into his pocket.

Edgar pats him on the back in a gesture of camaraderie, attaching the tracker beneath the collar of his jacket. Primus holds the plastic tube up to the light and then sits down on the floor with his knees pulled up to his chest. He starts to prepare a small glass pipe.

A young man standing beneath the storm lamp creates a small aluminum foil cone with shaking hands.

Edgar studies Primus's thin face from the side, taking in the lines on his cheeks and the long, lank hair hanging down over his shoulders.

Working as an agent on the drugs squad, he sees this kind of thing on a regular basis.

Crack cocaine can't be smoked because the salts make the melting point too high. But adding ammonia and benzene separates the mixture, creating a layer of near-pure cocaine at the very top. Once the solvent evaporates, the user is left with a white, crumbly mass that, when smoked, provides a brief, intense rush.

Primus unzips his jacket, takes out a lighter from his inner pocket, and hunches over the pipe.

Edgar notices that the tracker has slipped down from his collar and is on the verge of falling off. Realising he will have to fix it, he shuffles closer.

Primus's mouth starts to water as he heats the pipe with his lighter. A swirling cloud of steam builds in the glass bowl. He leans back and inhales. Tears start streaming down his cheeks as his jaw seems to tense and his lips turn white. He whispers anxiously to himself, the little pipe shaking in his hand.

Edgar crouches down beside him, placing a hand on his shoulder. 'You OK, man?' he asks, attaching the tracker properly this time.

'I don't know,' Primus mumbles as he heats the pipe again. 'Damn it, this isn't working, you take it.'

'Thanks, but . . .'

'Go, go, before it's gone,' he says impatiently, pushing the pipe into Edgar's mouth.

Before Edgar has time to think through the consequences, he breathes in the steam and watches the bowl of the pipe turn clear.

The effect is immediate: his muscles become heavy, and he slumps down against the wall beside Primus. Panic bubbles up inside him, and he realises he should stay still and wait for the rush to subside before trying to track down Joona. An intensely euphoric rush spreads through his body. His penis stiffens, his heart racing and his lips tingling.

'I'm on all kinds of medication,' Primus explains, his voice low. 'And sometimes when I smoke, it just slams into my head and makes my jaw tense up . . .'

Edgar listens to his voice. His mind is perfectly clear, and he knows this sensation is just from the drug, but he still smiles to himself.

The crotch of his jeans feel tight.

All around him, people are talking softly in the darkness.

A woman wearing delicate plaits smiles at him.

Edgar leans back, closes his eyes and feels someone unbuttoning his jeans, pushing a warm hand inside gripping his penis and squeezing it gently.

He breathes in, unsteadily, through his nose. His heart is racing.

The sense of pleasure is so overwhelming that nothing else seems to matter.

The hand starts moving up and down with soft movements.

Edgar opens his eyes, blinking in the darkness, and sees Primus lean forward to take him in his mouth.

He shoves him back and gets up on shaky legs, pulling up his jeans and buttoning them over his erection as he staggers out of the container.

A terrible fear of losing himself propels him forward, though he knows that what he is about to do is wrong.

His legs feels like jelly, his pulse thundering in his ears.

Edgar walks quickly, turning into the passageway and bypassing the line of men outside one of the containers, barging straight inside and pausing in front of one of the women. Her brown eyes seem guarded, the corners of her mouth chapped. Without a word, he grips her upper arm and pulls her to one side.

'Seems like someone's in a hurry,' she says.

He gives her all the cash he has, and catches the look of surprise on her face before he turns her to face the wall. He reaches beneath her short pleather skirt and pulls her red underwear down to her knees.

His erection is almost painful.

With shaking hands, he unbuttons his jeans and pushes into her.

He can't believe what he is doing. He knows he doesn't want this, but he also can't stop himself. The drug is like ice water in his veins, making every strand of hair on his body stand on end, endorphins pulsing through him.

Edgar thrusts into her, sobbing as he comes. It feels like the cascade and the contractions will never end.

63

Joona steps up to the bar beside the man in the hoodie. He bumps into him, catches his eye and apologises.

It isn't Primus, just a young man with a blond moustache and pierced cheeks.

Joona takes his plastic cup back over to the boxing ring.

Two men whose faces and torsos are pocked with scars are circling one another in the harsh glare of the lights overhead. Each of them is holding a broken bottle. One of the men is wearing jeans, the other a pair of black shorts.

Despite the energy of the audience, both seem fairly hesitant to attack, and their attempts to lunge at each other never end in a blow.

A large man with a shaved head and a tattooed neck taps Joona on the shoulder. He is wearing a green T-shirt and a pair of loose tracksuit bottoms.

"'Scuse me,' he says warmly, 'but . . . do you recognise me?'

'Maybe, I don't know,' Joona tells him, turning back to the boxing ring.

The man must be over two metres tall, outweighing Joona by a considerable amount. His enormous arms are covered in dark green tattoos.

Joona knows exactly who he is. His name is Ponytail-tail, and he was part of the so-called Brotherhood in Kumla Prison, though he was transferred to Saltvik just after Joona arrived.

'I'm sure we've met before,' Ponytail-tail tells him.

'It's possible, I really don't remember,' Joona replies, looking up at him again.

'What's your name?'

'Jyrki,' Joona says, looking him straight in the eye.

'They call me Ponytail-tail.'

'Sounds like something I'd remember,' Joona says, turning his attention back to the fight as the audience roars.

The man in the black shorts lashes out a high kick, but his opponent catches his foot in his free hand, stabbing his toes with the broken bottle before losing his grip.

'Shit, man, it's so weird, I really fucking sure I recognise you . . .'

Ponytail-tail starts making his way over to the bar, but after just a few steps he turns around and walks back to Joona.

'You usually here?' he asks.

'Not too often.'

'I'm so fucking slow, I can't work it out,' he says, scratching his neck with a smile.

'Maybe I just look like someone you—'

'Nah, I know I've met you before,' Ponytail-tail interrupts him.

'I've got to go.'

'It'll come to me soon,' he says, jabbing at his temple.

Joona starts walking past the ring towards the big hangar doors. He notices that the man in the black shorts is leaving a bloody trail behind him.

Ponytail-tail follows Joona, grabbing his arm. Joona turns around with a serious look on his face, and the enormous man holds up his hands in an apology.

'Just wanted to get another look at you,' he says. 'Give me a second.'

'You're making too big a deal of this.'

'You ever live in Gothenburg?'

'No, I didn't,' Joona snaps.

'OK, sorry,' the big man says, bowing so low that the hammer of Thor on the chain around his neck starts swinging.

Joona watches him turn around and head back towards the bar.

The crowd around the ring cries out in unison.

The fighters shuffle against the ropes. The man in the jeans gets a nasty gash on his hand as he tries to deflect the other man's bottle, sending a stream of blood down his arm. He manages to maintain his grip, and attempts to jab his own bottle into the other man's face, but misses every time.

64

Laura pushes away from the boxing ring, heading towards the entrance. A tattooed man puts an arm around her shoulder, and though she doesn't hear what he slurs into her ear, she could probably make an educated guess.

She shakes him off and can't help but imagine her ex seeing her here, surrounded by all these men, in a pair of leather trousers and a tank top. He probably wouldn't even look up from his phone.

A young man in the boxing ring falls flat on his back, his head hitting the floor with a loud thud. His bloody mouth guard flies out and lands in his hair.

The crowd boos and shouts.

Though the young fighter is being pelted with empty cups and rubbish, he doesn't move. The cutman is by his side, trying to get him onto his feet. He doesn't seem to know where he is, and his legs give out underneath him when he tries to walk.

Laura won big on the previous bout, but bet her entire winnings on the young boxer now on the floor.

She glances down at her receipt, crumples it and drops it to the ground. Her plan is to buy another beer and then head over to the group of men hanging around by the monitor towards the rear of the hangar.

She has just started forcing her way over to the bar when a tall man with long white hair stops her.

'Stefan Nicolic wants to buy you a drink in the VIP room,' he says.

'Thank you, but I'm fine, I'm leaving soon,' Laura replies.

'He wants to talk to you,' the white-haired man insists, without a hint of warmth.

'OK, fine, great.'

Laura follows him through the crowd, holding off a stocky man careening towards her and feeling his sweat-drenched T-shirt against her palm.

A group of people part as they see the white-haired man approaching, making space for them to reach a door at the very back of the hangar.

There are two men with bulletproof vests and guns standing guard outside.

Laura feels her pulse pick up.

She has absolutely no idea what Nicolic could want with her.

The man enters a code on a keypad and steps inside. Laura follows him up a small flight of lighted stairs.

They enter the VIP room through a burgundy bead curtain. The warm, subdued lighting inside gleams on the dark brown leather armchairs and the low coffee table, partially covered by a large book on birds.

The room smells strange, rancid.

Stefan Nicolic is over by one of the large windows, looking out at the boxing ring and the throngs of people down below.

A thin woman with an afro is standing by a sideboard laden with carafes, glasses and ice buckets. She is wearing shiny black sportswear and a pair of black beach sandals.

'Hi,' Laura says with a smile.

Silently, and without even a flicker of emotion, the woman polishes a glass with a white cloth and then sets it down beside the others.

Against the back wall, there is a golden eagle in an oversize cage with thick bars. Its dark brown feathers are ruffled and almost invisible in the gloom, but its golden head and curved beak catch a little of the light. The enormous bird seems to be following every movement in the room with its beady eyes.

As he turns around, Laura sees that Stefan is holding a pair of green binoculars in one hand.

Without a word, he moves over to the seating area and puts the binoculars on the table.

He looks like he hasn't slept in days, his eyes puffy and dark and his mouth slack. His grey-flecked hair is cut short, and his face weathered from fighting. It looks like his nose has been broken several times and his cheek is lashed with scars.

'Everything OK?' he asks, looking up at Laura.

'Yeah, absolutely . . . well, maybe not great since the first bout,' she replies with a nod to the window.

'I've never seen you here before.'

'No?'

'I've got a very good memory for faces.'

'You're right, this is my first time.' Laura smiles.

'Take a seat.'

'Thanks.'

Laura sits down and peers out at the brightly lit boxing ring and the dark crowds of people moving across the hangar floor.

'I like to introduce myself to anyone who loses money early on,' Stefan tells her. 'Some people think the matches are rigged, but they're not, I swear. We make big money no matter which way they go.'

He falls silent and grabs the other woman's attention, holding up two fingers for a second before sitting down in the armchair opposite Laura, knees spread.

'But if you've got a knack for telling how a match is going to go, you can leave here a rich man . . .'

The woman unhurriedly pours whisky from a carafe into two tumblers, takes a couple of ice cubes from the bucket with a pair of tongs, and adds some soda water from a tap.

Hanging from the light above the table are two small daggers attached to leather straps. They clink softly with every breath of air.

'For cockfighting,' Stefan explains, following Laura's eyes.

'OK,' she says, sounding curious.

'You fasten them to the cocks' legs, like spurs.'

Still expressionless, the woman brings the two glasses over to the table, handing one to Stefan and the other to Laura.

'Thanks.'

'Our odds are fucking good,' Stefan continues. 'You saw, but most gamblers lose periodically, too. That's why we also loan money . . . though the interest is high, I'll admit. I'd recommend very short-term loans – pay back tomorrow, or the day after next.'

'I'll think about it,' Laura tells him, sipping her whisky.

'You do that.'

Stefan swings his right foot up onto his knee and rests the glass on his ankle. His jeans are ragged and dirty at the heels.

The white-haired bodyguard points at Laura and purses his lips. 'I don't like her,' he says calmly.

'You think she's one of the cowardly bastards who showed up at my house?' Stefan asks.

'No, she looks more like one of the drugs cops, maybe CID . . . I reckon they've given her some money to make a few bets, but she won't take our offer for a loan, and won't do any drugs.'

The crowd around the boxing ring erupts suddenly, rattling the windowpanes. Stefan picks up the binoculars from the table and peers down into the hangar.

'René just lost the last of his money,' he says.

'Want me to bring him up here?' the bodyguard asks.

'May as well.'

'OK,' says the bodyguard, turning to leave.

Stefan lowers the binoculars to the table, picks up his glass and knocks back his drink avoiding Laura's eyes. The woman by the bar fills another glass with whisky, ice and soda water.

The eagle rustles in his cage, trying to get a better look. Laura recognises the stench of death throughout the room. At the bottom of his cage is a layer of droppings and a tangle of delicate bones.

Stefan puts down his glass and takes the new one from the woman, who carries the empty glass away, silently returning to her post.

'We used to have ring girls in bikinis, but with all this Me Too business, that kind of thing doesn't fly anymore,' he says, as much to himself as anything.

His black T-shirt is tight over his stomach, and his reading glasses are hanging from the neckline.

'Thanks for the drink,' Laura tells him, carefully lowering her glass to the table. 'I think I'll head back down. I've got a lot more money to go bet—'

'Not yet,' Stefan interrupts her.

65

Stefan Nicolic raises his hand slightly, letting Laura know she should remain seated. She hears footsteps and voices in the stairwell, and the tiny daggers hanging from the lamp start clinking again.

'I don't give a shit,' the bodyguard says as he steps into the room.

Behind him is a lanky man in a flannel jacket and brown shoes. He is somewhere around forty, pale and thin-haired.

'Jocke shoved me down a level,' he says. 'But I'll do the same to him – two levels, maybe three . . .'

'Shut your mouth,' the bodyguard snaps.

Stefan gets up, goes over to the fridge in the bar and takes out a dead dove hanging by a chain. He dangles it in front of the cage, and the eagle makes a clicking sound and starts pecking at the cadaver.

'I'll pay tomorrow,' the man whispers. 'I swear, I'll have the money tomorrow.'

'We said today,' the bodyguard points out.

'It's not my fault, I was supposed to get paid today, but it'll be tomorrow instead. Jocke shoved me down, and—'

The bodyguard hits him and he stops talking. The man is knocked to one side, blinking repeatedly and raising his hand to his cheek.

'That really fucking hurt,' he says. 'I've learned my lesson now, I . . .'

'Where's the money?' Stefan asks, his back to him.

'You'll have it tomorrow, I can call the boss,' he says, taking out his phone. 'You can talk to him.'

'It's too late.'

'No, it's not too late, it's just one day. What the hell, come on, you know me.'

'We're doing this now,' says Stefan, turning to face him.

Laura watches as the man puts away his phone and frantically starts searching his jacket pockets. He pulls out his wallet and roots through it with trembling hands, producing pictures of his wife and children.

'Don't be pathetic,' Stefan tells him.

'I just want you to look at my family.'

'One bullet, five empty chambers.'

'What?' The man smiles, his face faltering.

Stefan takes a revolver from the drawer in his desk, pops out the cylinder and tips the bullets into his hand. He drops five of them into a pencil case and reloads the sixth into one of the chambers.

'Please, Stefan,' he whispers.

'Think of it as a cancer diagnosis – the odds are pretty good, you've got an eighty-three per cent chance of survival . . . and the treatment only takes a second.'

'I don't want to,' the man whispers as Stefan passes him the revolver.

'I think he's understood the gravity of the situation now,' says Laura, her voice steady.

'Shut your mouth,' the bodyguard barks at her.

The lanky man is holding the revolver in his right hand. All the colour has drained from his face, and beads of sweat have started dripping from the tip of his nose.

'Mind the eagle,' Stefan tells him.

The bodyguard grips the man's shoulders, turning him by ninety degrees. He then steps out of the way, takes out his phone and starts filming.

'Do it now,' he says.

The revolver in the man's hand shakes as he turns it towards his temple. His breathing is quick, tears are now streaming down his cheeks.

'I can't, please, I'll pay you back with interest, I—'

'Just do it, and then it'll all be over,' Stefan tells him.

'No,' the man sobs, lowering the gun.

The bodyguard sighs, drops his phone into his pocket and takes back the revolver.

'You do it instead,' Stefan says, turning to Laura.

'This has nothing to do with me.'

'That's exactly what a pig would say,' says the bodyguard, holding out the revolver.

'I'm not going to shoot someone who hasn't done anything to me.'

'He's no one; he's just a pathetic little rat who sells dope and speed,' says Stefan.

'Fucking cop,' the bodyguard snarls.

Laura's head is ringing, and she feels a wave of nausea rise up from the pit of her stomach as she takes the heavy gun from the bodyguard's hand.

'So you want me to shoot a worthless pusher just to prove I'm not a cop? I thought that was exactly the kind of thing the cops did,' she says, her mouth dry.

Stefan laughs appreciatively, but his face quickly turns solemn. 'Just put the gun to his forehead and . . .'

'I'll shoot him in the knee,' Laura suggests.

'I'll shoot *you* in the knee unless you do what Stefan tells you to,' the bodyguard says.

The woman behind the bar is standing perfectly still, eyes on the floor.

Laura's mind is racing as she raises the gun to the terrified man. The dull metal catches the yellow light.

'Don't do it,' the man begs her. 'Oh, God, please don't do it . . . I'll have the money tomorrow, you can have it tomorrow, I swear.'

Laura lowers the gun and wonders whether she could shoot the bodyguard instead, though she knows the gun could click five times before it actually fires if luck isn't on her side.

'Fucking cop,' the bodyguard shouts.

Laura slowly raises the revolver and sees her finger curl around the trigger, fingertip turning pale.

The bodyguard gives her a shove in the back.

Stefan has cupped his hand over one ear in anticipation.

Laura's heart is racing as she presses the muzzle to the man's forehead.

His eyes are wide, snot running from his nose over his trembling lips.

Laura pulls the trigger. The cylinder turns, and the hammer makes a loud click. The chamber is empty.

The man drops to his knees, sobbing loudly and clutching his face.

Before Laura pulled the trigger, she thought she caught a glimpse of brass between the frame and the cylinder.

If that was the case, it means the bullet was in the third chamber.

She knows she was far from certain – it was only a glimpse, after all, possibly nothing but a reflection of the yellow bulb above the sofa, a trick of the eye.

The moment she pulled the trigger, she started to doubt herself, but she needed something to cling on to. There was no other way out.

She can't begin to process what this has done to her. All she feels right now is emptiness.

'Make sure I get my money tomorrow,' Stefan tells the man, taking the gun from Laura's quivering hand.

'I promise.'

Laura watches as Stefan locks the revolver in the drawer of his desk. She realises that she needs to find a weapon, that she may have to defend herself if she can't talk her way out of here.

The bodyguard hauls the man to his feet and drags him through the beaded curtain. She can still hear him sobbing as they head downstairs.

Stefan slinks off to the bathroom, and the thin woman follows him in. She quietly locks the door behind them.

Laura gets up and grabs one of the small daggers hanging from the light above the table, trying to untie the leather strap. The knot is too tight, and it slips from between her fingers, making the lampshade sway and the two daggers clink together.

The pool of light swings up the walls and windows.

She hears the toilet flush.

Using one of the daggers, she cuts the leather strap holding the other. Laura tries to hold the lamp steady, but her hands are still shaking.

The lock on the toilet door rattles.

She sits down and pushes the small dagger into her boot.

Stefan re-emerges, and the woman returns to her post.

The lampshade is still swaying slowly above the table.

'Like I said, if you need to borrow any money, that's fine,' Stefan tells her, moving back to where he was standing by the window when she first entered the room.

'I'm planning to win,' Laura replies, getting to her feet.

When he fails to answer, she moves over to the beaded curtain. The eagle is the only one who watches her leave the VIP room.

66

The line of people waiting to get into the Eagle's Nest has grown even longer. Joona is standing by the bar, drinking a beer and trying to see the faces of the people streaming into the hangar.

His mind turns once more to the conversation Martin overheard between Primus and Caesar. Perhaps Primus knew that Martin was listening, and set a trap to lure him down to the playground in an attempt to save Jenny, leaving behind his fingerprints and putting him squarely in view of the CCTV in the process. Primus probably wouldn't have anticipated that Martin would be too paralysed by fear to do anything.

The best thing would be if they could convince Martin to be hypnotised again – there is no doubt he saw so much more than he told them during the first session.

Joona's thoughts are interrupted when he sees Edgar pushing his way over to him. His cheeks are scarlet, and when he reaches the bar, Joona notices that the skin on his arms is covered in goosebumps.

Edgar's hands jerk unnaturally as he searches his pockets for a frame of film to give to the bartender.

'We've got him,' Edgar whispers, licking his lips. 'I found him and put a tracker on him.'

'On Primus?'

'It was about to fall off, but I was able to secure it.'

Edgar takes a few deep gulps of the beer he's handed, then puts the cup down on the counter and wipes his mouth with the back of his hand.

311

'Are you OK?'

'Fine . . . Actually, I don't know, I was watching the dog fight. It was totally messed up, I thought I was going to hurl . . . I'm actually feeling a bit shaky,' he says, blurting out the words.

'Stay here,' says Joona, his voice calm. 'I'll try to get Primus out.'

'Nah, it's fine, I'll come, of course I'm coming.'

'It'd be better if you stayed here and kept an eye on the exit,' Joona insists.

'OK, I'll stay here,' says Edgar, scratching his cheek.

'I can see the tracker's signal – good work,' Joona tells him after checking his phone.

'He's wearing a red leather jacket,' Edgar calls after him, aware that he is acting strangely.

Joona pushes away from the bar, rounding the edge of the boxing ring. He sees one of the women inside take a high kick to the face, but she keeps fighting, hard, hitting her opponent in the throat and again on the cheek before they both crash into the ropes.

According to the transmitter, Primus is at the edge of the container dock.

Joona follows the throng of people through the open doors, out into the enclosed dock area. The air outside is still warm. He passes a drunk man urinating on the door to an outdoor toilet. There are discordant shouts coming from the salt depot.

Joona follows the signal into the secluded city of colourful containers. Stacked three or four deep, they form windowless neighbourhoods full of roads and narrow alleyways.

He sees people moving in all directions.

The floor is strewn with broken pill casings, condoms, empty blister packs, bags of sweets and bottles.

Checking his phone, Joona sees that Primus has moved.

He turns off into an alleyway.

Up ahead, two men are deep in discussion outside a red container. They both fall silent as he passes, waiting for a moment before continuing their conversation in hushed tones.

As Joona emerges into the open dock area, he sees that Primus has returned to the salt depot.

The white tyre tracks come together in the shape of an arrow, pointing towards the open doors.

Joona sees the crowd cleave in two to make way for a man carrying an injured dog. Its blood is running down his trousers, dripping onto the white ground.

The salt crystals crunch beneath Joona's boots as he pushes his way inside.

He hears a dog growl and bark.

The speakers crackle, and a voice announces that the next fight will begin in fifteen minutes.

A bookie flits through the crowd, taking bets.

Joona's eyes scan the short end of the hangar. He catches a glimpse of a red jacket on the other side of the space. He forces his way over and is hit on the arm as a group of boisterous men try to get into the fighting pen.

The air smells like sweat and old beer.

In one of the cages, a huge pit bull paces restlessly.

Joona sees a young man trying to climb up the steep pile of salt, only to slide back down to the floor.

He needs to make his way around the pen before the next fight begins, and is just about to clamber over a salt drift when someone grabs his arm.

Ponytail-tail stares down at him with wide eyes. Both nostrils are black with dried blood.

'You a mechanic?' he asks.

'No, but what you . . .'

A wave passes through the crowd, knocking into both men and causing them to stumble. Someone shouts aggressively in the distance.

'Fuck me, I just can't drop it,' Ponytail-tail mutters, staring at Joona.

'You can't remember everyone.'

Right then, Joona gets a clear glimpse of Primus on the other side of the pen. He is talking to another man, who is angrily kicking the riot fencing.

'I know it'll come to me soon.'

'Assuming you haven't got me confused with—'

'I haven't,' Ponytail-tail interrupts Joona, staring at him.

A trainer dressed in khaki has taken a black dog out of one of the cages, and its collar, straining against the dog's pull, stifles its raspy barking.

Joona sees that Primus has finished his conversation and started moving towards the exit.

'I have to go.'

As Joona turns to leave, he suddenly feels a piercing jab in his side, followed by a wave of searing pain. He looks down and sees that Ponytail-tail has thrust a knife into his torso from behind.

'I saw you in Kumla . . . you're the pig who . . .'

The enormous man pulls out the short blade and tries to stab him again, but Joona manages to hold him off. The crowd knocks them backwards. Ponytail-tail has a firm grip on Joona's T-shirt, and he thrusts the knife again.

'Die, you fucking—'

Joona twists his upper body and swings up to hit the bigger man just above his larynx.

Ponytail-tail immediately falls silent and staggers backwards, into the arms of two other men. He points at Joona, spluttering.

A circle clears around them.

The pain from the wound on his side is throbbing, and Joona can feel the hot blood trickling down his thigh inside his trouser leg.

He takes a step forward, searching for a weapon, but his right leg gives way and he stumbles, hip hitting the ground, breaking his fall with his hands.

The huge man flicks the blood from his knife and draws closer to Joona, wheezing. Ponytail-tail's gaze is steadfast; this is a man willing to take a great deal of pain for another chance to drive his knife into him.

Joona steadies himself onto one knee, his back scraping against the fence.

Ponytail-tail lunges straight at him, holding out his left hand in Joona's face in order to conceal what his right hand is doing. He jabs with the knife.

Joona dodges the blade by spinning around, managing to ram his elbow into the man's neck. He puts his weight into the movement, delivering a huge amount of force. Both men tumble over the fence, slamming into the ground in the fighting pen.

Joona rolls away and gets back onto his feet. His right hip and trouser leg are now slick with dark blood.

His field of vision seems to be shrinking.

He can no longer see Primus.

The crowd pushes up against the fence, shouting and throwing beer.

Ponytail-tail gets up, coughing, with one hand on his throat. He glances down at the knife.

The black dog is barking, pulling so hard the trainer is being dragged forward.

Joona knows that he is quickly running out of strength. His boot is full of blood, and it squelches with every step he takes. He needs to get to hospital, and soon.

Ponytail-tail points the knife at Joona, but can't utter a single word. He moves closer, using the gleaming blade to draw a horizontal figure of eight in the air.

Joona has to try to get behind him. He could bring Ponytail-tail's T-shirt up like a garrote and twist it so tight that it cuts off the circulation to his brain.

Ponytail-tail feints, thrusting the knife. Joona barely dodges it, but he can tell that he is moving too slowly to evade another jab. The blade swipes in the other direction, and he has no choice but to block it with his arm. The sharp edge gouges a deep wound on the side of his forearm.

The dog is still straining.

Joona cries out in pain as he throws himself forward beneath the knife, lifting Ponytail-tail's legs from the ground and throwing him onto his back.

The dog rushes towards them, leash trailing after it. It launches itself at Ponytail-tail and locks its jaws around his arm, pulling and shaking its head, refusing to let go.

Joona falls back against the railings, grabbing one of the bars to drag himself to his feet. He raises his head and sees Laura forcing through the crowd towards him.

The larger man is rolling around on his back, stabbing the dog in the throat until it eventually lets go.

Joona tries to get up, but collapses again; he has almost no strength left. He is losing too much blood, and his heart is racing.

'Joona, Joona!'

Laura is on the floor, reaching through the barrier to hold out a small dagger on a leather strap.

Joona takes it and gets to his feet. He is now so weak that he can barely stand, but he supports himself against the railings. He desperately tries to get a better grip on the dagger, but drops it and hears it clatter through the metal bars.

Ponytail-tail staggers towards him. One of his arms is torn to shreds as blood drips down from his hand.

'Fucking pig,' he hisses, his bloody hand gripping Joona's neck.

Joona tries to hold him off, but Ponytail-tail presses against his arm, forcing the knife against his torso. Their muscles tremble as Ponytail-tail's hand inches forward and the tip of the blade slowly pushes between two ribs.

The pain feels strangely distant.

Joona sees his dagger catch the light on the floor, and realises that he is still holding the leather strap.

The crowd around them roars, and several sections of the riot barriers fall over.

Joona's blood is now trickling down the knife, onto Ponytail-tail's hand. He yanks the leather strap and sees the small blade follow the movement of his hand. It swings up in a glittering arc and into his grip.

Everyone cries out.

Joona tries to hold back Ponytail-tail, and uses the last of his strength to drive the small blade through his forehead.

He hears a murmur, and the hangar falls silent. Ponytail-tail takes two steps back. His lips are pressed together, his tattooed neck straining. The dagger is lodged deep in his forehead, the long leather strap swinging in his face. He starts blinking spasmodically, then raises a hand and falls backwards. There is a heavy thud as his huge body hits the ground, and a cloud of salt dust swirls up into the air.

The crowd goes up in a roar again, drumming their hands on the fence and waving their betting slips in the air.

Joona staggers away, clutching his side. His breathing is quick, shallow. He can feel the blood pulsing between his fingers.

He catches a glimpse of Primus's red jacket outside the depot, disappearing behind one of the loading cranes. The red colour seems to double, growing and splitting right before his eyes.

Joona moves past the loader, feeling his heart working hard to compensate for his falling blood pressure.

Laura catches up with him, and Joona puts an arm around her shoulder for support as they walk away from the salt depot.

'Contact the evacuation team,' he pants. 'Tell them to pick me up by the German RORO ship.'

'You'll die if you don't see a doctor right now.'

'Don't worry, I'll be fine . . . You need to find Edgar and get out of here as fast as you can.'

'You sure?'

They pause, and Joona tries to press harder on the deep wound in his side. 'He's waiting at the bar by the exit,' he says, setting off again. 'He's high on something, he'll need help getting out of here . . .'

It is still really warm, but clouds have gathered overhead, and the cranes and barges are bathed in a murky grey light.

Joona lumbers towards the red jacket.

The lantern at the front of the RORO ship casts a swaying pool of light onto two figures standing at the edge of the dock.

Primus is talking to a younger man holding a brown faux leather gym bag.

Joona has to pause so he can bring his hurried breathing under control before he reaches them.

'Good fight,' Primus says when he spots Joona.

Without a word, Joona steps forward and shoves him with both hands. Primus falls back over the edge of the dock, into the dark water.

A deep splash instantly rises up from the surface.

The young man with the bag steps back in confusion.

Joona keeps moving, jumping straight over the edge. He sees his own reflection hurtling towards him before he breaks the surface and plunges into the cold water. He twists around as he sinks, catching a glimpse of Primus through the swirling bubbles and grabbing on to his hair.

The sound of two outboard motors thunders beneath the water. Joona kicks his legs and turns back towards the surface.

67

Her undershirt is damp against her back, sweat trickling down her chest and dripping from the tip of her nose. Mia looks over to the door as she slowly chews a piece of bread. Kim tears off a bit of dried meat and drops the remainder back into the bucket.

'Eat up,' Blenda tells them for the third time.

She tries to take care of them, reminding them to brush their teeth with straw and comb their hair with their fingers, teaching them long passages from Corinthians.

Blenda occasionally gets to help Granny with jobs other than digging the bunker, like carrying the Persian rugs out into the yard to beat them. She has even driven the lorry before.

Of everyone, Kim is the most afraid. She told Mia about a girl who was killed just for being thirsty, and another who was gassed to death.

During their break yesterday, Mia and Kim walked right over to the lorry parked at the edge of the forest. Granny kept an eye on them the whole time.

There was an old sheet of corrugated metal roofing on the ground, rusty and damaged after years of being covered in damp leaves, and Mia noticed that there were sections of it that could easily be broken off and sharpened into perfect shivs.

She pulled Kim over to the lorry again today, while Granny and Blenda were hanging laundry on the lines between the longhouses.

Mia could hear Granny's gruff instructions and Blenda's friendly responses as the gravel crunched under their boots.

'Let's go back,' said Kim.

'I just want to check something,' Mia told her.

They reached the shade beneath the trees and stopped, breathing in the smell of oil from the lorry. Mia stamped on the metal and looked back towards the longhouses. A white sheet billowed slowly in the soft breeze.

'What are you doing?' Kim asked anxiously.

Mia got down onto one knee, picked up a loose piece of metal and pushed it into the top of her boot, quickly trying to snap off another piece of the larger sheet.

Frightened, Kim tried to pull her back onto her feet, but Mia resisted, continuing to wiggle the piece of metal back and forth.

Rusty flakes came loose where it bent.

The clothesline creaked as a new sheet was hung out to dry.

The piece of metal broke away, and Mia quickly pushed it into her boot too. She got up, brushed the dirt from her knee, and walked away.

* * *

Mia can't afford to wait for someone to come and save her, because she knows there's no one out there who misses her enough.

She eats the last of her food and picks up a kernel of corn from the floor, popping it into her mouth before continuing her work.

Slowly, methodically, she sharpens the piece of metal on the concrete floor beneath her parka.

Mia has tried to talk to the others about escaping, but Kim is too scared and Blenda seems to believe that things will get better. She claims they will move back into the big house before too long, and that they will be given clean clothes and gold jewellery again.

'We'll die here if we don't do anything,' Mia tells them coolly.

'You just don't get it,' Blenda sighs.

'I "get" that everything we do is controlled by an old woman, and I know that she'll have no chance if we all work together.'

'No one is going to work with you,' Kim mumbles.

'But we can easily overpower Granny,' says Mia. 'Three of us is more than enough . . . I know exactly how to do it.'

'I don't want to know.'

Mia falls silent, still determined to convince them once the shivs are ready. She will teach them how to stab Granny in the stomach or throat, the softest points on the body. You stab at least nine times, counting out loud so that everyone can hear.

Mia spits onto the ground, hides her hands under her coat and continues sharpening the blade. The slow scraping seems to fill the longhouse.

'Stop doing that,' Blenda tells her.

'Are you talking to me?'

'Stop scraping or whatever you're doing.'

'I can't hear anything,' says Mia, continuing her work.

It will take her several days, but once the pieces of metal are pointed and sharp, she will tear some thin strips of fabric and dampen them to wrap around the base as handles.

She and Kim will each hide a blade in their clothes, and during their next exercise break, they'll cut the cable ties and continue their walk, holding hands and keeping the shivs hidden. Blenda will choose the right moment to snatch the stick from Granny, and that's when Mia and Kim will split up and attack her from the front and behind.

Nine deep stabs each.

Once Granny is dead, they'll clean themselves up and open the rest of the cages, grabbing some water and fetching the dog before setting off on the road together.

No one will be able to stop them then.

Mia's hands have started shaking with the effort. She sucks at her grazed fingertips and carefully hides the two blades. She crawls over to Kim and puts an arm around her shoulders.

'I know you're scared,' she whispers. 'But I'll teach you exactly what to do. I swear, I'll look after you. You'll get to go home to your parents, you can start playing handball again, and . . .' She trails off as she hears a car pull into the yard. The dog starts barking angrily, and for a moment Mia lets herself think that they have finally been found, that the police are here to take them away, but when she sees Blenda using the last of her water to wash her face and try to fix her hair, she snaps back and realises it's Caesar.

Granny lifts the crossbar and opens the door, then drags a mattress into the longhouse. It's dark, but the light from the yard glints off the hinges and fittings.

'I don't want to, I don't want to,' Kim whimpers quietly, pressing her fists to her eyes.

Mia tries to calm her down, keeping an eye on Granny all the while. She is wearing a flannel shirt and a pair of loose fitting jeans. Her deep wrinkles are like cracks in her face, and her nose is sharp and makes her look sombre.

The big amulet swings between her breasts as she hobbles inside. She irritably pushes the metal bucket to one side to make room for the mattress as she pulls it deeper in to the room.

Kim crawls away from Mia, cowering in the far corner of the cage.

Granny moves over to the other cage and points at Raluca, who immediately shuffles over to the opening and climbs out. Her long plait is full of straw, and her bare feet are visible beneath the dirty hem of her long skirt. She lies back on the mattress, and Granny uses a bottle to dampen a rag, holding it over her mouth and nose until she loses consciousness.

The door swings wide open as the wind blows, allowing more light from the yard to spill into the longhouse.

Granny's skin is rough and wrinkled, but the muscles in her neck are strong. Her forearms are thick, her hands big.

She grips Raluca by the chin, studies her with displeasure, and then uses her stick to get to her feet.

'Come out,' she tells Kim.

'I don't want to. I don't feel well.'

'We all have our duties.'

Granny attaches a pale yellow tip to a notch at the end of her stick. It looks like a small fang. She holds it up to the light from outside, then turns her narrow eyes to Kim.

'No, don't, please don't prick me . . . I'll come out and thank the Lord, I'll take the rag, I'll lie still,' Kim pleads, shuffling to the side of the cage.

But Granny pushes her stick between the bars, jabbing it forward and pricking Kim on the shoulder forcefully with the tip.

'Ow!' Kim rubs her shoulder, smearing the blood with her fingertips.

'Come out now,' Granny tells her, pulling the tip from the stick.

Kim crawls over to the opening, climbs out of the cage and walks across the room on unsteady legs. She is struggling to hold back tears and her restrained sobs almost sound like hiccups.

The wind pulls the door to the longhouse shut with a creak, submerging the room in darkness again.

'Lie down.'

Mia barely dares breathe. She is sitting perfectly still in the gloomy cage, watching Kim steady herself against the bars of one of the cages with one hand. She seems incredibly weak, dropping to her knees on the mattress and then slumping onto her side next to Raluca, calm and limp.

Granny sighs in irritation as she pulls down their clothes and underwear, straightening their bodies on the mattress.

She gets up to leave.

The door swings open, and light pours across the two women lying side by side on the mattress, dirty and thin, exposed from the waist down.

The dog barks and footsteps sound against the gravel outside. Something clatters into the wheelbarrow.

A man's angry voice shouts at Granny.

'What have I done wrong?' he yells. 'You give them everything, you do things right, you . . .'

'It isn't you,' Granny tries to reassure him. 'It's—'

'I'll slaughter them all if they don't like it,' Caesar interrupts her.

His footsteps draw closer over the gravel, Granny limping behind him.

'They're here for you, they're all yours, I promise, they're grateful and proud . . .'

Caesar tears open the door and strides inside, tossing his machete to the floor with a clatter and marching over to the unconscious women on the mattress.

'If you only knew how beautiful you are,' he growls.

The hinges creak as the wind blows, and Caesar turns his head. Mia catches a glimpse of his raised chin and pale lips in the light from outside.

When he turns back, his glasses shimmer for a moment on his dark face.

Without a sound, she shuffles to one side to avoid being caught in the light whenever the door next opens. She shrinks back, thinking that the shivs are still too blunt to be used.

Caesar drops onto his knees and rolls Kim off the mattress without even looking at her.

The door opens again, and the light from the yard seeps in over the concrete floor as he parts Raluca's legs.

When Caesar sees that her thighs are sticky with blood, he pushes her away and gets back onto his feet.

'OK, I understand, but this doesn't just affect me,' he says between quick breaths. 'I can bear my cross, I can bathe and become clean . . .'

He spits onto Raluca and wipes his mouth with the back of his hand.

'I know you think you're smart, that you can knock me off balance,' he says. 'But it won't happen, it doesn't work that way.'

Raluca had mentioned that she had stomach cramps earlier, but Mia doesn't dare say that no one knew her period had started.

'I wish we could live together in the house again,' he says, his voice ragged with emotion.

In the fading light as the door swings shut, Mia watches him pick up the machete from the floor.

She can't quite process what is happening.

'But if I forgive you, you'll think the law lacks authority,' Caesar continues.

In the small bit of light that remains Mia sees him grab Raclua's hair and pull back her head.

'This is how you want it,' he says, holding the blade to her throat. 'Or does anyone want to switch places with Raluca?'

Blood quickly spills from the deep wound, spattering against the edge of the big metal bucket.

Mia clamps her hands over her mouth to stop herself from screaming. She squeezes her eyes shut, her heart racing in her chest.

He cut Raluca's throat.

Killed her while she was unconscious, and all because she was menstruating.

Mia can't believe this is really happening. She hears the machete crash to the floor.

Her pulse is thundering in her ears.

When she next opens her eyes, Caesar is on top of Kim.

The mattress soaks up Raluca's blood, turning dark beneath her.

Kim has no idea he is raping her right now, but she knew it was going to happen, and she will be able to feel the pain between her legs when she wakes up.

68

Joona has only fragmented memories of what happened after he jumped into the bay. By the time the special ops team dragged him and Primus into their RIB, he was barely conscious. It was as though he had reached a precipice and was teetering on the edge. They raced across the bay to the power station, where a helicopter was just about to land to airlift him to the hospital.

A team of surgeons and anaesthetists were waiting for him at Karolinska Hospital. The knife had missed his vital organs, but he had lost a life-threatening amount of blood. Joona was in the fourth, most acute stage of hypovolemic shock. The damaged tissue and blood vessels were ligated, his abdominal cavity was drained, he was given a huge blood transfusion and treated with crystalloid solution and plasma.

But the very next day, he was up and walking the corridors, though he had to return to his bed after only thirty minutes.

He called Valeria in Rio de Janeiro yesterday evening. Her son became a father that same night, and though he didn't say a word about it, Valeria could tell that he was injured and asked whether she should come home.

'No, but I can come to Brazil if you need help with the baby,' he said.

* * *

He has just finished his lunch when there is a knock at the door. Margot and Verner step into the room wearing blue shoe covers.

'We weren't allowed to bring flowers,' Verner apologises.

'Edgar and Laura have both resigned, and you look like I've given you a beating,' says Margot.

'But we found Primus,' Joona points out.

'Good work.' She nods.

'And I got him out.'

'Incredible,' Verner mumbles.

'What did I tell you, Margot?' Joona asks, his eyes fixed on her.

'What do you mean?'

'You didn't think . . .'

'Of course I did, I'm the one who gave the green light to—'

'Margot,' Verner interrupts her calmly.

'What do you want?' she asks, smiling.

'Who was right?' Joona asks.

'You were right,' she admits, sitting down in the sturdy visitor's chair.

*　*　*

The continental heatwave that settled over Sweden is not letting up, and water levels are dangerously low, necessitating a nationwide ban on fires. There is talk of record-breaking temperatures and extreme weather, but the Swedes can't help but enjoy the hot summer days.

Joona leans against the Needle for support as they leave the hospital together.

The white leather seats in his Jaguar are blisteringly hot, and the blasting air conditioning sounds like a downpour on a metal roof.

Nils helps Joona fasten his seat belt before pulling out into the road and merging into the right lane.

'You know, when I was a boy, I had a teddy bear that could growl,' he tells Joona. 'I fought the urge to slice it open and take the speaker out for three days before I finally gave in.'

'What made you think about that?' Joona says, grinning.

'No, no, you look like your usual self,' Åhlén reassures him, flicking the lights to full beam.

Joona thinks back to when Lumi was a child. One morning she woke up and announced that she had had a dream about a teddy

327

bear, and he and Summa laughed and asked her all about it. Every morning after for some time, she declared again that she had had the dream, probably because she was pleased with their response the first time.

Åhlén turns off towards Sankt Göran's Hospital and pulls up onto the kerb, honking at a man, who quickly moves out of the way.

Joona thanks him for the ride and groans in pain as he climbs out of the car. He walks slowly towards entrance one, and after only a few steps in the stairwell, he pauses to catch his breath before taking the lift to the psychiatric ward.

When the special ops team pulled Primus Bengtsson out of the water, he claimed he was a fighting dog and tried to bite anyone who got near him.

After a brief discussion with the lawyer they drove him over to Sankt Göran's and stationed two plain clothes officers outside his room.

Joona leaves the lift and reports to reception.

A few minutes later, chief psychiatrist Mike Miller comes out to meet him. 'You found Primus,' he says.

'Yes,' Joona replies. 'How's he doing?'

'Better than you.'

'Good.'

'Do you want me to sit in on the interview?'

'Thanks, but I don't think that will be necessary,' says Joona.

'Primus likes to come across as confident, but you can't help feeling sorry for him; he's a sensitive person, remember that.'

'I'll do whatever it takes to save lives,' Joona replies.

They walk down the corridors together, past locked glass doors and empty day rooms, eventually reaching the visitors' room.

Joona greets the two officers waiting outside and shows his ID to one of them.

Dr Miller enters yet another code and opens the door to let Joona inside. The room is only partially lit, and the cool air smells like hand sanitiser.

A plastic bucket of old toys sits against one wall.

Primus Bengtsson is sitting at a small table with a floral waxed tablecloth. His hair is tied up in a ponytail, and he is wearing a soft

denim shirt that hangs loosely over his jeans. His grizzled face is listless, his eyes half closed and his mouth open.

On the other side of the room, an orderly is sitting on the armrest of the sofa, playing on his phone.

Joona pulls out a chair and sits across from Primus.

Their eyes lock on each other.

Joona starts the recorder and begins by introducing himself, stating the date and time, and listing the names of those present.

'OK, but I don't want to be associated with his ridiculously small hands,' Primus mutters with a gesture to the orderly. 'Just look at him – who'd want to sleep with him? It's only biology . . . Eighty per cent of all women are pining for the top twenty per cent of men – the most handsome, the most successful . . . And since women are the ones who decide in this world, that means the majority of men end up being cheated on or left behind.'

Joona decides that he can use Primus's narcissism to his advantage. He can't afford to weigh every ethical concern at this stage. The investigation has narrowed to a spear, pointing straight through Primus to Caesar.

'You work for Stefan Nicolic,' he says.

'Work? I live off the leftovers and bones that fall to the floor.'

'We saw you handing over money to attendees at the Eagle's Nest.'

Primus licks his thin lips and looks calmly at Joona. His pale green eyes are like the water in a shallow lake.

'Stefan has to back the big wins . . . and I'm the runner boy there. I'm family, after all, and he trusts me . . .'

'Even though you're in touch with Caesar?'

'I have no idea what you're talking about. I thought you were drug enforcement.'

'We're investigating the murder of Jenny Lind,' Joona explains.

'And am I supposed to react to that?' Primus asks, scratching his forehead.

'She was murdered in the Observatorielunden playground.'

'I've never met anyone called Caesar,' he says, looking Joona straight in the eye, unblinking.

'We believe you have.'

'Look at yourself,' Primus says, gesturing to the mirror on the wall. 'When you leave here, you'll turn your back on the mirror as your reflection turns its back on you . . . But Caesar can do the opposite: his reflection walks backwards into the mirror, and suddenly he's in the room.'

'We know you've spoken to him – and we know you had fore-knowledge of Jenny Lind's murder.'

'That doesn't mean I did it, does it?' he says, grinning.

'No, but it makes you our prime suspect, and that's enough to hold you in custody.'

Joona can tell from a glimmer that has appeared in Primus's eyes and the way his cheeks have turned pink that he is starting to enjoy the attention.

'In that case, I don't have to say a word until I've spoken to a lawyer.'

'You know your stuff, that's good,' Joona says in praise, getting to his feet. 'I'll arrange for legal representation now – if you feel like you need help.'

'Though I do have to insist on defending myself,' Primus replies, leaning back in his chair.

'So long as you know that you have the right to legal counsel.'

'I'm my own lawyer, and I'll happily answer your questions, but of course I won't say anything that could have negative consequences for me or my sister.'

'Who killed Jenny Lind?'

'I don't know, but it wasn't me. That's not my thing, because I actually like girls . . . I mean, I won't say no to real hardcore stuff, and sometimes I've got loads of cocks on the go . . . but I would never hang a girl from a steel cable like some shark fisherman in Havana.'

'So who did it?'

Primus studies him with a look of triumph in his eyes, a narrow sliver of tongue visible between his lips. 'Don't know.'

'Your sister is terrified of Caesar,' Joona continues.

'He's Saturn, devouring everyone around him . . . and he swears he'll winch her up to the ceiling and saw off her arms and legs.'

'Why?'

'Why did Leopold want a kingdom?' Primus asks, scratching his neck. 'He's a Darwinist, a Chad, an Old Testament patriarch . . .' Primus trails off, getting up and moving over to the window. He looks out for a moment before returning to his seat.

'What's Caesar's surname?' Joona asks.

'He never said – and if he had, I wouldn't tell you for the reasons I mentioned earlier,' he says, restlessly bouncing one leg. 'Or are you going to wrap your arms around me and protect me when he returns?'

'We can give you witness protection if there's a threat against you.'

'Honey on a knife edge,' Primus mumbles.

'You say you've never met Caesar, but you have talked to him.'

'On the phone.'

'So he calls you?'

'There's a phone booth in the ward.'

'What does he say?'

'He tells me what he needs help with . . . and reminds me that the Lord is watching . . . that he implanted a camera in my brain.'

'What does he need help with?'

'I can't tell you without risking negative consequences for myself . . . All I can say is that I've taken some snaps for him.'

'Pictures of what?'

'I took a vow of silence.'

'A girl in Gävle called Mia Andersson?'

'Pure speculation,' Primus tells him, raising a finger.

'When did he start calling you?'

'This summer.'

'When did he last call you?'

'The day before last.'

'What did he want?'

'I'm going to plead article six of the European Convention on Human Rights.'

'What kind of voice does Caesar have?'

'Dark, powerful,' he replies, scratching his chest through his denim shirt.

'Does he have an accent of any kind, a dialect?'

'Nope.'

'Can you ever hear anything in the background?'

'A funeral drum would be fitting, but ...' Primus trails off and glances over to the doorway as someone passes in the corridor outside. A moment later, he tightens his ponytail.

'Where does he live?'

'I don't know, but I'm picturing a castle or a manor house, with grand halls and parlours,' he says, chewing on a thumbnail.

'Did he tell you he lived in a manor house?'

'No.'

'Has Caesar ever been a patient in this ward?'

'He's not the kind of person to be admitted anywhere he doesn't want to be ... He told me how he rolled out of Auschwitz in a first-class carriage ... like a fucking king,' Primus says, shivering.

'What do you mean, Auschwitz?'

'I've got Tourette's, so I say all kinds of things that don't make sense.'

'Was Caesar a patient at Säter?'

'Why are you asking me that?' Primus asks with a faltering smile.

'Because the forensic psychiatric clinic at Säter had a set of train tracks on the property, because they had their own crematorium, and because—'

'I didn't tell you that,' Primus interrupts Joona, jumping up so abruptly that his chair tips over. 'I didn't say shit about that.'

'No, but you could nod if I—'

'Shut up! I'm not going to nod!' he shouts, hitting himself on the forehead. 'You can't trick me into saying things I don't want to say.'

'Primus, what's going on?' the orderly asks, wearily getting to his feet.

'No one is trying to trick you,' Joona continues. 'You're doing the right thing by telling me what you know.'

'Please could you stop—'

'And no one can ... no one can blame you for doing what's best for you,' Joona interrupts him.

'You don't have my permission to tell anyone I talked to you,' Primus says in a shaky voice.

'OK, but in that case I need to know . . .'

'No more!'

Primus barges over to the window and slams his head into the glass several times, reeling backwards and holding on to the curtains to keep his balance.

The orderly sounds the alarm and rushes over.

Primus falls, taking the curtain rod down with him. It clatters to the floor, dust swirling in the air.

'Are you going to get up so I can have a look at you?' the orderly asks him.

'Don't touch me!' Primus shouts.

He holds off the orderly with one hand as he gets to his feet. Blood trickles down his face from the cut on his forehead.

'Damn you,' he says, pointing at Joona. 'I didn't say anything . . . I didn't tell you a fucking thing . . .'

The door opens, and another orderly enters the room. 'Everything all right in here?' he asks.

'Primus is just a bit anxious,' the other replies.

'Damn it,' Primus mumbles. 'Damn it . . .'

The second orderly pulls Primus away from Joona, over to the sofa. 'How are you doing, Primus?' he asks.

'I'm being nailed up on the cross . . .'

69

Primus wakes up in bed with the feeling that his tongue is swollen, his mouth watering. He swallows and thinks back to the way he manipulated the detective. He defended himself and stuck to the truth, albeit ingeniously encrypted.

It was like Boolos's logic puzzle.

No one can solve it.

But then the detective stepped into the room, closed his eyes, took a chance, and managed to draw the right card.

It's nothing to worry about.

He's fairly sure no one noticed how much it bothered him.

Everything is fine, though he did sleep a little too long as a result of the injection in his backside. He will have to hurry before Caesar gets impatient or angry. He'll do what he has to do, though he has no idea what the overarching purpose of the task is.

The left hand doesn't know what the right is doing.

Primus doesn't care that the Prophet calls him a dogsbody, a slave, a flesh fly; Caesar says he will be able to choose his own wives and concubines from a huge pile of virgins.

Or maybe it was a long line.

The Prophet said no to helping Caesar. He can stay in his creaky little house in Täby kyrkby, saving up for a sex doll.

Primus slumps down onto the floor, pushing his feet into his slippers and trying to look over to the door, but all he sees is the ceiling, the damp patch around the sprinkler.

The medication makes his eyes roll back in his head.

He slowly moves forward, arms outstretched. He blinks hard and can suddenly see the floor and the door again.

He quickly uses the toilet, spits some excess saliva into the sink, and pulls out from the cistern the pair of scissors he stole from the office.

He gets down onto his stomach by the door and peers out into the corridor.

There is an officer sitting in a chair outside.

Primus lies still, listening to the sound of his breathing, his fingertips on his phone, and the soft pings of notifications and likes.

After a little over an hour, the officer gets up and heads towards the bathroom.

Primus returns to his bed and presses the alarm button. Just a minute or so later, the lock at the door clicks and a night nurse called Nina comes into the room.

'Everything OK, Primus?'

'I think I'm having an allergic reaction to the medication; my head is itchy, and I'm having trouble breathing.'

'Let's have a look at you,' she says, moving over to his bed.

He hasn't quite decided what he is going to do next, but he grips her thin wrist with one hand, pulling her to him.

'Let go of my arm,' says Nina.

He gets up from the bed, noticing the fear on her face before his eyes roll back again. Suddenly, all he can see is the ugly grey plastic ceiling light.

'Not a sound,' he whispers, whipping the scissors blindly up to her throat.

'Don't do this.'

His eyes return to her, and he realises he has accidentally cut her cheek.

'I'll snip off your nose and fuck you like a pig until the blood starts squirting from your snout.'

'Primus, calm down. We can fix . . .'

'I need to get out of here, do you understand me?' he hisses, watching droplets of spittle land on her face.

'We can talk to the care manager in the morning, and—'

Primus picks up a sock from the bed and pushes it into her mouth. He stares at her face, her lips taut and chin creased, then pushes the sharp blade of the scissors against her eyebrows and nose.

'I always notice when you come in,' he says. 'You want me so bad, but you don't dare; you think you have to follow the rules here, but every time you come in I can smell your throbbing pussy, I know it's widening and getting wet . . .'

He spits onto the floor and turns her around, raising the scissors to her throat and guiding her towards the door.

'We're leaving now,' he whispers. 'If you come with me, I'll give you everything. I'll carry you around on my dick all day.'

They step out into the empty corridor, night lights illuminating the floor.

His eyes roll back again, and he sees the dark fluorescent lights on the ceiling as they walk.

Nina pauses, and he realises they must have reached the first door. 'Swipe your card, put your code in . . .'

He blinks firmly and can see her again, watches her hands tremble as she touches the glowing buttons.

He moves closer, cupping her breast with his free hand.

The door buzzes, and they step into the next corridor, passing the day room and the unmanned reception desk.

Primus pulls her through an emergency exit, taking the stairs down to the ground floor and emerging at the rear of the building. At first, all he can see is the dark night sky, and he walks into a flower box. He lets go of Nina and blinks several times until the buildings, street lamps and alleyways reappear.

'Are you coming with me?' he asks. 'It'll be an adventure . . .'

Nina steps away from him, pulling the sock from her mouth. He tosses the scissors, spits once again and attempts to smile at her. She stares at him with wide eyes and shakes her head.

'Whore,' he hisses and starts running.

70

It has been another blisteringly hot day, and the stifling heat did not subside until around eight in the evening.

Distant thunderclaps have been rumbling since afternoon.

Magda and Ingrid both finished ninth grade in June, and will be starting high school in Valdemarsvik in August. Neither of them has managed to find a summer job.

Combined with the heatwave, their summer boredom makes it feel like time has come to a standstill, the way it used to when they were little.

They ate dinner at Magda's house that evening. Her father cooked chicken skewers on the barbecue behind the little terraced house, and they sat down to eat them with potato salad and crisps at the white plastic table on the patio.

It is already after ten when Magda and Ingrid make their way into the wooded area behind the soccer field where Magda keeps her bright orange canoe. They drag it over the grass to the river, and Ingrid pushes it out into the water, holding it steady while Magda climbs in and takes a seat at the back.

A cloud of grey clay spreads through the water.

Ingrid sits down on the front thwart and pushes off.

They turn, heading upstream on the river running like a deep wound to the side of the small town.

All they can hear is the soft splash of their paddles and the grasshoppers chirping on the banks.

Ingrid thinks about her big sister, who moved to Örebro with her boyfriend in May. She cried when she said she would never be back.

Huge trees lean in over the water, forming a tunnel of lush greenery. They stop paddling and drift silently through the murky water.

Through the canopy, they catch glimpses of the bright night sky.

Magda trails her fingers in the warm river.

This is the third time they have paddled up to Lake Byngaren late at night. Technically, the local swimming spot has been off limits ever since the run-off from the factory was discovered years ago. The potatoes, vegetables, mushrooms and fish from Gusum are all deemed inedible; there are dangerous levels of heavy metals, arsenic and PCB in both the ground and the water.

Still, Magda and Ingrid love having the entire lake to themselves. They often paddle out to the small island in the middle to smoke and swim naked in the mirror-flat water.

'I *want* to glow in the dark,' Magda always jokes.

They leave the tunnel of greenery behind as the rounded bow of the canoe cuts through the placid water.

The girls paddle under a concrete bridge and hear the echo of the water on the damp walls.

Magda guides them to the right to avoid the rusty shopping trolley trapped between two rocks at the mouth of the tunnel.

They emerge on the other side, the meadow grass on the bank brushing up against the canoe.

'Hold on,' says Ingrid, paddling backwards so that the bow swings in to the bank.

'What's going on?'

'Can you see that bag up there?' Ingrid points.

'Come on.'

Among the weeds on the slope up to the main road above, there is a black Prada bag.

'It's so fake,' Magda tells her.

'Who cares?' Ingrid says, climbing ashore.

She grabs the rope tied to the bow, wraps it around a tree and starts making her way towards the bag.

'What's that stink?' Magda asks, following her.

A heavy vehicle thunders by on the road, making the branches of the trees sway in its tailwind.

Thousands of flies are teeming around a thicket of young birches and dusty nettles.

Ingrid grabs the bag, holds it up to Magda and starts scrambling back down the slope.

Magda moves closer to the trees where the flies are buzzing. Among the dry bushes, she can see three black rubbish bags. She grabs a stick and pokes at the one closest to her.

A cloud of flies swarms up into the air, carrying an incredible stench.

'What are you doing?' Ingrid shouts from the bottom of the bank.

Magda pushes the stick and rips into the plastic, angling it so that she can make a bigger hole. Hundreds of fly larvae spill to the ground, like a white paste.

Her heart is racing.

Covering her mouth with her hand, Magda tears a bigger hole in the bag. She whimpers when she finally sees the sawed off arm, nail polish still intact.

71

Pamela and Martin have finished eating, but they haven't got up from the table yet and their cartons of rice vermicelli, prawn and spring rolls are still in front of them.

Martin is wearing nothing but a pair of khaki chinos, and his neck is damp with sweat. He watches Pamela as the flickering candlelight dances over her face, the red glow of her hair bouncing across one cheek.

When she turns to look at him, he hurries to lower his gaze before their eyes meet.

'Have you packed?' she asks.

He shakes his head, but doesn't look up.

'I don't want any more electric shocks,' he says, turning to the hall to make sure no one is there.

'I really do understand, but Dennis thinks it'll be good for you,' she says. 'I can come with you if you're worried.'

A wave of anxiety makes him push back his chair and slump to the floor to hide under the table. He can't put into words the emptiness he feels from the electric shock therapy, like a panicked hunger for something unknown.

'It's just that we need you to get better now . . . and almost fifty per cent of people who have ECT totally lose their symptoms. They get better – can you imagine?' she says.

He peers at the strawberry-red fabric of her dress above her knees, her tanned feet and polished red nails.

Pamela picks up the tea light and crawls beneath the table with him, watching him with her warm eyes.

'And you've actually started talking more since the last session.'

He shakes his head, thinking that he actually improved because of the hypnosis.

'Do you want me to call the ward and tell them you aren't coming in tonight?'

He swallows hard. He wants to reply, but the lump in his throat makes it impossible.

'Please, Martin, talk to me.'

'I want to stay here, I can handle it . . .'

'I think so too.'

'Good,' he whispers.

'I know you get scared when I ask about the playground, but I can't help it – it's because I'm thinking of Mia,' she says. 'You were there, and you drew a picture of Jenny Lind when you got home.'

Martin tries to swallow his anxiety and tell himself that the boys aren't real. But despite the effort, his brain insists that names provoke them, that they want the names to carve them into a gravestone or whatever else they can get their hands on.

'Martin, talking isn't dangerous,' she says, placing a hand on his arm. 'You need to understand that. Everyone does it, and nothing bad happens to them.'

He glances towards the hallway and sees something hurry into the shadows behind Pamela's raincoat.

'I need to know whether it's the boys preventing you from telling me what you saw, or whether you really don't remember because of the ECT.'

'I don't remember anything,' he says.

'Are you even trying?'

'Yes, I am.'

'But you were there, you must have seen everything. You know who killed Jenny Lind . . .'

'No,' he says, raising his voice, tears in his eyes.

'OK, I'm sorry.'

'But when I was hypnotised, I started seeing things . . .'

It was like a bright light had just gone out, and he was left blinking in the darkness.

But when Erik Maria Bark told him to share what he saw, it really did feel like his eyes had started to adjust, except that he got stuck somehow, just as he was about to take in the first few shapes.

'Keep going,' Pamela whispers.

'I want to see the hypnotist again,' Martin tells her, meeting her eye.

72

Pamela puts the leftovers into the fridge, unhooks her bra beneath her dress, and is in the middle of pulling it out through one arm when the buzzer rings.

'That's Dennis,' she says. 'I couldn't get hold of him. He thinks he's taking you back to the ward.'

She tosses her bra into the bedroom before answering the door. Dennis is dressed in jeans and a Hawaiian shirt.

'I tried calling you – Martin isn't going to Sankt Göran's after all.'

'Oh, my phone is constantly running out of battery.'

He closes the door behind him and kicks off his shoes on the mat, muttering about the heat.

'Sorry to have dragged you over here for no reason,' she says.

They head to the kitchen together, where Martin is standing at the counter, filling a small jar with tiny pink dog chews.

'Hi, Martin,' says Dennis.

'Hi,' he replies without turning around.

'Martin didn't feel well after the ECT session,' Pamela explains.

'OK . . .'

'He doesn't want to go back to the ward.'

'How about this,' Dennis suggests, pushing his glasses back onto the bridge of his nose. 'I could take over as your care manager for now, so we can stay on top of all your medication.'

'OK,' Martin replies.

'And you can take your time looking for a psychiatrist you like.'

'Does that sound good, Martin?' Pamela asks.

343

'Yeah.'

He walks to the hallway and strokes the dog, who is lying among the shoes, waiting for him. Pamela follows him over, picking up the leash from the floor.

'Don't go too far,' she says, handing it to him.

'I think we'll walk to Gamla stan,' says Martin, opening the front door.

The Lout gets to his feet and lumbers over to the lift behind Martin. Pamela closes the door and returns to the kitchen.

'Is it going to work having Martin at home?'

'I really don't know,' she says, leaning back against the counter. 'But he has started communicating a lot more, and that makes a huge difference.'

'Fantastic,' Dennis says, without enthusiasm.

'I think the sense of being able to help the police is the key.'

'It could well be.'

A drop of water falls from the tap, making a metallic plunk as it hits the sink. Pamela's thoughts briefly turn to the bottles of vodka in the cupboard, but she manages to shake it off.

'Are you going to tell him about us?'

'I'll have to at some point, I know, but . . . it's just so hard, especially if you're going to take over his care.'

'I'm doing it for your sake. What I really want is for you to leave him and move in with me.'

'Don't say that.'

'Sorry, that was stupid of me, but I often think back to when Alice was small, before you met Martin. I was practically living with you, helping take care of her so you had time to study . . . I think that might be the only time in my life I haven't been standing on the sidelines, by myself,' he says, turning to leave.

73

Martin has walked around Hedvig Eleonora Church and down to Nybroplan. The dog stops to pee on a junction box and sniffs the ground beneath a rubbish bin. His black fur shines in the light from one of the shop windows.

Martin glances at the rack on a news-stand, reading the evening headlines as he waits.

The lead story in *Expressen* is about weight loss, but it is a smaller headline, about Jenny Lind, that catches his eye:

POLICE'S SOLE WITNESS IS MENTALLY ILL

Martin knows that he is the witness, and he knows that he is mentally ill, but it still feels strange to see it splashed across the front page of a newspaper.

He and Loke keep walking, and are making their way over Strömbron, towards Gamla stan when the dog suddenly lies down on the ground by the railings.

The dark water rushes by beneath them.

Martin drops to his knees and lifts the dog's heavy head in his hands.

'Are you OK?' he asks, kissing him on the nose. 'Are you tired? I thought you wanted a long walk today.'

The dog wearily gets to his feet. He shakes, then turns back, walking a few steps before pausing again.

'Shall we take the metro? Hmm, buddy?'

The dog takes another few steps and lies down again.

'I'll carry you for a while.'

Martin picks him up in his arms and walks back over the bridge, heading through Kungsträdgården Park.

He sees a group of teenagers in an alleyway, smoking and laughing. A few metres away from them, in the shadows from a tree, he spots two young boys with thin faces and eyes like saucers.

Martin takes a sharp right, crossing the road. He makes his way over to the metro station, then lowers the dog to the ground.

'You've turned into a little tub of lard,' he says, casting a quick glance back to the park.

They pass through the automatic doors and stop for a moment at the top of the escalator. A shiver passes down Martin's spine, and he turns around.

The doors rattle as a train passes through the station down below, then open again though there is no one outside.

As they close, Martin notices a small figure standing out in the darkness, peering in at him.

He is hazy, shaking.

Another train screeches into the station.

The automatic doors spring open yet again, but now the boy is gone.

Maybe he is just hiding around the corner outside.

Martin takes the short escalator down to the barriers and touches his card to the reader, hurrying to the next escalator.

Loke slumps at his feet, breathing heavily.

The second escalator is so long and steep that he can't see the end of it. Martin holds the dog by the collar, feeling every breath he takes through the taut leather. A warm, musty breeze from the tunnels hits them as they ride downwards. The machinery rumbles underfoot.

'Almost there,' he says as he spots the end.

Straining his eyes, he can see someone waiting at the bottom of the escalator.

He and the dog are still so far away that all he can make out are a pair of dirty, bare children's feet.

The glare of the ceiling lights seems to roll upwards as they continue down.

The child steps back.

A train thunders into the platform, brakes screeching.

Martin pulls the dog to his feet and tells him to get ready to step off the escalator. The boy is gone.

Martin knows this is just part of his illness, but he constantly struggles to accept that the boys don't really exist.

According to the display, the next train is eleven minutes away.

They walk to the very end of the empty platform, where Martin sits down on a red fire cabinet and the Lout drops to the floor.

Martin glances back along the platform.

There is a border of white tiles marking the very edge.

Hearing the slap of bare feet running, Martin gets up. He turns around, but there is no one there.

There is an electric buzz, a high-pitched whine pulsing along the tracks.

He feels suddenly anxious.

The metallic snaps on the tracks below remind him of the ice cracking on a lake.

He remembers lying flat on his stomach in the middle of the white landscape, peering down into the water through the hole in the ice.

Two large perch emerged from the darkness, cautiously approaching his float before darting away.

The glass in the station clock begins to shake.

Just four minutes until the next train. Not much longer.

Martin leaves Loke lying on the floor and walks over to the edge of the platform, staring into the dark tunnel.

He hears keys clinking, echoing between the walls, and footsteps again, but this time they sound heavier than before.

He squints in the direction of the escalator, but the platform is still empty.

Someone could be hiding behind the vending machine. Martin thinks he can see a shoulder, part of a pale yellow hand peeking from around its corner, but he knows it is probably all in his mind.

A faint, quaking roar grows louder. Dust and pieces of rubbish start shifting in the breeze.

He looks down at his feet on the edge of the platform.

The tracks, railroad ties and rocks seem to glitter in the gloom below.

Martin looks up and sees his own shadow on the rough wall opposite.

He thinks about the boys' sharp cheekbones and firmly closed mouths. The older of the two has a broken collarbone, making his arm hang at an angle.

Martin takes another step towards the edge, peering down the tunnel again. In the distance, a red light shines in the darkness. It blinks, as though someone has just passed in front of it.

The train is coming, its rhythmic thundering growing louder and louder.

He turns back to his shadow on the green wall across from him. It seems much broader than it did a moment ago.

Right then, it splits in two.

He realises someone must have crept up behind him, and before he has time to turn around, he feels a powerful shove between his shoulders, pushing him over the edge.

Martin lands on the tracks, hitting his knee and breaking his fall with his hands. The coarse gravel grazes his skin, making his palms sting. He gets to his feet and slips on the smooth rail as he turns around.

The train is heading straight for him, pushing a wave of dirty air ahead of it.

Martin tries to climb back up onto the platform, but his bloody hands struggle to grip the white edge.

The sound is deafening. The ground shakes.

He spots a yellow metal sign warning about live wires and manages to get his foot onto the edge of it. He uses it to heave himself up, making it onto the platform and rolling to safety just as the train rumbles into the station, brakes screeching.

74

White lines flash by down on the road, the tyres humming against the tarmac. Joona's right hand is resting on the wheel, and the bright summer light filtering through the pine trees twinkles on his sunglasses.

Säter Psychiatric Hospital is about two hundred kilometres northwest of Stockholm, between Hedemora and Borlänge. Court-mandated patients and others with particularly complex issues are sent there from all over the country.

Martin overheard Primus talking to Caesar about killing Jenny, and through Ulrike, they then learned that Primus could be found at the Eagle's Nest.

Joona only managed one interview with Primus before he escaped.

He clearly enjoyed evading Joona's questions and making his answers cryptic.

Primus has a narcissistic arrogance, and believed he was in complete control of the course of the interview. When he realised he had inadvertently revealed something, he was obviously shaken.

He gave Joona the first concrete lead on Caesar.

There is no record of anyone called Caesar being either convicted or placed in psychiatric care in Sweden during the past sixty years.

Despite that, Joona has no doubt that Primus was referring to Säter when he mentioned Auschwitz.

Everything that happened at the Eagle's Nest might have been worth it for that one small detail.

Before the interview with Primus, Caesar was just a name, but Joona is now convinced that the man was a patient at Säter at some point in time.

He thinks back to all of the names Primus used to describe Caesar during their brief meeting: Saturn, Leopold, a Darwinist, a Chad, a patriarch.

Each one is associated with some kind of superior, despotic masculine figure.

Joona turns off the 650 and drives through the Skönvik area of Säter. He passes the secure complex that closed down around thirty years ago, and was ravaged by fire thirteen years later.

The manor-like building looks like it is waiting to be demolished, with a collapsed roof and rusty bars covering every window. The main entrance has been boarded up, and there are chunks of plaster missing from the walls, revealing the bare brick below.

Joona drives on, and eventually pulls over, glancing at a map of the area and then turning around to park outside the modern clinic nearby.

These days, the hospital is a large complex with 88 patients and 170 staff members.

Joona feels the stitches in his side sting as he climbs out of the car. He enters the building and passes through security, pushing his sunglasses into his breast pocket, before making his way over to the reception desk.

The chief psychiatrist comes down to meet him. She is wearing an emergency alarm on the collar of her shirt. She is tall, in her mid-forties, with black hair and a furrowed brow.

'We're all too aware of how Säter has been covered in the media . . . Everyone imagines patients being drugged with benzodiazepines or psychopharmaceuticals . . . Anxiety therapy and psychologists retrieving repressed memories that never even existed.'

'Maybe,' Joona replies.

'Much of the criticism is justified,' the doctor continues. 'There were huge knowledge gaps in the old school of psychiatry.'

She swipes her pass in a card reader, enters a code and opens the door for Joona.

'Thanks.'

'We're still not perfect today, of course,' she says, showing him down the corridor. 'It's a process, and just recently we faced criticism from the Parliamentary Ombudsman for some of the measures we take. But what are we supposed to do with a patient who tries to scratch their own eyes out the minute we loosen their restraints?' She pauses in a pantry. 'Coffee?'

'Double espresso,' Joona replies.

The doctor takes out two cups and starts the coffee machine.

'These days, we've got a carefully considered foundation for quality-assured care,' she continues. 'And we're in the process of developing structured risk assessments . . .'

They take their cups to the doctors' office, each sitting down in an armchair and sipping their coffee in silence.

'You had a patient called Caesar here,' Joona says, lowering his cup to the table.

The doctor gets up and moves over to her desk. She logs in to her computer and then sits quietly for a moment before looking up.

'No,' she says.

'Yes.'

The doctor stares at Joona and, for the first time, a flicker of a smile seems to pass over her mouth.

'Do you have a surname or an ID number for this person?'

'No.'

'And when were they supposed to have been admitted? I've been working here for eight years, but our digital records go back fifteen.'

'Are there any other records?'

'I don't know, actually.'

'Who has worked here the longest?'

'That must be Viveca Grundig, one of our occupational therapists.'

'Is she working today?'

'I think she is,' the doctor says, picking up her phone and dialling a number.

A few minutes later, a woman in her sixties comes into the room. She has a narrow face and short grey hair. Her eyes are pale blue and she's smiling.

'This is Joona Linna from the National Crime Unit,' the doctor explains.

'From the police? And to think that I've been pining after doctors all my life,' Viveca says, making Joona smile back.

'The detective was wondering whether we have old patient records from before everything was digitised.'

'Of course, there's an archive.'

'I need to track down a patient called Caesar,' Joona explains.

Viveca looks away, plucking a stray hair from her blouse before bringing her eyes up to his again. 'That part of the archive was destroyed,' she says.

'But you know who I'm talking about, don't you?'

'Not really . . .'

'Tell me,' says Joona.

Viveca pushes her grey hair back from her forehead and studies him.

'It was when I first started here. Pretty early on, I heard about someone called Caesar in the secure unit, under the care of Dr Gustav Scheel.'

'What did you hear?'

She looks away. 'It was all nonsense . . .'

'Tell me,' Joona insists.

'I'm sure it was just talk, but when the secure unit was closing down, people said that Gustav Scheel was against it because he didn't want to lose a patient he'd become obsessed with.'

'Caesar?'

'Some people claimed he was in love with him, but that was just a rumour.'

'Is there anyone who might know the truth?'

'You should probably ask Anita, she's one of the nurses here.'

'Did she work in the secure unit?'

'No, but she's Gustav Scheel's daughter.'

Joona follows Viveca to the nurses' office on the next floor down. Through the walls, they hear the angry shouts of an old man.

'Anita?'

The woman standing by the fridge turns around, a cup of yogurt in her hand. She looks to be around thirty-five, with short, messy

blonde hair. Other than the blue mascara on her lashes, she isn't wearing any makeup. Her eyebrows are colourless, her full lips pale.

She puts down the yogurt and balances the spoon on the lid and wipes her hands on her trousers before greeting Joona.

He introduces himself, looking at her closely as he explains why he is here. The crease between her eyebrows deepens as she nods minutely.

'Yes, of course, I remember Dad having a patient called Caesar.'

'Do you remember his surname?'

'He was admitted without a name, as NN, but he called himself Caesar . . . It's entirely possible he didn't know his real name.'

'Is it common to have patients whose identities remain unknown?'

'No, I wouldn't say that it's common, but it does happen.'

'I need to see the archive.'

'But everything was destroyed in the fire,' she replies, sounding surprised that he didn't already know. 'Caesar was in the secure unit during the last couple of years before it closed . . . and the entire place burned down a few years later.'

'And you're sure it's all gone?'

'Yes.'

'You can't have been very old when your father was treating Caesar, but somehow you know all about his admission here.'

Anita's face turns solemn, and she seems to be weighing something before she speaks.

'Maybe we should sit down,' she eventually says.

Joona thanks Viveca for her help and takes a seat with Anita on one of the tall stools around a table with a vase of artificial flowers.

'My father was a psychiatrist,' she begins, moving the vase to one side. 'Fundamentally Freudian, I suppose, and he devoted a lot of his time to research . . . particularly the last ten years before he died.'

'Was he at Säter the whole time?'

'Yes, but with ties to the University Hospital in Uppsala.'

'And now *you* work here?'

'I have no idea how that happened,' she laughs. 'I grew up here, in one of the doctors' villas, and now I live five minutes away . . . I moved to Hedemora for a while, but even that's just twenty kilometres away.'

'That's often the way life goes,' Joona smiles briefly, before focusing again.

Anita swallows, lowering her hands to her lap.

'I was in my teens when Dad told me how Caesar became his patient . . . He woke up in the middle of the night and realised he could hear voices in the house, and when he got up, he saw that the light was on in my room. He found a young man sitting on the edge of my bed, stroking my head.'

The tip of her nose turns red, and she glances out towards the corridor, deep in thought.

'What happened?'

'Dad managed to get Caesar into the kitchen. It was obvious he was mentally ill . . . I mean, he knew that himself, because Caesar asked to be admitted.'

'Why did he turn to your father?'

'I don't know, but Dad was pretty well known back then, he was one of the few doctors who believed that anyone could make a full recovery.'

'But why did Caesar go to your house rather than straight to the hospital?'

'You couldn't just walk into the secure unit; people were admitted there as a last resort . . . But I think Dad took an interest in Caesar's case that night.'

'So he gave in to a threat purely out of professional curiosity?'

'"Gave in" might not be the right way to describe it.'

'Right . . . he realised the best way to take control of Caesar was to admit him as a patient in the secure ward,' Joona continues.

She nods. 'This used to be a place where the patients' rights ceased to exist. There was no transparency whatsoever; they often stayed here until they died, and then they were cremated and buried in the hospital graveyard.'

'What happened to Caesar?'

'He was discharged after less than two years.'

Joona considers the absent look on her face as she stares expressionlessly into space.

'What was your father's research about?' he asks.

Anita takes a deep breath. 'I mean, I'm not a psychologist or a psychiatrist, so I can't speak for his methods ... but Dad's primary area of focus was depersonalisation and dissociative identity disorders.'

'DID,' says Joona.

'I don't want to put my father down, but most people now would say that his view of the human psyche was quite old fashioned, that it belonged to another era,' she continues. 'One of his theories was based on the idea that someone who commits a violent act is traumatised by their own deeds, and affected by different kinds of dissociation ... I know he was busy writing a case study about Caesar, called "The Mirror Man".'

'"The Mirror Man",' Joona repeats.

'When the secure unit closed down, Dad stayed there,' she explains. 'All the patients were gone, but he wanted to compile all the research from his forty years as a clinical psychiatrist; his archive was huge ... But there was a fire one night, in one of the switchboards. My dad died, and all his research was destroyed.'

'I'm sorry,' says Joona.

'Thanks,' she mumbles.

'Do you remember much about Caesar yourself?'

'Can I ask what this is about?'

'Caesar is a suspected serial killer,' Joona replies.

'Oh.' Anita swallows. 'But I only ever met him once, that night when I was a girl.'

'I'm trying to see things from your father's perspective ... A mentally ill man breaks into his home in the middle of the night, and sits down on his daughter's bed, laying his hand on her head ... He must have been terrified.'

'But for him, it was also the start of something important.'

'As a case study?'

'I remember him smiling when he told me about that first meeting ... Caesar was sitting there stroking my head, and he

looked into his eyes and said, "The mothers are watching the children play.'"

Joona instantly freezes. He gets up from his chair, groaning in pain, and tells her he has to go. He thanks her for her help before hurrying down the corridor.

He thinks back to the hypnosis session, when Martin could remember the back of the university building and the red playhouse.

Erik slowly guided him towards the crime scene, describing the slides and the jungle gym.

Martin nodded and muttered that very same phrase: 'The mothers are watching the children play.'

Both Joona and Erik assumed that the words were simply part of Martin's attempt to imagine a playground, and Erik had reminded him that it was the middle of the night – 'the light is from a street lamp', he had said, trying to make Martin focus on his real memories of the playground, where no mothers would have been around.

But Martin was already in the real situation.

He couldn't see anything, but he could hear what was happening.

Martin heard Caesar speak that night in the playground.

Joona pushes the front door open and bolts towards his car as he tries to work out how he can get Martin to share more of what he remembers from that night.

75

Since Caesar disappeared, the days have all been warm and monotonous. Granny was out in the lorry yesterday, so they didn't get any food, but they were given salted fish and potatoes this morning.

Mia can't stop thinking about what happened. She can't make sense of it.

Caesar slit Raluca's throat and, just like that, she was completely extinguished. She was put to sleep and never woke up.

Caesar raped Kim, panting on top of her for a moment or two, then got up, buttoned up his trousers and went on his way.

Granny was here when Kim started to come to, and she made sure she got back into the cage, clutching her clothes.

She was still suffering from temporary blindness, and hit her head on the bars before curling up in her spot and dozing off.

Raluca's body was left where she had fallen overnight.

The next morning, Blenda was given the job of helping to cremate her in the oven behind the last of the longhouses.

It took almost all day, the sweet smoke hanging heavy in the air.

Blenda was crying when she returned to her cage, her face sooty. The smell of smoke still seems to be clinging to her, even now.

Kim has been in pain ever since the rape. When Mia tried to engage her and Blenda yesterday, she just sat still, holding her face.

'I don't get it, he keeps us in cages so we won't escape, but we're not worth shit to him. At first I thought this must be some kind of Boko Haram thing, only Christian . . . but now I'm thinking it's actually some messed-up incel revolution,' Mia told them. 'No one wants to have sex

with him, so this is what he does . . . It's so fucking sickening. I bet he's got a huge fanbase on 4chan. They probably worship him like a god.'

'Honestly,' said Blenda, leaning against the bars, 'have you ever met a guy who would seriously say no to this?'

'Having a bunch of sobbing girls in cages?'

'No, but the way it was before – like a harem, luxurious and—'

'It was never luxurious,' Kim interrupted her.

'Because you're used to fancier things, I bet,' Blenda snapped.

'There's no reason for us to fight,' Mia whispered.

The two shivs are now as sharp as she can get them without a proper whetstone. If she and Kim use enough force, they should work just fine.

Mia swapped her parka, which she has been using as a pillow, for Kim's shirt, making a series of small cuts in it and tearing the fabric into strips.

She has given up trying to involve Blenda in their escape, despite the fact that they need her to pull it off. Blenda just doesn't seem motivated enough, and might hesitate or change her mind when the time comes.

Still, since Blenda is the only one given any real freedom to move around the area, Mia has tried to ask her about the other longhouses, and what the route through the forest is like.

'I don't know,' she replies every time.

Mia knows there are girls in three of the other buildings – possibly as many as ten prisoners in total.

She has glimpsed their movements during her yard breaks, sometimes seen the whites of their eyes in the darkness, and she hears them crying and coughing at night.

Just yesterday, she saw a young woman in one of the doorways, looking in at them.

She was holding a spade in one hand, and her hair shone red in the sunlight. Granny shouted something, and she vanished.

'Did you see her?' Mia asked.

'She's got TB. She'll probably die soon,' Blenda replied.

Once Blenda fell asleep last night, Mia and Kim lay awake, whispering. Kim has changed since the rape, and now says she is willing to help with the revolt. She's listened to Mia's instructions, repeating them back to her.

Their break is almost here, and Mia's nerves have started to grow, an anxious weight in her gut.

She doesn't tell Kim that she has no real experience of attacks like this. All she has ever done is hang out with boys who have been to prison and joined gangs in an attempt to survive; boys who had to cut down their enemies to prove their loyalty to the leader.

The girls in the third longhouse have their break first today. Mia recognises their voices by now. Two of them almost always talk intensely among themselves, but the others are generally quiet, pausing whenever one of them needs to cough.

A helicopter passes over the forest, and Granny snaps at the dog when it starts barking.

The morning feels sluggish, as though everything is taking much longer than usual.

Mia gives Kim her shiv and makes sure she tucks it into the top of her sports sock, on the inside of her right shin, pulling her trouser leg down over the top.

She pushes her own into the top of her boot, double-checking that it isn't going to fall out.

If the circumstances are right, they're going to do it today.

It partly depends on the weather. Mia isn't sure whether a blade made from a piece of roofing tin will be able to pierce through thick clothing. Granny was wearing a denim jacket at breakfast, but the sun is now high in the sky, and the air in the longhouse is already stifling. If Granny is wearing the same blouse as yesterday, they shouldn't have any problem.

Mia has thought through the potential scenarios thousands of times.

She actually thinks she could manage it without any help, even if Kim can't handle her part. Mia is smaller and weaker than Granny, but if she can just get behind her back, she'll give it her all. She might only have time to stab her once before being knocked down, but that could be enough. If Granny is injured and bleeding, Mia would still have time to get back onto her feet and circle her until she gets another chance to stab her.

Kim is kneeling down, hands clasped as she prays, but she stops abruptly as they hear footsteps outside.

The dog is panting.

Granny lifts the crossbar, leans it against the wall and then props the door open with a rock.

Dust dances in the sunlight behind her as she carries a bucket of water into the building, the talisman around her neck clanking against the rim. She's taken off her jacket, and is wearing a thin blue shirt with the sleeves rolled up.

Kim crawls forward and holds out her arm. She lets Granny fasten a cable tie around her wrist, then climbs out of the cage onto the floor.

Mia follows her, has her wrist bound to Kim's, and climbs out.

They stand side by side, thighs tingling and feet tender. Mia can feel the shiv pressing against her leg inside her boot.

Granny pulls on a pair of yellow rubber gloves, lifts a sponge from the bucket and starts scrubbing their faces and throats. The warm water smells strongly of chlorine.

'Take off your tops as best you can.'

Mia lifts up her undershirt and Granny quickly scrubs beneath her arms, across her back and around her breasts.

The warm water trickles down inside her trousers.

She panics when she realises what is about to happen next. If Granny decides to wash them completely, they will both have to take off their shoes – exposing their weapons.

Mia pulls her undershirt back down and waits as Granny cleans Kim's upper body, scrubbing beneath her arms. Kim holds up her T-shirt and her grubby bra with her free hand, swaying against the sponge.

'Pull your trousers down.'

Granny wets the sponge again, wrings it out and moves back over to Mia.

'Make room,' she says.

Mia tries to spread her legs, and Granny shoves the sponge between her thighs. As she starts to rub, Mia closes her eyes and groans like she is enjoying it.

Granny stops immediately, hissing at the two of them to get dressed and return to the bench. She pulls off her gloves, tosses them to the floor and carries the bucket out of the building.

76

Mia smiles to herself as she hears Granny pour the water down the drain outside the sixth longhouse. She wasn't sure whether the old woman would hit her or not, but she couldn't risk the cleaning session going any further.

After a while, Granny returns, leaning on her stick and telling them to do a loop in the yard.

Hand in hand, Mia and Kim step out through the doorway. The bright sunlight is hot, their clothes sticking to their skin.

Granny is busy boiling something in a large pot outside the sixth longhouse, and Blenda is stirring it with a long ladle. Granny seems angry, muttering that she thinks some of the girls have secretly been having abortions, and that the Lord will single them out and start to cull them.

The musty steam drifts across the grass.

Mia guides Kim into the middle of the yard, feeling the blade move upwards with every step she takes.

Leaning against her stick, Granny watches them. They turn towards her, needing to find a natural way to move behind her before the end of their break.

'We do it if we get a chance,' says Mia.

'I'm ready,' Kim replies, her voice adamant.

Granny takes the ladle from Blenda and turns to face the pot. Mia pauses, reaching down into her boot and pulling out the shiv.

Her hands shake as she tries to cut through the thick plastic tie around their wrists.

The blade slips, and she almost drops the knife.

'Hurry up,' Kim whispers.

Mia watches Blenda pick up the shovel and add some coal to the fire. Granny barks instructions at her, the ladle clanking against the sides of the pot. Mia's pulse is roaring in her ears. She tries to angle the knife, sawing quickly, and hears the snap when the cable tie finally breaks and drops to the ground. She keeps the knife hidden against her body as they start walking again, still holding hands.

Granny peers down into the pot, stirring it with firm movements. Her strange necklace swings between her breasts as she churns.

The scraps of fabric around the handle of the shiv have dried and tightened, giving them a sturdy grip. It should hold up until it's drenched in blood.

They slowly move closer.

Blenda looks up at them through the steam.

Mia feels that Kim's hand has become sweaty.

Granny skims off the surface and empties the ladle over the rusty drain cover.

Mia's heart is pounding in her chest.

The dog comes over, circling them and sniffing between their legs, whining anxiously.

Granny's face is red and shiny from the steam.

They pass her, slowing down, then turn around and let go of one another.

Mia feels a sudden rush of icy adrenaline. The hairs on her arms are standing on end, and everything suddenly seems crystal clear. The seven longhouses, the stew, the blue shirt tight across Granny's back.

Kim pulls up her trouser leg and reaches beneath her sock. The blade of the knife flashes in the sunlight.

Mia meets Kim's eye, nods and moves quickly towards Granny, holding the knife close to her body. She is gripping it so tightly that her fingers turn white.

The dog starts barking. The gravel crunches beneath her boots. The wooden ladle clangs against the pot.

Kim is just behind Mia so that she can attack Granny from the front immediately after the first stab. She doesn't seem to realise she

is whimpering, and Granny lets go of the long handle of the ladle and starts to turn around.

Mia's legs are trembling, her breathing much too shallow. She focuses on Granny's torso, where her shirt is taut over her skin.

She has just pulled back her arm to gather her strength when she hears a bang.

Something slams into the side of her head, making the nape of her neck burn. As she falls, she catches a glimpse of Blenda holding the shovel in both hands. She drops the knife and sees it tumble over the gravel and disappear into the grate over the drain before she hits the ground and everything goes dark.

The screeching of fireworks seems to fill her ears.

Mia stretches out and feels herself fly like a missile ten centimetres above the ground, shooting between the trees and turning off onto the road to the quarry.

* * *

She wakes with a terrible headache, and realises she is lying flat out on the ground. Her mouth is dry, and the blood on her face is flecked with sand.

She has no idea how long she's been unconscious.

The sun is high in the sky and it looks like it's surrounded by a ragged circle of pink light.

As she slowly turns her head, two blurry crosses come into view. She blinks and thinks of Golgotha.

Kim and Blenda are standing in the middle of the yard, arms outstretched like Jesus on the cross. Kim's shiv is on the ground by her feet, and the shovel is lying in front of Blenda.

Mia tries to work out what happened.

Granny talks under her breath to herself and hobbles over to Kim and Blenda in the bright sunlight.

The dog follows her, lying down by her side and panting.

'What were you planning to do with the knife?' she asks.

'Nothing,' Kim replies, breathing through her open mouth.

'In that case, why do you have a knife?'

'To protect myself.'

'I think the two of you were planning to hurt Mia,' Granny tells them. 'And what do you do if the right hand offends thee?'

Kim doesn't reply, she simply stands still with her eyes on the ground. Her arms are shaking with effort, drooping slightly. Her Lady Gaga T-shirt is drenched with sweat around her neck and between her breasts.

'Arms out,' Granny barks. 'Can you handle that, or do you need help?'

'We can do it,' Blenda replies.

'Do you want me to nail them into place for you?'

Granny paces around them, straightening one of Kim's arms with her stick and then moving back in front of them.

Blenda sways, and has to take a step to the side to regain her balance. The dust from the dry ground whirls in the light.

'You hit Mia in the head with the shovel. What has Mia ever done to you?' Granny says to Blenda, before turning back to Kim. 'What were you going to do with the knife? Were you going to cut her face?'

'No.'

'Arms up!'

'I can't,' Kim sobs.

'Why did you want to hurt Mia? Is it because she's more beautiful than—'

'She was going to kill you,' Blenda shouts.

77

The apartment is stuffy, and Pamela's eyes are stinging. She took the day off work to search for any sign of Mia online, and has been sitting in front of her computer in her leggings and bra for hours.

She has visited hundreds of pornographic websites, men's rights groups and sites dedicated to posing, prostitution and sugar dating. She has scrolled through image after image of abused, exposed, and bound young girls.

But there is no sign of Mia, and no mention of Caesar anywhere.

All she has found is a serious hatred of women, a bottomless longing for power, and a desire to repress.

She feels queasy as she gets up and walks to the living room. Martin is sitting on the floor in one corner, wearing nothing but his underwear.

He has his arm around the dog, and is staring out into the hallway.

A series of huge black bruises have blossomed across his knees and shins. His grazed forearms have started to heal, but both hands are bandaged.

He still hasn't told Pamela what happened.

When he got home, covered in blood, she demanded to know what had happened to him, but all he whispered was 'The boys.' Since then, he hasn't said another word.

'Martin, do you remember telling me you wanted to see the hypnotist again?' She crouches down in front of him, trying to make him look her in the eye. 'I know you think the boys hurt you because of that,' she continues. 'But that isn't true; they can't really hurt you.'

He doesn't reply, simply hugs the dog tight and keeps staring at the hallway.

Pamela gets up and returns to her office.

She has just started to install some software that will allow her to visit the illegal marketplaces on the dark web when her phone buzzes.

It's Joona Linna.

She picks up immediately.

'Has something happened?' she asks, hearing the fear in her own voice.

'No, but I . . .'

'You haven't found Mia?'

'No, we haven't.'

'I heard you'd arrested Primus, that must be a breakthrough?' she asks. 'I mean, he was the one who did it, right?'

Pamela leans back in her chair, trying to calm her breathing. She can hear that Joona is driving.

'I interviewed him once,' he replies. 'But he escaped from Sankt Göran's last night. I don't know how it happened; we had an officer stationed outside his room.'

'One step forward, two steps back,' she whispers.

'Not quite – it's just a lot more complicated than we first thought.'

'So what happens now?' she asks, dizzy with anxiety as she gets to her feet.

'I need to see Martin again. To sit down with him and try to work out what he saw and heard.'

'Martin has been in an accident,' she says quietly. 'He's black and blue . . . and he's stopped talking again.'

'What kind of accident?'

'I don't know, he won't say a word about it,' she explains. 'But before the accident, he said he wanted to try hypnosis again.'

'I wanted to tell you that I have proof that he heard Caesar talking in the playground. It might be exactly what we need to get Martin to give us more information. He might not have seen Caesar, but he heard him.'

Pamela returns to the living room, pausing in the middle of the floor and looking over at Martin, who is still sitting behind the sofa, staring.

'I'll talk to him right now.'

'Thanks.'

* * *

Joona slows down as he turns off into the Karolinska Institute complex. The bright sunlight flooding through the windscreen flickers over his face, flashing in his sunglasses.

Thirty years ago, a man calling himself Caesar broke into psychiatrist Gustav Scheel's home and sat down on his daughter's bed.

'The mothers are watching the children play,' he said.

The very same phrase Martin said under hypnosis when Erik tried to coax him into sharing what he had seen at the playground.

Joona pulls over, leaving the car on the street by the entrance to the Department of Forensic Medicine.

The Needle's white Jaguar is parked so badly that the cars around it are trapped in their bays. The rear bumper has come loose on the left-hand side and is resting on the tarmac.

Joona walks quickly towards the entrance.

Nils has just received the dismembered body of a woman found by two teenage girls on the side of E22 outside of Gusum, some fifteen kilometres from Valdemarsvik.

She has a freeze-brand on the back of her head, just like Jenny Lind.

Joona heads straight up to the main examination room, greeting Åhlén and Chaya as he steps inside. The fans are whirring, but the stench in the room is still deeply unpleasant.

The head and torso of the unidentified young woman have been laid out on the plastic-covered autopsy table. Her body parts have reached an advanced stage of decomposition, now discoloured and seeping, dotted with fly larvae and pupae the colour of oxblood.

The police are currently trying to match her remains to the list of missing people from the past ten years, but any identification will be difficult.

'We haven't examined her yet, but a cursory look seems to indicate that she was killed by a blow to the vertebrae in her neck,' the Needle explains. 'Something like an axe, or a sword . . . we'll find out.'

'She was dismembered with an angle grinder post-mortem, and packed into four bin bags,' Chaya continues, pointing. 'Her head and right arm were in one bag, along with a few bits of plastic jewellery, a purse and a bottle of water.'

Åhlén has shaved the back of the woman's head, and he shows Joona an enlarged photograph on the computer screen.

The freeze-brand glows white against her darkened skin and the small yellow insect eggs nestled in her hair at the lower edge of the image.

The stamp itself is exactly the same, but the imprint is clearer this time.

What looked like an elaborate 'T' on Jenny Lind's body now resembles a cross. A strange cross – or a figure in a top hat and long coat, arms outstretched.

It's impossible to tell.

Joona stares at the image, thinking about freeze-branded cows, hallmarks and crosses on rune stones from the eleventh century. A memory flutters by in his mind, but he fails to catch it.

He feels a sting of pain behind one eye; a black drop falling into a black sea.

They now have three murders and one abduction on their hands. There is no doubt about it: Caesar has entered an incredibly active, deadly phase.

* * *

Pamela sits down on the floor, stroking the dog and studying Martin. His knees are pulled into his chest, and he has wrapped his arms around them. His forehead is creased, and he has a streak of brick-red paint on one cheek.

'You were in the playground,' she tells him, trying to read his face. 'You saw Jenny, you drew her afterwards . . . and Joona says he's sure you also heard Caesar speak.'

His mouth tightens in fear.

'Did you?'

Martin closes his eyes for a few seconds.

'I know I've asked you a thousand times, but I really need you to tell me what he said,' she says, a new sharpness in her voice. 'This isn't just about your fears now; it's about Mia, and I'm starting to get annoyed.'

He nods and looks up at her for a moment with sad eyes.

'This isn't going to work, is it?' she groans.

A couple of tears roll down his cheeks.

'I want you to see the hypnotist again – are you willing to try that?'

Martin gives another subtle nod.

'Good.'

'But they'll kill me,' he whispers.

'No, they won't.'

'They pushed me onto the tracks,' he whispers almost inaudibly.

'What tracks?'

'At the metro station,' he replies, covering his mouth.

'Martin,' she says, failing to mask the weariness in her voice. 'The boys don't exist. They're just a part of your illness. You know that, don't you?'

He doesn't reply.

'Take your hands away from your mouth.'

Martin shakes his head and turns to look at the hallway again. Pamela can't help but sigh as she gets up and heads to her office to call Dennis.

'Dennis Kratz.'

'Hi, it's Pamela . . .'

'I'm so glad you called,' he says. 'I've already told you, but I'm sorry for the way I behaved, it was inappropriate and it won't happen again, I promise . . . I don't recognise myself.'

'It's fine, let's just forget it,' she says, pushing her hair back from her face.

'I heard that Primus escaped, and . . . I don't know how you'll feel about this, but I thought I'd ask if you and Martin want to stay at my place in the country until everything calms down.'

'That's so kind of you.'

'Of course.'

She notices that Martin's large canvas with the unfinished painting of the house is leaning against the wall.

'I actually called to let you know that Martin will be going back to Erik Maria Bark,' she tells him.

'Not for more hypnosis?'

'Yes.'

She hears Dennis take a deep breath.

'You know what I think – there's a serious risk of re-traumatisation.'

'We have to do everything we can to find Mia.'

'Of course you do,' Dennis replies. 'I'm just thinking about Martin . . . but I do understand, I do.'

'Just this one last time.'

78

Erik Maria Bark is sitting at his varnished desk in the afternoon heat, looking out into his overgrown garden.

He is currently on leave from the Karolinska Hospital, but still sees patients at his home office in Gamla Enskede.

His son Benjamin came over that morning to borrow his car. Erik still isn't quite used to the idea that his boy is now an adult, living with his girlfriend and studying to become a doctor in Uppsala.

Erik's hair is unruly, flecked with grey, and he has deep laugh lines and dark circles beneath his eyes.

The top button of his pale blue shirt is undone and his right hand is resting between his keyboard and the open notebook on his desk.

After Joona's call, he spoke to Pamela Nordström, and they agreed that she and Martin would come over right away.

During their previous session, Erik failed to push away the blockage that seemed to be preventing Martin from sharing what he saw in the playground.

He remembers thinking that he had never hypnotised anyone so frightened before.

Erik knows that Martin heard Caesar say the same phrase the psychiatrist in Säter heard thirty years ago, and hopes that this time, he might be able to turn Martin's attention to whatever it is he doesn't dare see.

The pages of Erik's notebook flutter in the breeze and quickly fall flat again.

The fan at the very edge of his desk turns slowly from side to side.

On the floor along one wall are stacks of books dotted with colourful index cards, and reams of printed research papers and studies are piled up on a chair.

The door to his large filing cabinet is wide open, his own research on the metal shelves inside: VHS tapes, Dictaphone cassettes, hard drives, notebooks, journals and folders full of unpublished articles.

Erik picks up his Spanish switchblade from the desk, slices open an envelope and skims through an invitation to deliver a guest lecture at Harvard.

Hearing a rhythmic creaking sound through the open window, he gets up and leaves the office, walking through the waiting room and out into the shady garden.

Joona Linna is sitting in his hammock, sunglasses in one hand, rocking back and forth.

'How's everything with Lumi?' Erik asks, taking a seat beside him.

'I don't know, I'm giving her time . . . or, more accurately, she's giving me time. She thinks I should quit the force, and I think she's right.'

'But you need to solve this case first.'

'It's like a fire,' he says to himself.

'And you're sure you want to quit?'

'I've changed.'

'That's life – it changes us,' Erik tells him.

'But I've changed for the worse – that's what I'm starting to realise.'

'That's still life.'

'Before we go any further, I need to know how much this is going to cost me,' Joona grins.

'You'll get the friends and family rate.'

Joona looks up at the crown of the tree, at the dappled sunlight and the leaves that have curled up in the heat.

'Here are our guests,' he says.

A moment later, Erik too hears the sound of footsteps on the gravel by the front door. They leave the hammock and walk around the side of the brown-brick house.

Martin is holding Pamela's hand, glancing back over his shoulder to the metal gate and the street beyond. There is another man with

them. He is in his forties, and seems guarded, with a boxer's crooked nose under tinted glasses. He's wearing white trousers and a pink T-shirt.

'This is our friend who's been managing Martin's treatment lately,' Pamela says, introducing him.

'Dennis Kratz,' he says, shaking hands with the others.

Erik shows them into his clinic, taking the garden path around the house.

Walking alongside Dennis, Joona asks whether he has ever heard of a Dr Gustav Scheel.

Dennis puts his hand to his face and pinches his lips, as though he is trying to reshape his mouth, or change his expression between his fingers.

'He worked in the secure unit at Säter,' Joona explains, holding the door open.

'That was well before my time as a psychologist,' Dennis replies.

They pass the four armchairs in the small waiting room and continue to Erik's office. There is a pale-grey lambskin armchair by the wall next to one of the bookcases set in the wall, and the varnished oak floor is covered in stacks of books and manuscripts.

'Excuse the mess,' Erik tells them.

'Are you moving?' asks Pamela.

'I'm writing a book.' He smiles.

She laughs politely and they walk to the office with the others. Erik frowns and runs a hand through his messy hair.

'I'm glad you're willing to put your faith in me and give this another try,' he says. 'I'll do everything I can to make it more successful this time.'

'Martin wants to help the police find Mia. It's very important to him,' says Pamela.

'We're grateful for that,' Joona tells her. He notices that Martin smiles softly, but keeps his eyes lowered.

'He started talking a lot more after the last session . . . but things seem to have regressed now. I don't know whether I should tell you what . . .'

'Pamela, can I talk to you for a moment?' Dennis speaks up.

'Hold on, I just wanted to say that Martin—'

'Now, if that's OK?' he interrupts her.

She follows him out into the waiting room. He fills a paper cup with water in the visitors' cloakroom.

'What are you doing?' she asks, her voice hushed.

'I don't think you should tell the hypnotist about Martin's trauma,' he says, taking a sip.

'Why not?'

'Partly because Martin needs to tell him at his own pace, and partly because the hypnotist could use that knowledge the wrong way while making suggestions.'

'But this is about Mia,' she says.

79

When Pamela and Dennis return to the office, Martin is sitting on the brown leather daybed, pulling at the Band-Aid on his left palm with his teeth. Erik is leaning against the edge of his desk, and Joona is staring out of the window.

'Well, I think we should start over if that's OK with you, Martin,' says Erik.

Martin nods and then casts an anxious glance at the half-open door into the waiting room.

'It's usually most comfortable if you lie down,' Erik points out warmly.

Martin doesn't reply, but he kicks off his shoes, cautiously lies back on the daybed and stares up at the ceiling.

'If everyone else could take a seat and turn off their phones,' Erik tells them, closing the door to the waiting room. 'I'd prefer if you didn't say anything, but if you do need to speak, please do so quietly.'

He draws the curtains, checking that Martin is comfortable before rolling over in his chair and beginning the slow relaxation exercises.

'Listen to my voice,' he says. 'Nothing else matters right now . . . I'm here for you, and I want you to feel safe.'

Erik tells Martin to relax his toes, paying close attention to his movements. He tells him to relax his thighs, and watches as his legs lower slightly. He then works through each body part in turn, creating a link between his voice and Martin's actions.

'Everything is calm and quiet. Your eyelids are growing heavier and heavier . . .'

Erik makes his voice increasingly monotone as he leads Martin into a kind of receptive haze, eventually transitioning to the induction itself.

The fan on the table clicks and changes direction, making the curtains billow. A slice of golden light cuts across the room, over the piles of books and the stacks of papers.

'You are now calm and deeply relaxed,' he says. 'If you hear anything other than my voice, you will just become even more focused on what I'm saying.'

Erik studies Martin's face, his half-open mouth, his cracked lips and the tip of his chin, searching for the slightest hint of tension as he eases him into an ever deeper state of rest.

'I'm going to start counting backwards now . . . and with every number you hear, you'll feel a little more relaxed,' he says softly. 'Eighty-one, eighty . . . seventy-nine.'

As he continues to count down, Erik feels, as ever, like he and his patient are underwater. The walls, floor and ceiling have drifted away, the furniture slowly floating off into the darkness of the ocean.

'You are completely safe and relaxed,' Erik tells Martin. 'There is nothing to listen to but my voice . . . Imagine that you're walking down a long staircase, enjoying each step you take . . . and with every number I say, you take two steps, feeling even calmer and even more focused on my voice.'

Erik continues to count, and sees Martin's stomach rising and falling with each breath, like he is sleeping, though he knows his brain is fully active as it concentrates on every word he says.

'Thirty-five, thirty-four, thirty-three . . . When I reach zero, you will have returned to the playground in your mind, and you can tell me everything you see and hear without any fear whatsoever . . . twenty-nine, twenty-eight . . .'

Between the descending numbers, Erik adds instructions about the time and place to which they are returning.

'The rain is torrential, and you can hear it pelting your umbrella . . . nineteen, eighteen . . . you leave the footpath and walk over the wet grass.'

Martin licks his lips and starts breathing more heavily.

'When I reach zero, you will have walked around the back of the School of Economics,' Erik says softly. 'You'll stop and angle the umbrella so that you can clearly see the playground in front of you.'

Martin opens his mouth like he is trying to shout, but nothing comes out.

'Three, two, one, zero . . . What do you see now?'

'Nothing,' Martin replies, his voice almost inaudible.

'You might be able to see someone doing something that seems incomprehensible to you, but you are in no danger whatsoever. You are free to calmly tell me what you see.'

'It's just black,' Martin replies, staring up at the ceiling.

'But not in the playground, correct?'

'It's like I'm blind,' he says, sounding more anxious now, his head jerking to the left.

'You can't see anything?'

'No.'

'But earlier, you could see the red playhouse . . . describe that for me now.'

'It's just dark . . .'

'Martin, you are relaxed and calm : . . you are breathing slowly, and when I count down to zero, you will be sitting in the front row of a theatre . . . Over the speakers, you can hear a recording of the rain, and on the stage there is a set that looks like the playground . . .'

Erik pictures Martin sinking through the dark water of hypnosis. His face is studded with tiny, silvery grey bubbles, his mouth firmly closed.

'Three, two, one, zero,' he counts. 'The playground on the stage is made of paper – it isn't real – but the actors look exactly like the real people, and they move and speak in the exact same way.'

Martin's face strains, his eyelids trembling. Pamela recognises the pain on his face and wonders whether she should tell Erik not to push him too hard.

'I can see a faint light from a street lamp in the distance,' says Martin. 'There's a tree in the way, but when its branches sway in the wind, some of the light hits the jungle gym.'

'What else do you see?' asks Erik.

'An old woman wearing garbage bags . . . she's got a weird necklace on . . . and she's dragging a load of dirty plastic bags.'

'Turn back to the stage.'

'It's too dark.'

'But some of the light from the emergency exit sign reaches the playground,' Erik tells him.

Martin's chin trembles, tears running down his cheeks, and his voice is barely audible when he speaks again.

'Two small boys sitting in a muddy puddle on the ground . . .'

'Two boys?' asks Erik.

'The mothers are watching the children play,' he whispers.

'Who says that?' Erik presses him, feeling his own heart rate pick up.

'I don't want to,' Martin replies, his voice catching.

'Describe the man who—'

'That's enough now,' Dennis interrupts him, quickly lowering his voice. 'I'm sorry, but I need to bring this to an end.'

'Martin, there's nothing to be afraid of here,' Erik continues. 'I'm going to lift you out of the hypnosis in a moment, but first I want to know who you heard, whose voice that was. You can see him standing on the stage in front of you.'

Martin's breathing has become ragged, tears streaming down his cheeks. 'It's too dark, I can only hear his voice.'

'The lighting technicians turn on a spotlight and point it at Caesar.'

'He's hiding,' Martin sobs.

'But the light follows him, catching him by the jungle gym and . . .'

Erik stops abruptly when he notices that Martin has stopped breathing, his eyes rolling into the back of his head.

'Martin, I'm going to count back slowly from five now,' Erik tells him, glancing over to the medicine cabinet, where he keeps cortisone shots and a defibrillator. 'None of this is dangerous, but I need you to listen to my voice and do exactly as I say.'

Martin's lips are white, his mouth opening wide, but he isn't getting any air; his feet start to twitch, his fingers splayed.

'What's going on?' Pamela asks, panicked.

'I'm going to start counting now, and when I reach zero, you'll start breathing normally; you will feel relaxed . . . Five, four, three, two, one, zero . . .'

Martin takes a deep breath and opens his eyes as though he has just woken up from a good night's sleep. He sits up, licking his lips and looking thoughtful before glancing up at Erik.

'How do you feel?'

'Good,' he replies, wiping the tears from his cheeks.

'That wasn't quite what we were expecting,' Dennis mutters.

'I'm fine,' Martin tells him.

'Are you sure?' asks Pamela.

'Can I ask whether . . . whether Caesar is the man who killed Jenny Lind?' Martin asks, slowly getting to his feet.

'We believe so,' Erik replies.

'Because I might have seen someone, but as soon as I turned to the jungle gym, everything went dark. I want to try again.'

'We can discuss that,' says Dennis.

'OK,' Martin whispers.

'Shall we go?' asks Dennis.

'Give me just a moment, I want to have a quick word with Erik first,' Pamela replies.

'We'll wait in the car,' Dennis tells her, leading Martin out.

'I'll be outside,' says Joona.

Erik pulls back the curtains, opening the window onto the garden. He watches Joona step out into the sunlight, pausing with his phone to his ear in the middle of the lawn.

'I'm sorry that Dennis disrupted the hypnosis,' says Pamela. 'But I don't think you know Martin as well as he does, and you were pressing him really hard.'

Erik nods and maintains eye contact. 'I don't know why it keeps going wrong,' he says. 'Martin witnessed something awful, and now it's like he's trapped in his fear.'

'Yes, that's actually what I wanted to talk to you about . . . It's complicated, but what stops Martin from talking – according to him – are two dead boys, two ghosts . . . He feels controlled by them. He believes they punish him physically if he speaks,' Pamela

379

explains. 'Did you see his hands? They're grazed and his knees are black and blue . . . He might have been knocked down by a bike or something for all I know, but he's convinced the dead boys pushed him onto the metro tracks . . . I've been through this so many times, and he always says it's the boys.'

'Where do they come from?'

'Martin's parents and two brothers died in a car accident when he was younger.'

'I understand.'

'That's all I wanted to tell you – that this is incredibly hard for him,' she says, turning to leave.

Erik thanks her and follows her out into the garden, watching as she hurries towards the gate. He walks over to Joona, who is swinging in the hammock.

'What's going on with Martin?'

'He belongs to the segment of the population that is incredibly susceptible to hypnosis, but for some reason he still adamantly withholds from me what he sees,' Erik explains, sitting down beside him.

'You usually know how to get past patients' trauma.'

Joona leans back with his phone in his hand, pushing against the ground and making the hammock sway.

'Pamela told me that Martin has a paranoid delusion involving two dead boys who listen in on every word he says,' Erik continues. 'It's connected to a car accident from childhood that killed his parents and two brothers.'

'And now he's afraid of them?'

'To him, they're real; his hands are badly scraped, and he genuinely believes that the boys pushed him onto the tracks at the metro station.'

'Did Pamela tell you that?'

'She said that that's what Martin believes.'

'Did she say where this happened?' Joona asks, straightening up in the hammock.

'No, I don't think she knew – what are you thinking?'

Joona gets to his feet, takes a few steps forward and calls Pamela. She doesn't pick up immediately, and after a couple of rings, the call goes through to her voicemail.

'Hi, Pamela, this is Joona Linna again,' he says. 'Call me back as soon as you get this.'

'Sounds serious,' says Erik.

'Caesar warned Pamela not to cooperate with the police, so there's a chance he has been watching her and tried to silence Martin.'

80

After morning prayers, Mia and Blenda walk around the yard in the bright sunshine. Mia tries to keep up the same pace, but when Blenda decides she is walking too slowly, she yanks her arm, making the plastic tie cut into her wrist.

Granny is on the phone in front of the lorry. The driver's side door is open, and her curly wig has fallen to the ground.

Mia's head is still throbbing where Blenda hit her with the shovel, and it feels like her entire cheek is swollen.

She was lying on the gravel when she came to.

Granny forced Kim and Blenda to stand with their arms outstretched as she questioned them. In the end, Blenda admitted that she hit Mia with the shovel to prevent her from killing Granny.

Right there and then, Mia thought it was all over, but Granny lost her temper with Blenda instead.

'Mia doesn't have a weapon!' she shouted. 'I searched her clothes and there's nothing there. She didn't have a weapon, but you and Kimball did – both of you were armed.'

Mia realised that none of the others had seen her knife skid across the ground and into the drain.

Kim and Blenda stood side by side in the midday sun. They were both sweating and breathing heavily.

Granny pushed the sharp tooth into the notch on her stick, and clipped it into place.

Kim was shaking all over, and in the end she couldn't go on any longer. Sobbing, she lowered her arms and whispered 'sorry'.

Granny glared at her, then took a step forward and jabbed her with the stick beneath her right breast.

'Please,' she cried, dropping to her side on the ground, panting.

Mia and Blenda were ordered back to their cages. It was a long night, and they sat quietly, waiting for Kim. But she never came back.

Since then, there's been no sign of her, and Blenda is still refusing to say a word.

The smoke from the oven lingers over the roofs of the longhouses. Someone coughs over by the tap.

Blenda pulls Mia into the shade at the gable end of the main house and pauses. Her face is flushed from the heat, beads of sweat trickling down her cheeks.

Granny hobbles over to them, leaning heavily on her stick. Her dark, narrow eyes glimmer and she keeps her mouth firmly closed, deep furrows intersecting her thin lips.

'You'll both have to help out today,' she says, taking a key from the ring on her belt.

'Of course,' Blenda replies.

'Go and clean building seven – Blenda, you're in charge.'

'Thanks,' she says, reaching for the key.

Granny holds on to it for a moment, squinting up at her. 'Impurity is infectious, you know that.'

Blenda takes the key, pulling Mia after her towards the furthest building. The sun is high in the sky, beating down on her scalp.

'It wasn't my fault you and Kim got the blame. What was I supposed to do?' Mia asks quietly. 'I don't understand you. If you hadn't ruined everything, we'd all be free now.'

'Free from what?' Blenda snorts.

'You can't seriously want to stay here.'

But this time, Blenda doesn't reply, she just drags Mia over to the last of the longhouses. She pushes the key into the padlock, opens it and hangs it by the shackle after opening the door.

The stench hits them the moment they step into the longhouse.

Mia blinks, trying to make her eyes adjust to the darkness.

Thousands of flies swarm in a sluggish cloud.

The hot air is stale and heavy with the tang of ripe flesh and excrement.

Blenda retches, covering her mouth.

As Mia's eyes get used to the darkness, she notices a number of jet-black furs stacked up in huge piles against the walls. She looks up and whimpers when she sees the body hanging from the ceiling.

A silver cable is looped through a block on the overhead crane, stretching right down to Kim's throat. Her face is swollen and greyish-blue like clay.

There are flies crawling all over her mouth and eyes.

Mia only really recognises that it's Kim from her red tracksuit bottoms and Lady Gaga T-shirt.

'Bring her down gently,' Blenda orders, dragging Mia over to one end of the building.

'What?'

'Turn the handle.'

'I don't understand.'

Mia's eyes scan the room, and she realises Blenda must be talking about the winch attached to the wall.

'We're going to cremate her,' Blenda says.

Mia reaches for the winch and starts to turn the handle, but nothing happens. As she pulls harder, a vibration travels up the silver cable to Kim's body, making a buzzing cloud of flies lift away from her.

'You have to release the latch and . . .' Blenda trails off as a car horn blares outside. They hear the car's tyres roll across the yard, honking once more before it comes to a halt.

Blenda mumbles something and pulls Mia over to the door, peering through the crack. 'It's him,' she says.

As though in a daze, Mia follows her out into the sunshine. She feels queasy, and her legs tremble as they walk back towards the yard.

A dusty car has pulled up alongside the lorry, the grey bodywork above its wheels rusted.

'They must be in the house,' Blenda says with a dreamy smile. 'You've never been in there, but . . .'

The young woman with dark red hair crosses the yard. She is moving slowly, carrying a yoke with a heavy bucket balanced on each side. She pauses, carefully lowers them to the ground, and coughs.

'I think we should go back to our cages,' Mia says quietly.

'You'll understand . . .'

Granny opens the door just as Blenda starts dragging Mia towards the yard.

'Come in,' she says. 'Caesar wants to say hello.'

They climb the two steps up to the porch. Granny's leather jacket is hanging on a metal coat hanger. Mia follows Blenda down the hallway, over the bumpy marble-print vinyl.

The door to one of the rooms they pass is ajar, and Mia catches a glimpse of a small bedroom on the other side, shutters closed. There is a metal bed in the middle of the floor, thick restraints stretched across it.

At the end of the hallway, she can see a kitchen. Someone moves through the daylight flooding through the window.

Caesar steps into the hallway with a ham sandwich in one hand, slowly walking towards them.

Mia suddenly becomes conscious of the smell of sweat on her as they come to a stop. Her face is dirty and her hair greasy. Blenda has dried blood beneath her nose, and her thick hair is full of straw.

'My dears,' Caesar says as he approaches. He hands his half-eaten sandwich to Granny, then brushes his palms on his trousers and looks them over. 'Blenda I know . . . and you're Mia, special Mia.'

Blenda looks down at the floor, but Mia meets his eye for a few seconds.

'Those eyes! Did you see that, Mother?' He grins.

Granny opens a door and leads them into a larger room, around a two-piece folding screen covered in wallpaper.

She puts the sandwich onto a golden plate on the table, then turns on a floor lamp with a burgundy fringed shade. The curtains are closed, but the sun is seeping in through the small gaps between them.

All of the furniture and moulding on the walls has been sprayed gold. There are brown stains on the sofa, and the cushions are held together by glue at the edges, golden tassels hanging from the corners.

'Can I offer you anything?' Caesar asks.

'No, thank you,' Mia replies.

'It isn't all rules and punishment here,' he tells her. 'Mistakes will be punished, of course, but those who have faith are also rewarded, and given more than they could ever dream of.'

'It's all in the Lord's hands,' Granny chimes in quietly.

He sits down in an armchair with a plush yellow covering, crossing one leg over the other and studying Mia through squinted eyes.

'I want us to get to know each other and become friends.'

'OK.'

Mia realises that her legs have started trembling again. The mosaic-pattern on the vinyl flooring reminds her of a bathroom, and she notices that the cracks between the faux tiles are full of dirt.

'Relax,' Caesar tells her.

'She's got good teeth,' says Granny. 'And quite nice—'

'Just do it,' he interrupts her.

Granny breaks the neck of an ampoule, carefully taking out the creamy yellow tooth and turning her stick upside down.

'Hold on, I brought a present,' says Caesar, pulling a white plastic pearl necklace from his pocket. 'This is for you, Mia.'

'That's too much,' she says, her voice hoarse.

Blenda makes a strange cooing noise.

'Shall I help you?' Caesar asks, getting to his feet. He slowly circles Mia, draping the beads around her neck. 'I know it's hard to believe that this is your necklace now, but it is; these pearls are all yours.'

'Thank you,' she mumbles.

'Just look at her!'

'She's beautiful,' says Granny.

Mia's heart is racing as she watches the old woman click the tooth into place.

'Can't I stay awake?' she asks, turning to look at Caesar. 'I'd like to be able to thank the Lord and look into your eyes.'

He takes a step back and looks at her with a smirk. 'You want that? Well, you heard her, Mother.'

81

Mia resists the urge to throw up as Granny loosens the tooth from her stick with an uncertain smile. She knows that Caesar is watching her, and tries to stand tall while also keeping her eyes chastely on the ground.

'Special Mia,' he says.

She feels Granny's breath on her neck as she cuts the cable tie with a small pair of pliers. Mia rubs her wrist as her mind races. She tells herself she could pick up the heavy urn on the pedestal and smash it into Caesar's head, then open one of the windows and climb out.

'I'll take Blenda back to her cage,' Granny whispers.

'I know it's a bit uncomfortable for everyone right now,' Caesar says, rolling a lock of Mia's hair between his fingers. 'But soon . . . You have no idea what luxury awaits you.'

Mia struggles not to recoil from him. She hears Granny and Blenda leave the room and walk down the hall to the porch. The front door opens and closes, the lock clicks, and then the house is silent.

'I'll grab a carafe of port,' Caesar tells her, letting go of her hair. 'Shall I come with you?'

'No, you get undressed,' he says matter-of-factly.

He starts making his way towards the door, but Mia notices that he pauses behind the screen. She pulls her undershirt up over her head and the plastic beads drop back down between her breasts with a soft clink, catching on the protruding underwire of her bra.

Hearing his footsteps disappear down the hallway, she hurries over to the window on shaky legs and tears back the curtains. Her hands

are trembling as she unlocks the window and tries to push it open. It won't budge. She puts all her weight into it, pushing as hard as she can, until she hears the frame creak. It's impossible. She looks up and notices that the window has been nailed shut in at least ten places.

Panic wells up inside her; she can't stay here and be raped. She needs to get to the front door.

Mia tiptoes around the screen and pauses to listen.

She can't hear a thing.

She moves slowly towards the doorway, studying the light on the wall of the hallway. She can't see any movement, and steps forward and peeks out.

No sign of anyone.

Mia turns towards the front door and is just about to run that way when she realises she heard the lock click when Granny left with Blenda.

She hesitates for a second, then tiptoes towards the kitchen.

She hears glasses clinking, a cupboard door closing.

She tries one of the bedroom doors, but it's locked, and moves on down the hallway, struggling to keep her breathing quiet.

Caesar's shadow passes across the wall as he moves through the stream of light flooding in through the kitchen windows.

Mia reaches the next door.

One of the floorboards creaks under her weight.

She turns the handle and steps into a dark bedroom. A sheet of plywood has been screwed over the window.

She carefully pulls the door behind her and peers out into the hallway through a small gap.

Her heart is pounding.

Mia hears heavy footsteps and holds her breath as Caesar walks by, into the living room. She opens the door and runs towards the kitchen as quietly as she can.

A fierce thudding echoes through the walls of the house. She hears Caesar shout.

Mia knocks into a stool, and is about to fall over, but manages to regain her balance and reach the window. Her hands are shaking

as she tries to open the locks. She slips and splits her knuckle, but opens the window just as she hears Caesar running down the hallway behind her.

His feet stomping across the floor.

Mia climbs up onto the windowsill and jumps. The plastic beads crack against her teeth as she lands in the weeds.

She glances towards the dark woods, then gets up and starts walking.

Bees are buzzing around the tall lupins.

Behind her, Caesar roars through the open kitchen window.

Mia is making her way into the forest when she hears a sudden metallic snap among the nettles and cries out in pain. Glancing down, she sees that her ankle is caught in a fox trap. The shock pulses through her like an icy wave, and it takes her a few seconds to realise that the sharp metal teeth haven't actually penetrated her thick boot. Her foot is OK.

On the other side of the house, the dog starts barking angrily.

Mia tries to prise open the trap with her hands, but the spring is too strong.

They've untied the dog, and he charges around the corner of the house and stops just short of her, barking. The dog lunges towards her, then starts barking again, saliva spraying everywhere. Without warning, he sinks his teeth into her thigh and pulls back, making her fall.

Mia sees Granny limping through the weeds with her stick in both hands.

She tries to kick the dog away, but it continues to circle her, snapping at her shoulder.

By the time Granny reaches her, she sees that the little yellow tooth is already clipped onto her stick.

Mia tries to defend herself with both hands as Granny jabs with the stick, and the tooth sinks deep into her right palm. She feels a painful sting, and her hand immediately starts throbbing. She sucks the wound and spits even though she knows it's futile.

She is only half conscious as Granny drags her back into the yard.

Mia is on her back on the gravel, trying to stay awake as someone ties her to one of the sturdy legs of the bathtub.

Her eyelids feel heavy, constantly trying to droop. She squints and sees Caesar marching towards her with the machete in one hand. Granny is tottering along by his side, an anxious look on her face.

'I promise . . .'

'How are they ever going to respect the Lord if they don't respect the law?' he barks.

'They're stupid, but they'll learn; they'll give you twelve sons to—'

'Stop it, I've got more important things to think about than—'

A sudden ringing makes Caesar stop short, panting. He pulls out his phone, drops the machete to the ground and walks away before answering.

The call is brief. He nods and says something she can't quite hear before dropping the phone back into his pocket and running over to the grey car.

'Wait!' Granny shouts, hobbling after him.

He climbs in, slams the door and careers around the yard before racing away.

Mia's cheeks are hot, and the hand where Granny jabbed her is completely numb. She can also feel a strange tightness in her armpit.

Someone's feet crunch against the gravel, right by her face.

It's the woman with the red curly hair. She crouches down beside Mia, takes her hand and examines the wound on her palm.

'Don't worry,' she says in a low voice. 'She's given you a nasty jab, so you'll sleep for a few hours, but I'll be here the whole time. I'll make sure no one hurts you . . .'

Mia knows she is trying to comfort her, but she also knows that no one can protect her now. Whenever Caesar comes back, he'll chop her up in her sleep or kill her when she awakes.

'I have to escape,' she whispers.

'I'll try to find a way to cut the tie when you wake up . . . then you need to run along the road, not into the woods . . .' The young woman pauses and coughs into her hand. 'And if you make it . . .'

Mia sees her eyes well up as she stifles another coughing fit. The sunlight is making her red hair glow like copper. She has two small birthmarks beneath one eye, and her lips are chapped.

'If you do make it out of here, you have to call the police and tell them about us,' she says, coughing into her elbow. 'My name is Alice, I've been here for five years. I came a few weeks after Jenny Lind, you've probably heard about her . . .'

She coughs again, wiping blood from her lips.

'I'm not well. It's probably tuberculosis – I've got a fever and it's really hard to breathe – that's why they let me walk around like this; they know I'll never be able to run away,' she continues. 'But I'll tell you about all the others, and you'll have to memorise their names so that . . .'

'Alice, what are you doing?' Granny barks.

'Just making sure she's breathing,' she replies, getting to her feet.

'Look in the drain,' Mia whispers.

82

Tracy Axelsson has just returned from a trip to Croatia, and is back at work as a nurse's assistant at Huddinge Hospital. Joona has arranged to meet her in a café across from the hospital.

He keeps his phone clamped to his ear as he pays for his coffee. Pamela still isn't answering.

Tracy has already arrived, and is sitting with a mug of coffee in front of her. Her face is tanned, and she is wearing blue scrubs.

When Martin failed to share what he saw in the playground that night – despite being under deep hypnosis – Erik tried a different approach, using a technique called an intervention. He moved the events in the playground to a stage in an attempt to bypass Martin's fears.

Martin described an old woman wearing rubbish bags, with a strange necklace and handfuls of dirty plastic bags.

The police tracked down the homeless woman caught on camera that night and interviewed her. They also studied the footage of her from the night of the crime, and saw that she never once stepped into the blind spot.

The woman wasn't wearing a fur coat, and she didn't have a rat's skull hanging around her neck, as Tracy claimed.

Aron dismissed her inaccurate description of the homeless woman, reasoning that she was in shock, but when Martin described seeing a woman wearing a strange necklace, it became clear that the person Tracy saw was not the homeless woman after all, but an older woman in the blind spot.

A woman who was able to get to and from the playground without being caught on camera.

Perhaps she is the mother who was watching the children play, Joona thinks to himself.

Watching Caesar play.

Joona takes his coffee over to Tracy, introducing himself before taking a seat.

'I just want to say that I did call to check it was OK to go on vacation,' she says. 'The cops spoke to me once, that was it . . . No one has been in touch since to ask whether I've remembered anything else, nothing . . .'

'Well, we're here now,' Joona says warmly.

'I'm the one who found her, I tried to save her . . . but she died anyway, it was awful . . . It might have been nice for someone to check and see if I was OK, but I just went home and cried.'

'Usually, witnesses are offered support.'

'Well, if you did, I must've been too shocked to realise,' she says, sipping her coffee.

'I wasn't leading the investigation at the time . . . but the case has now been handed over to me and the National Crime Unit.'

'What's the difference?'

'I'll be asking a few more questions,' he says, glancing down at his phone. 'I read the transcript of your interview and, in your statement, you mentioned a homeless woman who refused to help while you were trying to save Jenny Lind.'

'Yes.'

'Could you describe her for me?' Joona asks, taking out his notepad.

'I already have,' Tracy sighs.

'I know, but not for me. I'd like to know what you remember now – not what you said at the time, but from your memories of that night . . . It was raining, and you were making your way home along Kungstensgatan. You went down the stairs and took the shortcut by the playground.'

Tracy's eyes well up, and she looks down at her hands. Joona notices she is wearing a signet ring on her left index finger.

'At first I couldn't work out what I was looking at,' she says quietly. 'It was pretty dark, and she looked like an angel floating above the ground.'

She falls silent and gulps.

Joona sips his strong coffee and thinks to himself that the image of an angel is a turn of phrase that must have come to her afterwards, something others would likely appreciate.

'What made you react?'

'I don't know.'

'It could be a minor detail.'

'The wire caught the light . . . and her feet were moving, like the last of her strength was running out . . . I ran over, didn't even think about it. It was just so obvious she couldn't breathe. It was insane. I pulled at the winch, but it wouldn't budge and it was dark and pouring down with rain.'

'You tried to lift her up, assuming she would be able to use her hands to undo the noose herself,' Joona replies, not mentioning the fact that Jenny was dead before Tracy even arrived at the playground.

'What was I supposed to do? I needed help, and then I saw a homeless woman staring at me, just a few metres away,' Tracy says, gazing out of the window.

'Where?'

She turns back to him. 'Next to the little Jeep – or whatever it's supposed to be – the car on a spring, the kind you can rock back and forth on.'

'And what happened?'

'Nothing. I screamed at her to help me, but she didn't react . . . I don't know if she couldn't understand what I was saying, or maybe something was wrong with her, but she didn't react at all . . . She just stared at me, and after a minute or two she went off up the steps . . . And in the end I couldn't hold Jenny anymore.'

Tracy falls silent, wiping away a tear with the back of her hand.

'What did she look like, the homeless woman?' Joona asks.

'I don't know, like any of them . . . rubbish bags around her shoulders, a whole load of old Ikea bags.'

'Did you see her face?'

Tracy nods and composes herself. 'She was haggard – wrinkly, I mean. The way people get from sleeping outside . . .'

'And she didn't say anything?'

'No.'

'Did she react at all to your shouting?'

Tracy takes another sip of her coffee and scratches her wrist. 'She just stood there, watching us. It felt like the more I shouted at her, the calmer she got.'

'What makes you think that?'

'Her eyes . . . At first, they seemed kind of wide, but then they became . . . not soft, exactly, but empty.'

'What was she wearing?'

'Black rubbish bags.'

'And underneath?'

'How am I supposed to know that?'

'Did she have anything on her head?'

Tracy raises an eyebrow. 'Right, exactly – she had an old black fur hat on, and it was completely soaked.'

'How do you know it was soaked?'

'Maybe I just assumed, because it was pouring.'

'Can you return to that night in your memory and tell me exactly what you see?'

Tracy closes her eyes for a moment.

'So, like . . . the only light in the playground was coming from one bright street lamp, and when she moved underneath it, I saw her hat glittering – like there was a drop of water on every single strand of fur.'

'What else did you see?'

Tracy's pale lips curl into a half-smile. 'I've already mentioned this, and I know it sounds crazy, but I swear I saw a rat's head around her neck, just the bone.'

'The skull.'

'Exactly.'

'How do you know it was a rat?'

'I just thought it was, since there are always lots of rats in that park.'

'What did the skull itself look like?'

'What did it look like? A bit like a white egg, but with two holes in it . . .'

'How big was it?'

'Like this,' she says, holding her finger and thumb about ten centimetres apart.

'Was she wearing any other jewellery?'

'I don't think so.'

'Did you see her hands?'

'They were as pale as bones,' she says quietly.

'But she didn't have any rings on her fingers?'

'No.'

'No earrings?'

'I don't think so.'

Joona thanks Tracy for her help, gives her the number for victim support and recommends that she calls them.

As he hurries back to his car, he replays his conversation with Tracy and the image he has of the woman in the playground.

In all of the interview transcripts, she was described as being homeless, likely drunk or on drugs. But after his chat with Tracy today, Joona no longer believes she was homeless.

He thinks that she murdered Jenny Lind, working alongside Caesar.

Tracy described her face as weather-worn, yet her hands were as pale as bone. But they only looked pale because she was wearing a pair of latex gloves. That was why they didn't find a single fingerprint on either the winch or the steel cable.

The reason she simply stood by and watched was that she wanted to make sure Tracy didn't save Jenny.

His phone buzzes as he opens the car door.

'Joona,' he answers.

'Hi, this is Pamela. I forgot to check my voicemail.'

'I'm glad you called. Two things, and I'll keep it brief,' he explains, climbing into the hot car. 'Martin told you he was pushed onto the tracks at the metro station . . . I believe that's when he hurt himself?'

'He doesn't want to talk about it, but . . . yes, that's what he told me.'

'When was this?' he asks, pulling the car away.

'Thursday night, pretty late.'

'Do you know which station it was?'

'I have no idea,' she says.

'Could you ask him?'

'I'm out walking, but I'll talk to him as soon as I get home.'

'I'd appreciate it if you called him right now.'

'I would, but he doesn't answer the phone when he's painting.'

Joona changes lanes on E20, passing Aspudden.

'When do you think you'll be home?' he asks.

'In less than an hour.'

The rough rock wall at the edge of the road flashes by, and soon he's crossing the bridge, flanked by its Plexiglas barriers.

'The second thing is that you should consider agreeing to police protection.'

There is a long silence on the other end of the line.

'Was it Caesar who pushed Martin?' Pamela whispers after a moment.

'I don't know, but Martin is our only eyewitness, and Caesar is obviously afraid that he can provide us with a good description,' Joona replies. 'Maybe at this point he knows that he can't count on just threatening you to stop Martin from talking.'

'We'll take all the protection we can get.'

'Good,' says Joona. 'Officers will be in touch this evening.'

'Thank you,' she says quietly.

83

Pamela is walking through Haga Park with her phone in her hand. The dappled sunlight makes the footpath feel like a narrow bridge over a glittering river.

It's clear that the police now consider the threat against them serious. She should have asked for protection much sooner.

When she left home earlier, she felt anxious, and called Dennis. He was in a meeting, but promised to pick her up at the North Chapel.

Pamela is now genuinely afraid, and debates whether to call off her walk at the cemetery and head home.

Caesar tried to kill Martin.

As she approaches the underpass beneath the main road, she slows down and takes off her sunglasses.

A group of people have gathered around a man lying in the bicycle lane. She can hear an ambulance approaching. A young woman keeps repeating that she thinks he is dead, covering her mouth with her hand.

Pamela steps onto the grass to avoid getting too close, but can't help but glance over at them. Between the people's legs, she looks straight into the man's wide eyes. She shudders and hurries down through the underpass with a sense that the people around him are all staring at her.

The sprawling cemetery smells like freshly cut grass.

Pamela leaves the footpath and takes a shortcut between the tall trees, noticing that the sun is shining on Alice's grave.

A magpie chatters in the distance.

Pamela drops to her knees and presses her palm to the sun-warmed stone.

'Hello,' she whispers, her finger tracing the inscription.

Pamela often thinks about the fact that her daughter's name has actually been cut out of the stone. All that remains are the grooves left by the letters.

Alice's name is an absence on the headstone, just like her body is an absence in the coffin.

She comes to the cemetery to talk to her daughter every Sunday, but Alice isn't actually here. Her body was never found. The police sent divers into the lake, but Kallsjön is 134 metres deep, with strong currents.

For a long time, Pamela fantasised that Alice had been rescued before Martin was found by the group of long-distance skiers. She pictured a kindly woman pulling her daughter from the water, wrapping her in reindeer skins and carrying her over to her sledge. She saw Alice waking up in the warmth of the fire in her timber cabin where the woman gave her a strong cup of tea and some soup. Alice had hit her head on the ice, and while they waited for her memory to come back, the woman took care of her as though she were her own daughter.

Pamela knows that those daydreams were simply a way for her to avoid letting go of hope.

Despite that, she stopped eating fish after the accident. She just couldn't escape the thought that they might be the same fish that had eaten Alice's body.

Pamela gets up and notices that the groundsman has hung the collapsible chair back in the tree. She walks over to get it, then brushes a few seeds from the canvas and sits down in front of the grave.

'Your dad has been trying hypnosis. I know it sounds crazy, but it's so that he can try to remember what he saw . . .' She trails off when she notices someone watching her from between the trees, half hidden behind a pale trunk. Pamela tries to make her eyes focus, and is relieved to see that it's just an older woman with broad shoulders.

'I don't know what's going to happen now,' Pamela continues, turning back to the grave. 'We've been threatened, and Mia is missing. The man who murdered Jenny Lind took her to scare us, all because Dad is trying to help the police.'

She wipes the tears from her cheeks and glances up again just in time to see the old woman disappear behind the tree trunk.

'It looks like we're going to be taken to a safe house now, in any case . . . otherwise we'll go to stay at Dennis's place in the country for a while,' Pamela says, forcibly steadying her voice. 'So I don't think I'll be able to come here for some time. That's all I really wanted to say . . . I have to go now.'

Pamela gets up and hangs the chair in the tree, then returns to the grave and hugs it tightly.

'I love you, Alice . . . I'm really just waiting to die so I can see you again,' she whispers, getting to her feet.

Pamela passes through the shadows beneath the trees, continuing down the slope to the footpath. She sees a flowerbed of pretty roses, and wonders whether she should pick a few to put on the grave, but holds herself back and keeps walking.

When she reaches the car park by the chapel, Dennis's car is already there, and she can make out his face through the reflections in the glass.

84

The tyres drone against the tarmac as Joona leaves the E18 after Enköping and continues up towards Västmanland and Dalarna.

'I've been trying to talk to Margot,' Johan Jönson tells him over the phone.

'You don't need to go through her. Caesar pushed Martin onto the tracks,' Joona explains. 'If we can find the CCTV footage, we've probably got him.'

'But where the hell am I supposed to look? Which station?'

'I don't know yet, but somewhere in central Stockholm.'

'There are maybe twenty stations there—'

'Listen to me,' Joona interrupts him. 'This is all that matters right now – you need to find that footage, and now.'

'They never want—'

'Get the prosecutor involved, anything, just do it,' he snaps.

Joona should be with Gustav Scheel's daughter Anita within the next forty minutes. She lives in a townhouse in Säter, just three kilometres from the hospital.

Anita was only a girl when Caesar broke into her bedroom, sat down on the edge of her bed and put his hand on her head. If her father hadn't told her when she was older how he first met Caesar, she likely wouldn't remember it. But he did, and Joona finds it hard to believe that she never asked for more details about it. There has to be more to her story. She might know more about Caesar than anyone else he has met so far.

Joona thinks back to his last conversation with Anita. She has learned to deflect any criticism of her father's research by distancing herself from it, even though deep down she's proud of his work.

Old-fashioned psychiatry always has a dirty sheen – that was what she tried to tell him. And yet she trained as psychiatric nurse, settled down in Säter, and now works at the very same clinic where her father once worked.

Joona overtakes a line of lorries. The wind buffets his open window as he passes between each trailer.

His gun is in the glove compartment, his bulletproof vest in a canvas bag on the passenger seat.

Caesar tried to kill Martin at a metro station in Stockholm. If that was captured on CCTV, then there is every chance they will be able to identify him – assuming he wasn't wearing a mask.

Perhaps both Caesar and the older woman were on the platform.

Perhaps they kill together.

Or maybe Caesar needs an audience, someone to act as a mirror – just like a child wanting their mother to watch as they play on a jungle gym?

Joona takes a swig of water and thinks back to his interview with Tracy.

He remembers her description of the egg-shaped skull the woman at the playground was wearing around her neck. There's no doubt in his mind that what she described was far too big to have been a rat's skull. It seems much more likely that it came from a marten of some kind.

The answer comes to Joona the moment the thought crosses his mind.

The woman's black hat wasn't made from fake fur. The fur was oily. The raindrops collected on the very tip of each strand of hair because it was water-repellant.

It must have been mink fur, he thinks, as a sudden, icy realisation dawns on him.

A shiver passes down his spine.

It feels like the entire case has just come into focus.

He swerves to the edge of the road and pulls over in the shade of an underpass.

Joona closes his eyes and travels back in time, to when he visited the Natural History Museum with his father.

He is eight, walking through the enormous skeleton of a blue whale. The echo of voices and footsteps bounce off the high ceilings above. Joona listens to his father as he reads from an informational plaque in front of a diorama of a stuffed mongoose fighting a cobra.

He is starting to get hot in his new padded jacket, and he unbuttons it and walks over to an image of a mink. In the glass case in front of him, there are three egg-shaped skulls. One of them has been turned over so that the underside is visible. On the curved inner surface, there is a pattern. A cross of sorts, part of the animal's bone structure.

Joona sits at the edge of the road, eyes closed, turning over the memory of that skull.

The pattern resembles a figure, with a pointed hood and outstretched arms, standing like Christ.

He opens his eyes, grabs his phone from the dashboard and looks for images of mink skulls. He finds one immediately. On the inside of the skull, he can see the faint outline of the figure with extended arms. It is a product of evolution, due to the gradual shifting of veins and brain tissue. The figure is present, to a greater or lesser degree, in all of the scientific drawings and photographs of mink skulls. It is identical to the symbol used to mark the victims.

Everything has come together, linking the details of the case from the mink's skull to the killer.

Joona knows that very few serial killers actively communicate with the police, but they all have their patterns, their preferences, the ways they structure their behaviour– and these leave trails.

He has no idea how many times he has studied Caesar's pattern and moved the various pieces of the puzzle. The sphinx hid the answer inside the mystery itself. What seems like a break from the killer's modus operandi is, instead, a logical and necessary part.

He starts the engine, checks the rear-view mirror and pulls back onto the road, accelerating hard.

Joona has always had the ability to travel back to perfectly preserved memories. For the most part, it is a dull, troublesome gift. It means he relives the past over and over again, down to the very last detail.

After Hedemora, the road straightens out and cuts through meadows and fields all the way to Säter.

Joona passes a roundabout with a sculpture of a large blue axe in the middle and enters a residential area where the low houses are packed tightly together.

He parks behind a red Toyota on Anita's driveway, climbs out of the car and walks over to the house – small, with red wooden panels and a steep tiled roof.

The water from the sprinkler splatters onto the concrete.

Anita must have seen him approaching, because she is waiting in the doorway in a polka dot dress with a thick fabric belt.

'You found your way all right,' she says.

Joona takes off his sunglasses and shakes her hand.

'I don't have much to offer, but the coffee's hot . . .'

She shows him down the hallway, into a kitchen with white-tiled walls and a round dining table with white chairs.

'Nice kitchen.'

'You think?' She smiles.

Anita tells him to sit down as she takes out two cups and saucers, pours the coffee and grabs milk and sugar.

'I know I've already asked,' Joona begins, 'but do you happen to have any pictures from your father's time in the secure unit? Any group photos from a retirement party or anything like that?'

She thinks for a moment as she stirs a cube of sugar into her coffee.

'There's a picture of me in his office . . . that's the only photograph I have from inside the unit . . . and that won't help you.'

'I'd still like to have a look.'

Anita's nose reddens as she pulls her wallet from her shoulder bag. 'It was my seventh birthday, and Dad bought me a tiny doctor's coat,' she says, placing a black and white photograph in front of Joona.

The young Anita's hair is gathered in two thin plaits, and she is wearing the white doctor's coat, sitting in her father's chair behind his enormous desk, which is covered with weighty tomes and stacks of journals.

'Nice picture,' he says, handing it back to her.

'He used to call me Doctor Anita Scheel,' she says, smiling.

'Did he want you to follow in his footsteps?'

'I suppose so, but . . .' She sighs, a deep crease forming between her honey-blonde eyebrows.

'You must have been around fifteen when he told you about Caesar coming into your house and sitting on the edge of your bed.'

'Yes.'

'Did you ask what he thought Caesar meant when he said that the mothers were watching the children play?'

'Of course.'

'What did he say?'

'He let me read a chapter of his case study, about how Caesar's original trauma was connected to his mother.'

'In what way?'

'The study is incredibly academic,' she replies, gently lowering her cup to the saucer.

Wrinkles run both horizontally and vertically across her forehead, as though she spends every waking hour brooding over something.

'Do you know what I think?' says Joona. 'I think you still have a copy of your father's case study of Caesar.'

Anita gets to her feet, taking her cup over to the counter. Without a word, she leaves the room.

Joona studies the radio on the table. It is old, with a telescopic antenna. The shadow of a bird passes over the window.

Anita comes back into the kitchen and places a stack of paper on the table in front of him. There must be at least three hundred pages, bound together at the spine with red thread. On the front cover, in the uneven keystrokes of a typewriter, he reads:

The Mirror Man
a psychiatric case study
University Hospital Institute for Psychiatry
Professor Gustav Scheel, Säter Secure Unit

She takes a seat, placing her palm on the cover and meeting Joona's eye.

'I don't like lying,' she says. 'But I've learned to say that everything was destroyed in the fire when Dad died . . . The truth is that almost everything was lost, but he had "The Mirror Man" at home.'

'You wanted to protect him.'

'This case study could be used as definitive proof of psychiatric abuse in Sweden,' she replies, her voice neutral. 'Dad could become the minotaur in the middle of the labyrinth, another Mengele, despite the fact that much of what he writes is very interesting.'

'I need to borrow the manuscript.'

'You can read it here, but you can't take it with you,' she says, a strangely absent look on her face.

Joona does not break eye contact as he nods. 'I don't have any opinions on your father's work; all I want is to find Caesar before he takes anymore lives.'

'But this is just a case study,' she attempts to explain.

'Is Caesar's real identity mentioned or hinted at anywhere?'

'No.'

'So the case study doesn't mention any names or locations whatsoever?'

'No . . . almost the entire thing is written on a theoretical level,' she says. 'And all of the descriptive examples took place in the secure unit . . . Caesar didn't have any identifying documents, and he was on foot when he arrived.'

'Is there any mention of mink, or animal rearing?'

'No, though . . . At one point Caesar talks about a nightmare in which he was trapped in a cramped cage.'

She rubs her neck and left shoulder through her dress.

'After Caesar showed up at your home and asked to be admitted, what happened?'

'He stayed in the secure unit. They kept him heavily medicated at first, and he was sterilised right away – that was still routine back then. It's awful, but that's just how it was . . .'

'Yes.'

'When Dad realised that Caesar had DID, he lowered the dosage and began the series of in-depth interviews that form the basis of his case study.'

'What did they talk about, briefly?'

'Dad had a very convincing theory that Caesar had suffered a double trauma,' she explains, running a hand over the manuscript. 'The first trauma took place at a young age, before he turned eight – which is roughly when the cerebral cortex matures . . . The second took place when he was an adult, just before he sought out Dad. The first trauma is what created the necessary conditions for his personality to split . . . but that didn't actually happen until the second trauma. Dad compared it to the case of Anna K, who was a woman with around twenty different personalities . . . One of them was blind, and her pupils didn't react to light during clinical examination.'

Joona opens the case study and skims through an abstract written in English before turning to the table of contents.

'I'll leave you to read in peace. There's more coffee in the pot,' Anita tells him, getting to her feet.

'Thanks.'

'If you need anything, I'll be in my office.'

'Can I ask you something before you go?'

'Yes?'

Joona brings up an image of a mink skull on his phone, enlarging it and showing her the cross-like shape. 'Do you know what this is?'

'Jesus, isn't it?' she asks.

As she takes a closer look, her face turns pale.

'What are you thinking?' asks Joona.

She stares up at him with frightened eyes. 'I don't know, I . . . it's just that the case study says that when Caesar was locked in his room at night, he often spent hours standing with his arms outstretched, like he was being crucified.'

85

Pamela locks the door behind her and walks down the hallway to her office. Martin's big canvas is on the easel again.

'I tried calling you,' she tells him.

'I'm painting,' he replies, mixing a little red into the patch of yellow on his palette.

'You said you were pushed onto the tracks at the station on Thursday,' she says. 'Joona needs to know which station you were at.'

'But you told me the boys aren't real,' he says as he paints, moving his brush in slow strokes.

'I don't want to worry you.'

He shudders, puts down the brush and looks up at her. 'Was it Caesar who pushed me?' he asks.

'Yes.'

'It was Kungsträdgården . . . I didn't see anyone, I just heard footsteps behind me.'

Pamela sends a message to Joona, then sits down in her desk chair.

'Dennis wants us to go out to his place in the country, and I said we would . . . but we're going to be given police protection instead . . .'

'But . . .'

'They're coming to pick us up tonight.'

'But I need to be hypnotised again,' he says quietly.

'You never see anything, though.'

'But he's there, I know he is. I heard him . . .'

'Caesar?'

'I think I saw a flash on his face . . .'

'What do you mean?'

'Like a camera flash.'

'He took photos,' she says, feeling a shiver pass down her spine.

'I don't know.'

'No, but I think he does, he takes photographs,' she continues. 'Can you try to describe what you saw?'

'It's just black . . .'

'But you think Erik Maria Bark might be able to find that moment, with the flash . . . ? So you can describe Caesar?'

He nods and gets up.

'I'll talk to Joona,' she says.

Martin opens the cupboard and takes out the box of dog treats, filling a small tub.

'I'll take him,' says Pamela.

'Why?'

'I don't want you to go out.'

Pamela wakes the dog and leads him into the hallway. He yawns as she clips on his collar.

'Lock the door behind us,' she tells Martin.

Pamela grabs her shoulder bag and opens the gate on the lift. The dog lumbers in after her, wagging his tail.

Martin closes and locks the security door.

The steel cables shake and rattle as they travel down to the ground floor.

The entire stairwell smells like warm brick.

She and Loke step outside and set off along Karlavägen, towards the School of Architecture, where Pamela once studied.

It occurs to her that Caesar could be anyone she passes; she has no idea what he looks like.

When the dog pauses to sniff a drainpipe, she glances over her shoulder to check and see whether anyone is following her.

She sees a thin man peering into a shop window.

Pamela moves on, passing the steep set of steps up to Engelbrektskyrkan and continuing onto the grass. Loke pees behind one of the trees and then trots over towards the little grotto blasted

into the rock. It served as a bunker during World War II, but is now a columbarium, where relatives keep their loved ones' urns.

He sniffs the rock wall.

Pamela looks back and realises that the man she spotted earlier is now striding along the street towards her.

It's Primus.

She instinctively pulls the dog into the dark entrance to the grotto and presses her back against the closed door of the columbarium.

Primus pauses on the pavement, searching all around. His grey ponytail swings between his shoulder blades. The dog wants to keep walking, and whimpers softly when she holds him back. Primus turns around, looks into the grotto and takes a step forward.

He can't see her, but Pamela holds her breath all the same.

A heavy lorry passes by on the road, making the bushes rustle. Leaves and rubbish swirl around in the entrance to the grotto.

Primus is now walking straight towards her, his eyes scanning the area. She turns around, opens the door to the columbarium and pulls Loke inside.

The air is cool and laden with the scent of old flowers and candles. There is a layer of gravel on the floor, and the bare rock overhead has been painted white.

The columbarium looks a little like a library, but instead of bookshelves, it is full of green marble boxes.

Pamela walks quickly, aware that the gravel is crunching beneath her feet. She passes the first row of boxes and ducks behind the second, dropping to her knees with her arms around the dog's neck.

She can't see anyone else inside, but the chairs have been pulled together, and the candles are burning in the thick cast iron candlesticks.

The door opens, swinging shut again after what feels like a long time.

The silence lasts long enough for Pamela to hope that Primus has given up when she hears his footsteps on the gravel. He moves slowly, then stops.

'I have a message from Caesar,' he shouts. 'He'd like this place, he's obsessed with his little crosses . . .'

Pamela gets up and thinks about the crosses on the Prophet's fingers. She pictures tiny crosses all over his body, on the walls, ceiling and floor.

The footsteps draw closer.

Pamela searches desperately for a way out, and has just turned around to run when Primus rounds the corner and appears in front of her.

'Leave me alone!'

'Caesar doesn't want Martin to be hypnotised again,' he says, holding up a sharp Polaroid.

In it, Mia's dirty face is illuminated by the bright flash. She looks tired and thin, and the photographer is holding a black machete. The heavy blade is resting on her shoulder, the sharp edge turned towards her throat.

Pamela stumbles backwards and drops her bag, the contents spilling out across the floor.

'He says he'll chop off her arms and legs, then cauterise the wounds and make her live in a box . . .'

As Primus takes a step forward, the dog starts to bark. Pamela crouches down to pick up her things.

Loke is barking like he hasn't in years, and makes a sudden, furious lunge forward.

Primus moves back, and the dog bares his teeth and growls. Pamela grips his leash and pulls him towards the door. As they step outside, she picks him up and starts running, without looking back.

* * *

Gasping for air, she lowers Loke to the ground by the door to their building, entering her code and dragging him into the lift, taking it up to the fifth floor.

The door to the apartment is ajar. Pamela locks it behind her and shouts for Martin as she searches the apartment. With shaking hands, she pulls out her phone and dials his number.

'Martin,' he picks up, sounding afraid.

'Where are you?'

411

'I'm going to ask to be hypnotised again.'

'You can't.'

'I have to – it's the only way.'

'Martin, listen to me, if Caesar finds out, he's going to kill Mia. This is serious, he'll do it.'

'Because he's scared . . . He knows I saw him when the flash went off.'

86

Erik Maria Bark is sitting in the shade beneath the big oak tree in his garden. He has his computer on the rickety table in front of him, and is trying to write a chapter about the clinical use of group hypnosis.

He hears the garden gate open and close and, when he looks up, he sees Martin hurrying around the corner of the house, heading towards the waiting room.

Martin sees him in the garden and changes course. He runs a hand through his hair and glances back over his shoulder before speaking.

'Sorry for showing up like this, but do you have time to . . .' He pauses abruptly as a car passes by on the road, stepping behind the lilac bush with a frightened look on his face.

'What's going on?' asks Erik.

'Caesar says he'll hurt Mia if I see you again.'

'Have you spoken to Caesar?'

'No, Pamela told me.'

'And where is she now?'

'At home, I think.'

'Aren't you supposed to be getting police protection?'

'They're picking us up tonight.'

'That sounds like a good idea.'

'Can we go inside?'

'Sure,' Erik replies.

He closes his computer and takes it with him as they head into the house, through the waiting room and into his office.

'No one can know I'm here,' says Martin. 'But I want to be hypnotised again. I think I saw Caesar in the playground, just for a second, in the flash from a camera.'

'You think someone was taking photographs in the playground?'

'Yes.'

Erik remembers that Martin was initially able to describe the rain, the puddles and the playhouse before everything went black. That would explain why he was blinded.

'We can definitely try again,' he says, starting the fan on his desk.

'Right now?'

'Yes, if that's what you want, absolutely,' Erik replies.

Martin sits down on the daybed and glances into the waiting room, one leg bouncing nervously.

'I'd like to split the hypnosis into two parts,' Erik explains. 'The first would seek to open a clear passage to your memories, the second to help you remember what happened as precisely as possible.'

'We can try.'

Erik pulls his chair over to the daybed and takes a seat. 'Shall we get started?'

Martin lies down, staring up at the ceiling with a tense frown.

'Just listen to my voice and follow my instructions,' says Erik. 'You'll soon feel a deep sense of inner peace. Your body will sink into a state of pleasant relaxation, and you'll feel the weight of your heels against the bed as you relax your calves, ankles and toes . . .'

Erik wants to try to channel Martin's inner stress into a deeper state of relaxation.

In moments of tension, what the mind actually longs for is release. Like a clock's true desire to stop ticking.

'Relax your jaw,' Erik tells Martin. 'Open your mouth slightly, breathe in through your nose and let it slowly seep out through your mouth, over your tongue and past your lips . . .'

Though Martin is already in a deep state of rest, Erik continues to take him down through the induction.

The fan clicks and changes direction. The movement sends a swirl of dust floating up towards the ceiling.

Erik counts backwards, taking Martin deeper and deeper past the level of cataleptic relaxation.

'Fifty-three, fifty-two . . .'

He has never taken a patient this deep before, and pauses only when he begins to worry that Martin's bodily functions might cease, that his heart might stop if he went any further than this.

'Thirty-nine, thirty-eight . . . you are sinking lower and lower, and your breathing is getting calmer and calmer.'

Erik has realised that Pamela was probably right when she said that Martin's delusion about the boys trying to silence him is linked to the loss of his brothers.

Martin may not have been present when his family were buried, perhaps he was still in hospital after the accident, or simply too shocked to understand what was happening.

The fact that his brothers appear to him as ghosts in his psychoses is likely down to the fact that, as a child, he never saw them laid to rest and was never really able to process that they were actually dead.

'Twenty-six, twenty-five . . . when I reach zero, you will be standing in a cemetery. You are there to bury your brothers.'

Martin has now reached the lowest levels of hypnosis, the point at which his inner censor is much weaker than usual, but where time and logic also begin to lose all meaning.

Erik knows that dreams can get in the way of real memories, that fragments from earlier psychoses can rear their heads, but he still believes that pushing Martin to these depths is necessary for what he wants to try.

'Eleven, ten, nine . . .'

Erik has no idea what the funeral for Martin's family was like in reality, but he decides to create a ceremony of his own, bringing together the service and the burial.

'Six, five, four . . . you can now see the churchyard. It's a peaceful place where people come to say goodbye to those who are no longer living,' Erik explains. 'Three, two, one, zero . . . You are now there, Martin. You know that you've lost your family, and you feel sad, but you also understand that accidents happen – without any deeper cause

or meaning . . . Your parents have already been buried, and you are here to say farewell to your two brothers.'

'I don't understand . . .'

'You're walking towards a group of people dressed in black.'

'It's been snowing,' Martin whispers.

'There is snow on the ground and on the bare branches of the trees . . . The people step back as you approach the freshly dug grave – do you see it?'

'There's a spruce branch marking it,' he mumbles.

'Beside the grave, there are two small coffins, and they are both open . . . You step forward and see your brothers. They're both dead, and it's sad, but you aren't afraid . . . You look down at them, you recognise their faces and say a final goodbye.'

Martin stands on his tiptoes and peers down at the two boys and their bluish-grey lips, their closed eyes and combed hair.

Erik notices that tears have started to spill down Martin's cheeks.

'The priest closes the lids and says that your brothers are going to rest in peace as the coffins are lowered into the ground.'

Martin notices that the sky is a dreary shade of white, like the ice on a lake.

The snowflakes rise up from the ground the way they do when you shake a snow globe.

They float up the length of the priest's trouser leg and coat, past his cylindrical black hat.

Martin takes a step forward and sees his brothers' coffins lying in the bottom of the grave. They are finally in hallowed ground, he thinks.

The tall priest takes off his hat and pulls out a doll's head that has been carved from a large potato.

'Ashes to ashes, dust to dust,' says Erik.

The priest holds up the hairless doll's head, pretending it is uttering the words from the Book of Genesis.

Martin can't tear his eyes away from its carved, painted face; its wide red nose, its sparse teeth and thin brows.

'Two men pick up spades and start shovelling earth onto the coffins,' Erik continues. 'You stand there until the grave is filled and the ground has been flattened.'

Martin is now so still that Erik can't tell whether he is breathing. Not even his fingers are moving.

'Martin, we are now going to enter the second part of the hypnosis. There is no longer anything standing in the way of your memories; your brothers are dead and buried, which means they can't punish you for speaking,' says Erik. 'I'm going to count back from ten, and when I reach zero you will be back in the playground . . . Ten, nine . . . you will be able to watch the murder without any fear whatsoever . . . eight, seven . . . the boys have no power over you now . . . six, five . . . you'll be able to describe Caesar in detail from the light of a camera flash . . . four, three . . . you're stepping into the darkness now. You can hear the rain drumming down on your umbrella, and you are approaching the playground . . . two, one, zero . . .'

87

The summer sun is reflected in the silver radio, sending a quivering pool of light onto Joona's cheek and his blond stubble.

He has raced through the case study, reading quickly but carefully, and is now scanning the references at the end of the document.

Johan Jönson is at Kungsträdgården metro station, and if he can get hold of the footage then they should be able to identify Caesar fairly quickly.

Joona closes the manuscript and runs a hand over the title page.

Gustav Scheel used his patient as proof of the existence of multiple personalities and to show that treatment was possible for such a disorder.

Caesar's real identity and origins are not mentioned at all.

Even so, Joona's investigation is nearing its climax – the last few pieces of the puzzle will soon fall into place.

Because even if Scheel's methods and theories now seem old-fashioned, Joona is starting to gain an understanding of Caesar's psyche, his suffering and inner struggles. That gives him everything he needs to predict Caesar's next move.

He thinks back to the last chapter, in which Gustav Scheel presents his final conclusion: that Caesar experienced a double trauma that split his personality in two.

If a trauma is significant enough and takes place before the age of eight, before the cerebral cortex is fully developed, then there will be an impact on the central nervous system.

Caesar was only seven when he experienced something so awful that his brain was forced to find its own way of storing and archiving

information. The second trauma took place when he was nineteen, when his fiancée hanged herself in their bedroom.

Caesar's brain had already developed an alternative way of processing difficult experiences after the first trauma, and the second led it to split into two independent halves.

One of the personalities was violent, accepting these traumas and living in the darkness around them, while the other led a normal life.

As things stand, one side could become an executioner or a torturer participating in violent conflict, while the other could devote his life to helping people, becoming a priest or a psychiatrist.

Towards the end of the final chapter, Gustav Scheel notes that Caesar was chaotic when he first sought help. After nearly two years of therapy, he had become more stable. He still stood with his arms outstretched like Jesus on the cross every night, but the two sides of him had just started to seek each other out in the mirror when the secure unit was closed down and the treatment came to an end.

Scheel writes that he would need many years to fully work through Caesar's trauma.

He argued that it was possible for multiple personalities to merge together to form a single whole, provided each part of the patient is aware of the others and there are no secrets left hiding anywhere.

The chair creaks as Joona leans back and massages his neck with one hand. He turns to look out of the window and sees two young boys carrying an inflatable boat along the pavement.

He reads through the final lines of the case study one last time. In them, Scheel claims that the only way to treat psychological trauma is to return to it and accept that what happened has a place in a person's life story.

This applies to every one of us: if we cannot bear to see ourselves reflected in our memories, then we cannot grieve that which has happened and move on. This may sound like

a paradox, but the more we attempt to ignore the painful parts of life, the more power they gain over us.

In the case study, Caesar is depicted as someone who took both divergent paths when he reached a fork in the road. One led to him becoming a serial killer, the other an ordinary man. While the killer is likely aware of his mirror image, the same cannot be said of his other self, since that knowledge would make normal life impossible.

Joona finishes off his coffee and is busy rinsing the cup in the sink when Anita comes back into the kitchen.

'Just leave that,' she says.

'Thanks.'

'So you've finished reading about Dad's abuses?'

'It was a different time, but to me it seems obvious he was trying to help Caesar.'

'Thank you for saying that . . . I mean, most people would probably see nothing but the implanted memories, the sterilisation, the restraints, the isolation . . .'

Joona's phone buzzes, and he turns it over and sees that Johan Jönson has sent him a file.

'Excuse me, I need to look at this,' he tells Anita, sitting back down.

'Of course.' She nods, watching him turn his attention to his phone.

All colour drains from the detective's face, and he gets up so abruptly that his chair slams into the wall. He brings his phone to his ear and strides into the hallway.

'What's going on?' she asks, following him out.

She hears the uneasiness in his voice as he repeats the address Karlavägen 11 down the line, telling them it is urgent – incredibly urgent. He knocks over the umbrella stand in his rush out of the house, and leaves the front door open behind him as he runs over to his car.

88

Pamela kneels down in front of the armchair where the dog is curled up. She strokes him, and he feebly wags his tail without opening his eyes.

'My hero.'

She gets up and heads to the bedroom, hanging her skirt and blouse in the wardrobe and pushing the slatted door shut. The apartment is quiet, the air still. Pamela shivers as a couple of beads of sweat roll down her back.

She is afraid that Caesar might have followed Martin to Erik Maria Bark's house, that he will hurt both Martin and Mia. Pamela can't get the image of Mia's dirty face out of her head, or the rough blade up against her throat.

She goes to the bathroom, takes off her underwear, drops it into the washing basket and gets into the shower. The hot water floods down over her head, shoulders and neck.

Through the patter of the water, she hears her phone ringing in the bedroom.

She just got off the phone with Dennis, explaining that they have accepted the witness protection unit's suggestions. He sounded a little disappointed, but offered to take care of Loke while they are gone.

He is coming over to pick him up in an hour.

Dennis has always been there for her, she thinks.

When Alice was thirteen, she went through a bit of a rough patch, screaming and shouting at Pamela and Martin every day as she cried and cried. She couldn't bear to eat dinner with them, and locked

421

herself in her room, playing music so loud that the china rattled in the cabinet.

Pamela remembers Dennis suggesting that Alice could try therapy with him, free of charge.

Sadly, it never came to pass. When she suggested it, Alice was furious and screamed that Pamela was evil.

'You want me to see a psychologist just because I can't pretend I'm the perfect daughter all the time?'

'Don't be so childish.'

She remembers Alice's angry face, and realises how stupid she was for not just wrapping her arms around her and telling her that she loved her unconditionally, more than anything else on earth.

Pamela lathers herself up and peers down at her tanned feet on the rough limestone floor. Her mind turns back to Primus.

She was so scared when he came around the corner that she dropped her bag and had to crouch down to gather up her things while the dog snapped at him.

It suddenly dawns on her that she never checked her keys were still in her bag.

It all happened so quickly.

She realises the door was ajar when she got home.

What if Primus has her keys?

She tries to see through the misty shower panel, but the door into the hallway just looks like a grey outline.

The hot water pours down onto her body.

Tiny drops of condensation cling to the cold water pipe.

The shampoo gets in her eyes, and she has to close them, straining to hear over the roar of the water.

She thinks she can make out a faint creaking sound.

Pamela rinses herself off, turns off the shower, blinks and looks out towards the bathroom door. Droplets of water roll down her body. She grabs a towel, eyes on the door. It's closed, but not locked. She should just lock it and wait here until Martin, Dennis or the witness protection team arrives.

The steam on the mirror starts to fade.

She feels sick with anxiety.

Pamela dries herself without taking her eyes off the bathroom door.

She can hear the rumbling of the lift through the walls.

She reaches out and turns the handle, pushing the door open and taking a step back.

The hallway is quiet.

From the kitchen window, soft light dances through the room.

She wraps the towel around her body, takes a step forward and listens for movement.

Filled with a strange, prickling sensation, she walks down the hallway. She glances over to the balcony and then hurries to the bedroom.

When she sees that her phone is not on the bedside table, she remembers that she was charging it in the kitchen.

Pamela quickly grabs some clean underwear, a pair of white jeans and a camisole.

She pulls on her panties, eyes still on the door.

In the kitchen, her phone rings again.

The minute she is dressed, she will call the protection unit, she decides.

A strange sound from the wardrobe makes her freeze. It almost sounds like a stack of shoeboxes falling over. She stares at the wardrobe door, her eyes lingering on the unmoving darkness between the slats.

It was probably just the neighbours on the other side of the wall.

She drapes her towel over the foot of the bed and continues to get dressed with shaky movements.

There is no one else in the apartment, she's sure of it, but the rooms and the furniture leave her with a niggling sense of fear. She would be much calmer standing on the pavement outside in the warm air, surrounded by other people.

Pamela buttons her jeans with her eyes on the hallway, thoughts drifting to the bottle of vodka in the kitchen. She could have a small glass, to take the edge off before she makes the call. Maybe a sip would be enough, just to feel the warmth in her throat and stomach.

She pulls her camisole over her head, losing sight of the hallway for a few seconds.

Her heart stops when she hears a click behind her and the wardrobe door swings open slightly.

The old ventilation duct above the clothing rod hisses loudly.

Pamela weighs going to the bathroom to hang her damp towel up when she hears a key in the lock.

She slowly moves forward, debating whether or not she has time to run to the kitchen and grab her phone.

The lock clicks and the door swings open.

Behind her, the wardrobe door slams shut in the sudden cross-breeze.

Her eyes scan the room for a weapon.

Someone is walking quietly down the hallway. Pamela hears the floor creak by the living room doorway.

She takes another step forward, pausing to one side of the door frame. She can see the light filtering through the kitchen curtains on the wall in the hallway. She might have time to charge out and reach the front door – assuming it isn't locked.

Something blocks the light on the wall.

Someone moves quickly through the kitchen, into the hallway, and starts making their way towards the bedroom.

Pamela backs up against the sailor's trunk, making it thud into the wall. She has just turned and is making her way around the bed when Martin steps into the room.

'Jesus! You scared the shit out of me!' she shouts.

'Call the police,' he says, anxiously rubbing his mouth. He is out of breath, his face pale.

'What's going on?'

'I think Caesar was following me . . . I was hypnotised again,' he says, clearly afraid. 'I saw him in the playground, I saw Caesar. I can't explain . . .' There are beads of sweat trickling down his cheeks, and his eyes are unusually wide.

'Try to tell me what happened,' she begs him.

'He's going to want revenge . . . I need to check the door, call the police.'

'Are you really sure you were being followed? You know that—'

'The lift just stopped,' he interrupts her, trembling all over. 'Listen, he's here, he's right outside . . . Oh, God . . .'

Pamela follows him into the hallway, turning off into the kitchen to yank her phone from the charger. She turns around and watches Martin slowly approach the front door.

He reaches out and turns the handle.

It isn't locked.

A shiver passes down her spine as the door swings open into the dark stairwell.

Martin is staring straight ahead at the wrought iron gate on the lift. He hesitates for a moment, then steps in and pulls the door shut behind him.

Pamela glances down at her phone, but doesn't have time to do anything before the door opens and Martin returns, carrying a heavy duffle bag in one hand. He locks the door behind him, hangs the keys on one of the hooks, and comes into the kitchen with a wronged look on his face.

'What's going on, Martin? Where did that bag come from?'

'Martin is going to die,' he replies in a dark voice, staring at her as though she were a stranger.

'Why are you saying . . .'

'Quiet,' he snaps, emptying the contents of the bag onto the floor.

Heavy tools clatter across the parquet. Pamela watches as a saw, several pairs of pliers, a machete and a dirty plastic bag fall from the bag.

'Put your phone on the counter,' he tells her without looking up.

Martin pulls a sticky plastic bottle out of the ziplock bag and unwinds the tape around the lid. Pamela tries to read the strange expression on his face, his oddly knitted brow and his abrupt movements.

'Could you tell me what you're doing?' she asks, swallowing hard.

'Absolutely,' he says, unrolling the paper towel. 'Our name is Caesar, and we're here to kill you and—'

'Stop it!' she shouts.

She thinks Martin must be experiencing some kind of paranoid psychosis, that he has stopped taking his medication, that he knows she cheated on him.

He unscrews the lid of the bottle, soaks the paper and walks towards her.

Confused, she backs up against the table. It rams into the radiator, making the last few grapes in the fruit bowl jostle quickly.

Martin moves closer.

There is a look in his eyes that she doesn't recognise, and Pamela instinctively knows that she is in real danger.

Her hand fumbles behind her as she grabs the heavy fruit bowl and swings it at him, hitting his cheek. Martin staggers to the side, leaning against the wall with one hand as he tries to compose himself, head bowed.

Pamela runs through the living room out into the hallway, but from the sound of Martin's footsteps, she realises he has made it there before her.

She glances over to the balcony.

The string of old Christmas lights on the railing glitters in the sunlight.

Martin steps into the room with the black machete in his hand.

His temple is bleeding, and his face is so tense that his features seem warped, just like they did when he told her Alice had drowned.

'Martin,' she says, her voice trembling. 'I know you think you're Caesar, but . . .'

He doesn't speak; he simply starts moving towards her. She runs back to the kitchen, closing the door behind her and glancing towards the hallway.

Right then, Pamela realises that Martin and Caesar are the same person.

She knows it is true even though she still can't quite believe it – it feels like thousands of small pieces have finally fallen into place.

The apartment is silent.

She looks at the closed door to the living room. Thinking that she can see the light shifting beneath it, she moves towards the hallway as quietly as she can.

She worries that her panicked breathing might give her away.

She could run over to the front door, grab the keys from the hook, and unlock the door so she can sneak out.

The floor creaks beneath her.

As she cautiously makes her way forward, she suddenly catches Martin's eye in the huge mirror.

He is standing perfectly still up ahead, waiting for her with the machete.

Without a sound, she moves back. She picks up her phone and unlocks it with trembling hands.

There is a loud crash as Martin smashes the mirror. The glass shatters as it hits the floor, scattering the shards everywhere.

If she can just get onto the balcony, she can try to climb down to the apartment below and call the police.

Pamela turns the handle on the living room door, pushes it open and peers inside.

She sees a rush of movement and a flash of Martin's tense face as the flat side of the machete hits her on the cheek.

She hears a crack, and her head slams into the door frame.

Everything goes black.

* * *

When she wakes, she is on the kitchen floor. The hammered iron light fitting is swinging overhead.

Pamela notices a mechanical clicking sound. It's coming from a winch that has been screwed to the wall.

'Martin,' she pants.

A long steel wire scrapes across the floor, rising up towards the light and looping through the ceiling hook, continuing downwards into the winch Martin is turning.

Pamela has only just processed what she is seeing when she feels the noose tighten around her throat, dragging her into the middle of the room. She rolls over onto her stomach, crawling after it, but doesn't have time to pull it over her head before the wire goes taut.

One of the candles from the chandelier falls to the floor, snapping in two.

Martin stops cranking the handle and turns to her.

He has pushed the dining table and chairs into the living room.

Pamela manages to loosen the wire around her neck slightly with two of her fingers, and starts crying with fear, trying to catch his eye.

427

'Martin, I know you love me . . . I know you don't want to do this.'

He turns the handle another half-revolution, and she has no choice but to pull her fingers out and stand on tiptoe in order to keep breathing.

With her right hand, she reaches up to the wire above her head, gripping it to maintain her balance.

She can no longer speak.

All she can do is try to draw in air through her strained throat. Her thoughts are racing, but she can't understand why this is happening.

The muscles in her calves have already started to tremble with the effort. She doesn't know how much longer she will be able to stand on her tiptoes.

'Please,' she manages to hiss.

Martin turns the handle, and the noose tightens around her neck, cutting into her skin. Her vertebrae pop, and Pamela barely has time to process the unnatural feeling of being lifted up by her head before she runs out of air.

She can hear the sirens of several emergency vehicles outside.

There is no way she can hold herself up with her hands.

The candelabra shakes and more candles clatter to the floor.

A gale seems to be rushing in her ears.

As her field of vision narrows, Pamela sees Martin run towards the hallway, open the door and disappear.

White streaks of rain are hitting the windows of the car. Alice has fallen asleep in her booster seat, and Pamela can't bring herself to let go of her tiny fingers.

She is only half-conscious as the police officers rush into the room. They try to lower her to the floor, but the winch is locked.

One of them grabs the machete from the counter, holds the steel wire against the wall, and manages to chop through it. Pamela drops to the floor, and the loose end of the wire whips through the light fitting, tumbling down beside her.

They loosen the noose and help her lift it over her head. She rolls onto her side, clutching her throat, coughing and spitting bloody saliva onto the floor.

428

89

After passing Enköping, Joona has been able to maintain a speed of 190 kilometres an hour.

He blasts the horn to warn the other cars he's passing.

Pamela still isn't answering her phone. He hasn't had any updates, and can only hope that the officers didn't arrive too late.

Grey tower blocks and power lines flash by outside.

He will be in Stockholm in twenty minutes.

Joona was talking to Anita in her kitchen when he received the message from Johan Jönson.

He sat down at the table, blocking the light so he could see the screen, and hit play on the footage from the CCTV camera.

A man in a pair of light-coloured trousers and a white shirt was standing alone on the empty platform. When he glanced back over his shoulder, his face came into view.

It was Martin.

Johan Jönson had found the film of the attempted murder.

In the video, Martin slowly moved towards the edge of the platform, peering down the tunnel and then staring straight ahead.

The tracks glittered.

The lights of an approaching train became visible deep in the darkness. Everything seemed to shake.

Martin stood perfectly still and then held out his arms like Jesus on the cross. A flash of light hit his face. He swayed slightly, but kept his arms outstretched.

Without warning, he jumped down onto the tracks, breaking his fall with his hands before getting up on unsteady legs and looking around in confusion.

The wavering headlights of the train surrounded him. He looked like he was panicking and scrambled up onto the high edge of the platform, then slipped back down. He barely pulled himself to safety before the train thundered into the station.

Joona called the National Command Centre as he left Anita's house and ran to his car.

During the drive back from Säter, he has been in constant communication with his colleagues. He knows that the officers are at Pamela's place, and they should have provided an update by now.

But now he knows the truth.

Martin and Caesar are the same person.

That is the answer to the mystery.

Now Joona needs to find Mia before it's too late.

He gathers his thoughts, combing back through 'The Mirror Man' in his head, remembering Caesar's nightmares about being trapped in a cramped cage.

There must be a bizarre connection to mink somewhere, but their attempts to find any mink farms, furriers, properties or plots of land with a connection to Martin or anyone by the name of Caesar have so far failed to yield any results.

A team from National Crime has widened the search to Denmark, Norway and Finland.

Joona has to slow down slightly as he takes the turn off towards Stockholm, pulling into the bus lane and driving over the traffic lines to get out onto the E4.

The evening sun is hanging low over the swaying treetops in Haga Park.

He passes one of the airport shuttles, accelerating ahead of it and trying again to get through to Pamela. This time, it only rings twice before someone picks up.

'Pamela,' she croaks.

'Are you at home?'

'I'm waiting for an ambulance; there are police everywhere.'

430

'What happened?'

'Martin showed up, and he attacked me – he tried to hang me, and . . .'

'Is he in custody?'

Pamela coughs, and it sounds like she's struggling to breathe. Joona can hear voices and sirens in the background.

'Is Martin in custody?' he repeats. 'Have we arrested him?'

'He ran off,' she says, her voice stifled.

'I don't know whether you've already figured this out, but he's living some kind of double life as Caesar,' Joona says.

'I just can't believe it, it's completely insane . . . he tried to kill me, he hanged me and . . .' She pauses to cough again.

'You need to get to hospital, you could be seriously injured,' says Joona.

'I'll be fine – they cut me down in time.'

'Just one more thing before I go,' says Joona, turning off towards Stockholm. 'Do you know where Martin could be? Where he might be keeping Mia prisoner?'

'I have no idea, I can't make any sense of this,' she says, coughing again. 'But his family is from Hedemora. He goes up there sometimes, to tend to the family graves.'

Joona realises that Caesar was on foot when he arrived at Dr Scheel's house following his second trauma.

Hedemora is only twenty kilometres from Säter.

He turns the wheel sharply to the right, crossing the lanes and getting off the main road just before the barriers.

The suspension groans as he drives up onto the grass, the car rocking. The glove compartment bursts open, and his gun falls to the floor.

A cloud of dust rises up behind the car, and gravel and small rocks clatter against the underside of the vehicle as he bounces up onto the turn off towards Frösunda.

'What's going on?' Pamela asks.

'Do Martin or his family still have property in Hedemora?'

'No . . . or I don't think so anyway, but I'm starting to realise I don't actually know anything about him.'

A lorry is approaching from the left over the bridge. Joona speeds up the ramp, sees the traffic lights up ahead turn red and cuts just in front of the lorry, making its brakes screech. The right-hand fender scrapes against the barrier. The lorry blasts its horn.

Joona accelerates over the bridge, then down the curved ramp on the other side. He ends up behind a horse trailer, and overtakes it with two wheels in the yellow grass at the side of the road. He swings back onto the road, heading north once more.

Joona hears an ambulance siren fading in the background of the call.

'Has he ever talked about a mink farm?'

'A mink farm? Does he have a mink farm in Hedemora?' Pamela asks.

Joona hears voices asking if she's all right, whether she is struggling to breathe, and telling her to hang up. The call ends.

90

The blue lights dance across the dark-brick walls and up the front of the building on the other side of Karlavägen, flashing in the restaurant windows.

'There's something I need to do,' Pamela splutters to the paramedic, setting off towards the garage.

The street is full of emergency vehicles and officers talking into radios. Curious passers-by have gathered by the police tape, filming the events in front of them on their phones.

'Pamela! Pamela!'

As she turns around, she feels a jolt of pain in her neck so sharp that she winces. Dennis has been allowed inside the cordon, and is running along the pavement towards her.

'What's going on?' he says, catching his breath. 'I called, and . . .'

'It's Martin,' she says, coughing. 'Martin is Caesar . . .'

'I don't understand.'

'He tried to kill me.'

'Martin?'

Dennis gapes at the deep wound from the cable around her neck. He looks so confused and despairing, his chin trembling and his eyes welling up.

'Where's your car?' she asks.

'I need to talk to you.'

'I can't do this right now,' she says, setting off again. 'My throat and neck hurt so much, and I need to get to—'

433

'Just listen to me,' he interrupts her, gripping one of her arms. 'I don't know how to say this, but it seems like Alice is still alive. I think she's one of Caesar's prisoners.'

'What are you saying?' Pamela asks, stopping dead. 'Are you talking about my Alice?'

'She's alive,' he says, tears streaming down his cheeks.

'I . . . I don't understand.'

'The police found a new victim, and she had a letter on her.'

'What? From Alice?'

'No, but it mentions Alice's name, that she's one of the prisoners.'

The colour drains from Pamela's face, and she sways unsteadily. 'Are you sure?' she whispers.

'I'm sure about the letter, and I'm sure the person it mentions is your Alice.'

'Oh my God, oh my God . . .'

Dennis wraps his arms around her, trying to reassure her, but she is crying so hard that her whole body is shaking and she can't quite catch her breath.

'I'll come with you to the hospital, and . . .'

'No!' she shouts, coughing again.

'I'm just trying to . . .'

'Sorry, I know, I know . . . This is all just so much . . . I need to borrow your car, I . . .'

'Pamela, you're hurt.'

'I don't care,' she replies, wiping the tears from her cheeks. 'Just tell me what the letter said. Does it mention where Alice is? I need to know.'

Dennis tries to explain that thirty minutes earlier, he was called in to offer psychological support for a young man as he identified the remains of one of Caesar's victims, believed to be his older sister, who had been found by the side of a main road.

A doctor by the name of Chaya Aboulela showed them into a small room that carried the strong smell of flowers.

The body was so badly disfigured that it was covered with a sheet, but the brother was allowed to inspect the girl's hand and the evidence bags containing the remains of her clothing.

He cried when he saw the brown bloodstains on the fabric, and tore open one of the bags, pulling out a pant leg and turning it inside out.

'It's her,' he said, pointing to a small hidden pocket he recognised on the inside of the right leg.

Dennis put an arm round the young man's shoulders as he pulled out some cash and a small scrap of paper.

My name is Amanda Williamsson, and I'm being held prisoner by a man called Caesar and his mother.

There are a number of us here, living in seven small buildings that weren't built for people. We're not allowed to talk to each other, so I don't know much about the others, but I share a cage with a girl called Jasmin from Senegal. Sandra Rönn from Umeå is in the other cage in my building, along with a sick girl called Alice Nordström.

I guess I must be dead if you're reading this, but please show this letter to the police. They have to find us.

And please tell Vincent and Mum that I love them. I'm sorry for running away, I was just so stressed and sad.

91

Though she doesn't really have the energy for it, Alice made sure she was given the job of cleaning out the cages. Each time she crosses the yard to fill the buckets with fresh water, she checks to see whether Mia has woken up.

The last time she passed, she saw that Mia reacted to her footsteps over the gravel, though she didn't actually open her eyes.

Mia is lying on the ground in her jeans and a filthy bra, tied to one of the bathtub's feet.

Granny stabbed her in the hand with her stick, and she started crying in fear when she went blind, just before losing consciousness.

Their vision usually comes back when they wake up.

Alice hasn't been able to find anything sharp enough to cut the cable tie yet, but she hasn't forgotten what Mia said about checking the drain. She just hasn't had a chance to lift the grille yet. Granny is busy cleaning the lorry, but is keeping a constant eye on her.

Mia needs to wake up and escape before Caesar comes back, because he'll almost certainly kill her while she sleeps if she's still here. That, or he'll force her to stand with her arms outstretched, putting a noose around her neck when she eventually gives up.

Alice puts down the buckets outside the second longhouse, loosening them from the yoke and leaning it against the wall. She coughs and spits on the ground. The air is still warm, but she feels clammy. She must be coming down with another fever.

Granny carries a vacuum cleaner across the yard, the mink skull she wears around her neck knocking against the hose.

Alice composes herself, trying to summon more strength, and steps into the darkness, turning towards the cage on the right.

'Move into the corner, Sandra,' she says, coughing into her hand. 'The water's coming.'

Alice empties the bucket of soapy water onto the floor of the cage. Sandra is squatting down, her dress gathered in her lap, the top of her head slightly bending the cage upwards. The water swills around her bare feet, hitting the wall behind her and turning the concrete floor dark.

Sandra takes the brush from Alice and scrubs the dried excrement from the corner of the cage.

'How's your neck?' Alice asks her.

'No better.'

'I'll see if I can find something for you to use as a pillow.'

'Thanks.'

The murky water runs down into one of the drainage channels. Strands of hair and other bits of rubbish catch in the filter.

'OK, time to rinse it,' says Alice.

She empties the second bucket of water onto the floor, and Sandra passes the scrubbing brush back through the food hatch.

'Do you have a fever again?' Sandra asks, noticing Alice's face.

'I don't think I'll last much longer,' she replies quietly.

'Don't say that, you'll feel better again soon.'

Alice holds her gaze. 'Remember you promised to find my mum when you get out of here,' she says.

'Yes,' Sandra replies solemnly.

Alice takes the empty buckets outside, closing the door behind her. She coughs and spits a gob of bloody phlegm onto the ground.

Blenda is severing the limbs from Kim's body and cremating her remains behind the seventh longhouse. The smell of burning, charred flesh is awful. The smoke blankets the entire yard, making the evening sun look like a glittering silver coin through the haze.

Alice carries the yoke in one hand, moving towards longhouse six. She sees Mia raise her head slightly and squint over to her.

There is no sign of Granny in the yard. Maybe she's in the trailer.

Alice starts filling the first bucket, gripping the rusty grille over the drain with both hands and lifting it clear. She lowers it to the ground beside the hole.

Granny emerges from the haze behind the lorry with a container of chlorine in one hand.

Alice starts filling the second bucket, and watches Granny climb into the trailer. She leans forward, reaching into the cool water in the drain. Lying flat on her stomach, she pushes her entire arm into the hole.

With her fingertips, she feels the pipe bend sharply. She slowly explores the sloping sides of the pipe, reaching some kind of wet fabric and then a solid object.

She pulls out the piece of metal and drops it into one of the buckets, replacing the grille over the drain and getting up. She glances over to the lorry.

Granny is still inside.

In the bottom of the bucket, she sees a long shard of metal that has been sharpened into a knife. The fabric around the handle has almost completely unwound. Alice crouches down and secures the buckets to the yoke, stretching her legs and moving over to the bathtub.

Mia raises her head and squints up at Alice with bloodshot eyes.

'Just lie still while I talk,' Alice tells her, casting another glance over to the lorry. 'Do you think you can get up and run?'

'Maybe,' Mia whispers.

Alice puts down the buckets and attempts to suppress her cough. 'You need to be sure . . . Granny will send the dog after you as soon as she notices you're gone.'

'Give me another ten minutes.'

'I'm almost finished cleaning the cages, and I don't know if I'll get another chance,' Alice replies.

'Five minutes . . .'

'You'll die if you stay here, you know that, don't you? Here's what we'll do: I'll leave the knife with you. Hide it under the bathtub before you run . . . Stick to the road, and jump into the ditch if you see any cars. Don't go into the forest, because there are traps everywhere.'

'Thank you,' says Mia.

'Do you remember my name?'

'Alice,' says Mia, attempting to wet her lips.

Alice quickly fishes the knife up out of the bucket, puts it into Mia's free hand and then gets up, making her way over to the first longhouse.

Caesar will kill them all once he realises Mia has gone. His violence has spiralled out of control since Jenny Lind tried to escape, and it feels like he's just waiting for an excuse to slaughter the entire farm.

After unhooking and setting down the buckets, Alice opens the door and turns back to look at the yard. In the smoky haze, she sees Mia get up on unsteady legs. She drops the knife, steadies herself against the edge of the bathtub and starts walking.

Alice carries the buckets into the longhouse and opens the two cages there.

'Go now,' she says. 'Follow the road and stay out of the forest.'

'What are you talking about?' asks Rosanna.

'Caesar is going to kill anyone left behind.'

'I don't understand,' Sandra says.

'Mia is escaping now. I'm going to open the other cages. Hurry up . . .'

She should take the knife from the bathtub and kill Granny, she thinks, letting the others out of the cages and then heading into the house to lie down in one of the beds.

Alice glances over to the door, sees the evening light quivering in the gap and hears the women in the cages behind her. The door creaks gently on its hinges. She closes her weary eyes and imagines she can hear music from someone else's headphones on a noisy metro train.

There are faint, agitated voices and dogs barking.

Alice opens her eyes again and notices that the light outside has taken on a dirty red colour.

She realises she must be having a fever dream and that she's probably about to lose consciousness.

A shadow flickers by.

Alice stumbles, but her shoulder hits one of the cages, helping her stay upright.

The dark room seems to be spinning.

Two of the four women have climbed out of their cages.

You need to hurry, Alice thinks, starting to move back towards the door.

It feels like she is floating, but the gravel crunching beneath her feet is deafening. Alice sees her hand rise, as though it were being pulled on a string. Her fingertips reach the door, and she pushes it open.

She can't help herself, despite the fact that she can see Granny through the crack.

The door swings out.

The women behind Alice cry out in fear. Outside, Granny is leaning against her stick, an axe in her free hand.

Shrouded in smoke from the crematorium, Mia is standing with her arms outstretched like Christ in the middle of the yard.

* * *

An hour later, the only light is coming from the lorry, which is parked nearby with its engine running. The front headlights are shining straight into the forest, and the tail lights on the trailer are bathing the house in red.

Alice tries to keep her balance beside Mia with her arms spread wide. The two women who left their cages in the first longhouse are standing a few steps away. Rosanna's thighs and knees were badly bitten by the dog, and she looks like she's in a lot of pain. She is bleeding heavily, and has stumbled several times now.

Granny has attached the tooth to her stick, and is holding the axe in her other hand. She glares at them with a mix of expectation and rage.

'We spoil you here, and you still try to escape. But we will find every lost sheep, we'll never give in, because you're all so valuable to us.'

Alice coughs and tries to spit, but she is now so weak that most of the blood drips down on her chin and chest.

'That's God calling to you,' Granny says, stepping in front of her.

Alice sways, raising her arms a little higher. Granny studies her for a moment, the axe swinging by her thigh, and then moves on to Rosanna.

'Do you need to rest?'

'No,' she sobs.

'It's only human to feel tired.'

The dog is circling them. Granny cocks her head and gives them a wry smile.

Alice thinks back to the only time she ever went to the main bedroom. Beside the double bed, there was a cot full of small white bones, thousands of tiny animal skulls.

But on the very top, she also saw the small skulls of two human children.

The smoke is still swirling around the seventh longhouse, forming billowing clouds in the darkness, like huge pillowy craniums.

Alice comes to, her hands growing hot. She quickly raises her arms again.

Granny hasn't noticed.

Her heart is beating hard, sending icy adrenaline through her veins. She needs to find a way to stop herself from slipping into a fever dream.

Rosanna's injured leg gives way, and she drops to her knees without lowering her arms. Granny swings the axe up onto her shoulder and watches her for a moment.

'I'm getting up, I'm doing it now,' Rosanna pleads with her.

'Where is the cross? I don't see the cross.'

'Wait, I . . .'

But the axe hits her forehead, practically splitting her head in two. Alice closes her eyes, feeling dizzy. She lifts up off the ground and floats away with the smoke, over the treetops.

92

Erik wakes with a splitting headache on the floor of his office. It feels like there's a sun-warmed rock beneath his back.

He peers up at the light on the ceiling and tries to remember what happened.

Martin came to see him, asking to be hypnotised one last time before he and Pamela were taken to a safe house.

Erik closes his eyes for a moment.

Martin was in a deep hypnosis when he suddenly rose up from the bed with wide eyes, grabbed a bronze ashtray and slammed it repeatedly into Erik's head.

Erik crashed into the table, taking a stack of manuscripts with him as he fell to the floor and lost consciousness.

The house is now quiet. The evening sun is filtering in through the curtains.

His phone is on the desk. It is likely still recording.

Erik decides to call Joona before heading to the bathroom to inspect his wounds, but when he tries to sit up, he feels a burning sensation in his right shoulder.

He can't lift his upper body even a centimetre from the floor.

He groans loudly from the pain. He closes his eyes and lies perfectly still, opening them a moment later and cautiously trying to raise his head.

The Spanish switchblade he uses as a letter opener has been driven through his shoulder and into the oak floor.

The heat he can feel beneath his back is from the blood spilling out of him.

Erik knows he needs to slow his breathing. If he keeps perfectly still, he may be able to delay going into circulatory shock.

He tries to relax as he replays what happened in his mind.

As an intra-hypnotic suggestion, Erik had conducted a funeral for Martin's two dead brothers. It was an attempt to make him see that they no longer had any power over him.

That was a big mistake.

The brothers not only prevented Martin from remembering and talking – they also guarded the passage to a completely different side of him.

That meant that when they entered the second stage of the hypnosis session, Erik inadvertently opened a door that had remained closed for many years.

He slowly led Martin back into his memories from Observatory Grove Park.

'You're stepping into the darkness now,' Erik said softly. 'You can hear the rain drumming down on your umbrella, and you are approaching the playground . . . two, one, zero . . .'

'Yes,' he whispered.

'You stop by the playhouse.'

'Yes.'

'Time comes to a stop, and as a camera flash goes off, the light slowly spreads through the night. It reaches the jungle gym and doesn't fade away . . .You can now see Caesar.'

'There are layers of glass, but I can see a man in an old top hat in the reflections . . .'

'Do you recognise him?'

'He's cutting a face into a potato with a paring knife, and . . . his wet lips are moving, but I think it's the carved face that's actually talking . . .'

'What is it saying?' asked Erik.

'That I'm Gideon and David, Esau and King Solomon . . . I know it's true, and I can see my own face as a child . . . It's smiling and nodding.'

'But what do you see in the camera flash?'

'Jenny.'

'You see Jenny Lind in the playground?'

'Her legs are kicking. She loses one shoe and starts swinging . . . the noose tightens and blood starts running down her throat, her chest . . . her hands are fumbling . . .'

'Who is taking the pictures?'

'The mother . . . watching the children play . . .'

'Is the mother alone with Jenny in the playground?'

'No.'

'Who else is there?'

'A man.'

'Where?'

'In the playhouse . . . he's looking out through the window.'

The hair on Erik's arms stood on end when he realised that Martin was seeing his own illuminated face reflected in the glass.

'What is the man's name?'

'Our name is Caesar,' he replied calmly.

Erik's heart began beating harder, faster. This was, without doubt, the most remarkable thing he had ever experienced as a hypnotist.

'You say your name is Caesar, but if that's the case, who is Martin?'

'A reflection,' he mumbled.

Dissociative identity disorders are included in *DSM-IV-TR*, the most widely used reference book in psychiatry, yet many practitioners are reluctant to make that diagnosis.

Erik doesn't believe in the existence of multiple personalities, but, in that moment, he had no intention of questioning Caesar as an independent individual.

'Tell me about yourself, Caesar,' he said.

'My father was a patriarch . . . He had a logistics company and a mink farm when I was growing up. It was through the mink fur that the Lord rewarded him and made him a wealthy man . . . He was chosen, promised twelve sons.'

'Twelve sons?'

'Mother couldn't have any more children after me . . .'

'But you had two brothers, didn't you?'

444

'Yes, because . . . one evening, my father came home with a woman he'd found by the side of the road. He told me that he would have more sons through her. Silpa screamed a lot when he first put her in the basement, but when my half-brother Jockum arrived, she moved up into the house . . . and when little Martin was born, she demanded that my mother give up her place in the bedroom.'

He opened his mouth as though he couldn't breathe, his stomach tensing.

'Just listen to my voice . . . you're breathing calmly, your body is relaxed,' said Erik, placing a hand on Martin's shoulder. 'Tell me what happened to your mother.'

'Mother? She suffered my father's wrath . . . she had to stand in the yard for eleven hours like Christ on the cross . . . before she moved into the basement.'

'Were you with her in the basement?'

'I'm the firstborn,' he said, his voice almost inaudible. 'But one night, my mother snuck up into the house and woke me so that . . .'

Martin's mouth continued to form words and sentences, but Erik could no longer hear what he was trying to say. His hands clenched and relaxed, and his chin began to tremble.

'I can't hear you.'

'They were all dead,' he whispered.

'Return to that moment, when your mother woke you.'

'She told me to follow her out, to start the engine in the lorry and wait until she came back.'

'How old were you?'

'Seven and a half . . . I'd started learning to drive in the yard by then . . . I had to stand up to reach the pedals, Mother said it was just for fun, that she would watch me as I played . . . but I saw her put a ladder against the house. She waved to me, climbed up there with the hose and pushed it into the gap of the ventilation window in the bedroom.'

'Who was inside?' asked Erik, conscious that his back was clammy with sweat.

'Everyone . . . My father, Silpa and my brothers,' he replied with a listless smile.

'Mother put me down in front of the TV to watch a video while she dragged the bodies out . . . and once she was done, she came back in and explained that everything was OK.'

'In what sense was it OK?'

'Because my father wasn't the one who was meant to have twelve sons, it was me . . . And I looked at my own face reflected in the TV screen where I saw a man in a top hat – and I saw that I was happy.'

Erik had assumed that Martin had invented Caesar in an attempt to transfer the murder and his feelings of guilt to someone else, but at that point he realised that it was Caesar who had Martin inside him.

'You were only seven and a half – what did you think when she said you would have twelve sons?'

'She showed me the picture inside the mink and said it was my sign. She said it was me in my confirmation gown . . . with outstretched arms and a pointed bonnet.'

'I don't quite understand.'

'It was me,' he whispered. 'God created a paradise for his sons . . . and the mothers are supposed to watch them play.'

Erik made sure to keep Martin on the same level of deep hypnosis, and cautiously led him through the past.

Caesar talked about his strict Christian upbringing, his work and education on the farm. Some parts were almost inaudible, like when he described the deliveries of feed – by-products from meat and fish processing plants.

'When the old driver stopped working, a young woman called Maria took over. I always kept my distance when she came, but Mother saw me looking at her . . . Then, one day, Mother invited Maria in for coffee and gingerbread. She fell asleep on the sofa and Mother took off her clothes and said that Maria would give me many sons . . . We kept her locked in the basement, and I slept with her every night she wasn't bleeding . . . by the next summer, she had a small bump, and moved up into the house.'

His smile disappeared and saliva began trickling down his chin from his open mouth. With a slurred, absent voice, he explained what happened next. Erik couldn't make sense of everything, but tried to piece together his words as best he could.

Maria had clearly started pleading with him to let her go, for the baby's sake, and when she realised it was never going to happen, she hanged herself in the bedroom. Caesar was left in shock, and started losing his grip on reality.

'I was a piece of grass tossed into a river,' he mumbled.

Erik learned that Caesar had left the farm and started wandering the roads in a kind of fugue state. He didn't remember anything until Dr Scheel began talking to someone inside him, someone he didn't know. This person was called Martin, just like his youngest brother, and Martin was unaware of anything that had happened before he arrived at the Säter secure unit.

'I had to share a body with him,' he slurred. 'Sometimes . . . sometimes I can't control when I get sucked in and switched off.'

'Is that how it feels?'

'My field of vision shrinks, and . . .'

He mumbled something incoherent about mirrors placed in front of other mirrors, creating an endless wormhole expanding and shrinking like the bellows of a bagpipe.

Then he fell silent and refused to answer any more questions for quite some time. Erik was just about to lift him out of the hypnosis when he started talking about what he did while Martin was establishing a life for himself in Stockholm.

Caesar returned to his mother on the farm and they started travelling around in the lorry together, abducting young women. He described their looks, the ways he loved each and every one of them, and how their lives had ended.

To Erik, it seemed as though Martin, unbeknownst to himself, had been living a double life. He travelled a lot for work, and likely went to visit his mother whenever he got a chance.

As the years passed, Caesar began stalking women on social media, documenting their lives and getting as familiar with them as he could in order to photograph them.

It wasn't entirely clear what he was saying, but the mother seemed to be the one who actually abducted the women, taking them to the farm and drugging them before they were raped.

'Doesn't Martin know what you've been doing?'

'He doesn't know a thing, he's blind . . . He didn't even realise I'd taken Alice.'

'Alice?'

'Martin couldn't do a thing . . . and when the lorry pulled away, he walked right over to a spruce branch marking thin ice and stamped a hole right through it to die.'

Erik peers up at the ceiling and feels a sharp pang of anxiety as he remembers that Pamela thinks Alice drowned that day. He tries to reach the knife in his shoulder, but it's impossible; he can no longer feel his fingers, and cannot move his right hand. His breathing has become rapid, and he realises he will bleed out soon.

Erik had tried to keep Caesar talking, but he could see that he was rising from the hypnosis.

'Caesar, you feel deeply, deeply relaxed . . . You are listening to my voice; any other sounds simply make you focus even more on what I am saying . . . I'm going to come around to Martin again in a moment. When I reach zero, I will be talking to him again . . . But before that, I want you to tell me where the women are.'

'It doesn't matter, they have to die anyway . . . there won't be anything left, not a single stone, not . . .'

His face began to strain, his eyes opening and staring blindly, his mouth seeming to search for words.

'You are sinking deeper, becoming more and more relaxed, breathing more calmly,' Erik continued. 'None of what we have been talking about is dangerous or frightening; everything will be fine once you tell me where the women are . . .'

Martin was still deep in a hypnotic trance when he rose up from the bed, his hand clamped over one ear. He knocked over the floor lamp, grabbed the bronze ashtray and brought it down on Erik's head.

Beads of sweat are now rolling down Erik's cheeks, but he feels so cold that he has started to shiver.

His heart is racing.

He closes his eyes and hears someone in the garden outside his office. He tries to call for help, but his voice comes out as nothing but a gasp between each shallow breath.

93

The car rumbles as Joona accelerates around a lorry with a full load of timber. He has spent the drive north searching in vain for breeders and mink farms in the Hedemora area, and has already passed Avesta when he finds an old discussion forum that mentions an unregistered farm by the name of Dormen, selling Blackglama furs at low prices.

When he searches for more information about Dormen, he discovers an abandoned farm in the forest close to the Garpenberg Mine, no more than ten kilometres from Hedemora.

This must be it.

Joona is driving at 160 kilometers an hour. He sees a cement factory flash by on his right as he calls Roger Emersson, the commanding officer of the National Task Force.

'I need you to authorise an operation right now.'

'Last time I did that my best friend was killed,' Roger says.

'I know. I'm sorry, and I wish that—'

'It was his job,' Roger says sharply, interrupting Joona.

'I know you've been briefed on our preliminary investigation. I'm confident that I've managed to locate Caesar,' Joona explains, thinking to himself that everything is taking much longer than it needs to right now.

'OK.'

'I believe he's at an old mink farm close to the Garpenberg Mine near Hedemora.'

'Understood.'

'I'm on my way there now – there's a risk that this has developed into a fairly extensive hostage situation.'

'You can't handle that?'

'Roger, now's not the time for an argument; I need to know that you understand how urgent this is. I need to be able to trust you.'

'Relax, Joona – we're coming, we're coming . . .'

Joona leaves the main road at Hedemora and races through the darkness, rushing by huge fields dotted with eerie irrigation machinery.

He tries to slow down as he turns off onto a ramp to the right, but the tyres still screech on the tarmac. The dry bushes at the edge of the road scrape against the side of the car. He accelerates down a straight stretch, driving out onto a narrow bridge over the Dalälven River and catching a glimpse of the water down below, glittering in the darkness.

The wheels thunder as he crosses the bridge. His phone rings, and he picks up as the lights of Vikbyn flash by.

'Hi, Joona, this is Benjamin Bark, Erik's son . . .'

'Benjamin?'

'My dad's been hurt . . . I'm with him in the ambulance, no need to worry, he'll be fine . . . but he said I had to call you to say that Caesar and Martin are the same person . . .'

'What happened?'

'I found Dad in his office with a knife in his shoulder. None of this makes any sense to me, but he says that this Caesar guy is heading for his mink farm now, to destroy all the evidence and disappear . . .'

'I'm almost there.'

'There are traps everywhere in the forest – I was supposed to warn you about that, too.'

'Thanks.'

'Dad was pretty confused, but just before they put the oxygen mask on him, he said something about Caesar having taken a girl called Alice.'

'Åhlén just told me the same thing.'

* * *

450

Joona turns left after Finnhyttan and continues down the narrow forest road. He sees a dark lake shimmering between the trees.

The car's headlights sweep ahead, pinning down the steel-grey trunks lining the road. A deer pauses for a moment by the side of the road before bounding off into the darkness.

Martin could easily have been discharged and readmitted to ward four without Pamela's knowledge, Joona thinks.

Patient confidentiality would have kept his movements secret.

Still, he must have a car somewhere – in a garage or a long-term parking space.

He's been able to lead a double life up to this point, but now Caesar is desperate. He probably thinks that both Erik and Pamela are dead, and knows it won't be long until the police find a way to track him down. That's why he wants to destroy all evidence and escape.

Joona drives past a tall steel gate at the rear of the enormous Boliden mine. The spotlights on the fence posts illuminate the old open-cast pit.

In the distance, he catches a glimpse of the modern industrial buildings through the trees before everything is shrouded in darkness again.

He makes a sharp turn, continuing deeper into the forest.

According to the satellite images, the farm is isolated in the middle of the woods, and comprises a main house and seven long, slender buildings.

The road grows narrower and more uneven.

Joona realises he is approaching the mink farm, and slows down, switching the headlights to half-beam and eventually pulling over to the edge of the road.

He grabs his gun from the floor below the passenger seat and finds two spare magazines in the glove compartment, then climbs out of the car, pulls on his bulletproof vest, and starts running along the road.

The warm night air smells of pine and dry moss.

A jolt of pain radiates from the wound in his side each time his right foot strikes the ground.

After a kilometre or so, he spots a faint light in the distance, and slows to a walk. He turns his weapon's safety off and cocks it.

Without a sound, he moves slowly forward.

There's no sign of Caesar, but he can see a battered Chrysler Valiant in front of the house, the driver's side door flung open.

Parked in the middle of the gravel yard, there is a lorry with a semi-trailer attached, engine running.

The smoke and exhaust fumes glow in its tail lights, spreading like a cloud of blood through the breathless air.

If it weren't for Benjamin's warning, Joona would almost certainly have approached through the trees, but he sticks to the narrow road instead.

The dilapidated wooden house emerges from the darkness, and he can make out the narrow buildings built to house the mink cages to the right.

The hazy air in the yard pulses slowly in the light from the lorry.

Joona sees three women standing perfectly still in the gloom, arms outstretched as though they were being crucified.

The pose is identical to the pattern in the mink skulls, the brands on the girls' necks, Martin's pose on the platform and the way Caesar stood in his room at the secure unit.

As Joona cautiously makes his way forward with his gun lowered, he notices an elderly woman behind the three others. She is sitting on the edge of an old bathtub with a walking stick across her lap.

One of the women sways and manages to regain her balance. She raises her face, and her curly hair swings back from her cheeks.

She is the spitting image of Pamela – she must be Alice.

Joona approaches the outer edge of the faint circle of light, noticing that Alice is trembling all over. Her legs are shaking, and she is struggling to keep her arms outstretched.

The old woman wearily gets up and juts out her chin.

A dog starts barking in front of the house.

There is still no sign of Caesar.

The task force team won't be here for another half hour, at the very least.

Alice takes a step forward and lowers her arms, her chest rising with every pained breath.

Joona raises his gun as the old woman drops the stick and approaches Alice from behind.

Something catches the light by her side. She is holding an axe in her right hand.

Joona takes aim at her shoulder, placing his finger on the trigger.

His cover will be blown if he has to shoot her. And that means that he will have to deal with whatever happens next on his own.

Alice pushes back her hair from her face, sways and then turns to face the old woman. They seem to be talking to one another.

Alice clasps her hands in front of her, pleading. The old woman smiles, says something and swings the axe above her head.

Joona pulls the trigger, hitting her in the shoulder. The blood from the exit wound spatters onto the edge of the bath behind her.

The axe continues its downward swing.

Joona shoots her again, in the elbow this time, as one of the other women pulls Alice to safety.

The blade passes right by her face.

The old woman has now let go of the handle, and the axe thuds to the ground and into the darkness.

The two shots ring out between the buildings.

The dog starts barking angrily.

Alice falls onto her side.

The old woman staggers backwards and bends down for her stick, blood gushing from her gunshot wounds.

Joona can hear terrified cries from the long, narrow buildings.

As he runs forward into the light with his gun drawn, he realises that the woman helping Alice to her feet is Mia Andersson.

'Joona Linna, National Crime Unit,' he says, keeping his voice low. 'Where's Caesar? I need to know where he is.'

'He's been loading things from the house into the lorry,' Mia replies. 'Going back and forth and . . .'

'He took Blenda, she's in the cab,' the third woman says, finally lowering her shaking arms.

With his gun trained on the lorry parked in front of the house, Joona pulls out his handcuffs. 'Who's Blenda?'

'She's one of us.'

Alice is leaning against Mia, gazing up at Joona with amazement. She coughs feebly and looks like she's about to collapse. She wipes her mouth and tries to say something, but fails to make a sound. Mia holds her upright, telling her repeatedly that everything is going to be OK now.

The old woman stares down at the blood dripping from her fingertips with a blank look on her face. The knuckles on her left hand have turned white from clutching the walking stick tightly.

'Drop the stick and give me your hand,' Joona tells her.

'I'm injured,' she mumbles, slowly looking up at him.

Joona glances over to the house and the lorry, takes two steps forward and sees that there is a dead woman in the bloody bathtub.

'Give me your left hand,' he repeats.

'I don't understand . . .'

Right then, a man cries out from the forest behind the lorry. He screams in pain, then quickly falls silent.

'Watch out!' Mia shouts.

Joona sees the sudden movement from the corner of his eye, and he ducks, trying to avoid the stick, but feels something sharp graze his cheek.

Using his gun, he knocks the stick from the old woman's hand, kicking out her feet from beneath her at the same time so that she lands on her back.

She bites down on her tongue as her head hits the ground.

Joona quickly scans the area, then rolls the woman over onto her front with his foot, placing one knee between her shoulder blades and locking her left hand to the bathtub with his cuffs.

He turns back to the lorry, wiping the blood from his cheek. The glowing cloud of exhaust fumes billows softly.

'Her stick is poisoned,' Alice coughs.

'What kind of poison? What's going to happen?' he asks.

'I don't know, it puts you to sleep. I don't think she had time to refill the ampoule, though . . .'

'You'll probably just feel tired or lose your vision for a while,' says Mia, pulling Alice's arm around her shoulders.

The old woman gets to her feet, though she is unable to stand straight. Blood trickles from her mouth. Growling, she uses all her strength to try and move the bathtub, but it doesn't budge.

'How many people are locked up?' Joona asks.

'Eight,' Mia replies.

'And they're all inside?'

'Mum,' Alice gasps.

94

In the gap between the lorry and the trailer, Joona can make out two figures. Pamela's face catches the light.

Joona quickly trains his weapon on them and realises that she must have jumped into the car immediately after their call earlier and tracked down the mink farm the same way he did.

A branch breaks underfoot. The dark ferns sway.

Pamela slowly emerges from the forest edge, and Joona sees that the person behind her is Caesar. He is pressed up against her back, holding a knife to her throat.

Joona moves towards them with his gun raised.

Caesar's face is hidden behind Pamela's. She stumbles slightly, and a sliver of his cheek becomes visible through her hair.

Joona's finger twitches on the trigger.

If Pamela can just get a little further away from Caesar, he might be able to take a shot that grazes his temple.

'Police!' Joona shouts. 'Drop the knife and step away from her!'

'Mother, look at me,' says Caesar.

He pauses, dragging the blade a few centimetres across Pamela's throat, making blood spill down onto the neck of her top. She doesn't react to the pain, simply stares straight ahead at her daughter with wide eyes.

The blade of the knife is still resting on her skin. If Caesar cuts an artery, she'll have no chance of making it to hospital in time.

Joona takes another step forward. He catches only a brief glimpse of Caesar's shoulder behind Pamela's, but maintains his line of fire.

'Take me instead!' Alice shouts, staggering forward.

Joona grips his gun with both hands, taking aim at Pamela's left eye. He moves the sight horizontally over her cheek to her ear.

The gravel crunches beneath Alice's feet.

Pamela pauses and looks Joona straight in the eye. She presses her throat against the knife, and he realises what she is about to do. The blood is now streaming down her skin.

Joona is ready.

Pamela pushes harder against the blade, forcing Caesar to lighten its pressure slightly.

That split second is all she needs to jerk her head back and to one side.

Joona pulls the trigger and sees Caesar reel as the bullet tears off his ear.

His head snaps to one side as though he has just been hit by a powerful left hook, then he drops to one knee behind the covered side of the lorry.

Joona can no longer see him, and moves quickly to the left, but Pamela is in the way.

She is standing perfectly still, staring at her daughter. Caesar has fallen, and is lying in the darkness behind her. The sole of his shoe is the only part of him Joona can see.

'Pamela, get away from him,' Joona shouts as he charges forward with his gun raised.

Caesar gets to his feet behind her, clutching what is left of his ear. He looks down at the knife in confusion, dropping it to the ground.

'Pamela?' he asks, his voice trembling with fear. 'Where are we? I don't understand what . . .'

'Shoot him!' she shouts to Joona, taking a step to one side.

Joona takes aim at his chest, and has just pulled the trigger when there is a sudden, deafening blast.

The air is knocked out of him, and he is thrown back as the sound of the explosion rings out around him.

Shards of glass from the windows hurtle through the air.

The interior of the house shoots outwards, tearing down walls and breaking away roofing tiles. The wall panels splinter, roof trusses are blown to pieces and thrown skywards.

A second later, the initial shock wave is followed by a ball of fire, expanding so quickly that it ignites the debris thrown into the air.

Joona lands on his back and rolls over onto his stomach, covering his head with his arms as shards of glass and burning splinters of wood rain down on him.

The dry forest floor at the edge of the yard catches fire.

A heavy wooden joist rams into the back of his head, and everything goes dark.

* * *

He hears Alice calling to her mother as though from another world.

Joona comes to and tries to get to his feet. The wrecked house is ablaze; the roof is collapsing, and embers swirl up into the air. The echo of the explosion sounds like waves repeatedly breaking against the beach. He gets up, a shower of splinters and dust falling from his clothes.

Joona's gun is gone, and Caesar is nowhere to be found.

All around him, the ground is alight with tiny fires, illuminating a large area around what used to be the house.

Pamela staggers forward, calling for Alice and digging through the smoking rubble.

The huge cloud of dust is still falling over the yard, and glowing embers float through the murky air.

There is no sign of Alice, but Mia and the third woman get up from the ground. A lone sneaker lies beside a burning door.

'Did you see where Caesar went?' Joona asks.

'No, I . . . I got something in my face and passed out,' Mia replies. 'What about you?'

'I can't hear anything,' the other woman cries in confusion.

Mia's nose is bleeding, and she has a deep gash on her forehead. Trembling, she pulls a long shard of wood from her right upper arm.

'Mia?' says Pamela.

'What are you doing here?'

'I came to get you,' she says, swaying.

Pamela moves forward, bleeding heavily from a wound on her thigh. Her trouser leg is soaked through. She drags a section of wall with remnants of golden wallpaper still stuck to it out of the way.

Another smaller explosion goes off in the longhouse furthest from them. The door flies up into the air, flames licking at the gable.

'Can you get everyone out of the cages?' Joona asks Mia, picking up a section of water pipe from the ground.

'I think so,' she tells him, glancing down at the blood trickling along her arm and dripping from her elbow.

The flames in the furthest building have now reached the roof of the neighbouring longhouse.

'Are you sure you can manage?' Joona asks. 'Because I need to find Caesar.'

'I can do it, I can do it,' Mia replies.

The old woman is sitting with her back to the bathtub, a look of apathy on her bloodied face. Her face is studded with splinters, and both of her eyes have been punctured, bloody lumps of grey vitreous humour mixing with the dust on her cheeks.

Joona strides towards the lorry.

The shell of the main house collapses, sending a wave of flames and embers high into the air. He feels the heat hit him. The entire forest edge is on fire now, black smoke rising into the night sky.

The lorry lets out a heavy hiss and starts rolling forward. Behind the wheel is a young woman he has never seen before. The engine revs strangely, the enormous wheels turning as the remnants of a window frame crack beneath its tyres.

Joona runs forward and jumps over a warped sink. The heavy plates in his bulletproof vest thud against his ribs.

'Alice!' Pamela shouts, limping after the lorry.

95

The trailer flattens one of the gateposts before turning, with a roar, onto the forest road. Joona runs through the burning wreckage of the house, the smoke making his lungs sting and the pain in his torso growing worse, cutting through him like a knife with each step.

'Alice!' Pamela shouts, her voice breaking.

Joona jumps over a ditch, cuts through a tangle of nettles and comes out onto the road, barely grabbing one of the posts holding up the nylon exterior just as the driver accelerates.

The driver grinds the gears.

Joona drops the metal pipe but manages to hold on to the lorry, letting himself be dragged along behind it. With his free hand, he reaches up to the tailgate and hauls himself into the trailer.

He gets to his feet on the shaking floor, and finds himself standing next to an old grandfather clock.

The tyres throw up a cloud of dust behind them.

The trailer lurches, and Joona has to cling onto one of the struts to prevent himself from falling.

The entire lorry is full of furniture.

The larger pieces have been stacked along the sides, the smaller boxes, chairs and lamps in the middle, along with a full-length mirror in an elaborate golden frame.

In the fading light of the burning house, he spots Caesar at the very back of the trailer. He is sitting in an armchair, one arm draped over the armrest, and is checking his phone.

One of his cheeks is slick with blood, and the shredded remains of his ear look like tiny spikes.

Alice is standing beside him, a piece of duct tape over her mouth. She has been bound to one of the vertical posts, a cable tie around her throat. Her nostrils are black with soot, and Joona can see that she is bleeding from one eyebrow.

The trailer sways again, and she grips the post with both hands in an attempt to protect her throat.

The lorry thunders through the forest, and it suddenly becomes very dark.

Joona realises that the woman they called Blenda must be driving. He caught a glimpse of her face in the driver's cab as he was running.

Branches and brush whip against the sides of the lorry, and the faint glow from the lights mounted on the back of the cab is seeping in through the nylon.

'My name is Joona Linna,' he says. 'I'm a detective with the National Crime Unit.'

'This is my lorry, and you have no right to be here,' Caesar replies, pushing his phone into his pocket.

'A task force is en route. You won't be able to get away this time. But if you turn yourself in now, it will help you at trial.'

Joona pulls out his ID and holds it up, continuing to walk towards Caesar, stepping over piles of mink fur bound with string. He moves a golden chair and pushes past the huge mirror.

'Your laws are not mine,' Caesar tells him, lowering his right hand from the armrest.

Alice doesn't dare pull the tape from her mouth, but she tries to catch Joona's eye, shaking her head.

Joona moves past a display cabinet and hears the china inside clinking softly with the vibrations. He holds up his ID again, giving him a reason to keep moving forward. Caesar studies him with a guarded look through his dusty glasses.

A few sections of gold plastic cornicing have been stacked between an upholstered headboard and a sofa standing on end.

The drawbar between the cab and the trailer groans, and the floor starts to shake beneath Joona's feet.

He pauses in front of a bucket containing hundreds of Polaroids of young women. Some are asleep in their beds, but others have been captured through the cracks in doorways or through windows.

461

'You know it's over, don't you?' he says, trying to see what Caesar is hiding down the side of the armchair.

'It isn't over; there are plans for me. There always have been.'

'Let Alice go, and we can talk about your plans.'

'Let Alice go? I'd rather decapitate her.'

Joona's eyes are fixed on Caesar's forearm. He sees his muscles tensing, his hand gripping something, his shoulder rising by a few centimetres.

Just as he steps over the bucket, Caesar lashes out with the machete. Joona had been expecting the sudden attack, but there is still a huge amount of force behind it.

The machete quickly swings upwards from the shadows below. Joona throws himself out of the way. The blade passes him by, chopping the slender neck of a floor lamp with a dull metallic clang. The fringed shade drops to the floor.

The trailer lurches to one side with a shudder.

Joona stumbles back.

Breathing through his nose, Caesar follows him, swinging the blade again.

The back wheel of the trailer drops into the ditch, making the floor tilt and some of the furniture slam together. The steel struts holding up the nylon flaps ring loudly.

Rolls of tape spill out of a cupboard.

The door swings shut.

Caesar regains his balance, moving towards Joona and slashing with the machete. Sparks fly as the blade hits one of the metal bars on the roof.

The tyres beneath them are rumbling against the ground.

Joona backs up, pushing over the display cabinet between them. Glass and china shatter across the floor.

A sudden jolt passes through the entire trailer as the lorry crashes through a tree by the side of the road. Joona staggers forward, and Caesar falls onto his back. The severed tree trunk rolls across the roof of the trailer, tearing the fabric.

Loose sheets of paper and napkins swirl away in the wind.

Alice's neck is now bleeding where the cable tie has cut into her skin.

Joona braces himself against the back of a chair. He can feel a strange icy sensation spreading from the scratch on his cheek.

Caesar gets up, still gripping the machete in one hand. The sharpened edge looks like a line of silver running down the black blade.

'Listen, I know all about your illness. You can get help,' Joona tells him. 'I read Gustav Scheel's case study. I know that Martin is inside you, and I know that he doesn't want to hurt Alice.'

Caesar wets his lips with his tongue like he's trying to identify a flavour he doesn't recognise.

Joona realises that his vision is starting to fail him.

One of the lights on the back of the cab is gone, and the other is swinging loose on its cables, flickering. The trailer is almost pitch-black now. The black treetops flash by against the dark blue sky.

Caesar grins, and his face seems to double, drifting apart as Joona's vision blurs.

'Time to play,' he says, vanishing behind the headboard.

Joona slowly moves forward, towards the overturned display cabinet. He blinks in the darkness, trying to make out any movement. Shards of glass and china crunch beneath his feet.

Caesar has switched sides, and swings the blade towards him again. The machete passes right in front of Joona's face, slicing into the sofa and causing the stuffing to burst out.

The fluttering nylon side curtain catches on something outside, and is torn away. A roll of brownish-yellow marbled vinyl flooring falls over the tailgate and thuds down into the ditch.

Alice pulls the tape from her mouth, coughing and sinking towards the floor. The cable tie is hitched to a horizontal bar preventing her from moving much, but she stretches one leg and reaches Caesar's phone with her foot, pulling it back towards her.

Joona can no longer see Caesar among the furniture, and he realises that it must be because the poison is affecting his vision. The icy chill from the scratch on his cheek has spread across his face, reaching his ears.

The trailer sways again, and Joona grabs on to a desk to maintain his balance. He blinks, but the outlines of the furniture are indistinguishable from the darkness.

Alice switches on the phone's flashlight, illuminating Caesar, who has crept up beside Joona.

'Look out!' she shouts.

Caesar lunges at him with what looks like three machetes – one sharp blade and two shadows. Joona manages to pitch his body back, so that the tip of the knife only just nicks his bulletproof vest.

But as it comes down next to him, the heavy blade takes off a chunk of the corner of the desk.

Joona moves back.

Alice follows Caesar with the light from the phone. Illuminated from behind, his hair glows, the taut lines on his cheeks deepening. Caesar steps over the display cabinet and disappears behind the large mirror.

Joona slowly moves forward, rubbing his eyes with his thumb and index finger.

A pothole in the road makes the furniture shake.

Caesar is nowhere to be seen, but Alice is shining the light on the back of the mirror. Her eyes are dark and focused.

Joona sees himself in the trembling glass, surrounded by furniture and boxes. He takes three quick steps forward, towards his own reflection, and kicks straight through the mirror, hitting Caesar in the chest.

Caesar is thrown backwards, landing on his back in a burst of glass.

Joona doesn't even notice that he's cut himself.

The trailer careers to one side so abruptly that Alice cries out in pain. The light from the phone plays across the walls.

Joona moves around the gold frame of the mirror and sees that Caesar is already on his feet. Alice turns the light back onto him just as he gets ready to swing the machete. The heavy blade comes from above this time, but rather than ducking away from it, Joona steps forward and thrusts the heel of his left hand into Caesar's chin. His head snaps back and his glasses fly off. Joona follows through the movement, locking Caesar's arm that's holding the knife in the crook of his own.

The two men reel to one side together.

With his right fist, Joona hits Caesar in the face and the throat until the machete clatters to the ground.

There is a loud bang, and the entire lorry shakes. Bright light fills the trailer. They have just broken through the steel gate at the rear of the old mine. Powerful spotlights illuminate the entire area from high above.

Joona forces Caesar to the floor, ramming a knee into his chest. He holds on to his arm, twisting it upwards as he falls.

He hears a crack as Caesar's elbow breaks.

Caesar cries out, landing on his stomach, and Joona puts a foot on his shoulders.

Alice has managed to grab the machete, and uses it to cut the cable tie around her throat.

The lorry is speeding along a wide gravel road. The dust behind them is illuminated by the floodlights.

Joona glances up ahead, and though his vision is failing, he knows that they are approaching the steep drop into the abandoned mine pit.

'Alice, we need to jump,' he shouts.

As though in a dream, she steps over Caesar, swaying with the bouncing trailer and meets Joona's eye. Her face is beaded with sweat, her cheeks feverish and her lips almost white.

The gearbox screeches and Blenda turns to the right, smashing into a decommissioned dumper truck and heading straight for the pit.

'Jump!' Joona shouts, taking out his cuffs.

He blinks firmly, but Caesar is nothing but a shadow on the floor.

Alice moves slowly, hesitating at the very back, looking out over the gravel landscape, the dusty road and the slope to the left.

The machete swings limply in her hand.

The brakes pump and screech, but fail to work. The front bumper has come loose, and is scraping against the ground, smouldering.

Joona leaves Caesar and runs over to the back of the trailer, towards Alice, just as his vision vanishes for good. They crash through the last fence, leaving the crumpled sections in the dust behind them. Engine roaring, the lorry races towards the huge pit.

96

In the car's headlights, Pamela sees splintered trees and flattened grass verges.

She isn't far behind the lorry.

Dennis's car was parked outside the police cordon on Karlavägen, and as they drove north, Pamela searched for mink farms in the Hedemora area, remembering that Martin once told her he used to play in an old mine as a child.

She rounds a curve in the road, accelerating and driving over smashed branches on the narrow forest road. The rough ground rattles against the underside of the car.

Memories of what happened when she and Dennis arrived at the mink farm race through her mind like fever dreams.

They had just left the car by the side of the lorry when Caesar took them by surprise. They turned and tried to escape into the forest, but Dennis suddenly stopped dead, crying out in pain.

Pamela was on her knees, trying to prise open the fox trap, when Caesar stepped forward. He hit Dennis on the head with a rock, then grabbed her hair and dragged her to her feet, pressing a knife to her throat.

Pamela knows that she is driving too fast to really control the car; a sudden bend comes out of nowhere, and she skids in the loose gravel.

She brakes, trying to turn the wheel, but the car spins off the road. The tail end smashes into a tree, and the windows shatter.

Pamela groans in pain from the wound on her leg.

She changes gear, reversing back onto the road, then accelerating on.

As she approaches the brightly lit mine, she sees that the metal gate has been razed to the ground. She drives straight over it and spots the lorry a hundred metres or so up ahead, through the swirling dust.

The rough gravel crunches beneath the tyres.

The lorry turns sharply, hitting an embankment and tipping onto its side. The connection breaks, severing the trailer from the cab.

The lorry slides across the ground, smashing into an old loader. The windscreen shatters and the metal exterior crumples.

The loose trailer with the torn nylon cover starts to move backwards, towards the pit. Its broken axle scrapes against the ground.

Pamela presses the accelerator to the floor, driving over the last few sections of mown-down fence.

Something catches on the front axle, and she loses the ability to steer, skidding as though she were on ice. She brakes, and the car spins around, the front fender hitting a pile of blasting mats and coming to a stop. The headlights crack, and Pamela's head thuds against the window to her side. She stumbles out and starts running after the trailer, which is slowly rolling towards the edge.

'Alice!' she screams.

The rear tyres roll over the edge of the pit, and there is a loud thud as the underside of the trailer hits the ground.

It slowly slides backwards towards the drop before stopping, teetering like a seesaw.

Pamela stops running and realises her entire body is shaking as she approaches. The air is heavy with the scent of diesel and hot sand.

There is a creaking sound, and the trailer's wheels lift up off the ground as it rocks forward.

Inside, Martin stands up, clutching his elbow.

The cover around the trailer is almost entirely gone, and the steel frame looks like a cage around him.

The large grandfather clock tips and plummets into the pit. She hears it hit the edge down below before continuing to fall and slamming into the bottom.

'Not this, not this,' Pamela whispers.

She feels like she is about to faint when she reaches the edge and peers down.

There is no sign of Alice or Joona. She takes a step back and tries to compose herself, but her mind is racing.

The trailer lurches again, the steering arm clattering against the ground. The torn fabric on the trailer flaps softly in the breeze.

'Pamela, what's going on?' Martin asks, sounding afraid. 'I don't remember what . . .'

'Where's Alice?' she shouts.

'Alice? Are you talking about our Alice?'

'She was never yours.'

The trailer tips again, and a plastic bucket slides across the floor by his feet.

Rocks have started to break away at the edge of the pit, hurtling downwards.

The chassis groans under the strain.

Martin takes two steps towards her, and the trailer regains its balance, though it suddenly slides another half-metre or so towards the drop with a screech. He falls forward, steadying himself with one hand, then gets up and stares at her.

'Am I Caesar?' he asks.

'Yes,' she tells him, looking into his terrified eyes.

Martin looks down and stands still for a moment, then turns his back on her. Holding on to the struts around the trailer, he walks slowly towards the pit. As he passes the mid-point, the trailer begins to tip, and the wheels lift off the ground in front of Pamela. Furniture and broken glass begin to slide across the floor, tumbling down into the darkness.

Martin pauses and holds on tight as the entire trailer starts to tip over the edge.

Part of the rock beneath it breaks loose, clattering down against the sides of the pit.

There is a deafening screech, and then it is as though the abyss has stirred to life, noticing Caesar's scent and swallowing him whole.

The trailer is gone.

The silence before the front end of the trailer smashes into a rock shelf some thirty metres below feels impossibly long. The trailer flips, continuing down into the darkness and slamming into the bottom of the pit in a cloud of dust.

Pamela hears the crash echo between the rock walls as she turns away. Hand shaking, she covers her mouth, glancing over to her car, the broken fence and the gravel road down the slope.

She sees two figures appear from behind the overturned lorry cab, coming up the slope to the side of the road.

Pamela takes a step towards them, pushing her hair back from her face.

Joona is moving slowly, his eyes closed, but he seems to be holding Alice upright with an arm around her waist.

Limping, Pamela runs over to them. She doesn't know whether she actually calls her daughter's name, or whether all of it is just in her mind.

Joona and Alice pause as she reaches them.

'Oh, Alice, Alice,' Pamela says over and over again, sobbing. She cups her daughter's face in her hands and looks deep into her eyes. A feeling of unimaginable mercy seems to embrace her, like warm water.

'Mum.' Alice smiles.

The two women drop to their knees in the sand, hugging one another tightly. In the distance, the sirens are drawing closer.

97

The glare from the ceiling light obscures the 'CNN Breaking News from Sweden' banner on her grubby phone screen.

Black-clad officers with helmets and semi-automatic rifles are moving across a gravel yard surrounded by forest.

Filthy young women are being led towards ambulances, while others lie on stretchers. In the background are the remains of a collapsed house, ripped apart by an explosion.

'The nightmare is over,' the anchor reports. 'Twelve young women were held prisoner on this mink farm near Hedemora, some for as long as five years.'

Drone footage shows a number of burnt buildings among the trees as the anchor explains that the police have not yet released any information about the suspect.

One of the young women speaks to a journalist at the scene while being tended to by paramedics.

'There was one policeman who found us, he saved us . . . God,' she sobs. 'I just want to go home to my mum and dad.'

She is led away to a waiting ambulance.

Lumi pauses the news report, closes her eyes for a moment, then calls her father.

She leaves the university studio as it rings, and is already walking down the hallway when Joona picks up, sounding anxious.

'Lumi?'

'I just saw the news about the girls who . . .'

'Ah, that . . . It turned out pretty well in the end,' he says.

Her legs feel so unsteady that she has to pause and sit down on the floor, her back to the wall. 'You saved them, right?' she asks.

'A team effort.'

'Sorry for being so stupid, Dad.'

'But you were right,' he says. 'I should leave the force.'

'No, you shouldn't. I . . . I'm proud to have you as my dad; you saved those women, who . . .' She trails off, wiping the tears from her cheeks.

'Thank you.'

'I'm almost too scared to ask whether you're hurt,' she whispers.

'A few bruises.'

'Tell me the truth.'

'I'm in intensive care, but there's no need to worry. Just a few stab wounds, a bit of shrapnel from an explosion, and some kind of poison they can't identify.'

'Is that all?' she says drily.

* * *

Five days have passed since the events at the mink farm. Joona is still in the hospital, but has been moved out of intensive care, and is no longer confined to bed.

The bombs Caesar placed in the other longhouses never detonated.

Twelve women were rescued, though Blenda died two days later from the injuries she sustained when the lorry rolled over.

Caesar's broken body was found at the bottom of the old mine pit. Among the wreckage of the trailer and the shattered furniture, the officers also discovered a box containing his brothers' skeletons and hundreds of mink skulls.

Granny was taken into custody and is now in isolation. The prosecutor has taken over the investigation.

Primus was arrested outside his sister's house.

The crime scene investigation is still ongoing, and it remains to be seen exactly how many women died or were killed on the mink farm over the years. Some were cremated, while others were buried or dumped in garbage bags in unknown locations.

Besides having tests run, going to rehabilitation sessions and having his bandages changed, Joona has been spending most of his time in meetings with the prosecutor.

Valeria has rebooked her plane tickets and is on her way home. She was so worried about him that she actually cried when they spoke on the phone.

Erik Maria Bark came to visit yesterday. He has regained almost all movement in his shoulder, and was in a fantastic mood as he told Joona all about the new chapter he has planned for his book – based on the old 'Mirror Man' case study.

Joona is wearing a pair of black tracksuit bottoms and a faded T-shirt with the words 'Life Regiment Hussars' across the front. He has just been to see the physiotherapist, who taught him some exercises that will rebuild the strength in his torso and back.

As he limps down the corridor, he thinks about the discovery of the two young boys' skeletons, and the bizarre fact they were never buried or cremated. He needs to talk to Nils about their decomposition. He wonders whether they had in fact been buried at some point, or whether, like the mink skulls, the flesh was boiled off them.

Joona enters his room, puts the sheet of exercises down on the bed and walks over to the window. He lowers his water bottle to the windowsill and looks outside.

The sun peeks out from behind a cloud, filtering through the rough glass bottle. The dappled light falls onto his hand and the surgical tape over the stitches on his knuckles.

Hearing a knock at the door, Joona turns around just as Pamela steps into the room. She is leaning on a crutch, wearing a knitted green cardigan and a checked skirt, her curly hair tied up in a ponytail.

'You were asleep last time I came,' she says.

She props her crutch against the wall, hobbles over and hugs him before stepping back and giving him a solemn look.

'Joona, I really don't know what to say . . . What you did, the fact that you . . .' She trails off, her voice breaking, and lowers her face.

'I just wish I could've put the pieces together sooner,' he says.

She clears her throat and looks up at him. 'You were the first person to do it. You're the reason I have my life back ... It's more than that, more than I ever could have imagined.'

'Sometimes things work out the way they're meant to,' he says, smiling.

She nods and glances back to the doorway. 'Come and say hello to Joona,' she calls out to the corridor.

Alice cautiously steps into the room. Her eyes seem guarded, her cheeks flushed. She's wearing a pair of jeans and a denim jacket, and her hair is down, spilling over her shoulders.

'Hi again,' she says, pausing a metre or so from the door.

'Thanks for your help in the trailer,' Joona tells her.

'I didn't even think about it, there was no other option,' she says.

'But it was very brave of you.'

'No, it ... I'd been locked up so long that I almost started to accept that no one would ever find us,' she says, looking up at her mother.

'How are you both?' Joona asks.

'Pretty good, actually,' says Pamela. 'Both black and blue, bandaged and stitched up ... Alice had pneumonia, but she's on antibiotics now, so her fever has gone.'

'Good.'

Pamela peers over to the door again, catching Alice's eye. 'Mia didn't want to come in?' she asks, her voice low.

'I don't know,' she replies.

'Mia?' Pamela calls.

Mia steps into the room and squeezes Alice's hand before making her way over to Joona. Her blue and pink hair is hanging loose over her cheeks. She has on red lipstick and her eyebrows are filled in, and she's wearing a camouflage print tank top and a pair of black trousers.

'Mia,' she says, holding out a hand.

'Joona.' He shakes her hand. 'If you knew how hard I'd been looking for you these past few weeks.'

'Thank you for not giving up.' She doesn't go on, her eyes welling up.

'How are you doing?' he asks.

'Me? I got lucky, I came out of it in OK shape.'

'She's going to be my sister,' Alice tells Joona.

Mia looks down, smiling to herself.

'We've agreed that I'm going to adopt Mia,' Pamela explains.

'I still can't believe it,' Mia whispers, hiding her face in her hands for a moment.

Pamela sits down in a chair and stretches her injured leg. The sunlight coming in through the window hits her weary face and makes her hair shine like copper.

'You talked about putting the pieces together,' she says, taking a deep breath. 'And I know I can see the whole picture now, but I still can't believe Martin did these things. It just doesn't make sense: I know him, or I knew him – he was a good person.'

'I know, I feel the same way,' says Alice, steadying herself against the wall with one hand. 'I mean, at first I kept begging Caesar to let me go. I called him Martin, I tried to talk to him about Mum, about our shared memories, but he didn't react. It was like he had no idea who I was even talking about . . . and then after a while, I started to think that Caesar just happened to look a lot like Martin, but that he wasn't him . . . I couldn't make sense of it.'

Joona runs a hand through his hair and frowns.

'I've spoken to Erik Maria Bark a lot about this, and I think we have to accept that while Martin and Caesar shared a body, in purely psychological terms, they were separate people,' he says. 'Martin probably had no idea Caesar even existed, despite being locked in some kind of unconscious battle with him . . . But Caesar was aware of Martin; he hated him, and refused to accept his right to exist.'

'Is that true?' Pamela asks, wiping a couple of tears from her cheeks.

'I don't think there's any other explanation,' says Joona.

'We survived, that's all that matters,' says Pamela.

'Mum, can I wait outside?' asks Alice.

'We're going anyway,' Pamela replies, getting to her feet.

'I don't want to rush you, I just need to get some air,' says Alice, passing her the crutch.

'We can talk later,' says Joona.

'I'll call you,' Pamela tells him. 'But I just need to ask if you know anything about the trial.'

'It looks like it'll start in mid-August. The prosecutor is going to request that it takes place behind closed doors,' he explains.

'Good.'

'No journalists, no members of the public, only those directly involved – the victims and witnesses.'

'Us?' Mia asks.

'Yes.' He nods.

'Is Granny going to be there?' Alice asks, her cheeks turning pale.

98

The doors to the secure courtroom at the Stockholm District Court are closed, the artificial lighting glaring on the bulletproof glass around the near-empty gallery.

At the front of the room, the judge sits at a pale wooden table alongside three lay judges and the clerk.

The prosecutor is a woman in her mid-fifties who uses a walker. She has a symmetrical face and large, dark-green eyes, and is wearing a light-coloured suit, a pink clip in her blonde hair.

Granny is sitting perfectly still in her baggy prison uniform. She has a bandage over both eyes, and her right arm is in a cast. Her mouth is firmly closed, and the deep furrows around her lips make it look like they have been sewn shut.

Neither she nor Caesar were registered anywhere, and since she refuses to give her name, she is referred to throughout as 'NN'.

The evidence suggests that she, like her son, was born and raised on the mink farm in Hedemora.

Throughout the main proceedings, the old woman has refused to say a word, even to her legal representative. After the prosecutor submitted her application for a summons, the defence lawyer announced that the accused admitted to some of the circumstances, but denied having committed any crimes.

The hearings involving the witnesses and plaintiffs have been going on for two weeks now. Many of the young women who were held captive have struggled to talk about their experiences. Some sat with

their arms wrapped around themselves, eyes downcast, and others cried or clammed up, shaking.

Today, on the last day of evidence, Joona Linna is called to the stand.

The prosecutor slowly makes her way over to where he is sitting, the rubber wheels of her walker rolling silently across the floor. She takes a photograph from a folder, but has to pause because her hand is shaking so much. She waits a moment and then holds up the image of Jenny Lind that was shared in the media when she first disappeared.

'Could you tell us about the investigation that led to the raid on the mink farm?' she asks.

The room is completely silent as Joona explains the case in detail. Other than his voice, the only sound comes from the whirring of the air-conditioning unit and the occasional cough.

Granny cocks her head as though she were listening to music in a concert hall.

Joona concludes by emphasising Granny's active role in the abduction of the women, in holding them captive, and in their abuse, rapes and murders.

'Martin found the victims on social media and started stalking them . . . but she was the one who put on a wig and a black leather jacket and drove the lorry,' he explains.

'Did she do so under duress, in your opinion?' the prosecutor asks.

'I would say that they coerced each other . . . in a complex interplay of fear and destructive influence.'

The prosecutor takes off her reading glasses, accidentally smudging her eyeliner.

'As we have shown, the abuse went on for a long time – perhaps over several generations,' she says, looking up at Joona. 'But how could that have continued when Martin needed to go into full-time care?'

'He wasn't forcibly admitted, and he wasn't given forensic psychiatric care,' Joona replies. 'That meant that like most of the others in his ward, he could be discharged or given day release virtually whenever he wanted it . . . all without informing any relatives or family, because of patient confidentiality.'

'We have been able to match each incident with a registered discharge from the ward,' the prosecutor tells the judge and the lay judges.

'He also kept an unregistered car in a private garage in Akalla, the same Chrysler Valiant we found on the mink farm during our raid.'

Joona continues to answer questions for another two hours, and after a brief break, the prosecutor presents her closing arguments to the court, calling for a sentence of life imprisonment.

The defence lawyer doesn't attempt to home in on any particular details, or to sow any doubt, and simply repeats that the accused acted in good faith and denies any wrongdoing.

The room empties out while the court considers the verdict. The prison guards lead Granny away, and Joona heads out through the secure doors to the courthouse café with Pamela, Alice and Mia.

He buys coffee, juice, sweet buns and sandwiches, telling them to try to eat something, even if they aren't hungry. 'It could be a long wait,' he explains.

'Would you like anything?' asks Pamela.

Alice shakes her head, clamping her hands between her thighs.

'Mia?'

'No, thanks.'

'Not even a bun?'

'OK,' she replies, taking it from Pamela.

'Alice? At least have some juice.'

Alice nods and takes the glass from Pamela, taking a sip.

'Imagine if they let her go,' Mia mumbles, picking the lumps of sugar from her bun.

'They won't,' Joona reassures her.

They sit quietly for a while, listening to the cases being called in over the loudspeaker and watching people get up and leave the café.

Pamela nibbles at her sandwich and sips her coffee.

When they are eventually called back to hear the verdict, Alice remains seated.

'I can't do it, I never want to see her again,' she says.

* * *

Three weeks later, Joona finds himself walking down a corridor in the women's wing of Kronoberg Prison. The plastic flooring glitters like ice in the cold glare of the strip lights. The walls, skirting and doors are all dented and scratched. A warden wearing a pair of blue latex gloves throws a sack of dirty laundry onto a trolley.

In the interview room for the National Board of Forensic Medicine, the forensic social worker, psychologist and forensic psychiatrist are sitting in their usual places, waiting for Joona.

'Welcome,' says the psychiatrist.

The old woman known as Granny is strapped into a wheelchair in front of them. The bandages around her head are gone, and her grey hair is hanging limply by her cheeks. Her eyes are closed.

'Caesar?' she whispers.

The nurse says something calming to her, patting her hand.

Three weeks earlier, when the court finished its deliberations and the involved parties were called back to the courtroom, Alice and Pamela stayed behind in the café. Mia followed Joona back into the room, and sat beside him as the judge explained the court's verdict.

The old woman showed no emotion whatsoever as she learned she had been found guilty on every count.

'You will undergo a forensic psychological assessment before any appeal hearings or sentences are handed down.'

Since then, the psychologist has been assessing her general intellectual capacity and personality, while the forensic psychiatrist has been examining her to ascertain whether she has any neurological, hormonal or chromosomal issues.

The aim is to determine whether she was seriously mentally ill when she carried out her crimes, whether she is at risk of reoffending, and whether she needs forensic psychiatric care.

'Caesar?' she asks again.

The psychiatrist waits until Joona is sitting before he speaks. He clears his throat and repeats why they are there, introducing everyone in the room like he always does and clarifying that none of them have a duty to maintain confidentiality as far as the court is concerned.

'Once Caesar lets me go, everything will be fine again,' Granny mumbles to herself.

The thick straps of her chair creak as she tries to pull her arms back. Her hands turn pale before she eventually gives up.

'Could you explain why you killed Jenny Lind in the playground?' the psychologist asks.

'The Lord had Judas Iscariot hanged . . .' the old woman calmly replies.

'Do you mean that Jenny was a traitor?'

'Young Frida ran off into the forest first, and got caught in a trap . . . I helped her come home and settled her down.'

'How?' asks Joona.

The old woman turns her head and squints at him. Only the white acrylic of her temporary prosthetic eyes is visible.

'I sawed off her feet so she wouldn't be tempted to run again . . . After that she changed her mind and admitted that she had a friend's phone number written on a scrap of paper . . . And since I knew she was lying when she said Jenny didn't know about her plans, I swapped the paper for one with my son's phone number on it, and left the girls on their own . . . I wanted to know if they had a phone hidden in the forest, I wanted to show them that the Lord sees everything . . .'

Jenny Lind probably took Granny by surprise when she suddenly took action after all those years in captivity, Joona thinks to himself. Caesar had lied about having friends within the police, so Jenny likely thought she had no choice but to get in touch with Frida's contact. When she found the note, she didn't hesitate for a moment. She set off into the forest right away.

'We now know that Jenny called your son when she got to Stockholm, and that he arranged to meet her in the playground, but why were you there?' Joona asks.

'It was my fault she escaped. It was my responsibility.'

'But Caesar showed up anyway,' he says.

'Only to make sure she was reprimanded the way he wanted . . . The whole world would see her shame.'

'Could you tell us what happened in the playground?' the psychologist asks.

The old woman turns her glossy white gaze to him.

'Jenny gave up when she saw it was me waiting by the jungle gym ... All she asked was that we didn't punish her parents,' Granny explains. 'She stood like a cross and let me put the noose around her neck. She thought Caesar would forgive her if she showed that she accepted her punishment, but he didn't have any love left for her, and he didn't say a word when I started to turn the handle.'

'Did *you* want to forgive her?' the psychologist asks.

'She drove a knife into my son's heart when she escaped ... Nothing could stop the bleeding; he was suffering. After that he became impatient. He put them all into cages, but it didn't help. He couldn't trust them anymore.'

'And what was your role in all of this?'

She leans forward with a smile, her hair falling over her face and her narrow white eyes visible through the grey locks.

'Can you understand why Jenny Lind wanted to escape?' the psychologist asks when she fails to answer.

'No,' she says, raising her face again.

'But you know that none of the women came to the farm voluntarily.'

'First, you have to subject yourself ... happiness comes later.'

The psychologist makes a note in his pad and flicks through his method book. Granny closes her mouth, making her sharp wrinkles deepen.

'Do you consider yourself mentally ill?' the psychologist asks.

She doesn't reply.

'Did you know that Caesar had a serious mental illness?'

'The Lord chooses his keystones without asking permission,' she says, spitting in his direction.

'I think she could do with a break,' the nurse says.

'Did Caesar ever talk about Martin Nordström?' Joona asks.

'Don't say that name,' Granny snaps, tugging at her restraints.

'Why not?'

'Is he the one behind all this?' she asks, her voice raised. 'Is he the one trying to ruin everything?' She pulls so hard on the straps that the wheels of her chair creak.

'What makes you say that?'

481

'He's always hated my son, following him everywhere,' she shouts. 'Because he's a jealous bastard . . .'

With a roar, she manages to pull one of her arms free. Blood spills from her broken skin.

The nurse quickly fills a syringe with medication and attaches a needle.

Granny growls between shallow breaths, sucking the blood from the back of her hand and trying to loosen the strap on her other arm.

'Caesar?' she shouts, her voice breaking. 'Caesar!'

Epilogue

Valeria and Joona are sitting at the table in her tiny kitchen, eating Hamburg steaks with boiled potatoes and cream gravy, pickled cucumber and lingonberry jam. The fire crackles in the old cast iron stove, projecting quivering stars of light across the white walls.

Joona has been living with Valeria ever since she got home from Brazil. Everything is the same as ever, aside from the photograph of the newborn girl on the fridge door.

On Monday, the trial finally drew to a close. Granny was sentenced to psychiatric care with extraordinary conditions applied to any future parole proceedings, and placed in unit thirty at Säter.

The blind old woman is violent and kept in isolation, away from the other patients, on a restraint bed bolted to the floor. During her waking hours, she screams and cries for Caesar to let her out of the basement.

As they eat, Joona tells Valeria about the case that took up so much of his time while she was away. He describes everything, from the first murder that came to light to Caesar's death in the mine, explaining how each strange piece of the puzzle eventually fell into place.

'Incredible,' she whispers after he concludes.

'So he was both innocent and guilty.'

'I understand what you mean, and I can see how that's the missing piece to the puzzle, as you put it . . . That makes sense, but I'm still struggling to see how Martin and Caesar could share one body.'

'You don't believe in DID or multiple personalities?'

'I don't know, to be perfectly honest,' she says, giving him a smile that makes her chin crease.

'The background to all of this is that Caesar was born at home, and his birth was never registered, so no one knew he existed or what he had been subjected to . . . His entire life revolved around his strict, punishing father and his obsession with having many sons and populating the world,' Joona explains.

'But his mother wasn't willing to be brushed aside.'

'Caesar wasn't even eight when he helped her kill his father and the rest of the family. She told Caesar he had been chosen by God and that he would take over his father's role and that now he was responsible for having twelve sons.'

'How did she do that?'

'She found proof of his chosen status in the mink skulls . . . She thought she could see an image imprinted on them of her son in his confirmation gown, standing like Christ on the cross.'

'The freeze marks,' Valeria whispers. 'I've got goosebumps now.'

'They clung to it, both of them. For them, it was true, it had to be true . . . and it was all right there in the Bible,' Joona goes on.

Valeria gets up and feeds more wood into the stove, blowing on the embers and closing the door. She fills the coffee pot with water.

'I often think that the more patriarchal religions haven't been all that great for women.'

'No.'

'But it's still a pretty big leap to go from being chosen by God to becoming a serial killer,' she says, sitting down again.

Joona tells her about the first woman they held captive, about her suicide after she became pregnant, and about Caesar's time in the secure unit at Säter. He shares Gustav Scheel's theory, that Caesar's personality split in two in order to preserve both the young boy who loved his half-brothers and the child who had helped to kill them – the youngster who knew it was wrong to keep a woman locked in the basement and the boy who exploited that right.

Caesar's grandiose image of himself as the progenitor was his way of escaping the pain of these unbearable traumas.

But Martin's happy life with Pamela and his stepdaughter Alice were a constant threat to that mental manoeuvre.

'Caesar grew to hate Martin.'

'Because he was his opposite – a kind, modern man,' says Valeria.

'And it was Martin who Gustav Scheel registered, who he gave a new life.'

'I understand,' says Valeria, leaning back in her chair.

'We're fairly sure that Caesar started the fire at the secure unit in an attempt to kill his doctor and erase any links to Martin.'

'Because if he did that, he would be the only one who knew the truth?'

'Yes, that was the idea, but the strange thing is that Martin was involved in the struggle after all ... For Caesar, their battle was conscious, and for Martin it was unconscious – something that became particularly evident when Caesar abducted Alice and handed her over to his mother during their fishing trip. Martin responded by stamping through the ice, not knowing that what he was really trying to do was drown Caesar.'

'But he didn't succeed,' Valeria whispers.

'Martin was saved, but he ended up suffering from a paranoid psychosis where his two dead half-brothers were watching over him ... It's difficult to know for sure, but going into full-time care might have been his attempt to lock up Caesar.'

Joona gets up, hitting his head on the ceiling light. He fills two cups with coffee and brings them back over to the table.

'But we can't deceive ourselves.'

'Nope, that's the rub,' Joona says, sitting down. 'Caesar made sure he was allowed to leave the unit, meaning he could continue like usual. And everything probably would have continued that way for years if Jenny Lind hadn't escaped. Caesar lost his footing, became offended, and started fantasising about awful punishments.'

'So that was why he tried to get Primus involved,' Valeria nods, blowing on her coffee.

'He called him using the Prophet's secret phone – and this is the interesting part ... Martin was in the ward when he called Primus, but he couldn't hear his own voice because it belonged to

Caesar . . . and that part of him was blocked off,' Joona continues. 'All he heard was Primus's attempts not to be dragged into their murder.'

He thinks about the fact that Jenny made it all the way to Stockholm in three days, borrowing a phone from a convenience shop and arranging a meeting in a playground.

'But outside of the ward, Martin and Caesar used the same phone?' Valeria asks.

'Martin was at home with Pamela, but whenever his mother called it was Caesar who answered,' Joona explains. 'I don't think Martin was even conscious of what drove him to take the dog out in the middle of the night, but when he got to the playground, Caesar took over again . . . What we saw on the CCTV footage wasn't a witness frozen in shock – it was Caesar, making sure the execution was carried out properly from a safe distance.'

'So it's always Caesar who wins out?'

'Actually, no, because Martin was waging a subconscious battle against him. He drew what he'd seen that evening, and allowed himself to be hypnotised in an attempt to reveal Caesar. And my guess is that it wasn't Caesar who threw Martin onto the tracks in the station, either. That was Martin trying to kill Caesar.'

'Without even realising it.'

'Oversimplifying slightly, you could say that Martin came to as the trailer was teetering on the edge of the mine,' Joona says. 'He realised that he and Caesar were the same person, understood what he had done, and made the conscious decision to sacrifice himself in order to stop Caesar.'

* * *

Joona is shown into Saga's suite, where he sits down in one of the armchairs and gazes out through the window at the bare rocks and the rough surface of the sea.

'There's already a bit of autumn in the air,' he says, turning to look at her.

She has a silver-grey blanket wrapped around her and a book from Norrtälje City Library in her lap.

Joona tells her about the resolution of the strangest case he has ever worked on.

Saga doesn't ask any questions, but it is obvious she is listening to how the details mirrored one another, coming together to form the answer.

Joona explains that Caesar didn't know he had been sterilised while he was at Säter, but that his inability to live up to his own self-image as a patriarch gradually became his motive for controlling the women and wielding his sexual power over them.

When he eventually gets up to leave, Saga picks up the novel from her lap. It's a copy of Joseph Conrad's *Lord Jim*. She opens it and takes out a postcard that came with the book, tucked between its pages like a bookmark, handing it to Joona.

The black and white photograph, dated 1898, is of the old cholera cemetery in Kapellskär.

He turns it over and reads the four sentences on the back, handwritten in black felt tip:

I have a blood red Makarov pistol. There are nine white bullets in the magazine. One of them is reserved for Joona Linna. The only person who can save him is you.
Artur K. Jewel

Joona hands the postcard back to Saga, and she tucks it into her book before looking up and meeting his eye.

'The name is an anagram,' she says.

Author's Note

The Mirror Man is intended as entertainment, but crime fiction can also be a platform for discussions about humankind and the world we live in.

Like so many other authors before us, we have chosen to isolate a particular global problem and place it in a limited situation in which a solution is possible. This does not mean that we are not aware of the reality.

The unreported statistics are likely enormous, but according to both the United Nations and the World Health Organisation, over a billion women globally have been subjected to sexual violence. More than forty million women are involved in prostitution, fifty million women are forced to live as slaves, and 750 million women are married before their eighteenth birthday. Eighty-seven thousand women are murdered every year, half of them by either their partner or another family member.

If you enjoyed *The Mirror Man*,
then why not join the
LARS KEPLER READERS' CLUB?

When you sign up, you'll receive a never-before-seen short story by Lars Kepler, plus access to giveaways, news about upcoming books, and exclusive writing delivered straight to your inbox. Simply visit:
www.themirrormanbook.co.uk

Keep reading for a letter from Lars Kepler . . .

Dear Reader,

Thank you for picking up *The Mirror Man*.

As you may know, Lars Kepler is the pen name for the Swedish writing couple Alexander and Alexandra Ahndoril. We are married, we love each other, and we have three daughters, but those things don't necessarily mean you can write books together. Quite the opposite, many would say!

For us, at least, writing together seemed completely impossible until we had the idea to create a third writer, Lars Kepler. With him arose an enormous creative flow and a new literary universe, which surprised us with its darkness. The first book we wrote as Lars Kepler was *The Hypnotist*, and even before it was finished, we were convinced that it was the beginning of a long series.

We share everything throughout the writing process, from the first idea, through all the research and plot building, to the writing itself, down to the very last word. When we flip through the manuscript afterwards, we can't tell who did what. There is not a single sentence that only one of us has written.

Our starting point is to let each novel function as a standalone. Each book should focus on an overarching case with a clear beginning and end. But if you follow the whole series, you get to know the main characters' lives and follow their stories on a deeper level.

The Mirror Man is the eighth book following Detective Inspector Joona Linna and Saga Bauer. We have no templates for our writing or our mysteries – we just try to write books that we would love to read ourselves. They must be full of both darkness and heart. With *The Mirror Man*, we wanted to create a frightening, psychological labyrinth and at the same time maintain the fast, propulsive pace of a breakneck thriller.

A woman is hung on a playground in the middle of the night. The police can't see the murder itself via surveillance cameras, but they can see a man standing at a distance, staring straight at the playground until the perpetrator is gone.

When the witness is identified, he turns out to be a mentally ill man who has no memory of the night. Joona Linna asks Dr Erik

Maria Bark to hypnotize the witness to help him remember. What emerges is the gateway to a nightmare.

We always sit next to each other when we type; the atmosphere becomes electric in the small room, the only sound the rattling of the computer keyboard. When we wrote *The Mirror Man*, sometimes it became so intense that we had to leave our study and go out on the balcony to calm down and just breathe for a while before we could return.

For us, our writing is primarily about empathy and correcting the world through fiction. Hand in hand with our readers, we will find our way out of the labyrinth and solve the mystery of who the Mirror Man really is.

If you would like to hear more about our books, you can visit **www.themirrormanbook.co.uk** where you can become part of the Lars Kepler Readers' Club. It only takes a few moments to sign up, there are no catches or costs.

Bonnier Zaffre will keep your data private and confidential, and it will never be passed on to a third party. We won't spam you with loads of emails, just get in touch now and again with news about our books, and you can unsubscribe any time you want.

And if you would like to get involved in a wider conversation about our books, please do review *The Mirror Man* on Amazon, on Goodreads, on any other e-store, on your own blog and social media accounts, or talk about it with friends, family or reader groups! Sharing your thoughts helps other readers, and we always enjoy hearing about what people experience from our writing.

Thank you again for reading *The Mirror Man*.

All the best,
Lars Kepler

THE SPIDER

Three years ago, Saga Bauer received a postcard with a threatening text about a gun with nine white bullets – one of which is waiting for Detective Joona Linna. But time passed and the threat faded.

Until now.

A sack with a decomposed body is found tied to a tree in the forest. A milky white bullet casing is found at the murder scene. And soon the police are sent complicated riddles from the killer – a chance to stop further murders.

Joona Linna and Saga Bauer must fight side by side to solve the puzzle and save each victim before it's too late. But the violent hunt becomes increasingly desperate.

Maybe this serial killer is unstoppable.

Maybe they're already caught in the web . . .

COMING SUMMER 2023

Originally published in Sweden by Albert Bonniers Förlag in 2020
This edition published in the UK in 2023 by
ZAFFRE
An imprint of Bonnier Books UK
4th Floor, Victoria House, Bloomsbury Square, London WC1B 4DA
Owned by Bonnier Books
Sveavägen 56, Stockholm, Sweden

A CIP catalogue record for this book is
available from the British Library.

Hardback ISBN: 978–1–83877–646–6
Export ISBN: 978–1–83877–647–3
Paperback ISBN: 978–1–83877–648–0

Also available as an ebook and an audiobook

1 3 5 7 9 10 8 6 4 2

Typeset by IDSUK (Data Connection) Ltd
Printed and bound in Great Britain by Clays Ltd, Elcograf S.p.A.

Zaffre is an imprint of Bonnier Books UK
www.bonnierbooks.co.uk

THE MIRROR MAN

Lars Kepler

ZAFFRE

Lars Kepler is a No.1 bestselling international sensation, whose Joona Linna thrillers have sold more than 15 million copies in 40 languages. The first book in the series, *The Hypnotist*, was selected for the 2012 Richard and Judy Book Club. *Stalker* went straight to No.1 in Sweden, Norway, Holland and Slovakia. Lars Kepler is the pseudonym for writing duo, Alexander and Alexandra Ahndoril. They live with their family in Sweden.

Also by Lars Kepler

The Joona Linna Series
The Hypnotist
The Nightmare
The Fire Witness
The Sandman
Stalker
The Rabbit Hunter
Lazarus

THE

MIRROR

MAN